Jeremiah Kent Swartzell

AWAKEN

THE

DARK

Book One in "The Shadow of Death Trilogy"

For more information, address: valleyofshadowstrilogy@gmail.com

Cover design by Danielle Swartzell

ISBN: 979-8-9917507-1-4 (paperback)

ISBN: 979-8-9917507-0-7 (hardcover)

To my wife, Danielle for your never-ending support in this endeavor. A better help-mate a man could not find than a wife who keeps them centered and focused.

Prolouge

The Valley of Elah, Israel 1025 B.C.

An unkindness of ravens soared high above the Valley of Elah, appearing certain that by day's end there would be plenty of corpses to pick at. The ravens circled patiently above the formations of men, recognizing it as an overture to the massacre that would result from the clash of iron and bronze.

Tsalmaveth's gaze went from the ravens above as he looked out through his helm at the throng of Israelites standing on a hill on one side of the valley. The afternoon sun reflected from the smattering of bronze armor among the Hebrew soldiers and made it difficult to see without squinting. Tsalmaveth preferred the dark, but this body of Goliath's he now inhabited cast the largest shadow of any one man in all the land of Canaan.

A slight breeze wormed its way down the valley and brought the stench of the five-thousand Israelites standing a few hundred yards away to his nostrils. One thing Tsalmaveth despised about inhabiting a body was the human senses. In this case, the smell of this hated enemy caused him great annoyance.

Behind Tsalmaveth stood an entire army of Philistines from each of the five city-states in Philistia. It had taken his servant Lox a great while to rally the support of each of the five Lords, who independently ruled these cities and their surrounding settlements, because they favored marauding and attacking on their own timing and were loosely confederated when it came to conquest pursuits. For this reason, Lox was only able to muster a force of seven to eight thousand troops to this campaign, most of them being from Gath, Goliath's stronghold.

He looked over his left shoulder and saw Lox standing there in his drab black robes wearing a hood that covered his eyes. In Lox's hands was a stone box that had been his prison for ages after Michael and Azrael had bound him to it, cursing him to exist as a prisoner, being let out only once for a brief foray in Egypt hundreds of years ago where Elohim used his power to destroy the captors of Israel. At the thought of the name, Elohim, he spat on the ground three times.

Ever since Lox had retrieved him from the Ark of the Covenant, when the Israelites lost it for a brief time to the Philistines, he had been communing with Lox and planning their next steps, researching, and digging through archives the world over, searching for the key. The fear was that Michael would return and confiscate the box once again. Fortunately, nearly sixty years had passed and there had been no sign of Michael or any of the hated angels of Elohim.

Again, he spat three times on the ground as the name came into his thoughts for a second time. There were few names that Tsalmaveth hated more than Elohim, the god who'd trapped him and now favored the seed of Abraham above all other men on the earth. It was a name he could almost taste and he loathed the mere mention of the god. It thoroughly disgusted him, the piousness these Israelites showed toward Him.

Each day for thirty-nine days, he would use Goliath's body and take to the valley daring the Israelites and King Saul to send out a champion to face him in single combat. He insulted, goaded, blasphemed their precious god, and openly challenged their customs hoping it would spark one of them to come forward.

Spies within their camp had gleaned information that King Saul had offered riches and a place in his family to the man that could slay Goliath and deliver the Philistines into their hands. None had even hinted at accepting the duel. They were all too scared, as they were more scared of Goliath and his imposing size and reputation for violence than their own king's wrath.

What kind of a king was Saul who could not inspire men to do courageous things? Tsalmaveth thought with a scowl. He'd expected that there would at least be one man that would want the fame and renown that a victory over the great Goliath would bring.

Was there not at least one? Tsalmaveth thought further, as he began his trek down from the ridge into the valley in between the two armies who had lined up in ranks across the countryside on this, the fortieth day.

As he reached the low ground between the two armies with his shield bearer, Tsalmaveth turned his spear tip down and slammed it into the dirt and said haughtily, "Why are you all coming out to fight?"

Tsalmaveth's voice was amplified by the acoustic quality of the valley, with rolling hills on both sides making it sound as if he were standing among them, although they were hundreds of yards away. He was well out of range of their archers even on the low ground he stood upon.

Tsalmaveth beat his chest loudly and called out, "I am the Philistine Champion, but you are only the servants of King Saul. Choose one man to come down here and fight me!" He paused for effect knowing that they had all heard this challenge before, but this time Tsalmaveth added, "IF the man kills me, then we will all become your slaves. But if I kill him, YOU will become OUR slaves!"

Tsalmaveth began to pace back and forth in front of the armies shouting as he went, "I defy the armies of Israel today! Send me one man who will fight me!" He heard a chorus of murmurs rise in the Israelite ranks, knowing that they were all voicing their fear of Goliath's power and behemoth-like size. Goliath was easily the tallest and strongest man in all of Canaan.

At once, Tsalmaveth stopped his pacing and shouted in his loudest guttural voice that echoed down the entire valley, "YOUR GOD IS NOTHING! No one dares to stand up against the Shadow of Death. Cowards! Where is your god now, Israel?"

Murmurs arose from the Philistines at his back, and he turned to see what they were clamoring about and realized they were craning their necks down the valley to the west.

From the west, traveling east, came a boy dressed in shepherd's clothing carrying a staff and sling. The boy stopped a hundred paces from Goliath in between him and the Israelites. The ruddy-faced boy looked to be so young that he'd barely begun to show signs of being a man, with no facial hair to be seen and skin as smooth as a newborn baby. Tsalmaveth chuckled to himself as the boy walked forward, his shield-bearer was in front of him by three paces. Then he started to laugh uncontrollably the closer the boy approached.

He sneered mockingly, the contempt in his voice unmistaken. "AM I A DOG," Tsalmaveth roared, "THAT YOU COME AT ME WITH A STICK?" He shouted curses at the boy, begging him to make the first move.

"Come over here, and I'll give your flesh to the birds and wild animals!" He yelled, his last words sounding like a growl through gritted teeth.

The boy squared his shoulders and replied stoically, "You come to me with sword, spear, and javelin. But I come to you in the name of the Lord of Heaven's Armies, the God of the armies of Israel, whom you have defied." He paused briefly and let the words echo. "Today, the Lord will conquer you, and I will kill you and cut off your head. And then I will give the bodies of your men to the birds and wild animals, and the world will know that there is a God in Israel!"

The boy turned slightly to the Israelite army behind him as if to direct this last part of the monologue at them as well, "And everyone assembled here will know the Lord rescues his people, but not with sword and spear. THIS IS THE LORD'S BATTLE, and He will give you to us!"

Tsalmaveth assumed this bluster was just that, vain bluster that would fold as soon as he crushed this little twerp into a pile of blood and bones at his feet. But there was a little prick of doubt as the boy shouted louder. When the boy finished the last word, he dropped his staff and began to run full speed toward him.

Tsalmaveth felt Goliath's heartbeat quicken slightly as he rushed forward to meet the boy in the open field, nearly forgetting to grab his spear from the earth. Raising the spear, he planted his feet hurriedly and threw it with such force that the air whistled shrilly. As it hurtled toward the boy who was just then loading a stone into his sling while on the run, it looked as if the little runt would be impaled on the spear. At the exact, right moment, the boy dove forward horizontally, his body only a cubit from the ground.

The spear whizzed by, missing him by mere inches and buried itself into the ground. The boy tightly rolled just before landing on the ground and skillfully came up to his feet, not ten paces from Goliath. As the boy rose to his feet, he swung his sling around and loosed a stone, sending it hurtling toward Goliath's head with such force, that it also made a whistling sound equal to Goliath's spear.

Tsalmaveth barely had time to utter a curse as the stone hit him just between the gap in the nose and face guard of his helm. On the edge of consciousness, he felt disconnected from Goliath's body as it fell more than ten feet to the stony ground and lay there looking up at the blinding blur of light in the early afternoon sky. With a ringing in his ears, Tsalmaveth heard the faint sound of iron scraping across the earth, as what little vision he had was darkened by a silhouette of the person standing over him. The boy blocked the sun and cast a shadow over Goliath as if portending death. The irony was not lost on Tsalmaveth, seeing a shadowy death descend upon him. The shrill scrape of metal became louder until he saw the shadow raise a sword above its head.

Tsalmaveth felt no pain as this was Goliath's body and he was only a visitor. Goliath within, however, was screaming out in agony and panic, unable to defend against his death that was coming at the hands of a shepherd boy. Even as he willed his body to recover it was to no avail.

From the Israelite ranks he could hear a growing chant as the soldiers learned who this young boy was. Chants of, "DAVID! DAVID! DAVID! DAVID!" could be heard echoing down the valley as the Israelite soldiers charged from their positions to pursue a shocked and fleeing Philistine army. The Philistines shrieked in horror at seeing their champion lying flat on his back before them. Fear now flowed from them as the Israelites swiftly moved across the landscape, eager to finish off their foe.

The boy did not flinch or even hesitate as he raised the mighty sword over his head, and the last thing Tsalmaveth saw while inside Goliath's giant body was the glint of the metal blinding him through blurry vision as the sword descended upon the neck.

——◆○◆——

After the battle...

Two ravens broke away from the unkindness that had descended upon the far-flung battlefield, now strewn over several miles. It was thoroughly littered with dead and dying soldiers killed during a chaotic retreat. The melee had been swift and final leaving little doubt as to who was the victor. Buzzards and other carrion birds joined the buffet without shame as the ravens complained momentarily before realizing there was no need to squabble. After all, the battlefield was so littered with the dead that it would take hundreds of birds and wild dogs to even make a dent in the display of carnage.

The pair of rogue ravens, clearly not swayed by the abundant flesh, flew to the northeast in a direct flight that soon brought them to the city they called home and to their master, King Adonizedek. Flying high over the houses below, they banked right and soared over the walls of a great fortress on the hilltop and soon came to a large ash tree that towered over the fortress itself looking down on the sprawling city below. As they came to rest on the upper branches, they soon heard the familiar voice of their master calling to them.

"Hugin. Munin. Come." he said cheerily, as the two ravens floated down to land on his outstretched forearm.

As they landed, Hugin moved up and across to the other shoulder, while Munin took up a place on the nearside shoulder. Their master's son, Thoros sat nearby on a bench looking at them as they maneuvered.

"Tell me what you saw?" King Adonizedek asked in a jovial tone.

Hugin was the first to squawk, "Battle! Battle!" the raven said excitedly.

Munin chimed in, "Boy! Boy! Fight!" it squawked while bouncing up and down.

"So there was a battle?" He asked before moving on, "Who won this battle?"

Hugin and Munin both squawked simultaneously saying different words.

"Hebrew!" Hugin said while Munin said, "Boy! Boy!"

He understood the meaning and asked, "A Hebrew boy won the fight? Whom did he fight?"

"Giant!" Munin said as Hugin confirmed, "Giant!"

"Goliath. They mean Goliath." Thoros said smugly.

"What happened to the giant?" Adonizedek asked gravely.

"Giant! Death! Death!" Hugin said excitedly.

"That fool of a cousin went and got himself killed."

King Adonizedek took it in stride, though he looked uneasy as he asked, "And what of the Philistines? Did they fall?"

The two looked confused before he realized that Philistines was not a word they'd mastered yet, so he rephrased, "The giant. He had friends with him. Many friends were there to fight. Did they fall?"

The pair turned their heads, listening to him intently as he spoke. Eventually they grasped the question, and both answered loudly, "All! Death!"

"And what happened to Lox, was he there?" Adonizedek asked in a panicked tone.

Munin squawked, "Lox Run!"

"Lox," Thoros moaned. "He's been attempting a military alliance with the Philistines for decades now."

King Adonizedek breathed a sigh of relief and nodded confirmation before asking the birds, "Lox. Can you find him?"

"Find! Find!" They squawked before adding their natural caws to the noise.

He held finger to his lips and whispered, "Quiet now my precious birds." The ravens immediately ceased and looked at him expectantly.

"I need you to find Lox and give him a message. Can you do that?"

The birds bounced up and down in tandem and waited for their master to speak. King Adonizedek raised both arms which was a signal for them to walk to his hands and perch on them. They each ambled down an arm and clinched onto his forefingers gently.

King Adonizedek raised his hands up and gently spoke, "Lox. Come home." With those words he waved his arms and sent Hugin and Munin to flight. They wasted no time in flying southwest towards the soon-to-be-setting sun. As they gained altitude, they began to squawk a word they'd heard over and over as they surveyed the battlefield today.

"David! David!" Hugin squawked.

Munin answered with, "David! David!" as the two ravens rapidly flew to carry out their master's will, while squawking the new name all the way.

CHAPTER 1

Jebus, Canaan 1010 B.C.

Fifteen Years Later

The air was bursting with excitement, but also tinged with a hint of dread, as Thoros ran through the streets at a blinding pace towards the Citadel and Palace grounds. The Citadel, nestled into Mount Moriah, was a shining example of his father's vision. It was the highest vantage for a twenty-day journey, rivaling the Assyrian fortress at Ugarit. From the top, one could see an approaching army from three days away.

An hour ago, Thoros heard a horn blow three times from the top of the Citadel Fortress which meant one thing, a marching army was coming. He didn't even need to see it with his own eyes to know it was the main force of the invaders coming from the north where they had laid waste to many cities.

Now they were surrounded by Hebrew lands, cut off from Damascus and Ugarit and Philistia. They had sent messages to the few allies they had left, to no avail, asking for help before the main Hebrew force arrived. Egypt, which had a grudge against the Hebrew, had not responded. The Philistines were too wrapped up in their own politics these days. The ever-advancing Israelites seemed unstoppable and perhaps the most troubling aspect of their conquest of Canaan was the way in which they had accomplished it. In a series of unexplainable events, they had destroyed every foe with little loss of life on their side.

In Jericho, Thoros' great uncle, Og of Bashan was beheaded after his city was torn to pieces by a great earthquake that caused the walls to crumble to the ground. Jericho's forty-foot walls were the tallest in Canaan and had never been breached by anyone. The few of his relatives that managed to escape said the invaders marched in silence around the walls once a day for seven days and on the final day, marched seven times, after which they blew their horns and shouted in unison as the earth began to quake beneath the city. The walls crumbled like sand and the horde of Hebrew charged over the rubble like a swarm of locusts.

Anyone who had not been crushed was put to the sword, including cattle and livestock. Nothing was left alive. To hear it told, it sounded as if the Hebrew had a powerful god-like ally helping them. Whispers in the streets of Jebus quietly spoke the name.

Elohim was this god's name, but other names were used interchangeably. Thoros had to confess that even he had a passing thought that there might be something to the rumor, but it made no difference to him which God they claimed because they had gods of their own. His father, King Adonizedek, was descended from a powerful god who ruled long ago in a faraway land. This god that the former slaves toted around in an acacia box, plated in gold, was surely no match for them. He had heard tell of it in the aftermath of Jericho.

Surely, they were only men; mere flesh and blood, Thoros reasoned, as he crested over the final hill leading up to the Citadel gates. However, the tinge of doubt prodded his psyche as he had seen enough battles in his life to know that this situation was not ideal for them. Lives would be at stake.

The guards opened the portcullis at the gate entry to the fortress for him as he entered, not breaking is purposeful stride. If he had more time, he would spend a little of it inspecting the battle readiness of the Citadel, but time was not something anyone had now, so he picked up his pace as he began the steep climb up the pathway to the Palace compound, trudging upward with a purpose. As he went, Thoros made mental notes of the fortifications and ploys that were in place should they have to fall back to defend as a last stand. He had to give Lox some credit for the design of this fortress because it really was a well-built defense system, even if it were a little ostentatious and flashy by his utilitarian standards. It seemed Lox's gift for building had become well represented as rumors of his involvement in the Tower of Babel had wormed their way into the conversations of those at court. Lox was careful to never confirm or deny such rumors, content to let the people talk and gossip. Ever since returning to Jebus fifteen years ago, Lox had thrown himself into the work of building up defenses.

Every terrace was filled with beautiful gardens and vines that masked arrow loops and chutes which hot oil and tar could be poured down directly onto the cobbled pathway. Any poor soul bottlenecked at the gate would have boiling pitch poured on them before being set alight. If the invaders happened to break through the first gate, they would meet another gate which would set them up underneath a 'murder hole', as Lox called it, where stones and boulders and more boiling pitch would be poured on them from overhead. Lox's imagination for ways to die was second to none.

By his own estimate they could withstand a full assault with only a few hundred soldiers. Still, there was little hope to outlast this siege because they were surrounded by land conquered by this enemy and in a few days, they would be surrounded by thirty thousand Hebrew men that believed a God was doing their dirty work. It didn't matter how soundly built this fortress was, even a fool could see this was coming to an end faster than anybody expected.

It took him at least twenty minutes but finally, he passed under the archway into a massive courtyard with vines and trees growing out of the stone surface. Olive and fig trees flourished on this high up perch where they were cared for by servants. Thoros made a hard right turn towards where the sentry tower was located for the northerly watch and climbed the flights of stairs to the top which was a full thirty cubits in height.

As he approached the sentry who was standing watch, Thoros could see out over the vast expanse that was now in control of Israel. Sure enough, without even using a looking glass, he could see the Hebrew force marching in a slow-moving column. He couldn't see the entire force because of the undulating hills and valleys. Luckily, the sun had been out in full force all day, or they may not have seen the bronze weapons and armor reflecting in the light because they dressed very plainly in brown and gray tones and were able to blend into their surroundings. Almost like a ghost army. Still, they were at least a three day march out from what he could estimate.

Thoros made his way across the courtyard to the where his father's throne room and council chambers were and entered in through the front portal and once inside, he took his seat on the right side of the table closest to his father's seat at the head. Across from him was his adopted brother Lox.

Brother was a strange word to use when describing Lox. Nobody, except his father, trusted him in any measure because he could be found in the middle of every plot and scheme or quarrel. Lox was more a burden than a brother, and Thoros had the suspicion that Lox had similar views of him. But nonetheless, his father loved him, so the King defended him whenever somebody made a comment or complaint. There had been many times they had nearly come to blows over pranks and schemes that always seemed to spell consequences for him while Lox seemed to slink off into his dungeon until the mood calmed in the court. Thoros, being the heir, constantly had the eyes of the court as well as his own father on him. He did not have the luxury of being so flippant, nor did he retreat to a dank hole when things got tough.

Thoros busied himself by scanning the room to see who was attending. Standing to his right was Ide, the finance minister. Across from him was Orvandil, who was a trusted advisor to the king, sharp witted, though a bit flamboyant for his liking and older than dirt. Over in the corner were two of his closer friends, Jarnsaxa the Archer and Siege Captain, and Bulwark the Stonemason and Blacksmith. They were having a discussion but paused long enough to give him a regarding gesture. Peppered around the room were various others who filled out the duties of ruling a city-state.

Slowly they began to stand in front of their seats at the table figuring the time for the king to enter was drawing nigh. He looked away from the table and could see two sets of eyes looking towards him between the cracks in an ante-room door. As he made eye contact, they burst through the door and ran over. Thoros guffawed and turned to embrace the children. His son Magni and his daughter Thrud threw their arms around Thoros and climbed him like a tree.

With one child on each arm Thoros bellowed, "Where is your mother, children? Is she letting you find your way into trouble?"

"Not a chance husband, they don't wait on my permission as you are well aware. They are your children after all." Siv strode across the room through the ante-room door with so much elegance that everyone in the room ceased their conversation and turned to watch her move.

Thoros was at a loss for words, as he always was when he was around her. He could shout and bellow on the battlefield and make his voice known at the council table but when she spoke, he was dumbfounded. Siv was as intelligent, skilled, creative, and as battle hardened as any man, yet still exuded the tenderness of a mother and helpmate. She was an incredible mother to their two children who were already as tall as his waist. Siv was only half Amalekite, her mother had been from a far-off land to the east named Cush, which gave her the dark, olive skin while her hair was a golden amber, and long and curly.

Breathtaking was the word that more than one man in the land had used to describe her beauty. And she had chosen him; the lumbering warrior with the square jaw and scarred physique. He snapped out of his stupor when his father walked into the room, followed by his two younger brothers, Baaldir and Vithas. King Adonizedek motioned for them to take seats on the side of the room. He likely wanted them to observe. They had no voice in court just yet, though Baaldir was coming up on his trials to initiate him into manhood in the next year or so. Vithas was still a bit younger and spent most of his time with his mother, Frigg. They would sit on the outskirts of the meeting and do their best to stay interested. Thoros remembered his adolescence and he couldn't blame them if they'd rather play with their friends than sit in a boring council meeting full of old men.

"Okay, you know the rules, no child monsters are allowed in the council chambers!" King Adonizedek said with a grin as he walked towards his seat at the head of the table.

Thoros turned towards his father; children still tucked under his armpits as they squealed with excitement at seeing their grandfather come into the room.

"Before you go with your mother, children, I want you to give your uncle Lox the meanest, scariest face you can muster. Ready? I'll do it with you!"

Magni and Thrud burst into laughter and began to growl at Lox making their best monster faces while Thoros roared at the top of his lungs with a convincing scowl.

He set the children down and pushed them towards Siv who led them away, "Good little monsters. Behave for your mother or I'll swat you one later."

"Vithas, you may go with Siv and find your mother." King Adonizedek added.

Siv motioned for young Vithas to come along, and he scampered over to her and grabbed her hand. She collected the children and walked over to Thoros and kissed his cheek. She said in a faint voice, "The children will be in bed in a few hours."

She placed her hand on his chest and gave him a knowing look. And just like that she was off, and he was left standing there wishing he were following her.

Lox, never one to stand on decorum, took his seat and slouched back nonchalantly and prodded Thoros, "Should you be here brother? The King said no child monsters allowed in the council chambers."

Thoros was satisfied with this reaction, so he turned to his father and said, "My apologies for the child invasion. We have serious things to discuss. High among them, the Hebrew force that will be at our walls in just a few days' time."

King Adonizedek nodded, "Indeed we do. Everyone please be seated. The question I need to put forth to you is whether you believe we can withstand an onslaught of more than 30,000 Israelite warriors?"

Thoros felt a chill run up and down his spine as everyone slid their chairs out and took their seats. The Israelites had been victorious over nearly every army they had fought against. His own family members and close friends had fallen under their swords. Whatever slave-like tendencies they may have had in battle when they entered the region, centuries had passed, and they were now honed into a deadly fighting force.

Thoros leaned forward, "We need to send riders out to Philistia to rally their support. Have we received any correspondence from them lately?"

Ide coughed loudly, "My prince, we have not heard from the Philistines but the last scout we heard back from said they were at the south of Philistia pressing their claim to some land bordering Egypt. We may not be able to count on them this time."

Thoros looked toward Jarnsaxa and asked, "How many archers do you have at the ready?"

Jarnsaxa cleared her throat, "We have five thousand my prince, and one thousand slingers also. We could conscript a few thousand more in a pinch."

Thoros responded, "Infantrymen, Jebusite or otherwise, number ten thousand plus one thousand Amalekite cavalrymen. That's a force half the size of our foe. We need help or I fear we may be outmatched." He didn't like to sound unconfident, but years of experience told him it was better to be direct and accept reality as it presented itself, not what he wished it to be.

For at least half an hour the members of the Court discussed the siege. The conversation ranged from troops, defenses and ploys to food stores and medical preparedness. Perhaps the most concerning thing about the timing of the siege was the severe drought they found themselves in. Several months without rain had all but emptied their cisterns and the underground spring had all but dried up to a measly trickle of water. Thoros could tell King Adonizedek, who sat silent through the whole meeting, was pondering the information but seemed a little distracted at the same time.

The room fell silent as the King pushed back his chair and rose from the table. In response, all those seated abruptly stood up so as not to be seated when the king was not at his own table.

King Adonizedek placed his hands on the table and leaned forward urgently, "I have heard enough for today. All those present are to do whatever is necessary to prepare, each of your jobs is vital to our survival, no matter how small or seemingly unimportant. The coming days are dark indeed and I believe to a man, that someone in this room has what it takes to defeat this foe and save our way of life!"

King Adonizedek stepped around his chair and turned to leave before saying over his shoulder, "I need some fresh air. Would the ranking members of the Inner Council join me?"

Thoros scanned the room as his father walked towards the veranda. The majority of those present began to discuss their strategies and a bustle of energy filled the chamber once again. Lox, Thoros, Bulwark, Jarnsaxa, and the two advisors Ide and Orvandil followed the King as he led the way.

Baaldir, his second brother, hurried off. No doubt this meeting had been a bore to him. He was not yet a man with a voice at council, but his father insisted that Baaldir join the Council meetings to listen and learn. It wasn't Baaldir's favorite activity by any means, Thoros could tell, though Adonizedek had been able to develop his intellect through these meetings and spending time asking his opinions and instructing him afterward. Thoros remembered that his father had done the same process for him as he was coming of age. He'd grown to appreciate the mentorship as he aged and started a family of his own. Baaldir would see that himself one day, he hoped.

On the way, Lox walked close to Thoros and queried, "Do my ears deceive me brother or are you admitting defeat? The great Thoros; bested by slaves?"

Thoros sighed, "Why must you always prod me? I know that you can be pragmatic. So, tell me, what good is hubris and foolhardy vanity? What would that do for the situation we find ourselves in? My uncle, Og of Bashan, was so defiant right up to the point that they took his head, as you well know. Goliath was bested by a shepherd boy of fifteen, with a sling no less. The boy used Goliath's own sword to sever his head. That boy is their greatest warrior to date. We had an advantage forty or so years ago, when they were still squabbling tribes trying to settle their conquered land, trading blows with the Philistines. Now that they are united with a king, we are steadily becoming overmatched. Our trade routes are sporadic and our willing allies even more so. So, tell me…Brother. What size tomb would you like? Your full height, or a head shorter?"

Lox feigned a humble expression, "Dear brother, I agree with you for once. But while you'll be playing hide the sword in the Hebrew, I'll be making plans. Besides, I am the only one here with actual practical experience facing these foes."

Thoros shouldn't have been surprised. Scheming is what Lox did best. "Making plans? What sort of plans are these? Should I be worried?"

Lox feigned an incredulous frown, "Oh, on the contrary brother; I intend to keep my pretty little head right where it is. You will see in time."

Lox placed his hand on Thoros' shoulder, "You could even wager your neck on it."

Thoros grabbed the back of Lox's collar, and then jerked it toward him, only half-playful. "How about we wager YOUR neck?"

They followed the King onto the veranda that overlooked the garden below. Once everyone had found a place King Adonizedek turned to address them. "I have had dreams and visions every single night for this past fortnight. I would like to share it with you all," The King said as he scanned the faces on the veranda.

"In my dream, I am walking through a field of wheat that stretches as far as the eye can see. After some time, I came to a well in the middle of the fields. I am rather thirsty, so I pull on the rope with a bucket attached to draw water from the bottom. When I pull the bucket up it is rather heavy and when I finally bring it up to the surface, I realize it is not full of water but of blood and bones. I drop the bucket on the ground and jump back, surprised to see this instead of water. As the blood hits the ground it spreads out onto the dry earth.

Abruptly, I find myself standing in the middle of a great city. I can't tell you what city it is, but it looks familiar to me in my dream, and I feel as though it belongs to me. Walls of timber surround it with a great hall at the center and houses with thatched roofs all around. It is built on the bank of a vast river. The river rages and waves crash over the ramparts.

Fire begins to rain down from the sky as people all around me run for cover as the thatched roofs burn like tinder. A great serpent circles around the city in the air. It is so large that its length nearly wraps around the city in a full circle. At the middle of the city there is a giant wolf gobbling up the citizens one by one while an eagle the size of an elephant soars high in the sky watching the carnage from above.

The wolf, seeing me standing there, starts my way. I prepare to fight, spear in hand as the wolf rears back as it snaps its jaw that is ten times the size of my body. As the wolf attacks, I ready my spear and then I wake up just as I am about to be eaten alive by the wolf."

Everyone sat there with their jaws hanging open as he finished telling of his chilling dream. Eventually, there was a stirring behind King Adonizedek and a crippled old man lumbered up to him, seemingly from the ether. Skald, the seer, was misshapen and hunched over, his fingers gnarled. He moved laboriously everywhere he went, the years of torment from the gods and their visions having twisted his body into tangles.

Skald circled around Adonizedek and looked at him up and down before closing his eyes and letting out a series of grunts and noises that sounded like he was saying, "Mmmhmm. Mmmhmm." All the while the old man's eyes darted around behind his eyelids.

Suddenly, Skald's narrow eyes opened, and he looked upon King Adonizedek before saying gravely, "There is calamity in our future. The end of all things. But it appears to me with a clouded veil covering the answers you seek. Though it is plain to see that the field of wheat is a new land of plenty. The blood spilled is the price that must be paid to achieve your destiny and possess that land. Perhaps that is the city you saw; I can't be certain. As I said, some of the details are covered from my sight."

Thoros scoffed, "More riddles, meanwhile we have an army bearing down on us."

Adonizedek was unphased by his son's skepticism. "I have long wondered if our time in this land is ending, but I have always hoped that our story would continue elsewhere. Still, the idea of an end to the world is a sobering one. I would like to find answers and keep myself open to possibilities. What do your bones tell us? "

Skald pulled a bag from his belt and lumbered over to a small table near Adonizedek and poured the bag's contents onto the table. Onto the table fell several chicken bones with characters scrawled onto them.

He studied them for a moment and made the same, 'Mmmhmm, Mmmhmm' noise before scooping them up and tossing them up into the air. They fell onto the table, and he studied them again. This time he was visibly shaken by what he saw. So much so that he picked them up again and tried a third time. The bones fell and he looked them over yet again.

This time he looked up at Adonizedek and Thoros before saying, "I see a looming shadow, a prince in captivity. I see the death of kings, and a son swallowed by The Void. I see enemies who become allies, an upending of the world by fire."

"More riddles!" Thoros repeated, "I don't have time for this. There is much to be done to prepare for the coming siege."

Thoros rose from his seat to leave the veranda, but Adonizedek motioned for him to be patient. Thoros returned to his seat and sat with a barely audible grumble.

His father asked Skald if he could elaborate but the ancient seer shook his head several times, "No, no, my king. The bones only show me a glimpse of what the gods have in store. I cannot say when, where, how, or even who this is meant for. However, take this reading with a warning, the shadow will cover the land, and none will be untouched. It will take great character and strong will to resist the pull of this darkness."

That last line was a very sobering warning. Nobody, including Thoros, had anything to say in response.

CHAPTER 2

The Citadel Fortress, Jebus

Among the bustling council chamber, Baaldir ducked through the first door he came to as his father dismissed them all while asking Lox and Thoros to stay behind. He wasted no time disappearing, looking over his shoulder to be sure nobody meant to stop him. His plan, if someone should try to stop him, was to pretend he didn't see or hear them and keep moving. This tactic had worked a few times. The only ones that Baaldir couldn't get away with this with were his mother and father.

He'd already been roped into the council meeting which interested him, only because of the impending doom of the Israelites bearing down on their city. His interest was in wanting to hear what his brother Thoros meant to do in the face of such odds.

The meeting had been a bore to say the least. No talk of strategy or battle plans and no talk of meeting them in the open field. Only talks of troop counts and granary stores. None of that interested him.

Baaldir knew what he would do if someone cared to ask. He would set up an ambush in multiple areas along their path and harass the advancing army the whole way to their gates where he would have traps and ploys waiting to burn and maim them. However, they would never ask him because a boy of thirteen wasn't allowed to speak, and if he did, none would acknowledge him. The only one that did was his father and occasionally Thoros. Baaldir's adopted brother Lox was always egging him on, and if he allowed himself to go along with Lox's urging, it normally ended up in discipline from his parents, and Lox would always have plausible deniability and escape unscathed. He was starting to think that was a talent only Lox had. Although, there had been times where he felt like Lox came through as a brother.

Baaldir made his way through the chamber and out into the palace proper, the afternoon was wearing on and he was hoping he could catch up with his friend Nathan before supper time. There weren't many boys his age in the court, so he'd made some friends with boys down in the lower city where most of the soldiers were housed. There they would throw rocks at targets, play fight, and pretend they were mighty warriors battling monsters that they'd think up.

Nathan's mother Ramah was nice and reminded him of his own mother. She would bake bread and pastries for them to eat. Nathan's father was a guard in the palace, whom he didn't know very well. From what little he'd talked to Nathan about him, he'd gathered that Nathan envied having a father like Adonizedek and a brother like Thoros. His father was nice enough, just the distant head in the clouds type, who would come up with a scheme to make them rich, wager his money on it and lose it all. This caused Nathan's mother lots of grief as she struggled to keep food in the house. Baaldir had heard his father call men like those fools. From time to time, he'd left a coin or two on the table, hoping to ease their burden only to find it sitting on the table waiting for him to take it back on his next visit. Nathan's mother was too proud to accept help, though she was never rude about it.

Baaldir remembered the first time he met Nathan out in the streets:

***

He was twelve then, Nathan was eleven and was a little small for his age. The other boys would push him around, steal his things and toss them over his head as he tried to jump and reach them, tears streaming down his face. The tears would send the boys into a frenzy, and their cruel response was to punch him and push his face into the dirt. They'd throw animal dung at him as he ran away. Baaldir had happened upon this one day as he was out playing on his own. Being much larger for his age, he was taller than the older boys and quite muscular for a boy of twelve, nearly thirteen years old. The boys tried to get Baaldir to join in on the harassment. Instead, he stood up for Nathan. This caused them to turn on him. For that he'd punished them, five of them, with his fists. They quickly ran away, not wanting to risk being more seriously hurt.

Helping Nathan up off the ground, they walked to the well and drew some water to wash up. Nathan was rather shy and hurried off home after but thanked him for stopping the bullies as he ran off.

Afterward, Baaldir went walking in the city and soon got lost in a section he was unfamiliar with. Turning down an alleyway, he realized that he'd found a dead end. As he started back in the direction he'd come, he was met by the same five boys he'd just tuned up. This time they were carrying sticks. Big ones, meant for doing damage.

The boys wasted no time exacting their revenge on Baaldir. He'd had the element of surprise before and had only fought one or two of them at a time in the last encounter. This time they were prepared, and he was the one at a disadvantage. One by one they hit him and beat him down to the ground. They began to kick him, crushing his ribs, his hands, and his legs, and ripped at his tunic and hit his face. It was all he could do to deflect the most brutal blows only to receive another on a different body part. Shouts of, "C'mon! Teach him a lesson!" and other vulgar insults came from each of them as their rage was slaked.

Suddenly, when he feared they would kill him, he heard two of them scream and cry out in pain. Their screams transformed into dull grunts as he heard loud crashes on the other side of the alley. Baaldir's face was already swollen and so bloody that he couldn't fully make out what was happening. All he knew was that the attacks had abruptly stopped.

Soon, he heard two of them shouting. "Run! Run!" As they fled the scene, their voices trailed off.

Then he heard his brother's voice. "Baaldir. Can you hear me? You're going to be okay. Let's get you home," as Lox picked him up and carried him cradled in front of him, purposefully moving through the streets.

The next he knew he was waking up in his bed, bandaged and bruised from head to toe. Lox sat there reading a scroll which he rolled up and then leaned forward when he realized Baaldir had awaken. "Good to see you awake Baaldir, you've been out for a few days."

"What happened?" Baaldir asked, trying to sit up.

"You were beaten pretty badly, and we were worried your injuries were more than surface level. Don't try to sit up, boy," Lox said, motioning urgently for him to lay back down.

"I want you to know that those boys will be dealt with," Lox said matter-of-factly as he got up to leave the room, saying he'd send his mother in to see him. But soon, Baaldir drifted off to sleep again and did not wake for quite a while.

It had taken Baaldir a few weeks to recover after he'd received five broken ribs, a broken forearm, and several cuts on his face, apart from the massive bruising and swollen tissue all over his body. One of the cuts would leave a scar. He didn't mind that one, it made him look older and was like his brother Thoros' scar. His wounds had healed, and he no longer remembered how badly they had hurt.

***

Baaldir snapped out of his reminiscence as he went through the gates into the lower city, noticing that no one was idle. Everyone was either preparing to leave ahead of the siege or to defend the city. The whole of the city would likely be hearing of the impending siege in the matter of an hour, some would panic.

He felt kind of guilty that he was off to play. That's something he'd realized early on that even at a young age he was attentive to the actions and motivations of others. His father called it empathy which was something that meant he could put the shoes of another on his feet and relate to what they were thinking and feeling. Perhaps that was why he jumped into action to help Nathan that day.

After he'd mostly recovered from the beating, he finally worked up the nerve to go out in the city again. His father insisted that guards accompany him, which he would duck as soon as he was able to shake them. One day he happened upon Nathan throwing a ball against a wall, playing catch with himself. He walked up and introduced himself. Nathan replied with his name and asked if he'd like to play catch with him. Then, Nathan realized Baaldir's arm was in a sling with the yellowing bruises blanketing his skin. Instead, he asked if Baaldir wanted to come to his house to eat some pastries his mother had made just that day. That was the first time he'd made a true friend outside of the occasional one around the court. They were inseparable afterwards. Baaldir would run to meet him after his lessons and play catch or hide-and-seek and chase stray cats with broomsticks.

One day, Nathan asked Baaldir if he'd show him how to fight, which he had agreed to enthusiastically. Even though Nathan was smaller in stature, it was fun to have someone near his age to spar with. Nathan was quick to study and was extremely fast and agile, which made up for the small size and he was deadly accurate throwing a stone at short distances.

After crossing a few more neighborhoods, Baaldir finally made it through the city to Nathan's house. He knocked on the door a few times and heard some arguing within. They ignored the knock and kept arguing. It sounded like Ramah and Nathan's father arguing about money and another venture that had turned out to be a failure.

"Why can't you just be happy with what we have? WHY must you always fall for these schemes?" Ramah yelled, her voice cracking between tears.

"I'm just trying to give you what I promised you Ramah! There must be more to this life than just scraping by while they stand over us and rule over our every movement."

"But I don't want those things, I want you. I want Nathan. And I want a roof over our heads and clothes on our backs. Ahmet! That is all I ever asked for and you continue to put that behind your foolishness!"

"I don't have to listen to this Ramah. You'll see it one day. Everything I've done and even the risks I've taken were for you and Nathan."

"Oh, I'll see one day? You are the one who is blind! You'll never change. And I'm cursed to love a man like you!" Ramah burst into tears.

"I must go to the palace. My post begins in an hour."

"You're working tonight? I thought you had the night off; I was preparing a meal for us!"

"I took a shift from Musa. We need the money."

"We need the money because you lost last week's pay when you thought it was wise to invest in a scheme to buy grain and resell it! We are in the middle of a drought Ahmet! How foolish can you be?"

Ahmet yelled something back that was inaudible when Baaldir heard the crash of a clay pot slamming against the wall. He assumed Ramah had thrown it as she screamed, "Get out! Get out! Get out!"

Baaldir sensed Ahmet coming to the door, so he ducked around the corner of the house just as the door opened and slammed shut. Nathan's dad stormed off in the direction of the palace.

From behind him he heard Nathan, "Sorry you had to hear that."

Baaldir turned to see Nathan sitting on a crate in the alley, kicking the dirt with his foot.

"I'm sorry Nathan, I didn't mean to eavesdrop. Are you okay?"

"Yeah, I'm okay. Just the same old argument." Nathan looked anything but okay.

Baaldir suddenly remembered why he wanted to find Nathan. "Hey. Do you want to check something out I found the other day?"

Nathan shrugged, and said, "Sure, what is it?"

"I found a secret shaft near the spring that goes under the city. I overheard some of my father's men talking about it the other day. Wait till you see it!" Baaldir said as they ran off in the direction of the Pool of Siloam.

A voice of a woman yelled out into the street, "Nathaaannnn! Supper is ready!"

"Ah! That's my mom Baaldir. I must go." Nathan said, stopping in his tracks.

"Okay, I suppose it can wait." Baaldir said with a shoulder shrug.

"Tomorrow then?" Nathan inquired.

"I have lessons most of the day. Maybe the day after would be better."

Nathan's mother yelled melodically into the street once again sounding like a songbird, "Nathaaaaan!" Then a little pause before, "Nathaaaaaaan!"

"I must go! See you in a couple of days!" Nathan said over his shoulder as he ran from the alley toward his house.

Meanwhile, after the council meeting...

Lox and Thoros left the king's chamber in a hurried procession as all the officials made their way to see to the tasks that were discussed before and during the meeting. Orvandil and Ide had stayed behind to converse with Adonizedek about other matters, as they often did. What they talked about was anyone's guess, but he imagined it would be somewhere between religion and gold. The pair of elderly advisers had made a tidy business in causing the superstitious commoners of Jebus to part with their coin in exchange for a blessing from one deity or the next. In this way they exacted almost no taxation on the populace. Ide often referred to the racket as voluntary taxation. In exchange, Adonizedek insured that each man, women, and child felt safe and had food on their tables which was provided as a charitable ration by the various temples surrounding the Citadel.

There was almost no crime to speak of on the streets because everyone had been provided for, or to put it in Orvandil parlance, "Showered with so and so's blessings" for their devotion. There were employment opportunities and homes for all. In the past, when the population was burgeoning, they were set to work building homes and marketplaces for commerce to take place. Every single inhabitant had it made as far as Lox was concerned.

He chuckled sarcastically as he thought about how his last thought was past tense. Months of siege and a drought that stretched past a year would soon take care of the horn of plenty feeling in the city. It was all on a razors edge of falling to pieces. He was now certain that this was what the three elder men were discussing as they left the hall.

The Israelites, no doubt, had assessed the state of things given the strain that a drought would have on Jebus and had set their siege at the exact right moment to exploit it. He had said as much when he pleaded with Adonizedek to strengthen their tie to Philistia but the king fancied Orvandil's advice over his when it came to the supply chain and coin. Now they were about to be completely cut off and nary a word from Philistia regarding their plight had been received.

It served them right, Lox thought coldly.

"I need to go find my wife and help her wrangle the little monsters for bedtime," Thoros said as he turned to leave.

"Very well, I have some things to attend to down below," Lox explained to Thoros who was already making his way across the courtyard. Thoros threw up a hand as he turned part way and waved goodbye.

Lox decided to head down towards the stables using a narrow staircase that served as an evacuation route from the palace. This was a detail he'd added late in the construction, and it was not drawn onto any plans. If by chance, an enemy were to have access to the scrolls showing the layout of the palace and its fortifications, they would be blind to this hidden staircase. It was so easy to miss that if someone didn't know the staircase was there, they'd pass right by it. Due to an optical illusion that caused it to look just like the façade of the palace garden, even Lox sometimes had difficulty seeing it. In a matter of a few minutes, he descended to the ground where it exited into a small room that had an iron gate, which was locked. Producing a key, he inserted and twisted it to release the latch inside the gate. It swung freely toward him, and he stepped through into a much larger room meant to hold the citizens of Jebus should retreat to the Citadel be necessary. It was estimated that up to one thousand could inhabit the large room at any given time.

Naturally, the women and children would be the first to occupy as the men prepared to defend the fortress. A gauntlet of stations covered a retreat. From the inside, the door would lower into place concealing the people from the carnage outside. The door was made of stone and, once in place, it could only be opened from the inside using pulleys and levers. This allowed for the weight to be managed by several able-bodied people at the ends of the ropes.

The door was so formidable and placed in such a way that anyone wishing to break it down would have to spend considerable time under the rain of arrows and boiling tar. This meant that everyone inside was completely safe from the onslaught. At least those lucky enough to make it into the fortress would be spared. The Israelites would need to make it up to the summit to defeat Adonizedek and his armies. Lox liked to think this was impossible given his ingenuity and skill at building and ploys, but he had nearly been on the wrong end of the sword once before years ago in Jericho against these very same foes. Had he not escaped during the night just before the final day, he would've been slain just like all the others. Instead, he'd watched from the hills the next morning as Jericho became a pile of smoking rubble.

In a few moments Lox came to a junction where he could go left and reach the stables, or right, and head to the prison. Instead he stopped for a moment and realized he had made suitable time, so he decided to double back to a room he kept to himself, to which he alone held the key.

Once inside Lox looked around for a moment. It was a spacious room with a library of scrolls and various artifacts and weapons adorning the walls. There was a door on the other side that he made his way to. It had no handles or keyholes to be used to open the door. Holding out his palm, he pressed against the emblem of a winged serpent that protruded from the flush surface of the door. Lox turned it clockwise 180°, then turned it counterclockwise 360°. Finally he turned the emblem clockwise 180° to bring it back upright. The door hissed and popped as inner gears and bars moved with each turn. As the emblem found its final place the door opened and swung towards him slowly. He pulled it towards him and ducked through the opening.

Once through, Lox turned back and pulled the door shut. Then he turned a lever on the door to set the bolts into the stone wall, locking the door behind him. He walked down a set of stairs that descended deep into the ground and at the bottom, opened into another room that was lit by slow burning lamps filled with oil. This room was also not on the plans, and he used it to house anything that he would not want prying eyes to see, such as powerful potions, poisons, and antidotes.

He took one lamp from the wall hanger and walked across the room to another door where the same emblem of a winged serpent adorned the center. This door opened freely into the next section. He normally left this unlocked but could easily turn a handle upward to latch the door and it would need a key to open from the other side.

Lox entered a long hallway that was dark, except for his lamp. Passing by rows of empty cells made of iron bars, he came to a junction and heard a stirring in the darkness ahead and the sound of chains rustling; his guard dogs as he liked to call them, but they were far more dangerous than dogs or even lions.

The beasts were dumb, near blind, had strong noses and were fierce as wolves; perfect for a dungeon such as this and their imposing size made them formidable guards should any try to enter or exit. They smelled him coming as he approached, and he could make out the shapes looming in the distant darkness. Instinctively, they shrank back to their places as he walked by knowing that to come near the master was punishable by flogging.

He had found the two of them on an island far away in the land of the Ionians where they were born male and female twins, and he had snuck into the cave where they were nested and stole them while mother was away hunting. He remembered hearing the mother's cries of despair as he rowed towards his anchored vessel. From the moment he brought them back to Jebus he raised them to be cruel and to respect his authority. They hated him and loved him at the same time.

Lox passed by the cells where his prisoners were kept just out of the reach of his beasts. They barely stirred when he stopped and looked through the bars at him. He thought that they looked too skinny but only because they might be able to squeeze between the bars, so he reached into his satchel and pulled out a small loaf of bread, tore off a third of it, and tossed it into the middle of the five boys. They descended upon it, clawing, and scraping to be the one to reach the food that they had been deprived of for days. In mere seconds, the bread was torn to pieces and each one retreated with his take to separate corners.

He reached into his pouch one last time and retrieved a cloth. The pair of one-eyed beasts stirred as soon as he pulled it out. They could smell the contents concealed in the cloth as Lox unwrapped the objects, revealing two hocks of pork. He tossed one to each of them and they immediately went to work on them.

Lox was in a generous mood, so before leaving, he broke the bread in half and tossed it into the cell where the captives reconvened their ravenous struggle for food. Those boys had long forgotten their life before he'd taken them from their beds at night. Each of the five were responsible for Baaldir's injuries and he doubted that after what he had put them through, that they even knew whether they were man or animal any longer. Soon they would be serving Tsalmaveth. That was their fate now.

He passed by the two giant beasts and up a set of stairs into a grand room he had turned into a temple of sorts, deep in the dungeons away from prying eyes. As he walked toward the altar, he noticed a stirring in the dimly torchlit corners and alcoves. He could feel eyes on him as movement stirred in the shadows. Upon reaching the altar, twelve gaunt-faced men dressed in black cloaks converged on the center to surround the altar. These were known to him as Shades, servants of Tsalmaveth, made to be his eyes above and to search the Shadow Realm for The Key that would bring about the resurrection of Yaldabaoth, the enemy of Elohim.

The Shades were a recent addition to Tsalmaveth's evolving plan to finally locate the Key that had eluded him for millennia. As was explained to Lox, the Key was an essential component in the plan. Tsalmaveth's goal was not only to finally sever his tie to the box through acquiring a permanent vessel, but also to find The Key which he would then use to release Yaldabaoth from his underworld prison. Creating the Shades served to give him a network of spies that could walk in the Shadow Realm while simultaneously monitoring the natural world for signs or evidence of the location of this Key that he desired.

The way Lox understood it, The Key would be guarded closely and like-ly the only way to locate it would be through the use of the Shadow Realm, which Lox was unfamiliar with. He'd never seen the Shadow Realm before, but it was he who had found reference to it and The Key decades ago in a remote reliquary of scrolls and artifacts far to the east in the magical land of China.

For decades after opening the stone box, Lox and Tsalmaveth scoured palaces, observatories, reliquaries, and libraries the world over until one day they came across a multiple-volume collection of scrolls, written in an ancient language that resembled the symbols on the stone box. This turned out to be the boon of information they'd been searching for as Tsalmaveth was coincidentally able to fluently read the symbols on the scrolls.

It was there that they formed the plan to inhabit Goliath's body and use him to strike the first blow against Elohim and his special pets, the Israelites. The hope was that this would draw out The Guardian of the Key. Upon defeating the Guardians, the Key would likely be revealed to Tsalmaveth. When the plot to use Goliath was defeated, they had returned to Jebus and begun their subterfuge within, building networks the world over, and fortifying Jebus was the cover for all of it.

Lox placed a box on the altar and pulled the top off. A thick cloud of black smoke exited and took the form of a human above the altar, but it did not have a face where a face should be. Just a black void that looked deeper than a bottomless pit. The being moved around the room and circled back to a place on the other side of the altar. The Shades swayed back and forth as the being began to speak. His name was Tsalmaveth. The Shadow of Death.

"How have the preparations been going Lox? Where is my army of Shades?" Tsalmaveth said, almost accusatorially.

Lox was quick to answer, "Master, I have several candidates in a cell now. But they are not broken yet, soon I will bring them to you. I have five now not including those standing here."

"Five?!" Tsalmaveth scoffed. "Paltry sacrifices. I require an army not an entourage. YOU need to bring me more and bring them to me SOON!"

Tsalmaveth paced the floor in front of the altar. "I am impatient to begin the next phase. Don't forget what I've promised you, power beyond your imagination."

"I will bring more, Master. It's just that it's been difficult to find them and even more difficult to kidnap them without anyone knowing. I can't risk being found out or everything we've worked towards will be jeopardized. And the temple under the mount is so close to being completed and King Adonizedek is none the wiser."

"You must branch out to other regions then. Tyre, Ugarit, Egypt, the Far East if you must. I will not wait much longer; I've waited more than a thousand years."

Tsalmaveth stopped pacing and looked toward Lox. "If you do not bring me what I require I will withdraw my favor from you."

Lox winced, "We are two days away from having an Israelite army on our doorstep. Leaving will be nearly impossible. I'll have to find ways to get around the siege."

"Israelites you say?" Tsalmaveth said with emphasis on the word 'Israelites'. He sounded almost giddy with his shadowy fingers tickling one another in anticipation, a derisive chuckle escaping from the void. "Oh, that'll do just fine! Have you ever met an Israelite who was not devout? They all worship one God and dismiss all others. You must bring them to me. They are just the sort I need for my army. And I have a score to settle besides."

Lox hadn't expected this reaction from Tsalmaveth. "Israelites? How many?"

Tsalmaveth brought his arms up in front of his face, his hands with what passed for fingers came together at their tips and he smiled a dark and vacant grin. "Israelites indeed. Bring them to me Lox. By the hundreds. Use my Shades to help you steal them at night and bring them back through the tunnels to my dungeon."

Hundreds, Lox thought. How would he ever break that many? He didn't want to risk Tsalmaveth's wrath so he simply replied, "It will be done Master."

"Do not fail me Lox, I have high hopes for you." Tsalmaveth said as he dispersed into a smoke cloud and reentered the stone box. The Shade next to Lox secured the lid and placed it underneath the altar.

Lox thought back to when he'd first learned of the box after the Philistines had captured the Ark in a battle near Shiloh:

***

1090 B.C.: Philistia after the battle at Eben-Ezer

After a victorious battle against the Israelites, the Philistines had captured the infamous Ark of the Covenant from the Israelite priests at Shiloh. In their celebration they hastily carried it back to their land and over the course of seven months moved it between each of the five cities of Philistia. In each city they experienced plagues of rats, and many grew tumors on the outsides of their bodies. Still others died outright after touching the Ark. This was the first time Lox had seen the Ark up close as he followed the procession touring the cities. The last time he'd seen the Ark was from a distance before he'd nearly lost his life in Jericho a few hundred years ago and escaped by the skin of his teeth.

In Ashdod, the Philistines placed it in the temple of Dagon to celebrate their capturing of the Israelite god. The ark was meant to be an offering to the half man-half fish deity. They worshipped this deity, being a people that traversed the ocean before coming to Canaan a hundred years ago. At the urging of Lox, they had become a scourge of the Israelites and had dominated them on and off again for a hundred years.

They had originally attacked the Pharoah in Egypt, being known as the Sea People, and were eventually defeated by Ramses III. This event had opened an opportunity for the Cretans who had emerged from the collapse of the Mycenaean culture in Crete toward the end of the era. Driven to the sea by war and famine, they had brought their knowledge of seafaring with them and after several meetings with Cretan clan leaders, he convinced them to expand their settlement off the coast of Canaan and permanently make their home next door to the Israelites. Thousands of men and their families flocked to Canaan in an invasion that was impossible to stop. Within a generation they had grown to more than one hundred thousand and were able to field a force equal to that of Israel having founded five major cities in their newly formed country called Philistia. These Cretans had become known as Philistines over the last hundred years or so.

The next morning, the people panicked as they found that the statue of Dagon was toppled over and broken in half overnight. Several men were slain in gruesome fashion and lying around the temple grounds. Apparently, they had tried to open the lid of the Ark and had paid with their lives. Panic set in around the city and soon the Ark was packed up and carried away from the temple. Goliath of Gath had urged that it be brought to his city for safe keeping.

Naturally, Lox accompanied the procession carrying the Ark. He remembered hearing whispers of the contents over the years. Legend held that it contained artifacts from the Hebrew's time in the desert. This was likely the reason those men had tried to open it, hoping to find a great treasure or a powerful weapon that would explain the Israelite god's power and maybe even allow them to use it in subduing the Israelites.

Lox wanted to see for himself but did not want to experience the same fate of the last men to touch it. He overheard Goliath talking about how to open it on their journey to Gath. Lox had his doubts but was resolved to observe from a distance as the big lout attempted it.

Upon reaching Gath they took it to Goliath's Hall and placed it in the center of the large main room. After a series of orders an entourage of slaves walked in and stood before him.

"You will now open this box," Goliath said, "The first man to open this box will be given his freedom. Do it now," he ordered. The slaves, knowing what box sat before them, hesitated and some even backed further away in fear. The offer to give them their freedom was no good if they were too dead to see it.

Goliath raged, "Oh you fear death? Do it now or I will be the one to do the smiting!" He pounded the butt of his spear on the stone floor to emphasize his point. It was clear that they believed him as all of them began to creep toward the Ark, timidly at first but more confidently the closer they approached.

The first one to reach it lunged for the lid and was able to push it ever so slightly before his body went airborne, his neck simultaneously twisting his head backward as Lox heard a series of snapping sounds. Not one second later, two more slaves attempted to push the lid open and were only able to move it a bit further before being killed. The other slaves watched in horror as one of the slave's limbs were pulled from all directions by an unseen force. The invisible beings pulled each limb from its socket one by one with a snapping and popping sound, blood gushing in all directions. The third man to touch it spontaneously combusted and was burnt to ash in an instant, his ashes falling to the floor in a messy pile even before his screams faded.

The panic that ensued was nothing short of astounding as Lox watched the slaves halt their advance and run toward the door only to be stopped by the guards, their spears leveled to thwart their escape. Goliath shouted curses and threats as he rallied them for another ill-conceived attempt. One by one, under threat of execution the slaves tried to open the Ark, only to be punished for their trespass with their lives. It was within this mayhem that he heard a voice clear as day.

"Son of Cain. Come forth!" Lox wasn't sure he'd heard anything at all as the noise around him faded into a dull hum.

"Son of Cain. Come forth!" the voice said again.

Upon hearing those words, a second time, he was now able to see two radiant beings standing like sentries in front of the Ark. Lox had never seen such beings before standing as tall as the roof and glowing red-hot. There were four heads on each of them. The first head facing him was that of a man. The second was an ox, set over the right shoulder. The third was an eagle facing him from the back with a long neck that allowed it to look forward. Finally the fourth head was that of a lion over the left shoulder. Multiple arms and wings covered their upper body, each being covered completely with eyes of every color under the sun. In one hand they each held a fiery sword that blazed white hot and radiated an intense heat that would make anyone within ten feet uncomfortable.

The voice called again, this time coming from one of the beings, "Come Forth, Son of Cain."

The other being followed with, "It is time for you to play your part, Author of Chaos."

'Son of Cain' and 'Author of Chaos?' That was the first time he had heard those words addressing him though he felt an excitement stir amid the trepidation. Then he realized that he was walking forward as if his mind was separate from his body. Those around him were now frozen where they stood, unmoving and oblivious to the beings guarding the Ark.

Goliath, filled with rage, was tossing a man toward the Ark who was suspended in mid-air with a horrified look on his face. Still others were in varying stages of obliteration having touched the Ark. There were so many things happening at once that were now frozen in place as though time had stopped.

Lox involuntarily walked toward what he assumed would be his own demise, not able to stop his own feet from stepping forward. As he approached, the two beings parted to the sides, but they did not move as if with feet. Instead, each of them moved in a sort of glide, their bottom half taking on the appearance of fiery wheels. Lox passed by them and felt a blinding heat touch his face and eyes. It was everything he could do to keep his eyes open as he saw an eagle head from one being's shoulder snapping at him, and the other's lion head roaring while angrily gnashing his teeth, spittle flying from its jaws. These beings were clearly not happy with him and his proximity to the Ark, but they let him by while protesting the intrusion as if some other force was blocking them from attacking him.

As he stepped forward the lid of the Ark began to levitate over his head. Upon reaching the Ark, he felt himself reach into the box and pull out a hewn stone box from inside. The box was hot to the touch, he could feel his fingertips sizzling as the flesh burned and blistered. Had he been in control he would have dropped the box well before injury, but instead he extracted the stone vessel from the Ark to the detriment of his own skin. The pain was excruciating as he yelled at the top of his lungs. He saw other artifacts inside as well: a bowl with a white airy looking grain of some type, a rod that had leaves growing from it as though it were rooted in the ground, and a tablet containing Hebrew characters. He couldn't read them quickly enough but was able to make out the inscription of one of them loosely translated 'Thou shalt not Steal.' The irony was not lost on him as his body withdrew the stone box from the Ark.

No sooner had his burnt hands cleared the outer wall of the Ark than the lid slammed down tight as if the intrusion was only tolerated for this purpose and not one second longer. The Ark was closed again, and the two beings propelled him away from the center of the room. As his body slammed against the stone wall, Lox fell to the ground nearly losing grip of the box, which was no longer burning his hands, to his relief. As he reaffirmed his hold on the box, the action in the room continued as if he had never moved from his place on the outer edge of Goliath's chamber. The slaves were killed, maimed, and vaporized one by one, as Goliath continued his foolhardy attempt to open the Ark.

Lox heard the same voice from before calling out to him, "Leave this room, Son of Cain. Do not come back until you've learned the part you must play!"

The command from the unseen voice was absolute and he felt compelled to heed the order. At this point his body was no longer his own. Lox picked up a cloak, wrapped the box into it and slinked off through the rear door. Once outside his legs began to run. Lox ran faster than he'd ever thought was possible and for three days he did not stop. At one point he felt like he was out of his body while watching himself run like a man possessed.

Finally he stopped at the top of a mountain far to the north and collapsed in front of a dilapidated hovel that looked as if it were abandoned years ago. The high altitude had caused the temperature to drop, and it was all he could do to drag himself, exhausted from three days of involuntary running, into the drafty hovel. There he fell asleep shivering and slept for at least an entire day. When he awoke his strength returned somewhat, being of strong constitution and no stranger to strenuous living. The first thing he did, with his injured hands, was collect firewood and build a fire in the hearth to warm himself. Then he found plants that had healing properties and made a salve for the burns and wrapped them with strips of cloth that he'd found in the abode.

The stone box sat across from him on a rickety old table. It spoke to him, almost calling him to it. The moment he touched the box he could feel the heat coming from it. Picking it up, he turned it over in his hands and he saw that on it were inscriptions chiseled into the lid and onto each side. Lox knew every language, but this one was different; the characters were foreign to him but somehow felt familiar. The lid seemed to be sealed with wax and took some prying to make it budge, made more difficult by his injured hands. Upon opening it, he remembered seeing the familiar smoke exit the box and meeting Tsalmaveth for the first time.

"Son of Cain, we meet again." The shadowy figure said, his face an abyssal void that would devour anything that focused too hard on it.

Lox, hearing this name again to describe him said curtly, "Who is Cain and what do you mean by 'we meet again'? "

"I was there at the beginning, Son of Cain."

Lox was more confused now than ever before, "I don't understand what you mean, shadow. What beginning?"

"I am Tsalmaveth, the Shadow of Death. You and I have a shared destiny which you will see unfold before your own eyes. All will become clear to you, Son of Cain. There is much work to do, and I require your help to do it since I am bound to this box until a vessel is obtained by which I can subsist. Until then, you are my arms. Do you understand?"

***

Lox recalled that he didn't understand then, but he'd shaken his head in the affirmative and over the next several months he stayed there under the instruction of Tsalmaveth, learning of the underworld and all the workings therein. Tsalmaveth felt comfortable speaking freely here away from civilization. This seemed like a favorable thing to Lox who kept up a façade with King Adonizedek that he was working to build up a resistance to Israel that would not implicate Jebus or King Adonizedek. Still, any time he inquired on the origin of the Son of Cain, as he was called, Tsalmaveth would brush it off and offer him unclear and confusing responses. Lox was told to be patient and to expect a great reward if he played his part and helped bring about the resurrection of Yaldabaoth. That was the goal, as far as he'd been told. He asked over and over to go back to Jebus to begin their preparations, but Tsalmaveth kept saying cryptic things about the timing and having to wait for 'the one' to be born. According to Tsalmaveth, time was on their side. Lox instead spent his time obtaining copies of scrolls of ancient mysteries to educate himself on the power he'd stumbled upon. He found references to Cain going back thousands of years. He'd never known his father and those beings, whatever they were, had called him 'Son of Cain.' Lox couldn't be sure, but his assumption was that he was somehow linked to Cain by blood or some other means.

It was nearly 60 years later, and only after the death of Goliath at the hands of David, that he made his way back to Jebus with the stone box hidden in his cargo. Most men lived and died in that span of time. But not the rulers of Jebus or Lox himself. They were ageless, connected to a powerful lineage. It was almost as if he'd never left, except that Adonizedek had fathered more children. Baaldir and Vithas were the new additions to the palace in the years to follow, as well as many daughters who were since married off to faraway kings and lords. Lox had been introduced to them as a blood brother to Thoros. He was not the boy's brother but took on more of an uncle type role with them.

Since then, he'd built the temple to Yaldabaoth, his new god, and soon the new underground temple would be completed, ready and waiting for the coming of Yaldabaoth, whom Lox had started to believe may be the key to his finally finding and taking revenge on the peoples that brutally murdered his mother. Tsalmaveth had promised to give him powers beyond his imagination in exchange for his building the material infrastructure to prepare for the rise of Yaldabaoth. He had since learned that Yaldabaoth had a huge following in Babylon and in Egypt. None of them had ever met Tsalmaveth, but he was revered for the chaos he'd caused in Egypt centuries ago. The building of the fortress around the palace had been at the behest of Tsalmaveth who showed him hidden passages and caverns that connected a wide swath of Canaan to Mount Moriah. Lox had built it up in graduating levels to conceal the tunnels below Mount Moriah and connect them to the fortress. His dungeon was directly connected to the new location for the temple in the dark bowels of the mountain. Neglect had been his friend in this endeavor because neither Adonizedek nor Thoros cared to venture into the dungeon.

For the first time in a long time, he felt like his life had a direction rather than that of a rudderless vessel. Now his purpose was to bring the resurrection of Yaldabaoth from his prison and in doing so, gain the power to right the wrongs done to him over his long life and maybe find the answers to burning questions.

Recently, he'd found a reference to an amulet that gave the wearer great power. It reminded him of one he'd given to a woman he loved long ago. He intended to retrieve and use it to increase his power in hopes that would entice Tsalmaveth to bestow his power on him. He'd asked overtly and been brushed off with excuses that didn't make sense to him, but he'd continued to work on the tasks the Shadow of Death required regardless, hoping that one day he'd become worthy. Apparently, Yaldabaoth had other plans for him beyond the power of Tsalmaveth. This was according to the Shadow of Death. He couldn't decide if he believed it or if it was just another excuse to string him along. Though he buried any thought of resentment as Tsalmaveth could read people like no other.

Lox learned through research that Tsalmaveth was bound by Michael, an archangel that served the Israelite God. Michael had placed him in the box and sealed it with lamb's blood and wax. He hadn't been seen since the early days of man, though rumors of his appearance in Egypt at the time the Hebrew left captivity persisted in many scrolls.

Soon, it would be made known to the world again. The Shadow of Death could not be conquered because it was an aspect of death itself. If something so powerful served Yaldabaoth, then he wondered how powerful Yaldabaoth was. Maybe powerful enough to go toe to toe with the Israelites god. How poetic would that be to witness the battle between two powerful gods who were arch enemies?

Lox looked to the Shades who were standing there looking at him with vacant stares. "Our Master requires souls. See to it." With that the Shades dispersed to carry out the will of Tsalmaveth.

Meanwhile nearby...

Hiding in the dark corners of the dungeon, Ahmet had spied on Lox several times during his rituals in the temple. Having found a secret vantage above the temple, he would climb into it crouched, and from there he could peer through a slit that allowed him to see the altar.

Ahmet couldn't understand why but he was drawn to it. What had started out as a fearful curiosity had formed into a type of secret obsession. It was frightening to see the brutal nature of it, and he wasn't one to do dangerous things, but he could sense the power, and it intrigued him. One time he'd seen Lox torture a slave on the altar. A black cloud had formed above the altar and descended into the man. Afterward the man was no longer a man. He was what he'd heard Lox call a Shade. The Shade then used the dagger that Lox handed him to cut out his own tongue. With the blood the Shade had traced over a stone carving of the Hebrew word Tsalmaveth. The black smoke went back into the stone box that Lox held and was placed somewhere near the altar. He was curious to see what was inside the box, but he didn't dare enter the temple for fear that he'd be found by the Shades, and they thoroughly scared him.

This time, Ahmet had witnessed something he'd not seen yet. Instead of performing a ritual, Lox had summoned a creature from the stone box that appeared to be a man, or rather, the shape of one. Ahmet couldn't quite make out their conversation, but it appeared that the being had given Lox a task and sent the Shades out to see to it. Usually, the throng of Shades concealed the placement of the box from his view. This time, he watched as the Shades dispersed leaving Lox standing there alone. From his hiding place he watched as Lox took it and inserted it into a cutout in the altar. He pulled a lever on the side of the altar that, to a passerby would just look ornamental. The opening covered up by the false door made the altar look seamless. Lox exited the temple and went in the direction of the stables.

Ahmet didn't move for several minutes. He thought about the being that had come from the box and for a moment thought about going to the altar and opening it. But he didn't dare, for fear that those Shades would return, and he'd be exposed.

As he waited his mind kept going back to his wife Ramah. He feared his mishaps had finally caused her to see him differently. The latest argument had been worse than ever before. So bad that he feared that she would never forgive him. He only wanted to provide a better life for her which was why he risked his pay to buy in on a shipment of grain. The game was to buy it wholesale from a Phoenician merchant and sell it in the city of Jebus at a profit. He'd given a man named Japheth his share, as had several others. Japheth then told everyone the shipment would come in on the next ship and he'd have it by the following week ready for sale. The problem was, there was no grain shipment. Japheth had been taking coins from as many as he could, promising them different rates of return over different time periods. Japheth would pocket the money and when someone came looking for their return, he would pay them what he told them he'd pay. Japheth was effectively using Ahmet's investment to pay someone else back on the other side of the city. It all came unraveled three days after Ahmet had given him all his savings. Japheth was found out and arrested, his money seized by the treasurer. He'd been put to death the next day and with him, any chance that he'd recoup his loss. Japheth kept no paper records, so everything was word of mouth and by memory.

Ahmet couldn't believe his run of rotten luck. He'd invested in a vineyard that went sour last year at the start of the drought. That was the first time Ramah had gotten angry with him, and he'd promised not to risk their funds like that anymore. This time it really seemed like a sure thing, which it was obviously not, hindsight being what it is.

A few minutes passed until he felt safe enough to exit his hiding place. He had to get back to the prison above before his shift started. There would be no time to check in on Vlulor and Flagor before heading to his post for the night. He always gave himself time to play with them and feed them but tonight would be an exception because he hadn't expected to have to hide for so long.

Lox was generally cruel to them, and Ahmet pitied them. Lox was, for all he knew, unaware of his interaction with them. However, the beasts would not allow him to pass by them, which had made him curious about what was on the other side of them.

One day a year ago, Ahmet had found a way to slip past them and had stumbled upon the temple and seen the prisoners in a pen outside of it. He remembered the dread he'd felt that night and had not returned for quite some time after. If not for his curiosity toward the two one-eyed giants chained up underneath, he wouldn't have returned at all.

Part of the reason he was able to enter the temple area was because he'd found a key to a door that another jailer had left lay about carelessly. It now was kept on his belt, lost to anyone else. During a boring shift he found himself alone and decided to explore, trying to find any door he did not already have access to, hoping for the key to unlock it. He'd heard many inklings of the secret passages below the prison and his curiosity had gotten the better of him. So far, he had done an excellent job of only going there when the chance of anyone else coming by was zero.

Ahmet suddenly realized something that Lox had said to the being; the Israelites were due any day on their doorstep. A siege was imminent.

As he was leaving the temple he glanced back at the altar and thought he could hear someone call his name in a faint voice, almost a whisper.

CHAPTER 3

Goshen, Egypt: 1513 B.C.

More than five hundred years before

*C*omplete and total darkness stretched into its third day as Moses and Aaron ran through the affluent districts of Thebes, hurrying to reach Goshen to warn the people of Israel of the coming calamity and instruct them on how to protect themselves; Aarons staff glowed to light the way.

This darkness was the type that a person could feel. It covered everything and left every single person and animal blind and unable to move about. Not a sound except fearful wails and cries for help could be heard echoing through the desolate streets. Miraculously, the Israelites that lived in Goshen had been spared from this plague just as they were the other eight plagues. It was an invisible dome had been erected over their homes that protected them from the horrors.

Each plague was intended to directly attack a corresponding Egyptian god or goddess: The first plague of blood that turned the rivers red was a direct attack on Hapi and Osiris, who were the gods of the Nile. This was followed by a plague of millions of frogs that covered each home and made travel on the streets impossible. This plague was intended as an affront to Heqet, a local goddess of fertility. Six more plagues had rained down upon the citizens of Egypt over the last few weeks including: lice, flies, livestock pestilence, painful boils, hail and finally locusts that destroyed their wheat harvests and rendered their god , Seth, meaningless.

The current plague of darkness was intended to show Egypt that Elohim was in control of the sun, not Re or Horus. They were powerless, false gods that could not stand against the one who created the sun and placed it in the firmament of Heaven. Pharoah's magicians and alchemists had tried everything from sacrifices to cutting themselves to relieve their afflictions and those of the people of Egypt. But this was beyond their understanding and every attempt had been a failure to the point that Pharoah had begun *to execute his mystics as they failed for the last time. Through all of this, Pharoah's heart was hardened like a stone and would not budge from his defiance to Elohim. This pained Moses, to see a man who had grown up with him in the palace be so set upon his own destruction and that of his own people. Had he allowed the Hebrew to leave, thousands upon thousands of lives would have been saved. However, Pharoah was altogether deceived and willfully ignorant of the causes of this misfortune.*

Moses and Aaron carefully negotiated the streets finding that there were people strewn about huddled in fear unable to even sense when someone was close. The darkness stuck to their bones and hung from them like a stone around their neck. Cries of panic and pleas for help continued to echo all around them as the pair walked down the main thoroughfare that led straight the Palace that Moses had called home nearly forty years prior.

Moses and Aaron had just come from their final visit to Pharoah, resulting in a final refusal to free the Hebrews from bondage, sealing the fates of every living firstborn creature in Egypt, from humans down to the lowly livestock. None would be spared. According to a messenger, Elohim was releasing an old foe from captivity to exact His vengeance on the people of Egypt and Pharoah whose heart was set against Elohim and His will. This foe was called Tsalmaveth. The Shadow of Death would visit all of Egypt tonight.

The next morning...

The sun rose in the East for the first time in three days. Wails of grief and anguish could be heard all around the surrounding districts and all the way up and down the Nile River.

Moses was working on fastening up his sandal straps when he heard a knock on the door. Aaron, who was preparing a plate of dates and some aish-baladi bread from the night before, answered the door from his seat. "Who's there?"

From the other side of the door, muffled by the crudely made board and batten panel, a man answered. "I am here on an errand, and I am looking for Moses. I need to speak to him urgently."

Moses motioned to Aaron that it was okay to open the door. They'd tried to keep their location secret, even from their own people, for fear that Pharoah would send soldiers to arrest them if his dwelling had been known. Only a handful of people even knew which one they'd stayed in last. Aaron had sought out abandoned hovels throughout Goshen, which they alternated every few days. Most Israelites didn't even know their location, which turned out to be a good thing. There had been reports every night, up until the darkness plague, where soldiers had combed the streets of Goshen searching for the pair, the two brothers who'd made a fool of the Egyptian gods. Pharoah, a god in his own right, had ordered the searches.

Aaron stalled, clearly skeptical that someone meant them harm after the previous night's events. "Brother, we ought to be careful. I've taken great pains to conceal our movements. This could be a trap," he said worriedly.

Moses arose and walked the short distance to the door and looked at Aaron and cracked a nervous smile. "Our movements were clearly not as secret as we hoped, Brother." he said as he released the latch that was the only thing holding the rickety door closed.

"If this is a trap then we are clearly caught in its snare." he calmly said, letting the door swing inward on the leather straps that fastened it to a pole on the door frame.

Before them stood an extremely tall man, a whole head taller, and then some, compared to any of the tallest men in Egypt. He stood there like a statue, his brown cloak covering him with a low hanging hood that concealed his eyes from Moses and Aaron.

Moses tried to be cordial but his tone betrayed suspicion. "I am Moses, whom you seek. And to whom am I speaking?"

"I am called Michael by some. What I have to say should be uttered indoors away from the eyes and ears of others."

Moses had no intention of refusing entry to such an imposing man as he stood aside and motioned for Michael to walk through the door. Michael moved decisively as he ducked under the lentil and entered the home. He was barely able to fit under the roof, though now his great height was magnified ten-fold by the close quarters of this hovel. His head reached to the top of the thatched roof overhead as his wide shoulders filled the limited space.

Moses pushed the door closed behind him and fastened the toggle that latched it closed. As Michael turned to face them, he drew back the hood, revealing his face for the first time. A bright glow illuminated the room as it emanated from him in waves that carried a low humming frequency.

Seeing the luminous display in front of them said more than any order of words could say. Moses and Aaron simultaneously fell to their knees and placed their foreheads on the ground, reaching back and blindly removing their sandals. His next words were contrite, knowing that the place they knelt on was holy ground. "Your servant is here, Lord. What would you have me do?" His voice quivered and lost its luster in the presence of an Angel of the Lord.

As the glow subsided, Michael wasted no time. "This morning, Pharoah will announce that the people of Israel shall be released. The show of power from The Most High last night has convinced him, though he will pursue your people after and meet his end. The Lord will provide a way to escape and deliver you from him."

Aaron was clearly relieved. "Finally, our people will be free. But what is so pressing that an archangel of the Lord would come to our humble dwelling to speak to us? Apologies for being so forward, I meant no disrespect."

Michael, showing no inclination that he felt that Aaron's question was unwelcome nor unexpected, moved his hand in a sweeping motion and pointed to the table. On it sat a box made of stone where nothing but a fruit plate had existed moments before.

"Inside this box is the tool that was used for your deliverance. It was taken from a place far away from here with significant risk. This Shadow of Death

was guarded by Azrael, the Angel of Death. He guarded it because though it is his own shadow, it has a persona of its own that cannot be allowed to roam freely. This box keeps it contained. It cannot travel far from it without a willing host and to be permanently bound requires a dark ritual. Any man who encounters this will be affected. You must take great care that no man opens this box lest they risk being corrupted."

Moses, recovering from his nearly prone position on the floor, looked the box over. He could feel an uncomfortable heat coming from it. It was slightly rounded like a jar but had four distinct sides to it. The top was tightly sealed with wax and what appeared to be blood. Michael didn't seem to mind that he was touching and looking it over with curiosity. If he did, he did not convey any disagreement and seemed content to allow the mortals to wonder at this simple box.

Moses spoke wondrously, "Is that...?"

"Lambs blood? That is correct." Michael replied, finishing his question.

"Pardon my questions, but why bring it here? Wouldn't it be safer with the Lord's angel, Azrael?" Moses asked.

He knew truly little about the inner workings of Elohim and his angels. But he couldn't fathom that Azrael was not a safer wager than a mere mortal such as himself.

Michael clearly expected Moses, a human, to have many questions and doubts, "An Angel of the Lord will draw the darkest foes to this box, not since the garden of Eden has this evil been felt in the world, as the Shadow of Death's location has been concealed from all who would seek to use it to locate The Key. Opening the seal was like a cosmic signal that awoke a rising darkness; one that even the Angel of Death cannot protect against. This event has set into motion an event that will culminate in an ultimate battle that will stretch over many lands across the world. Your deliverance comes with a heavy price, one that the Lord now requires a covenant to satisfy. Until the appointed time, this being must stay in this box, hidden from the world. Your people must carry it with you and at that appointed time, must take it and hide it. The question isn't whether this darkness will be released, but when. For Elohim's plan to work it must be done as He requires. If you do exactly as you are asked, His plan will work. Do it not and your people will suffer for it and the world will suffer in turn. The darkness that has awakened will stop at nothing to find The Key."

Michael clearly took Moses and Aaron's dumbfounded silence as confusion. He softened his demeanor slightly by relaxing his squared shoulders and explained further. "The entire underworld is aware of this evil and will be doing everything it can to obtain this power. It must not happen until the appointed time. It must be done by your people; in return, the Lord will make you a holy people and will prosper you if you heed his commandments and follow his laws. Your descendants will number the stars, which is the promise He made to your ancestor Abraham centuries ago."

He walked over to the box sitting on the table, picked it up and walked toward Aaron, holding the box out for Aaron to take. "You will be the High

Priest that will be responsible for the spiritual journey of His people. Your priests, the Levites, will also be the guardian of this box. This warning I give you: the darkness in this box will tempt and torment anyone who stays with it too long. It wants to be released but can only be if the seal is broken. Only your strongest willed priests should handle this box. It will test even the most devout among you."Aaron, taking the box, trembled at being handed an object from an Angel, and an Archangel no less.

Moses and Aaron looked at each other and then turned their eyes back toward Michael, but he was gone without a trace. They could sense a faint vibration coming from the stone box, almost like it was responding to being alone in the presence of mortals, daring them to withstand it.

The Palace Gardens, Jebus 1010 B.C.

In the late afternoon heat, too dry to even sweat, Adonizedek and Thoros sat in the garden under the shade of a tree watching his grandchildren play among the trees and ornamental plants and ferns. Birds chirped loudly, lost in their own conversations above their heads. Siv and Frigg sat nearby conversing, the look on their faces betraying the anxiety of the pending siege. The sun was beginning to set and in two days' time, the Israelites would be at their doorstep. Birds continued to chirp a few melodies that differed in pitch and speed but still somehow melded into unison while his ravens flew high overhead, careless of the struggle that was about to ensue. This was the struggle of men, not of birds. Adonizedek envied his ravens, Hugin and Munin in this, although they understood the goings on of men more than most animals. He'd even taught them to speak several words, and they could communicate adequately, especially when they wanted food and could even recite the names of his grandchildren upon seeing them, which thrilled the little ones to no end. In his own way he was able to commune with them to receive simple messages and they were stellar at understanding commands.

"How are the preparations coming son?" Adonizedek inquired.

"About as well as can be I suppose. The walls are strong, we have food and water, though not unlimited supplies due to the drought. I'd say we could outlast them by two months. Three to four months if we ration tightly."

"It's not enough. I've seen sieges that lasted ten years." Adonizedek said as a matter of fact, remembering a tale of a battle far away where thousands of ships landed and besieged a great city. It took ten years before the city fell. This according to their allies, the Philistines who had sailed from that battle and instead of returning to their home in Crete, began their journey along the coasts of Canaan to finally revive some of their settlements near Egypt where they quickly established a major foothold in the region.

If it weren't for the Philistines, Israel may have attempted this siege a hundred or so years ago. Instead, the Israelites had to contend with a powerful enemy on their doorstep that was responsible for much of the upheaval around the Great Sea cities. The Philistine's weapons were made of iron instead of bronze, their bows powerful, and their ability to take to the sea and land anywhere made them a scourge on the known world for centuries, though after a few hundred years the advent of iron weapons had largely permeated the whole of the known world. Eventually, their weapons advantage was countered as other enemies adopted the use of iron in place of bronze which in turn meant that they were forced to seek out more civilized pursuits. Their empire of five cities projected power to the whole of Canaan and stood as a backstop to Israel's conquest, or at least an annoying deterrent.

Lox had only returned to the court about fifteen years ago with a vision to build a fortress. The courtyard they sat in was a newly built structure that was protected by the high elevation of Mount Moriah. The system of walls and corridors, built right onto the side of Mount Moriah, provided a striking view of the land of Canaan. He'd said then that a battle was brewing and soon they would need to defend themselves. Lox told the tale of how David of Israel had defeated Goliath, a distant cousin of his, in single combat in the Valley of Elah. A boy of fifteen had beaten the mighty Goliath with nothing more than a sling and Goliath's own sword.

Since then, this warrior named David had become a victorious commander of a band of men that some called The Gibborim, which consisted of a minimum of one-thousand elite warriors led by David's favored officers. These fearless men could ride horses, use bows and slings, and their prowess with a sword or spear was unmatched, at least so far. This was the assessment of his spies which he'd sent out after Lox's warnings. They were to follow him everywhere he went and report back his whereabouts and deeds.

David was a specter that people had begun to see around every corner. Adonizedek even had to confess that he'd found himself worrying about it, though he countered that with stoic principles such as only worrying about things you can control. Which was why he had allowed Lox the freedom to design and build and spare no expense in the building of this fortress. When the siege came upon Jebus, they would be ready, or so he hoped.

Thoros responded, almost as if reading his father's mind, "Still no sightings of David. Last our spies heard he was near Damascus pressing a claim to a trade route with part of the Israelite army. He is not currently in the ranks of the army marching toward us."

Adonizedek responded, "My hope is that this force is meant to choke us off from the outside and soften us up. If David were with them, it would mean they intend an assault." This was his best assessment given what he knew of the elusive David.

The focus, as Adonizedek now saw it, given his recent dreams, would be to outlast them as long as possible and search for a way to survive, either by coexisting with them or by leaving this city altogether and searching for a new life elsewhere.

Adonizedek had long thought that their time as a giant race was ending in Canaan. The dreams he'd been having were a recurring dream that gradually became more detailed every time he experienced it. For more than a thousand years he'd watched as less and less of the Anakim and Rephaim survived. His own race, the Assyr were no different. Those in his family had intermarried with Amalekites, Kushites, Moabites, and even Philistine and Egyptian nobles to secure their place in the ever-changing world of Canaan and Mesopotamia. War, and unrest, cosmic calamities, and plain poor luck had brought about a decimation of the Assyr over the last few hundred years. A ten-thousand-year period where they numbered in the millions at times was ending. His estimate was that between those in his court and others who had journeyed north that there were less than a thousand original Assyr left in existence. The Assyrian bloodline had been so far removed from Adonizedek and his family that he couldn't see where they diverged from. Some Assyrian lineages no longer claimed any kinship with his kind which he supposed was just the natural course of things as the race of men grew increasingly numerous on earth.

His father Nimrod's attitude was one of defiance toward higher powers that had led to his downfall in Babel a few thousand years ago. Adonizedek had learned to be humble as a result and he recognized that the Israelite god was not to be trifled with. He actively encouraged his citizens, the Jebusites, to worship Elohim, though they called him El, or Elyon. Legends held that the Jebusites were closer in relation to the Israelites whose patriarch Abraham had ties to this very city and the Mount Moriah region. He hoped that his reverence for Elohim would earn him some favor at least some grace in case of a defeat against Israel.

Thoros looked unsure about what David's absence meant. "I wouldn't be so sure they would bring thirty thousand soldiers to bare on us if they didn't mean to attempt an assault. No doubt, David will be amongst them. The only question is, at what point in the siege?"

Adonizedek acquiesced, "Too true son, too true. An old man can hope though."

"In two days, we will know what kind of a siege this will be. My hope is that we are ready for either type," Thoros said as he rose to leave. "I must take the children to bed with Siv. Good night, Father."

Adonizedek rose as well and embraced his son. "Good night son."

———◆○◆———

Later in the Palace Residence...

In the wee hours of the morning, before sunrise, Thoros sat on the edge of the bed while Siv lay sleeping on her side with her back to his. He turned and brought his right knee up onto the bed and shifted so he could see her sleeping. Her flowing hair landed on the small of her back as his eyes traced her shape. Her silhouette could easily be mistaken for a set of rolling hills at her hips and her shoulders with a valley between them at her waist. He thought about waking her, but she seemed to be peacefully resting so he let her be. He was always late to bed and early to rise. He'd been that way for his whole life, and he couldn't sleep peacefully knowing that the Israelites would be knocking on the door in less than two days.

Siv stirred as she turned towards him and he felt her hand on his back, "What troubles you, love?" she said.

"I cannot sleep knowing all that must be done and what is coming to our doorstep." Thoros replied, turning toward her once again.

"You'll need your sleep love, come back to bed, keep me warm," she said seductively.

Thoros hesitated, all he could think about up to the point that she touched him was all that was yet to be done and redone in preparation for the siege. The uncertainty affected him so that the only way to be at peace was to do whatever he could to make himself certain.

Thoros looked at Siv, who was propped up on her arm looking at him with shimmering eyes and a peaceful smile that disarmed him instantly with just a glance. She lifted the covers and beckoned him with her eyes.

Siv laughed softly, "If you won't sleep then neither shall I. Come to bed Thoros."

Her last command was absolute, and he was powerless to disobey.

Two Days Later...

Baaldir and Nathan shimmied through a fissure that had long ago opened just below a man-made shaft under the wall near the Spring of Gihon. It was just wide enough for a full-grown person to lower themselves down into an area about the size of Nathan's home. From there they were able to squeeze through into a narrow path that led deeper into the ground. The torch Baaldir lit when he reached the bottom of the shaft was their only light as they reached the place he was talking about. The ceiling of stone was just above their head and Baaldir had to partially squat down to avoid hitting his head.

"Woah! How did you find this, Baaldir?"

"It was an accident really. I'd heard people in court talking about finding old cisterns and spillways that were carved underneath the city. I was exploring on my own one day in an abandoned dwelling and my foot fell right through the floor. I dug at it using some old tools and uncovered the shaft. It must have been sealed up and covered by someone long ago. I haven't had much time to explore but I found this here and I figured you had to see it." Baaldir said excitedly.

Before them was a trickle of water flowing from the stone which looked like a slow-moving waterfall coming from the spring above. The waterfall certainly was not impressive as it was apparent that several months of drought had all but dried up the underground spring.

Nathan was dumbfounded at first. "Where in the world is that water coming from?"

"Best I can tell, its coming from the Gihon Spring above. The pool above is fed by the spring. This must be why it doesn't overflow." Baaldir explained.

Nathan took the torch and looked down the stream as it flowed into the darkness, "I'd wager my father's weekly pay that this leads to the Pool of Siloam on the other side of the city." Nathan making jokes about sensitive subjects was his way of coping.

Baaldir grabbed the torch, stepped into the stream which came up to his calves and looked back at Nathan, "How about we find out? Maybe we can find other shafts." He didn't wait for Nathan to follow, figuring that Nathan wouldn't stay behind in the dark.

"I don't know Baaldir, what happens if we lose our torch?" Nathan protested as he jumped into the cold stream, the water coming up to his waist.

"Don't worry, Nathan. I'll bet we can't even make it that far. We'll just go as far as we can and turn back. I'm guessing the stream will narrow and we won't be able to continue," Baaldir reassured Nathan.

Nathan did not look convinced but trudged along through the water, nonetheless. They waded for several minutes, having to duck under openings and climb through areas that departed from the stream. Some parts of the stream were no more than a puddle, others were deep enough that Nathan's toes barely touched. Baaldir had to help him through those areas since his swimming skills were nonexistent. They finally came to a place where the stream disappeared into the stone. Baaldir moved the torch around the cavern and noticed that it had opened into quite the large cave.

"It's a dead end Baaldir, let's go back." Nathan was starting to sound nervous. He'd followed Baaldir but now seemed to be second guessing that decision.

"Hold on a moment, there must be a way through." Baaldir pulled himself up from the stream and walked to the edge of the cave. Nathan, not wanting to be too far from the torchlight, soon followed, protesting all the way.

"Baaldir, we've been down here for more than an hour, how much longer can that torch last?"

Baaldir attempted to reassure Nathan. "It seems to still be burning strong; I'll get us out of here. Don't worry, friend."

At that point Baaldir relented and decided their exploration had come to a good stopping point. Nathan was a very timid boy and Baaldir had resolved to try to push him gently towards being more confident. He would coax him along into daring acts, careful not to push him into dangerous situations like he'd found himself in so many times before. For the most part, Nathan went along with him. Occasionally he would dig his heels in and refuse. That point was coming, he could sense the change in Nathan's demeanor. Still, Nathan had come a long way in the last year and like his brother Thoros liked to say, 'adversity builds courage'. Baaldir liked to repeat that to Nathan often and he certainly tried to emulate that sentiment whenever hard things presented themselves. In another year he would be sent out on his own journey alone, not to return until he'd experienced and learned three truths.

The first part was to test the limits of his physical body. The second, which was connected to the first, consisted of testing the limits of his mind, and third, and perhaps the most elusive of quests, to view his own soul and find his purpose in life. Thoros was gone for three years on his mission quest. The journey was different for every man in his clan, and some hadn't returned.

"Let's come back when we are more prepared. I want to explore further," Baaldir said, snapping out of his contemplation and entering the stream again to trudge back the way they came.

Going back seemed to go faster as they weren't concerned with the surroundings as much. Nathan took the lead this time, walking with a purpose, hastily splashing through the stream and up and over obstacles. In less than a half-hour they were climbing back up through the shaft and into the abandoned house. Baaldir pulled himself up and pulled the wood cover back over the shaft.

Nathan sighed relief and said, "Remind me why I let you get me into these crazy things?"

"Adversity builds courage. That's why." Baaldir said playfully pushing him on the shoulder as they walked out into the alley from the shanty.

They were both laughing as they exited next to the northeast wall and started back to the center of the city nearer to Nathan's house. From their side Baaldir heard a familiar voice.

Baaldir said quietly, "I'm going to go the other way. I have some things to do for my brother."

"Okay Baaldir, I'll see you tomorrow." Nathan said as he turned and ran off toward home.

Baaldir turned his attention to the voice he'd heard. It sounded like Ide. As he snuck up to the corner he peered around and saw him standing there talking to Lox. He thought this was peculiar because those two openly argued and insulted one another in the Court. It was no secret their disdain for one another. Why then were they meeting in an abandoned part of town? Baaldir got as close as he dared to them, just close enough to hear Lox speaking. But could only make out bits and pieces of the words.

From what Baaldir could gather Lox said, "We need Israelite captives." The last part he whispered but it sounded like a number.

Ide's eyes widened as he shook his head, "I'll need a lot more coin." Baaldir heard a string of unintelligible words followed by Lox pulling a coin purse from his belt and handing it to Ide, who pocketed the purse after shaking it a few times to judge the weight.

"The siege will begin tomorrow," Lox offered. Followed by more unintelligible words from Ide.

Lox looked over his shoulder, his expression showing he sensed someone watching them. He nonchalantly went back to his conversation with Ide who hadn't picked up on the same sense.

A series of words that couldn't be understood followed as they soon finished their meeting. Ide bowed and went on his way. Lox hung back, leaned against the shanty, and kicked a pebble with his feet.

"You're a terrible eavesdropper lad. You can come out now." Lox said in his direction. Baaldir's heart skipped as he realized he'd been found out. He stepped out with a sheepish look on his face in front of Lox.

"What were you doing out here with Ide, I thought you despised him?" Baaldir asked his adopted brother.

Lox passively chuckled, "You'll learn one day that you cannot operate in the world without help; even from those you don't like. Even an enemy can become an ally given the right circumstance."

Baaldir thought about prying a little further as to what they were talking about, but he knew well that Lox would only tell him what he wanted him to know. He'd also become familiar with Lox and his schemes, even being on the receiving end of those schemes from time to time. Lox talking to a rival in an abandoned shanty neighborhood and handing him money was just Lox being Lox and nothing more. He resolved himself to ignore it and move on with the conversation.

"So, Israelites are nearly here?" Baaldir asked, changing the subject.

"They are, but don't worry. Your brother has some surprises for them. As do I," Lox said knowingly.

Baaldir hadn't encountered Israelites before but the stories of their conquest of Canaan were well known throughout the Court and the city of Jebus. Nathan and he would take turns pretending to be King Adonizedek and confronting him on the battlefield where the other one had to fight David to survive. In their version, David always lost. But the reality of history told a different story. David was almost inhuman according to those in the Court, some even thought he was the offspring of Elohim, a local god that had been worshipped here for more than a thousand years, sent to exact punishment on those that angered him.

His father worshipped Elohim also, in the tradition set forth by a former king whereby a burnt sacrifice was offered on the heights of Mount Moriah above the Citadel fortress. It was said that the Israelite ancestors inhabited this mount many centuries before leaving for Egypt. Back then they were just a small tribe numbering in the hundreds.

They were gone for more than twenty generations before escaping slavery in Egypt and journeying back to Canaan to begin their conquest, numbering in the millions. The last four hundred years had proven that the Israelites were here to stay. The last ruler of Jebus to confront the Israelites was also called Adonizedek. That confrontation had ended with his death by beheading in a cave. Shortly after, Baaldir's father assumed the mantle and the title Adonizedek, Lord of the Righteous, ruler of Jebus. Afterwards King Adonizedek quickly settled with the Israelites to stay out of their affairs if they stayed out of those of Jebus. There had been an uneasy peace between them for centuries now.

It wasn't until the Philistines stole the Ark of the Covenant from the Israelites during a battle that their ire was directed at Jebus. For the last several decades, King Saul had been joining the tribes of Israel into a united country. With the rise of David, this confrontation between the Israelites and Jebus was guaranteed to happen, according to his father. Jebus was the only stronghold left in Canaan untouched by Israel. Now they had come to eliminate it and claim it as their own. If Baaldir had anything to say about it, he wouldn't give them an inch of ground without shedding their blood. That is what his brother Thoros would do.

Lox and Baaldir walked on for a time not really saying anything, just the occasional platitude or small talk. Until, finally Lox said, "That boy you are with all the time, who is he?"

Baaldir answered uneasily, "His name is Nathan. What's it to you?" he added curtly.

"Easy, young prince, just curious." Lox said defensively raising his hands palm out and gesturing.

Baaldir had learned that short answers were best with Lox. If he was asking a question, it was for a purpose. What purpose, Baaldir couldn't fathom but he'd heard from his brother that Lox was the kind that was always a step ahead of everyone else. Also, if he was asking a question about Nathan, it meant that he likely already knew the answer which made his spine tingle.

"Why are you curious, Lox?" Baaldir asked.

"Oh, no reason. It's just that he is a commoner and a prince such as you should not keep such company. I've seen you spend days on end with him and also, with the siege upon us you should stay close to the palace."

Baaldir scoffed, "The palace? More like a prison. I like it out here in the city. And Nathan has been a good friend."

"Ah. What about those street rats that beat you last year? Have they given you any trouble lately?" Lox asked, sounding concerned.

Baaldir shrugged, "I haven't seen hide nor hair of them since. It's like they moved out of the city or something. Father said they were never caught and punished."

"Interesting. Well, wherever they went they won't likely cross your path again. Maybe they left the city altogether," Lox said.

This was another thing that Lox did that needled at him. He'd make an overture to a happening, then follow it up with alluding to an outcome without clarifying if it was a guess or a fact of the matter. It made him uneasy. In the span of five minutes, Lox had pried about his friend, gave his opinion on said friendship, asked a question about the boys that beat him, and made a statement on their whereabouts as if he knew something. Nothing was ever nothing with Lox.

Baaldir, being only thirteen, was easily dismissed as too young to understand. This was the mistake that every adult made about him, apart from his own father. This was certainly the truth when it came to Lox. It only took a few times of being disciplined for an action that Lox had encouraged with his wile to catch on to him. Baaldir had never told Lox that he'd caught on, he just simply made himself scarce around Lox to avoid getting caught up in his ridiculous manipulation.

Being skeptical of Lox came naturally to him as he grew. He knew that with Lox, if he spoke about two things as though they were not related even though they clearly were, then it meant that he was involved in both things simultaneously. This was the case now, so he resolved himself to tread more carefully and not give Lox any more information than he needed. Which in this case, was nothing more.

"I don't care if they do, I'll be ready for them," Baaldir said, referring to the boys, making sure to sound like a careless teenager. He could play games too.

"This Nathan fellow, who are his parents?" Lox asked.

More questions about Nathan. Baaldir lied, "I couldn't tell you. His mom is nice though, according to Nathan. What do you care, Lox?"

"I don't care, just making conversation with the young prince," Lox said nonchalantly.

Baaldir was done with the questions as he parted ways with Lox at an intersection, "I want to go to the wall and watch the Israelites coming in. I'll see you later," he said, as he ran off toward the south gate, not waiting for Lox to reply.

Lox shouted after him unenthusiastically, "Wait, I'll come with you."

Baaldir pretended not to hear him and kept running. He ducked through an alleyway and came out onto another street. Then Baaldir ducked through another that would eventually bring him onto the main road that ran straight from the palace to the south gate. That is where Thoros would be. Baaldir briefly looked back over his shoulder and saw that Lox hadn't followed.

Lox's questions, his statements, and his proximity to his secret passage to the dark river made his senses tingle. Maybe he was overly suspicious of Lox since he didn't trust him very much. As he walked, he figured he'd take mental notes on the weirdness of Lox. One, he knew something about those boys that attacked him, but what, he didn't know. Two, he'd asked way too many questions about Nathan, which meant he really was interested and not just making small talk. Third, he was meeting with Ide in the slums and passing off coins to him in secret. And last, he happened to be in the slums right next to the shaft he'd found in an abandoned well house.

These things separately were not anything out of the ordinary for Lox. But the overlapping nature of the details made the whole of them extraordinary. He resolved then that he would wait for an opportunity to return to explore the dark river under the city and instead see what he could find out about Lox's plans. Also, he wanted to map out at street level the part they'd explored already. He had a profound sense of direction and had memorized the slight turns along the way. Baaldir figured he could come within several feet of their furthest point and that would give him an idea where the river led too. He would also search for other entrances in the cisterns, being so low from lack of rain. His theory was that the channel they found would fill up from inside the ground as runoff from the mountains collected. Then this would feed the spring and the wells in the lower city.

Baaldir soon made it to the section of the wall that Thoros and the military were occupying ahead of the siege. He could see his brother standing up on the wall looking out to the South watching the coming horde of Israelites. He stood like a statue as Baaldir heard, for the first time, a shofar sound in the distance. The Israelites were here and by tomorrow they would begin their attempt at conquest.

CHAPTER 4

The Lower City, Jebus

Among a steady flow of palace workers returning home for the evening, Ahmet walked toward his home as the sun began to set. He'd heard a shofar sound to the south which told him the Israelites were making camp outside their walls. His shift had ended for the evening, and he would be expected to form up in ranks for further orders in the morning and would likely have to fight if it came to it. To a man, his colleagues were all excited about the prospect of fighting the fabled Israelite army. Ahmet couldn't decide where he landed on that sentiment. Part of him was eager to defend his home, and another part of him just wanted to find a way to take his family to safety.

The last few days had been better at home after he resolved to apologize to Ramah and promised not to take impulsive risks with their income any longer. Still, he found himself thinking about the shadow being that appeared from the stone box. He had just visited briefly with Vlulor and Flagor the last few days and did not stick around to see if anything else happened in that temple. Ahmet had witnessed enough in that temple while hiding to know that Lox was not to be trifled with. Further, whoever that being was, Lox was obedient to him. That caused him a sense of dread that he couldn't really understand because it also felt like a nearly inexorable force pulling him closer. It took all his will not to enter that Temple after seeing what he saw the other night. He instead focused on making good on his promise to Ramah to be more present at home and in their marriage. The last few days had actually been wonderful at home. Tonight, he would make it home just after dark and in time to eat some supper with Nathan and Ramah before bed. A good life, one he would fight for, he decided at once.

Ahmet watched as the sun traveled down behind the buildings that lined his street. At the end of this road was his home and he could see the light coming from the window and smoke coming from the fire in the hearth within.

Ahmet took two or three steps and slowly came to a stop as two cloaked men appeared from the shadow of an alleyway, blocking his way. His blood ran cold as he heard footsteps behind him. He turned just in time to see a burlap sack being pulled over his head and cinched tight while others tied his feet and hands together. Ahmet tried to struggle until he heard a familiar voice which froze him in fear.

"Take him to Tsalmaveth, the Master has need of this man."

Ahmet heard Lox, near his right ear, in a deep voice, "We'll see if you really are what the Master says you are."

With that, the Shades picked him up and carried him, holding him in such a way that resistance was impossible. The first thing he thought about was that he'd promised to be home for dinner and now he would be proven a liar once again. The second was the name, Tsalmaveth. He now knew that this was the name of the creature he'd spied on and was about to meet. He heard doors open and shut and felt them descend stairs. They made no sounds, apart from faint raspy breaths, and through the burlap he was able to smell a hint of sulfur mixed with the rank breath indicative of poor hygiene.

After what seemed to be a long walk, they finally sat him down and pushed him to the ground as they ripped off his hoodwink. It took only a second to realize that he was in the temple in Lox's dungeon. He looked up from the ground as Lox squatted and picked up the hoodwink before reaching down to cut the ropes on his legs and hands. Lox then motioned for Ahmet to rise to his knees as he then strode around the altar and reached into the void that Ahmet knew held the stone box. Lox pulled the lever and retrieved the box and set it upon the ledge of the brazen altar. Removing the lid, the familiar black smoke trailed from it and traveled down to the ground, hovering in place before beginning to form into the shape of a man. This was like what Ahmet had seen just two days ago.

In a matter of seconds, a deep black figure stood towering before him. A full six cubits tall, this figure dwarfed even Lox who was as big as any of the rulers of Jebus. The smoke emptied fully from the stone box and poured into the figure of Tsalmaveth standing before him.

Ahmet trembled as Tsalmaveth spoke, a deep voice he'd never heard echoed about the temple, "Look at our little eavesdropper, we finally meet!" he said, sounding almost joyful.

"Ahmet, is it?" Tsalmaveth inquired in an amicable tone.

Ahmet was speechless and he couldn't stop trembling as Tsalmaveth spoke to him. He was so riddled with nerves at the sight of Tsalmaveth that he couldn't remember what he'd asked.

Lox stepped forward and kicked Ahmet in the gut, causing him to double over on the ground clenching his stomach.

"When the Master asks a question, you answer!" Lox said ferociously, spittle flying from his mouth.

Tsalmaveth feigned shock. "Lox. This isn't that kind of meeting. I simply wanted to introduce myself to this remarkably interesting man who readily spies on our rituals. Do restrain yourself Lox."

Lox bowed and stepped back to the side of the altar as Ahmet recovered from the kick and brought himself to his knees and looked up at Tsalmaveth.

"Let us try this again. Ahmet, it is nice to finally meet you in person." Tsalmaveth said, speaking Ahmet's name in a long drawn out set of syllables that sounded like two different words.

Ahmet had slowly regained his composure even as his hands were trembling. After a moment, he was finally able to understand and respond, though with a stutter that seemed to appear whenever he was nervous or fearful.

"P-p-pleased t-t-to meet y-y-you." he said passively, trying to sound cordial while averting his eyes to the ground at Tsalmaveth's feet. All the while, Ahmet was thinking, *Curses! Curses! They knew all along that I was here. This is bad!*

"Apologies for Lox's rude behavior just now. His zeal is commendable if a little misguided at times. Please do not be fearful. I brought you here to speak with me."

Ahmet couldn't tell if Tsalmaveth was being sincere and wanted to continue the small talk, so he figured he'd cut to the chase, his nerves finally calmed.

"I'll be okay. What could you possibly want from me?" he said, boldly at first but trailed off as his resolve withered.

"Straight to the point, I like it!" Tsalmaveth said pretending to clap his hands as smoke playfully merged and returned to his form once again.

Tsalmaveth leaned forward, "What I want from you is service, Ahmet."

"Service? I'm not sure you have the right person; how could I possibly be of service?" Ahmet said, hoping that this was all just a ruse.

"All I require is service, the next few weeks will be pivotal in my plans and you, Ahmet, are to be a part of those plans."

Ahmet looked visibly confused as he turned Tsalmaveth's last statement over in his mind. *Service? Plans that I am a part of? What kind of plans, and why am I to be a part of them?* Those, and a hundred other questions raced through his mind in the matter of a few seconds.

Tsalmaveth continued, clearly sensing his confusion. "Before me stands a man who has tried, and tried again to make something of himself, someone worthy of the beautiful wife he somehow won in a stroke of luck that he hasn't seen since. This man has made promises and did not deliver on them, and he is afraid that his wife will wise up one day and leave him in the gutter where he should have ended up years ago."

Tsalmaveth flitted around the the other side of the altar and drew closer to him, "This man has been pushed around and defrauded by swindlers repeatedly. He fears his son will look at him with shame and hopes that the boy does not end up like him as he wonders if he will ever measure up. All the while, he sees his neighbors improving their lives. Meanwhile, he struggles just to get by day to day. When is it his turn? When will his languish and struggle finally be rewarded?"

Ahmet stood there dumbfounded as Tsalmaveth read him like a scroll. With a shaky voice he spoke, "How?"

"Every man casts a shadow Ahmet. Within that shadow is a glimpse at your destiny made up by your choices. Most men ignore it or never notice it altogether. Their lives pass by, and they turn to dust, and never once do they realize the potential that exists if they look within themselves and really see the darkness created by this shadow. This shadow is created by light, and it follows a man throughout his life. I am looking for a man with the courage to stare at his shadow and reach out and grab his destiny. Are you that man Ahmet?"

Ahmet heard the question, but his mind was racing through all the times he'd noticed his own shadow and he'd been too afraid to look at it. It was not lost on him that the shadow that Tsalmaveth was speaking of was not a literal one but a spiritual one. Perhaps if he'd had the courage to stare at his shadow, he wouldn't have wasted his whole life up till this point.

"What would you have me do?" Ahmet finally managed.

Tsalmaveth swirled around above and came back down to sit atop the altar, "Your service to me, at this point, comes in the form of service to that man over there," he said with his smoky fingers pointing to Lox. "Do what he tells you, without fail. Prove yourself to me, and you will be rewarded beyond your wildest imagination. Will you commit to this, Ahmet?"

Ahmet couldn't have said no if he wanted to after this Being read him so accurately, "I will do as you ask," he said simply.

"Wonderful! You'll see, Ahmet. This night is the night your destiny changed forever." Tsalmaveth said enthusiastically.

Then, Tsalmaveth began to swirl above them until his form became a dark cloud and began to trail back into the stone box.

"There is no time to waste. Bring me what I need," he said as the smoke disappeared into the vessel, the lid closing itself and sealing tightly.

Ahmet was left standing there staring at Lox and the half dozen Shades that stood around the altar. Lox walked back to the altar, picked the box up and placed it underneath.

Then, Lox walked around and stood in front of Ahmet and looked down at him and said, "You will do what I ask without fail or hesitation. Do you understand?" Not waiting for him to answer, Lox he punched Ahmet in the stomach and sent him to the ground doubled over and gasping for air. "That is so that you remember. You are mine. Now, get up, you've just been promoted to head jailer."

Lox tossed a purse of coins at him, and it fell to the ground in front of him with a dull clink as he walked out to the room. Speaking over his shoulder, Lox ordered, "Follow me, Ahmet. We have much to discuss."

Ahmet picked up his coin purse and stumbled to his feet and followed, dumbfounded at this turn of events. The Shades looked on with stone-faced expressions and made no move to leave their post around the altar.

Head Jailer? Wait until I tell Ramah about my promotion! Ahmet thought as he quickened his pace to catch up with Lox and leave those frightening Shades behind.

Meanwhile at the South Gate of Jebus...

The sounds of wood being cut and clanging of metal echoed back to Thoros who stood upon the walls watching the swarm of Israelites file into the sandy area outside the South Gate. This was the most fortified area because the western side of the wall heading towards the fortress nestled into Mount Moriah was generally untraversable. The stepped stone walls terminated into jagged rocks and series of steep grades that made the wall seem a great deal taller. The only possible area for an attempted assault was from the valley on the eastern side where the slope up to the walls was more gradual.

It was no wonder that this city had only been under siege a handful of times in those last thousand years dating back to the reign of Melchizedek, the King of Righteousness. The terrain on which Jebus was built heavily favored the defenders and the attackers could expect heavy losses if they tried a full-frontal assault. The assumption had been made that the Israelites would instead rely on siege ploys to attack the gates, and so far, that had proven correct as he watched the beginnings of a siege camp springing up. From the tower he could see them felling pine trees and oaks to strip down and build rams and barriers to protect advancing soldiers from the rain of arrows. He expected they would daub wet clay on the outside to give it some resistance to the fire. With enough pitch covered arrows, the barriers would ignite. The question was whether they would ignite before the swarm of enemy warriors could make it to the stepped stone wall.

The stepped stone walls were an ancient form of barrier that was formed by laying layers of stones of varied sizes upon one another, graduating upward in a very steep incline with a parapet providing the men on the top with cover from enemy arrows.

The newer Citadel Fortress at the foot of Mount Moriah had hewn stone walls that jutted upwards fifteen to twenty cubits. It was fortified with guard towers and choke points that made it easier to defend and also led to the fortified area around the Gihon Spring. Still, the terrain made the lower city of Jebus defensible. Thoros assumed they would likely have to fall back to the fortress at some point, but he hoped to slow them and make them pay for every inch with their own blood. Thoros looked along the wall and saw Jarnsaxa instructing the archers in the tactics they had agreed to employ. Bulwark was busy stacking stones with his masons to shore up the weakest areas.

Yesterday his scouts had returned to report on the actual size of the Israelite army. It was made up of mostly foot soldiers as it were, numbering twenty thousand men and five thousand archers and slingers accompanied them alongside chariots and mounted warriors. The total size was fairly accurate compared to the preliminary estimate from a few days ago. When asked about their leadership, Thoros was surprised and cautiously relieved not to hear one name in particular.

David, the mighty warrior and general of Israel was not among them. Still, this worried Thoros more than if they'd reported he was at the head of the columns. Perhaps the greatest warrior in Canaan, apart from himself, was nowhere to be found and that meant he was likely closer than he'd like him to be. There was no way that David would sit out the battle for the last great stronghold in Canaan. But where was he? This question would have to nag him in the days to come. For now, he focused his attention on the army unfolding in front of him. The next few weeks and months would decide whether their way of life would persist or be smothered by the horde of Israelites.

Thoros paced back and forth on the wall between the two towers that fortified the gate, thinking and strategizing. The Israelites would be ill-advised to try a full-frontal assault since the road leading up to the gate was narrow and only opened into a wider area closer to the wall. This area was largely in range of archers and only a small number of troops could occupy it at any given time without being in range of the arrows.

The thing that worried him about the Israelites is that for the last four-hundred years they had surrounded Jebus with their conquered lands. The impregnable nature of the city walls had forced the tribes of Israel, mainly the tribe of Benjamin and Judah, to seek diplomatic solutions. Before they had united under King Saul the Israelites were twelve independent tribes of cousins who would at times squabble and skirmish over pastures and resources. This fact had insured that the Israelites could not form a force large enough to assault Jebus.

There were so many moving parts to the diplomacy between these tribes that he had only just begun to take an interest in a few years back. Particularly once the very famous David came on the scene and turned these tribes into a disciplined army. Before David, King Saul would call up the banners of the tribes and they would send their own independent armies for the defense against the Philistines, their mutual enemy. Under the command of David, they now had a standing army and would use it to expand their influence beyond the borders of Canaan.

Before David, the agreement between the tribes and Jebus was that they could have permission to access a very holy sight above the city on the mountain top of Jebus once a year. This sight was only reachable by first passing through the city and then through the fortress. This was the only path for them to access the place where a stone altar said to have been used by their ancestor Abraham was located. This altar was built long ago under the rule of Melchizedek, who also worshipped the Israelite god at the time. Most people did not realize that the name Melchizedek and the names Adonizedek were titles, not birth names. Melchizedek was rumored to have the birth name of Shem, son of Noah.

Thoros' father had assumed the title Adonizedek four hundred years ago after the sitting king was beheaded in an ill-fated attempt to unite five city-states together to drive out the invading Israelites. The power vacuum created had to be filled and his father, Odin, son of Nimrod was the man to fill it, receiving the title of Adonizedek, Lord of Righteousness, King of Jebus.

Thoros stopped pacing when he saw Baaldir in his periphery. His brother was no doubt coming to see the mighty Israelite army gathering for the siege. The boy was only thirteen, but even Thoros recognized that Baaldir was far more advanced than the average boy of his age. Baaldir was just about to embark on a three-year journey to initiate him into manhood and then assume his place in the Court of Adonizedek. As a boy of thirteen he was not allowed to take part in battle which Baaldir no doubt disagreed with as he was more than capable with weapons and martial ability. If they survived this siege, there would be countless other opportunities for Baaldir to prove himself in battle. Thoros remembered being his age and having the same desire to push his limits and prove to everyone that he was a force to be reckoned with. His opportunity came at the age of twelve on a caravan traveling to the Far East. The caravan was set upon by bandits and a skirmish ensued that left several dead. Thoros wet his blade for the first time and from that point on his boyhood was gone whether he was ready for it or not. He wanted Baaldir to have the opportunity to at least grow into the kind of man he would become rather than be thrust into it and have no choice but to be a hardened warrior. Perhaps this was a naïve way of looking at things in a world as brutal as this where you either become hard as stone or else be worn away.

Baaldir bounded up the steps and stood next to Thoros on the wall as they both looked out over the growing Israelite siege camp.

"When do we fight the Israelites?" Baaldir asked, drawing his knife from his belt.

Thoros chuckled, "We? You will be at the fortress young Baaldir. This is no battle for a boy, even one such as you." He pushed Baaldir playfully and then pulled him in by his shoulder. "There will be many battles to wage when you've completed your initiation." Baaldir ducked away from Thoros' arm and stepped into the middle of the rampart.

"I am ready now brother," he said throwing his knife skillfully into a sack of sand at fifteen paces. "See brother? I can help. You were younger than me when you became a warrior."

Thoros was just about to compliment him on his knife skill and rebut him yet again when another knife flew by and perfectly stuck into the wooden pommel of Baaldir's knife.

"Until you can do that at thirty paces, I don't want to hear anything about fighting on this wall. You hear me little brother?"

They both turned to see Siv walking up to them. Siv was a master with knives. There was little doubt that young Baaldir had learned his skills from her in the courtyards of the palace. She was dressed in a simple tunic that split at the legs allowing her powerful thighs to move and flex as she walked up to him. Thoros felt the saliva pool in his mouth as he stood there dumbfounded. He swallowed in one gulp and smiled as she walked up and kissed him full on the lips. Then she turned to Baaldir and pulled him into her bosom and planted a sloppy kiss on each cheek. He squirmed and wriggled free wiping the wet kisses from his cheeks, red-faced. This was the reaction she was looking for judging by the radiant smile on her face.

"Agh! You know I hate that!" Baaldir complained.

"Which is why I do it!" Siv said laughing as she walked over to the knives and withdrew them from the sack, sand pouring out at her feet. She freed her knife and placed it in a sheath on her outer thigh and flipped Baaldir's knife around to hold the blade and handed it to him, hilt first.

"How go the preparations husband?" she asked, turning to look outward at the growing Israelite camp.

"As well as they can be I suppose. They will have a tough time breaching these walls." Thoros said confidently. "We've a few surprises for them tomorrow that will hopefully show them just how hard this siege will be."

Thoros watched as the sun began to set to his right, a sense of foreboding tickled his mind. "It is getting late, why don't you take our little brother back to the palace? I have a few more details to tend to this evening."

Siv leaned in for a kiss and then whispered in his ear furtively, "the kids are with your mother all night, don't keep me waiting for too long."

As she turned to leave Thoros grabbed her hand and pulled her tight to his chest and kissed her deeply. "I'll be home within the hour," he said as she pulled away slowly leaving her hands trailing on his forearms.

"Let's go Baaldir!" she said, smacking him on the back of the head and putting her arm around his shoulders. The two of them walked down the stairs side by side and crossed the small yard to the main road that led back to the palace compound.

Thoros took one more look to the south and watched the Israelites as they set up tents across the landscape. In the morning, the siege would be in full effect and his main concern was resources. While their granaries were at a respectable level, the cisterns were low throughout the city. The pool of Siloam not far from here had been dry for weeks now. Most of the residents had to go to the Gihon Spring to the northeast to obtain the water they needed for cooking and bathing. Many of the houses near this end had been vacated in favor of living closer to the spring.

Thoros contemplated the variables for a few moments longer and then decided that there was not much he could control about them at this point. The only thing left to do was stay alert and fight like a demon to protect his city. He looked behind him and saw that Siv and Baaldir had disappeared into the city.

After one last look at the siege camp in the distance, he bounded down the stairs and headed toward the palace, thinking he may be able to catch Siv and Baaldir along the way. Tomorrow was unsure. He decided to only focus on what was here today.

CHAPTER 5

South of Jebus

Horse hoofs beat the too-dry ground and sent dust billowing. David and Jonathan rode like the wind with several other mounted warriors. The Philistines were at their heels just a few hundred yards behind, no doubt grateful for the thick dust cloud that was rising to betray the fleeing Israelite warriors.

They had traveled end around Jebus, to avoid being detected, but to no avail. While Philistia wasn't mobilizing against them now, they kept a garrison that rode through the countryside looking for enemies or opportunities to exploit a caravan of travelers. Time would tell if the Philistines would be drawn into this war.

If history served as a reminder, their involvement was imminent. Since their arrival by boat near two centuries ago they had been a thorn in the side of the people of Israel and their judges. It was curious the mass arrival of thousands of them on the southern border of their territory via the Great Sea. His spies had gleaned that they hailed from an island called Crete. They had first settled in Ashkelon, attacking Egypt, and pillaging from them. Apparently, the Sea People, as the Egyptians called them, were a confederation of tribes not unlike Israel.

From coastal and island towns all around the Great Sea they formed a formidable force. For a time, they focused on Egypt and eventually, when defeated by Ramses III, they settled further inland. Ashkelon, Ashdod, Gaza, Gath, and Ekron were their main settlements in their newly formed Philistia. Eventually they developed into full-fledged cities burgeoning with population and commerce. They had close ties to the Phoenicians though the Phoenicians were more interested in trade. They regularly traded with Israel and other Canaanite people peacefully, being the only source for the purple dye that the priests and royalty used to make the rich color for their vestments. The purple dye apparently came from a type of snail that could only be readily found on their coasts just to the north of Israel near Lebanon in the city of Tyre.

The rest of his cavalry, four-hundred strong, were grazing and watering their horses several miles from there in the hills of Ephraim near his home. He'd ordered them to wait there until he was able to assess the siege progress. Most of them were what others called 'Gibborim' which translated loosely to 'Mighty Men'. They were fiercely loyal to him and were some of the most skilled warriors in the known world.

Someone shouted, "There's a hiding spot out of view, if we can make it there, they may ride past us!"

David made for it at once. They might have a chance since it was just around a bend and out of the line of sight of the Philistines. He motioned to one of the men, who happened to be the fastest rider. "You there! Leave us and keep riding. Kick up as much dust as you can and get to Jebus!" Maybe they would see the dust and not realize it was only from one horse.

David and Jonathan and the rest of the party rode their horses into a large grouping of rocks with a small clearing just before a cave entrance. They were out of sight by the time they heard the shouting soldiers speed past. All was quiet as their pursuers fell for the ruse as they rode out of view, not a one looking back.

They needed to find a way through the countryside to join the main army at Jebus, laying siege to the city this last month. The allied encampment was bustling on the southwest corner of the sprawling city, waiting for David and his men to return from subjugating a distant enemy. The recently conquered enemy consisted of the surrounding nomadic tribes that had been attacking the trade routes. In just a few short years he had made vassals of nearly all surrounding people, bringing peace and safety to the twelve tribes of Israel. It had been two years since he returned home; two years since he and Saul, the king, had reconciled.

Jebus was the only city-state within the boundaries of Israel that was left unconquered. They had lived in relative peace with those within the city for a few hundred years, but the tension was always high, and the ruler and his cohorts were the last known Anakim in the entire region. This was problematic because their strength and wealth were well-known for a hundred-day ride in every direction. Israel had only existed in this way for less than a generation. In olden days, the tribes were ruled by judges who upheld the law and ensured adherence to their commitment to The Almighty, the one true God, Elohim. But after a few hundred years the judges had become corrupt and so wicked that people had asked for a king to unite the tribes and help protect the realms they had carved out. They were at constant odds with the Philistines who were allied economically with Jebus.

Samuel, who was the only upright judge left in all the tribes, became the next Prophet and he anointed Saul to rule as king. However, years into Saul's reign, he became a lukewarm king when it came to honoring Elohim and obeying his commands; so, at an early age, David, who was a lowly farmer was anointed as the next king of Israel. The anointing had come at a time when Saul's health and demeanor were troubled but manageable. Before long, David had become more popular than King Saul. Eventually this caused Saul, filled with hatred and jealousy, to try and kill David. For years he ran from Saul; all the while engaging Philistines in skirmishes to protect Israel. It was after one such battle that David, having realized Saul was close by and hunting for him, went into hiding again, this time in a cave not unlike the one they now hid inside. This was where he had spent at least two of the eight years in hiding. David walked his horse over to the mouth of the cave and descended the embankment.

"We'll wait here until morning and then continue to Jebus. Let's tie our horses up and go check out this cave. We should be able to build a fire inside to keep warm." David said.

Several men including Jonathan joined him and brought some food, water and torches with them. Bats flew in and out of the cave as dusk began to fall. Once inside they lit up their torches and revealed a massive cave the size of a palace. David walked at the head; his steps deliberate. He had always loved these caverns. Not far from here had been his home for those years and ultimately it played a role in restoring his position in Saul's court.

Most people did not realize that the caves were connected to each other. With some skill and a willingness to brave tight spaces at times, a man could make his way through and exit out several places. He'd wager there were hundreds of cave entrances just like this one, all connected in some form to each other.

The men set to gathering up wood from outside and getting a fire going. After, they shared some rations amongst themselves and settled in to get some rest. Before long most of the men were sleeping, three men to a watch kept an eye on the horses and watched for intruders. David and Jonathan took the first watch.

An hour or so had passed and, being too exhausted to say any more words between them, they listened to the sounds of the cavern: the steady drip of water all around, the occasional screech of a bat, the pounding in the distance deeper into the cave.

Pounding, like a steady hammer blow, a drumbeat, David thought.

"Do you hear that?" David asked.

Jonathan was not acquainted with the normal sounds of this cavern, so he was relatively oblivious to the faint pounding.

"Hear what? All I hear is water and bats."

David was up on his feet standing on a boulder looking into the darkness, his musical ear attuned to the sounds that came between the familiar ones.

Jonathan asked again. "What are you..." David raised his hand to signal for silence.

Bang. Bang. Bang. Tink, Tink, Tink.

The strange sound continued like that in a constant loop.

"What is that sound, David?" Jonathan asked, apparently after his ears had focused on the noise.

"I don't know brother, but it's inside these caverns," David said as he walked over them to the next three on watch and woke them quietly.

"We are going to check something out deeper in the cave. I need you to keep watch for the duration of the night. The men rose and nodded, wiping sleep from their eyes. He woke the rest of the men and informed them that they would need to go with him.

Once all the men had assembled David spoke, "Follow me, extinguish all but one torch. Move quietly." David turned away and disappeared headlong into the darkness of the cavern on the edge of the chamber.

<hr />

Below Jebus, near the pool of Siloam...

"Hand down the pack!" Baaldir shouted from the bottom of the shaft as he rearranged the supplies they'd already brought down. Nathan handed the pack down and scuttled down the shaft into the small room at the bottom.

For a month, the city had been under siege by the Israelites. So far it had been just a lot of skirmishing, positioning and generally trying to tighten the siege and choke of supply lines, with which the Israelites had succeeded. Jebus had received no supplies, food or otherwise since the first week of the siege. Not far from here the Jebusite army led by his brother stood atop the walls taunting the Israelites who had spent many days building siegeworks. Some of them were contraptions that Baaldir had never seen or heard of. One of them could hurl a barrage of stone through the air. So far, the Israelites had only tested it, unsuccessfully, at a long range. To use these, they would need to move them closer and risk retaliation from those upon the walls.

For now, the Israelites were holding, drilling, and building with the occasional attempt at using ranged attacks from a safe distance. He overheard the court discussing that they thought an assault was imminent within the next few days.

During the last month, Baaldir had been required to spend more time in the palace and wasn't allowed out into the city very often. The few times he'd seen Nathan they'd spent their time planning and mapping out the areas they'd already explored at street level. They now had a crude map that he could refine further once they explored it for real. The Dark River, as he and Nathan named it, had been calling to him like a siren ever since they first explored it, but he ignored it, partly because the prying of Lox had made him nervous about spending too much time pursuing it. The last thing he wanted was for someone to catch on and close it up or claim it as a mystery for adults to solve. This was his and Nathan's discovery and whenever they found out the significance of it, they would present it to the court and receive accolades. Baaldir even hoped that Nathan would find favor and be allowed to attend lessons with him and train with him in the palace. He had asked his mother to talk to his father about bringing Nathan on as a student, but she was non-committal. She had, however, allowed Nathan to come to the palace to play a few times in the last month.

Apparently, Lox had put Nathan's father in charge of the operation of the prison. This troubled him just as the prying questions had. No doubt Lox knew who Ahmet was and it was a mystery as to what Lox meant by it. In thinking of Lox, he realized he had seen hide nor hair of Lox in a few weeks except for in passing. He claimed he was studying for a solution to the siege and would have a strategy to share soon enough. Baaldir, being a skeptic in all things Lox, didn't believe for a second, he was studying scrolls and strategizing. Baaldir kept these apprehensions to himself mostly. He'd only hinted to Nathan the weirdness in the timing of Lox promoting Ahmet just as the siege began. He left it alone when he saw how Nathan's mother, Ramah, seemed happier now that Ahmet was able to better provide for the family, and was home for dinner every evening. Baaldir was happy for them even if he was skeptical of the real reasons for the sudden good fortune.

Nathan found his way down to the channel that gradually flowed under the stone into the Pool of Siloam, which had nearly dried up.

What a difference just a few weeks made, Baaldir thought.

They each checked over their packs of supplies which were likely overkill, but he figured it couldn't hurt to be overprepared. In the pack he'd placed some bread and dried fruit, a blanket rolled up, a rope, a knife, and fire starting implements such as flint, tinder and a pouch filled with talc powder. He doubted they could find fuel down here for a fire, so he'd managed to lash a few split logs to Nathan's pack. Nathan's pack carried comparable items, and he'd also made sure to bring pastries that his mother had made this morning.

"Well I'm ready if you are," Nathan said nervously.

Baaldir picked up his pack and slung it over his back and stepped into the nearly dry riverbed which was little more than wet stone at this point. Nathan held a torch and handed him a second one. The light from the flame flickered and danced on the cavern walls as they began their exploration under the city once again. It was considerably easier to walk without the knee-deep water, so Baaldir was able to focus on the surroundings as they trudged further. One thing he realized is that the channel seems to have been carved by human hands instead of being a natural occurrence. With more light they were able to see the hand tool marks made by a large hammer or a pick. In some places the channel narrowed, and the ceiling lowered. A month ago, they would've had to pass under nearly submerged in water but now they could walk by with little effort. During the last month, Baaldir had been frustrated that his duties at the palace were so all-consuming, but now he was relieved that the wait had made it easier for them to pass.

Baaldir's instinct told him they were heading Northeast toward the Gihon Spring and the fortress that protected his home, the palace. Before long they reached the furthest extent of their last attempt. Using the torches, they examined the walls and searched for an answer as to where the cavern would lead. The water seemed to pool here so he followed the moisture as it trickled down the wall to their feet. As he held the torch higher up the wall, he noticed the flame flickered and pulled toward him, and then pulled away from him. This told him that air flow was coming from somewhere above.

Baaldir spoke for the first time since they began their search. "Did you see that, Nathan?"

"See what?" Nathan asked inquisitively.

"The flame!" Baaldir exclaimed, "It is showing us the direction we must go by following the air flow."

Baaldir, not waiting for Nathan to respond jumped up onto the wet rock and carefully balanced himself. Once up on the rock he slowly stood upright and found a shaft that was about three cubits high above his head. If he reached, he could grasp the top and pull himself up.

"Here, hold on to the torch." he said excitedly as he set his pack down at his feet. Nathan grabbed the torch and stood on the tip of his toes, finally seeing what Baaldir had seen.

"Is it another shaft?" Nathan asked.

"Seems so. I think it may be a continuation of the channel. I'm going to pull myself up and see what I can find. Try to shine some of the torch light up once I get up there."

Baaldir shimmied up the shaft and easily pulled himself up onto another level of the water system. This made sense since they would be headed up the slope of Mount Moriah the deeper, they went. The dim light from the torches below showed him just enough to recognize the hand-tooled rock cutting like below.

"It's a continuation alright! Can you hand me my pack and the torches? I'll help you up," Baaldir said.

Nathan pulled himself onto the rock and precariously balanced himself holding both torches. Baaldir reached down with his long arms and was able to grab the bottom of the torches one by one. He placed them upright against the wall of the channel and then reached down for the packs. Then, with help, Nathan pulled himself up into the newest part of their exploration.

"Can you believe this was all cut by hand?" Nathan asked, wondrously looking around the narrow channel.

This part of the channel was a little wider than a large man's shoulders, but only just. His brother and father would have difficulty squatting and walking through here; Baaldir was nearly too large for passage as it was.

Baaldir shrugged, "It doesn't surprise me. This city has been built one on top of the other for more than a thousand years according to my father. Most people probably think the Pool of Siloam is just a natural occurrence, when all this time it was connected to the Gihon Spring by someone long ago. Fascinating."

The two of them, invigorated by their newest discovery, trudged down the damp corridor. Baaldir ran his hands along the walls, feeling the undulation with his fingers, recognizing texture that was clearly man-made apart from that which was a natural occurrence. Now that he knew there were possibly other channels, he looked more closely at the surroundings hoping to find another branch, or a separate corridor to explore. So far it seemed to have made a turn northward if his senses were correct. They walked for a hundred cubits before he realized the corridor had widened into what appeared to be a room of sorts. The channel ran deep and led toward another tunnel that appeared to be carved. This cavern seemed to be mostly natural surfaces judging by the rippled stone and jagged rocks hanging above their head. Baaldir climbed up out of the channel and found that he could stand up comfortably. Nathan hopped out a little further down the channel.

"Wow! Look at this Baaldir," Nathan said from his right. Nathan stood there holding his torch up to the walls. On them Baaldir saw what he would call symbols or markings. The language was unknown to him, but it appeared to be some kind of signature or something.

"Perhaps this was a signature from the one who carved this?" Baaldir offered as a theory.

"I'll wager it's a riddle leading us to a treasure!" Nathan offered as an alternative.

Baaldir stood there wide eyed, "Well whatever it is it sure has been here a long time." He slowly walked to the perimeter of the room using his torch to scan the walls as he went. After five paces, he stopped abruptly. Before him were three paths. One went to the right from the man-made channel and had water trickling across the stone in the direction they had come. This was no doubt their route to the Gihon Spring. He would have followed it to see where it led if not for these other two paths which appeared to be leading north and northwest away from the Spring. He imagined that these led underneath the mountain and possibly to parts outside the city walls. Not only had they found an aquifer that supplied water to the southern part of Jebus, but they had also found a series of tunnels that led to infinite possibilities in his mind. He imagined ancient people digging and tunneling and chiseling their way through stone and layers of sediment for a purpose unknown. Maybe as shelter or a place to hide from dragons or serpents. His mind ran wild at the possibilities.

"We should take one of these tunnels and see where it leads." Nathan said, more enthusiastically than Baaldir expected. Apparently, Nathan had found some interest after these last series of finds.

"Take your pick, right or left?" Baaldir said standing between the two.

"Let's go this way." Nathan said plunging down the left tunnel. Baaldir hadn't expected him to take the lead but silently laughed at the new vigor his friend now possessed. He followed along behind and kept his eyes out for more clues as to their heading and what could be more tunnels or shafts to the city above. Baaldir's sense of direction was thrown off so he took the talc powder and made markings on the side of the walls that would clue them in on how to get back to that room they had found. It would not be good to find themselves lost should these tunnels split off elsewhere. One could get good and lost within just a few turns. He used the talc every few paces and made an arrow pointing the way back, incredibly pleased with himself that he had thought to bring it. He had originally thought it might come in handy if he had to climb a rock wall or something, using it to obtain a better grip on the stones.

They walked for a hundred or so paces before coming to another small room that had three more tunnels. Baaldir realized they were going deeper into the ground the more they walked. The tunnel to the right went upward, the one in the middle continued their heading, and the left one traveled deeper still.

"What do you think Nathan? Which way?" Baaldir asked, hoping to encourage him to continue to lead the way.

Nathan shrugged, "Your guess is as good as mine. We ought to head back. It was afternoon when we came down here, I'll bet its nearly dinner time now."

"Go back? No way! We've stumbled upon an important find; we can't turn back now." Baaldir said persuasively. "Besides, what if there really is treasure?"

"I don't know Baaldir, what if what we find is a monster that is hungry?" Nathan asked, seriously.

Baaldir drew his knife from his belt, "Don't you worry about that. Whatever we find, I'll be ready. You can count on that."

Baaldir could tell Nathan wasn't convinced so he appealed to him with bargaining. It was a technique he'd seen Lox use time and again to get people to move in a direction of his choosing just a little further than they intended to go. It worked on more agreeable personalities like a charm. He didn't want to manipulate his friend but figured this was a harmless use of the tactic.

"Let's just take one of these paths and see where it leads. We can turn back when we come to the next one. I just want to see where this goes a bit further." Baaldir said, fully intending to turn back as he said. This was the difference between him and Lox. Lox would manipulate someone into an action and once that was achieved, he would push further and manipulate further. Baaldir resolved never to be that kind of man, he would only use it to lead someone in a positive direction.

"Fair enough Baaldir. Why don't we just continue straight as we were going?" Nathan said, allowing Baaldir to take the lead again.

Baaldir, pleased at the success of his argument stepped forward. He noticed his torch was getting low and stopped to momentarily light another one that was lashed to Nathan's pack. Baaldir held the nearly spent one in his other hand and walked ahead, a torch in both hands. Sure enough, after a hundred or so paces they came to another junction. The torch in his left hand flickered and burned out so he tossed it to the side as he walked back to the tunnel they'd come from, marking it with chalk.

"Okay, let's head back now. It might take a while to return to the topside and I don't want my mother to be worried for me," Nathan pleaded.

Baaldir agreed, intent on doing as he said. Their next expedition would be much easier since they had marked their path. He would try and draw a map to chart where they'd gone and what areas they needed to explore yet. Overall, this had been a bigger success than he'd expected.

"Okay Nathan, lead the way back," Baaldir said.

They started back the way they came when suddenly Baaldir heard something in the distance behind them. "Stop! I heard something."

Nathan stopped and dropped his shoulders, clearly, he was having none of it, "Really, Baaldir I need to get going."

Baaldir held up his hands to his lips and signaled for Nathan to be quiet for a moment. He listened intently, hoping to hear the faint sound he'd just happened to hear a moment before.

A few seconds later he heard it: *Tink, Tink, Tink. Tink, tink, tink.* Then the sound would trail off only to begin again a few moments later.

"Did you hear that?" Baaldir asked.

Nathan did not look happy to admit but nodded affirmation, his face white as a ghost. Baaldir, with that confirmation turned and walked single-mindedly back toward the tunnel ahead. "Follow me close, Nathan. We will see what this sound is and then we will turn back if it is dangerous."

Nathan protested but followed nonetheless, not wanting to be left alone in the tunnels. Every few steps, he stopped to listen to the persistent sounds coming from deeper within: *Tap. Tap. Tap. Tink. Tink. Tink. Tink.*

Meanwhile on the street level...

After an entire day on the walls and drilling with the infantry, Thoros decided to walk back to the fortress near sunset via the stables, wanting to check on the preparedness of their calvary units and be sure that they had all bases covered. He expected an assault any time now that they had built up their engines and scouted the land over the last month. They would need cavalry to move quickly about the city should the walls be overrun in multiple places. He'd seen movements around the walls to the East, and to the North near the mountain. Thoros half-expected the Israelite army of thirty thousand to split into separate battalions and assault the wall in separate places. That is what he would do. He also expected them to try to attack at night, so he doubled the standing army on the walls throughout the night in preparation. He had decided on his walk to the stables that he would also send units out into the city to patrol on horseback around the perimeter streets.

The Israelites were taking their time preparing, clearing forests for their siegeworks. He'd been watching them test out things he'd never seen before and wondered where they got such ideas. Maybe their god had given them knowledge of a weapon. That thought made him shudder. He didn't like the feeling that he might be on the outmatched side. But still, he would fight to the last breath and continue to adapt and plan and execute until that day came. Maybe, just maybe, they could pull a victory from the jaws of defeat.

As he came upon the stables, he scanned the vast expanse of stables that lined the right and left of the middle corridor. All seemed calm now, since it was near supper time. Most of the groomsmen had checked out for the night. He was just about to walk through the big doors and cross the stables when he heard a man yelling and whip cracking down the outer corridor to his left. He heard the crack of the whip a second and third time.

His curiosity peaked, Thoros turned down the corridor and walked toward the prison. He was not aware of any work being done in this area and certainly not with slaves, in which they only had a few in the whole city. Thoros walked several steps and found an empty hallway and stood there for a moment and heard nothing. He thought that maybe he'd been hearing things. After all, he was a little tired from the long day that began before sunrise. Just as Thoros was ready to turn and head back to the stables, he heard someone talking to another up the corridor and knew instantly that it was Lox. Thoros walked purposefully down the corridor and sure enough found Lox standing in the corridor talking with a soldier that he'd promoted to prison captain.

Akhmed, he thought. Thoros was terrible with names but figured it was close enough.

Lox, seeing Thoros, dismissed the man and shooed him away as he turned toward Thoros. "Thoros! To what do I owe the visit to this damp and dark corridor away from the fight?"

Thoros was always skeptical of Lox even in the most innocent of circumstances. There was always a scheme or a plot afoot.

"I thought I heard something." Thoros said, unsure of himself. "What are you doing down here Lox? I could ask you the same thing."

"As you are aware, I oversee the prison and the security within the fortress. You have your soldiers, and I have mine. Its more out of character for you to be here than me, I'm sure you see that?" Lox looked uneasily as he said that.

Thoros was just about to give up his questions and return to his tasks before heading to dinner when he heard the faint crack of the whip through the door to his left.

"What was that sound?" Thoros inquired.

"What sound, I heard nothing." Lox said coyly.

Thoros listened and heard the crack of the whip again followed by a curse.

"That doesn't sound like nothing, Lox." He said as he burst through the door into a storage room full of crates.

"Thoros, I'm not sure what you think you heard but this is a storage room full of forgotten clutter. Come now, the heat must've gotten to you." Lox tugged at his shoulder and ushered him out of the room. "I was just about to go eat with the king; will you be joining me?" Lox added.

Thoros stood there for a moment and looked at the seemingly full room and thought perhaps Lox was right for a change. He'd been out in the heat all day and was dehydrated, having drank only a small amount of water all day. They had to ration it since the Gihon Spring was lower than he'd ever seen it. The Pool of Siloam near the south gate was all but dried up this last month of severe drought.

"You may be right, Lox. Lead the way. I could use some sustenance," Thoros acquiesced, walking past Lox, back into the hallway. Lox followed behind began to pull the door shut and as he did, the whip sound echoed again. This time it was audible as if only cubits away, inside the storage room. Lox winced that time at the noise, betraying the fact that he indeed heard the noise as Thoros had.

"Brother, it's nothing to be concerned with. Let's go to dinner." Lox said in a worried tone.

"Stand aside Lox." Thoros said as he shouldered his way past Lox and pushed the door open so hard it nearly broke the iron hinges attaching the door to the doorframe.

Lox sounded panicked and tried to stand in Thoros' way. "Brother, please let me explain. I've been working on something; a discovery and I wasn't ready to show to the king just yet."

"A discovery in a storage room? Stand aside Lox or I'll go through you." Thoros muscled past Lox and made for the back of the room. The room was bigger than it appeared with crates stacked like a maze. Lox chased behind him protesting and pleading in the same breath.

"Let me explain brother. This is a good thing for us. I'll show you," Lox said.

Thoros bumped into a stack of crates sending them sprawling and shattering on the floor. Grain and milled flour poured out onto the ground, piling up at their feet.

"What is this? Where did this grain come from? Here we are rationing food, and we have an entire room full of it!" Thoros pulled down another crate and opened it, all the while Lox tried to explain what he was seeing.

"This is an emergency supply Thoros. In case we have to fall back to fortress. I can't believe what you are insinuating!"

"Full of grain, I can't believe it." Thoros said as he pushed further into the room. As he rounded the last stack of crates he stopped suddenly and stood still with mouth agape, an incredulous look on his face. Before him was a doorway with a set of stairs that descended downward. Without thinking he tilted toward the stairs and began to descend. Lox was right behind him, barking out his usual explanation when he'd been caught in one of his schemes yet again. Thoros took the stairs two at a time and soon spilled out into a large half circle room cut out of the stone far under the city. There were seven doors built with arches around the half circle with torches mounted by each door shedding light on the entire area.

Thoros was fuming, "And just when were you going to tell us about this tunnel underneath the city? Is this what you've been doing? Did you build this?"

"No brother, I discovered it a while ago, but this was built long ago by another people who inhabited the city. Don't you see brother? This is a great find! It may just be our salvation should the need arise to escape."

"Escape? Where do these tunnels lead?" Thoros said, still angry but intrigued all the same.

Lox explained excitedly, "I've only been able to explore a few of the tunnels fully. I'm certain at least one of them leads out of the city and into the hill country."

Thoros was beginning to calm when he heard the crack of the whip and a shout of, 'MOVE YOU DOGS!' followed by another murderous crack of the whip. It was coming from the furthest door to the right. Thoros looked at Lox who just stared at the door as if he had hoped they would be clear before they came back through. Moments later, the soldiers appeared, leading a small group of slaves. From their dress and complexion, he could tell they were Hebrew. They were followed by the taskmaster and two other soldiers carrying spears. He was puzzled by this because he had not been aware of any capturing of Hebrews as they had yet to even assault the walls.

"Where did you get these prisoners Lox?" Thoros asked accusatorially.

"Oh, these? I kidnapped them." Lox said, apparently choosing to tell the truth rather than evade.

"Kidnapped? How?" Thoros said, his face turning red. He hated being surprised by Lox's schemes. It made him look like a fool not to have seen it.

Lox looked sheepishly at the slaves whom the soldiers had lined up against the wall and were standing at attention waiting for orders.

He finally answered timidly as if realizing he'd been caught in a lie. "My agents sneak into the Hebrew camp and steal them during the night."

Thoros could not believe his ears, "So what you are saying is that when you just stood here and told me you hadn't found a way out, you lied to me, stone faced. In fact, you have found a way out and have been using it to bring Hebrews into my city! Wait until my father hears of this. Incredible, Lox. You really are a piece of work!"

He stormed off down the tunnel, grabbing a torch and plunging into the darkness, heading in the direction that the slaves had come from, all the while cursing Lox and his stupidity. "We'll see just what you've been working on!"

Lox hurried behind shouting to the soldiers, "Wait here for my orders."

Thoros paid him no mind as he stomped down the dark handmade corridor. He spilled out into a large square room expertly carved from the stone and covered in onyx and black marble. Braziers burned throughout and stonemasons labored away shaping the marble and other stones. It appeared to be some type of temple. Probably for some god Lox picked up from parts unknown, as he was known to do.

Thoros, seeing this exorbitant and opulently adorned room, started to lose his temper. He walked over to a stack of cut marble and pushed with all his might, the marble shattering all over the floor. The masons scattered and ran up the tunnel away from the wrath.

Suddenly Thoros felt a wave of nausea run over him that stopped him cold as he stumbled backward. Next to him he heard a faint chant that seemed to be coming from Lox, but he seemed further away from him than just a few feet. It was all he could do to resist the pulling at his psyche.

"You are not angry about what you've seen here Thoros." Lox said, blood dripping from a dagger cut on his palm.

"You're right, I'm not angry. I just want to make sure our city is safe." Thoros said, somehow aware that he was saying this unwillingly but still feeling as though he wasn't angry.

"In fact, I think we should dedicate soldiers to protect what we've found, just to be safe, until we find out if a tunnel leads to the outside." Lox said, all the while chanting a foreign incantation in between the words.

"That's a great idea Lox, I wish I would've thought of that." Thoros said, with the existence of a tunnel needling at him but not sure why. He decided it didn't matter.

"On the count of three you're going to come to and walk calmly back the way you came and go up the palace for the evening. One. Two. Three."

The next thing Thoros knew he was waking up at daybreak next to his wife Siv to the sound of a horn in the distance.

CHAPTER 6

Deep in the Caverns, Near Jebus

Traversing the dank caverns for hours, diving through narrow holes and climbing over rock formations, David finally stopped for a minute to listen for sounds deeper into the caverns. He let his breathing slow and his heartbeat calm so he could hear in the darkness. The sound had stopped. He must've taken a wrong turn somewhere. They had gone further into the caverns than even he had previously gone. To keep track of where they had been he made a directional mark on rocks to point the way back from where they had come.

David used the torch to look around at all the formations around him. *No marks*, David thought. They hadn't been here before. He turned around and hopped up onto a ledge trying to get a better ear in the darkness.

Nothing, David thought.

Jonathan was kneeling, resting his legs. They had been following that noise for several hours and he wasn't sure how long but if he had to guess they were somewhere in the middle of the second watch. "Brother, I don't hear the noise anymore. Are you certain it was from inside the cavern and not outside on the surface."

David insisted. "I know what I heard. It came from deep inside. I spent eight years roaming these caverns and never once heard anything like that even with marching armies on the surface."

Jonathan prodded. "We cannot spend eternity roaming these caves. None present have eaten for more than a day and we risk getting lost in this cavern, without provisions. I'm not saying you didn't hear the sound. We all did. All I am saying is..." Jonathan's words were cut short as the sound returned.

Bang. Bang. Bang. Bang. Tap. Tap. Tap.

They were close, he now realized with a renewed sense of urgency.

David handed Jonathan the torch, "Here, take this torch. Hang back a bit so my eyes can adjust in the dark."

Then he turned and plunged through a narrow opening in the cavern rocks. Each step he took the noise intensified, the faint light from the torches giving him just enough light to make his way. He could now make out the sound of iron hammers hitting on stone, but it was slightly muffled; like it was on the other side of a cave wall. He looked back at the party far behind him; their torchlight just barely reaching him.

"Bring me the torch!" he ordered in a forced whisper. Jonathan ran forward, the dozen warriors at his heels. Taking the torch, he climbed over some boulders and looked over a ledge down into a bowl-like depression in the cavern. From this vantage he could direct light on the source of the pounding. David doused the flame instinctively and ducked down behind the rocks.

Darkness enveloped them for a moment until light came from the other side. He could see Jonathan and the others kneeling there wide-eyed, trying to hold their breath.

He whispered the words, "Don't move." while pointing over his shoulder.

David used the noise to move further up the embankment where there was better cover and a flanking vantage point and signaled for the others to do the same. They quietly crept over to him and made themselves as small as they could behind boulders with just their eyes cresting over to see down below.

"Move you dogs!" *Crack!* A whip rang out, as the sound echoed in the cavern. *Crack! Crack!*

"Filthy dogs! Faster!" *Crack!* The whip echoed around the cavern with each snap.

From his vantage, David could see a singular door through which a troop of guards led a group of slaves carrying a massive statue of which he couldn't quite make out the features. The taskmaster and guards drove the captives down through another door and disappeared into a dark hallway, the sound of the whip fading. David could tell by their attributes that they were Hebrew. Joab had given him reports that several men had gone missing from their tents at night. That had gone on for the last month, several men each day. There was no way to know what had become of them. Until now, it was assumed they deserted and went home. From the looks of it they had not been treated well; scarred on their backs and shoulders from the taskmaster's whips. It was plain to see they hadn't been fed properly or given medical treatment.

David suddenly felt his heart beginning to race, his blood beginning to boil. Four hundred years ago his people had escaped slavery in Egypt, after having been enslaved for as many years. Rage-filled and indignant, David turned away and slumped down next to Jonathan and the others. They looked at him, knowing what they had just witnessed down below.

David's breathing shortened into exasperated panting as the rage internalized into pain. He had to do something. But what could he do? They didn't know what they were up against. In that moment he remembered a song he had sang in the court of Saul's court years ago as a boy:

***

Oh Lord, you cause the work of my hands to prosper.
The rain comes and soothes the parched earth.
All good things flow from your fountain.
Your justice moves through the land like an ocean's tide.
You have given me victory over my enemies and caused them to seek peace with my house.
Thine own hand has caused the honeybee to prosper, and the land to overflow with honey.
Your mercy covers the land like the vintner's vines, and the wine is like none that I have tasted.

***

David finally calmed down and acknowledged Jonathan with a nod, but his mind was busy thinking, planning, strategizing; his right hand hidden in a pouch he kept on his belt with five smooth stones running between his forefinger and thumb.

He sat quietly as his breathing returned to normal. He looked at the others who were anxious, knowing what was just discovered. A few already had their swords drawn ready to charge.

David quietly said, "We wait." as he peered up over the ledge into the room below.

Almost as if on cue, a chorus of shouting came from the door the captives had come through carrying the statue. First a giant who filled the doorway burst through shouting. He was quickly followed by another slightly shorter and leaner giant. These men were every bit as formidable as Goliath whom he'd faced fifteen years ago.

They were arguing in some foreign tongue other than the common language of the region, so he was unable to understand them. The two giants took turns interrupting one another and the bigger man looked ready to resort to blows at any moment. A moment later David heard the crack of the whip followed by shouting and soon saw the guards leading the ragtag group of captives from the dark tunnel. This caused a new rupture of anger from the bigger man followed by what appeared to be, more explanation from the other man. The bigger man tore off down the tunnel and they both disappeared, shouting the whole way as the voices trailed off.

David looked at Jonathan and his men and took stock of what they had at their disposal. They outnumbered the guards but not if the giants came back. He could faintly hear shouting for a few moments and then it all quieted down. David watched and waited until finally, the larger giant came back, looking extremely calm. The giant was even humming as he walked past the men, entered the stairway and disappeared up to wherever that led. The other darkly dressed man stayed behind and he heard him tell the guards in the common tongue, "These men have worn out their usefulness. Kill them and dispose of the bodies discretely." The guards at once raised their spears and moved to conduct the order.

Then he added, "Take them to ground level. Burn their bodies in the pit. I don't want their filthy blood to stain my walking path." The man stood as he walked back into the dark tunnel with a purposeful gait.

"Yes, my lord," one of the guards said, standing at attention. As the man exited the room down the dark tunnel again, the taskmaster cracked a whip and shouted, "ON YOUR FEET YOU SWINE! GET UP! ALL OF YOU! UP!"

David looked at his men as the whip began cracking and didn't have to say a word to them in order for them to know what the plan was going forward. Jonathan was by his side at once and handed him a sword and a small blade. After twenty years of battle by each other's side they knew each other's tells.

Two of his men had been scouting the surrounding areas and had found a way down to one of the tunnels that led to one of the doors. Jonathan sent six men who quietly positioned themselves near the doorway where David could see them, as the guards rounded up the captives and started to drive them toward the stairs that would take them up to the ground level. David and Jonathan perched upon the rocks above the stone room, ready to pounce and time their attack with the others on the far side of the room

As David gave the signal to attack, both of them dropped down to the ground silently and tucked into a roll just as they reached the ground. David rolled to his feet and brought his blade slashing down onto the back of the first guard, followed by imbedding his dagger into the chest of the next closest guard as Jonathan's sword pierced the back of the same.

In seconds he and his men were upon the unwitting guards with such precision that it was hard to tell who made the first kill. None of the guards stood a chance in the ambush as David and his men hacked and slashed their way through with brutal efficiency. The guards didn't have time to draw a blade to defend themselves and most fell with wounds in their back and neck, having been unable to see the face of their killer.

Only the very rotund taskmaster remained as he turned and waddled for the tunnel, but just before reaching the door, a knife flew into the back of the man's shoulder. The taskmaster fell and unsuccessfully struggled for a moment trying to reach the blade imbedded in his back. David walked over and withdrew his blade, cleaned it off and tucked it into his belt. The man managed to roll to his back and with labored wheezing, looked at David with fear as though he'd seen death itself standing over him. The last thing he saw was David's foot descend onto his face with such force that his face was crushed beyond recognition.

Around them lay six dead guards and a now dead taskmaster. Nary a sound had been made during the attack. The captives, looking starved and tortured, slumped over and some fell to the ground. It was unclear if they even understood that they had just been rescued. Most of them looked vacant and removed from reality. A few of his men tried to give some of them some water, unsuccessfully.

"Hide the bodies." David ordered plainly as he surveyed the countrymen they'd just liberated.

Two men started to grab the taskmaster and drag him toward the caverns. He was so heavy that they could barely lift his torso off of the ground.

"Not him. Leave that pig of a man where he lay," he ordered, and they dropped the body with a thud and went to work dragging the soldiers into the caverns on the other side of one of the doors.

David helped Jonathan move one of the bodies. Jonathan, clearly concerned that the giants would return, suggested that they hurry and find a way to get these men out and to the camp as soon as possible. David walked cautiously over to the entrance to the far right where the impeccably dressed man had exited. He could feel a cold and damp flow of air coming from the long dark corridor. It made him shiver, but he couldn't tell if it was from the draft. He could almost feel the darkness in the air coming from the tunnel.

———————◆O◆———————

Meanwhile, nearby...

Nathan's heart raced as he fought back the urge to scream for fear that those men would hear him. He'd just witnessed several Jebusite guards being murdered by unknown men in a very gruesome attack that happened so fast, that the massacre was over in the blink of an eye. Baaldir and him had happened upon the scene just as the attack started.

The doorway they'd found led toward a stairway that looked to be an exit to the ground above. But they'd stopped short just in time and pulled back out of sight and hid themselves where they still had a vantage.

When the attack happened, Nathan ran for his life and couldn't control his body's instinct to move as fast as he was able, away from the danger. He ran through passages without thinking and was now good and lost, and Baaldir was nowhere to be found.

By the time he realized he was lost Nathan had no idea how long he had been running. Nathan tried calling for Baaldir in a loud whisper and received no response. He didn't dare shout or call out for fear that those men could be nearby.

His friendship with Baaldir had certainly turned his outlook on things around in the last year. Baaldir had taught him some fighting techniques and how to read characters and even how to do some arithmetic, sharing his palace lessons with him on their many days running the streets of Jebus.

But now, he could not find Baaldir, nor did he recognize any of his surroundings and to make matters more dire, he soon would be in the dark as his torchlight waned alarmingly close to being extinguished. He figured he only had a few minutes of light left, at most.

Think Nathan, think! He encouraged himself to come up with a solution.

What did he have at his disposal? His pack was lying on the ground near where they'd witnessed the attack, otherwise he'd have another torch ready to use and supplies in case he was lost for a prolonged time, the only thing he had on his belt was a small knife and pouch with some pine tar in it that Baaldir had told him to wear.

Pine tar. Yes! That's it! Nathan thought, wanting to shout but holding it in.

It came to him suddenly as he began to tear off some strips of his tunic, smear some pine tar on the cloth, and carefully wrapped it around the base of the flame. The torch flame took to the cloth and began to burn a little brighter but didn't quite catch as it started to flicker and smoke. He carefully blew on it the way Baaldir had showed him when they used tinder to build a fire inside a makeshift fort they'd constructed in the slums. He briefly let out an excited gasp as the cloth heated up in the embers and ignited finally. He wrapped another at the top and soon had a burning torch again.

That should buy me a little time, Nathan thought excitedly as he tore off a few more strips and tucked them into his belt thinking maybe he'd be able to use them to prolong his torch.

Somehow, the act of solving this one minor problem had given him some clarity. He stood still and listened and investigated the darkness at the edge of his torchlight. What would Baaldir do in this situation? If they were lost together how would Baaldir figure out which way to go? Nathan quickly scanned his surroundings; he'd come to a junction which gave him a choice.

Right or left? Nathan wondered.

He used his torch to look in each direction, walking a few cubits down each tunnel. He had to decide before his torch quit on him. A moment of excitement came over him when he saw an arrow pointing to the right. Silently he thanked God that his friend had thought to use the talc to mark their path. If he followed them, he should be able to make it back to the original tunnel. It was no doubt nighttime, and his mother would be distraught.

Nathan moved decisively and now that he knew what to look for, he was able to navigate rapidly. He stopped for a moment and dabbed some pine tar on a strip of cloth and carefully wrapped it onto the torch, hopefully prolonging the torch's life. Just now he'd realized he was back to the channel where they'd first found the multiple tunnels. Now all he had to do was follow the trickling stream out of this cursed place.

He paused for a moment as he now had a choice before him. His friend Baaldir was likely lost as well. He wanted to get out of the cave, but he also was torn between seeing that his only friend was okay. He still had pine tar, and he had found an old torch that Baaldir had discarded.

Nathan took a few more steps down the stream toward the exit and then looked back over his shoulder. Baaldir would not stop looking for him, neither could he. With that realization he let out a loud sigh and set to work tearing more strips and covering them in pine tar. With those he fashioned another torch that would burn for a good long while. With luck he could trace his steps back to the place where they'd witnessed the ambush and perhaps find Baaldir along the way.

———◇———

Deeper in the Caverns...

The sound of footsteps bounced around the narrow corridor causing Baaldir to cram himself into a very small alcove until he was backed up against a wall, hiding from a group of terrifying creatures. Whatever they were, they seemed inhuman. Sure they looked like men, but their gaunt and pale faces accented by lifeless eyes made them appear like something from the depths of the underworld. They didn't move like a human, breathe like one, or have any sort of emotion.

Something about one of them pricked a sense of familiarity in the brief time he saw the withdrawn face as it passed by unaware of his presence. He couldn't quite put his finger on it, but it was almost as if he'd met the creature before.

As Baaldir focused his breathing and tried his utmost to avoid discovery, he racked his brain trying to get a handle on his location in this god forsaken place underneath the city. During the hours prior he had stumbled his way through the darkness without a torch because it had flamed out when he'd entered a pocket of poor-quality air some time ago. That was one thing he now remembered from his survival lessons: the fact that caverns can have areas with little to no breathable air that can even be toxic if inhaled.

Before that, he was searching for Nathan, who'd panicked and fled at the sight of the Israelites attacking the guards. It all happened so fast, and he'd lost both his way, and Nathan, in the process.

Before they were separated, they had found a doorway that led to a set of stairs but retreated after realizing that the room was occupied. A troop of prison guards with a very brutal taskmaster were driving a dozen slaves up the same set of stairs. From the looks of it the slaves were Israelites, judging by their tattered clothing and features he'd come to know as Hebrew from his lessons.

The attack happened so fast, and he was in awe of the speed at which the attackers moved and how decisively brutal they had been. Had he been armed he probably could've intervened but something about those men told him that he was no match for them; not a dozen of them. One he could take. Two or three, maybe. But twelve skilled warriors would even be tough for his brother to handle.

Baaldir wondered if he really had heard his brother's voice which is what led him to the exit of the tunnel. He'd swore he heard Thoros and Lox arguing but when there was no sign of them, just a group of ill-fated soldiers and one overly-fat taskmaster.

After the ambush and subsequent massacre, Baaldir watched the men drag the bodies and place them in the caverns behind rocks. Their supposed leader had told them to leave the taskmaster, who'd borne the brunt of the leader's ire during the attack, where he lay. Baaldir had to confess that he didn't fault the man for his brutality. Slavery in Canaan was common, but it was not something his father condoned. The only people that worked within the palace were paid wages and provided a home for their families. They served his family but were not owned by his family. In fact, his father detested slavery. The only slaves that were allowed were lawbreakers and criminals. Baaldir was not so naïve, even at the age of thirteen, to think that other forms of slavery were not prevalent in every society within Canaan. But he'd heard his father decree many times that active slave trade was banned, and a punishable crime itself, within the walls of Jebus.

Baaldir had realized Nathan was gone minutes after the attack. He could see the stairs a few cubits away that must've led to the ground above but thought of nothing but turning back to find Nathan, hoping that he was hiding close by. However, an hour after beginning his search his torch died, and he'd slowly found his way blind through the tunnels and stumbled into some semblance of a structure below the city. He now found himself in a dank corridor with candles being the only poor light available.

It was quite the predicament he found himself in after realizing his choices were either to return to the tunnel and feel his way through the dark, or try to stealthily move through an unknown complex. Baaldir knew one thing, and that was that he absolutely had to find a way out before those dangerous looking men found him. If he could find his way up to the city, he could find more supplies and go back to the start and try to find Nathan. Neither choice seemed possible. Baaldir could not see in the dark and he could not be sure he'd be able to advance without being detected, especially not knowing what lay ahead.

In the tunnels, even though he couldn't see, he'd used talc powder to mark the walls. If somehow, he could find a torch, he may be able to find the markings and use them to retrace his steps. Of course, that could also prove to lead him in circles endlessly around the caves as he wasn't sure if he'd crossed over areas multiple times.

Candles lined the corridor; he could use that to see a few feet in front of him, but it would likely be hard to keep the candle lit as a small puff of air could blow it out and he'd be left in the dark all over again.

The corridor went to the left where he'd seen those creatures go and it went to the right to parts unknown. Not a soul had passed by in several minutes of hiding. He could see the tunnel entrance just a few cubits away and decided he would take his chances with the candle.

His course decided, Baaldir appeared from his hiding spot and quickly obtained a tapered candle and started for the tunnel to retrace his steps. With any luck he could at least trace his steps back to their supplies that he'd left behind a rock near the room where they got separated. He decided that would be the first aim, then go to look for Nathan. He'd have a torch, food, water and other implements that could help him; that was the best-case scenario.

The candle went out almost as soon as he entered the tunnel. He swore under his breath, doubled back, and relit the candle with another. This time he used his hand in front of it to shield the flame from the cool draft. This seemed to work, but it severely limited his range of motion and ability to see more than a cubit or two in front of him. He stealthily tiptoed away from the corridor and hopefully those creatures and it occurred to him that these creatures were beneath his home, likely unknown to anyone. Israelites at the gates and sub-human creatures beneath the city was enough to make him shudder at the thought.

Surely these weren't agents of his father's. This had Lox written all over it. Which, now that he thought of it, explained Thoros and Lox's voices in the cavern. It explained the use of slaves, which was a constant source of contention between his father and Lox. It made him wonder now why Lox was engaged in palace intrigue with Ide, a supposed adversary in the court. That explained how this could exist without anyone above knowing about it; especially if Ide were controlling the purse strings which would be easy to do in his position as treasury advisor.

The more he thought about Lox the more he distrusted him which saddened him because there were always moments when Lox came through as a member of the family. But these were always followed by a contradiction that showed he was self-absorbed and constantly tiptoeing on the line of what was acceptable and unacceptable in society. Lox lived in the gray areas of most issues and seemed to make his bed there at night.

Baaldir slowly walked back through the tunnel. He was able to see white markings where he'd smeared the talc, just barely. At least this told him that he'd been that way before even if it wasn't leading him where he wanted to go. With any luck he would make it back to his supplies, and there he could regroup, make new torches, and start a proper search for Nathan.

One foot in front of the other, he trudged ever so carefully into the cave, spending most of his time cupping one hand around the flame so as not to give it a chance to blow out. He couldn't really tell which way he was heading but he figured it to be south which should lead him back to the parts he'd explored with Nathan just a few hours before.

A half hour or so later he was starting to think he would never find his way out when he heard a loud scream echo off of the tunnel walls. It sounded like a cry for help, and it sounded like Nathan. He couldn't quite hear the words, but it sounded like: "Stop! Get away from me! Help! Help!"

It was close, remarkably close, Baaldir realized.

He quickened his pace, not worrying about the candle, trying to decide the direction. Nathan frantic voice echoed again and he darted left down a tunnel and then right at a junction. As he rounded a corner, he didn't have time to stop and assess the reason for the cries from Nathan. Three black cloaked figures surrounded Nathan, who was using two torches to keep them at bay as they tried to attack. They were all brandishing daggers and from the look of it, Nathan was badly wounded already. Baaldir didn't realize he'd drawn his own dagger until he'd plunged it into the shoulder of the first attacker. The other two turned to him and hissed, spittle flying from their mouths. Their eyes were black as night and oozing a black pus that putrefied the air.

Another one lunged at Baaldir before he could pull his dagger from the first creature's shoulder blade. He was able to block the stab attempt with his forearm and felt a burning sensation as the creature sliced his skin open. However, the attacker unrelentingly slashed at him and Baaldir took a bad gash across his chest and stomach as blood poured from the wounds and soaked his tunic. Baaldir head-butted the creature in the face and sent it falling backward holding its nose, now gushing blood like a sieve in turn.

No sooner had he fended off the second, the third tackled him and picked him up with such force that his feet left the ground as he tumbled. The creature landed on him and immediately went toward his chest with the long-jagged blade. Using the weight of its body to attempt to plunge it into his chest. Baaldir fought with all his might to stop the blade. It took everything he had at the unbelievably bad angle to stave off the attack. Locked in a battle of wills he was determined not to relent, but the more he pushed, the more the frothing demon of a man pushed back seemingly unable to tire and was not even breathing hard. Baaldir felt weight of the attacker and knew that he would lose this fight if he didn't find a way.

Just as he felt the dagger pierce his chest, Baaldir summoned one last ounce of strength while managing to create some distance between his chest and the blade using his forearms as a frame. His strength surged and then waned again rapidly as his wounds continued to bleed. He looked the attacker full on in the face and realized with surprise that this attacker was none other than the ringleader of the boys he'd fought with a year ago that fateful day. The one's that Lox had told him would be dealt with. The same one's his father had said disappeared into the ether without a trace. This face was not human though, not anymore. It was more likened to the undead creatures he'd heard about when Skald told scary stories to the children around a firepit.

Seconds later, his salvation came, as a torch swung like a club into the side of the face of the man. The torch hit with such force that the side of the face was embedded with embers and tar that smoldered as the man writhed in pain on the other side of the small room, trying to remove the embers from the skin.

Baaldir, now filled with adrenaline, was on his feet and on top of the one he'd stabbed first. The creature was still alive and futilely trying to reach the dagger in his shoulder. Baaldir put his knee between the shoulder blade, pulled the blade out, and with both hands upon the hilt, plunged it into the skull. The creature let out a slight whimper and then spit blood from its mouth, breathing a last shallow breath before exhaling abruptly. Baaldir screamed a blood-curdling shout that even made the hairs on his own neck stand on end. Now ready for more battle, he pulled the knife from the dead attacker and turned to face the one who'd nearly killed him, ready to finish him off. However, it was gone, fleeing the fight with the third creature.

Baaldir shouted another guttural cry that would strike fear in hearts of lesser men on a battlefield. His war cry soon turned to frustration as he paced around trying to figure out the direction of their escape. After a moment he allowed his heartbeat to calm and started to breathe normally again. That was when he suddenly realized Nathan hadn't said anything this whole time.

"Nathan!" Baaldir cried as he saw him. He ran to Nathan who lay against the stone wall holding a wound on his stomach tightly. He was barely conscious but managed to say, "I don't want to die."

"You aren't going to die. I'm going to get help. Just stay with me Nathan!" Baaldir went to work trying to stop the bleeding, tears flowing down his face. "Hold on Nathan. Just hold on!"

"Tell my mother I love her Baaldir. And tell her I'm sorry." Nathan said weakly.

"You can tell her yourself Nathan, don't you dare die on me, you hear?" Baaldir said as he shook the near lifeless body of his closest friend.

"Don't leave me Nathan! I'm going to get you to help!" he said as he took his jerkin off and used it to tie around Nathan's waist and cinched it as tight as he could; so tight, he thought he heard a rib or two crack. Hopefully, that would stop the bleeding or at least slow it down. He wondered if it was too late as he carefully put Nathan on his shoulder and grabbed one of the torches that was miraculously still lit, tucked his dagger into his belt and then hurriedly ran into the tunnels hoping to find a way out. His own wounds were bleeding terribly but he still had enough strength to carry his dear friend.

"Stay with me, Nathan! I'll get us out of here. Stay with me!"

CHAPTER 7

The Israelite Siege Camp

David walked briskly towards Joab's tent in the siege camp. They had returned an hour ago to cheers among the ranks. By the time he reached the camp it was daybreak as the sun rose above the horizon. He was exhausted but there was no time to waste after what they had witnessed in the caverns. They had brought back twelve of their kinsmen from captivity after a long, dark trek back through the caverns. When he reached the tent, the guards posted at the entrance parted to allow him entry.

"We are back here, my lord general," David heard Joab call from the back room of the tent.

Joab was David's cousin and his most loyal captain who had stayed by his side when King Saul had sent assassins after him. He was well respected by his men for his willingness to lead into battle and never retreat until the last man had moved safely away from the skirmish. For this reason, David had convinced King Saul to give Joab control of the siege of Jebus, while he and Jonathan went north with Abner to press their claim to the trade routes between Mesopotamian cities and Israel. During this last campaign they had subjugated the city of Damascus and made them a vassal state to Israel. Abner had returned to Hebron with plunder while David left a few thousand troops there to solidify their claim and see to the restoration of trade throughout the region.

He received messages from Joab nearly every other day telling of the siege which had been fairly tame so far, as they had spent their energy on building massive siegeworks and preparing tactical ploys. However, the reports of mass desertions had also hurt the morale of the army according to Joab. Now, David at least had an idea what had become of them.

He entered the back room of the large tent and found Jonathan and Joab and a few officers gathered around a map of the city. They all stood up straight as David walked through the opening.

"David the giant slayer! Welcome to my humble abode. I must say it was a surprise seeing you stroll into camp this morning. Last I heard you had taken a scouting party out for a ride, next thing I know you are walking up from the south."

David walked over and embraced Joab, "We decided to extend our scouting expedition just a little further, cousin. I hear you were recently married. Am I correct?"

Joab proudly responded, "It's true, the night before you sent me here to lay siege."

David smiled, "Please accept my congratulations on your wedding. Let us see what we can do to bring this siege to a victorious end so you may return to your wife and start your family."

David turned, "Jonathan, what can you tell me about the men we brought back with us?"

Jonathan shrugged, "Brother, there is not much to tell. All but one of the men had their tongues removed. The only one with a tongue still intact is unconscious now from dehydration and exhaustion. They've all been starved half to death. Mere shells of the men they once were."

Joab spoke up. "David, my lord, I am so relieved you were able to save some of these men. By my estimates we have lost more than three-hundred men, missing from their tents at night. There has been no way to know what had become of them until just now. We had assumed desertion to be the cause."

"I am thankful to The Almighty that we were led into that cavern and were there to be of use rescuing them," David offered, "So you are saying there may be as many as three hundred men in captivity within the walls?"

Joab shrugged, "There is no way to know for sure; it could be more. We should try and find a way to ask these men some questions. They've been through a great ordeal but any detail they can confirm would be a great help."

Jonathan was next to speak, "I'm afraid those men will not be of use to us. I would count them lucky if they survived the week after what they've been through. In the meantime, we need to move forward with the siege. I see the siegeworks have been built? What is the plan to take the city?"

Joab listened to the prince's question and then responded, "The danger is not so much in taking the city, as we will have softened them up with our improved siegeworks so that the victory will be overwhelming. The real danger is in laying siege to the Citadel Fortress once the city is taken. They can defend that fortress with only a fraction of the men they have now. It is the greatest feat of engineering I have ever seen."

"That is a very good point," Jonathan said. "What if we moved the siege equipment within firing distance? That could take away some of their defense abilities."

Joab replied, "That is true, my Prince. The only flaw in that plan is that the fortress has an extreme advantage in being situated atop Mount Moriah. This gives them greater range than our siege weapons. We would risk being picked apart by their archers and whatever ploys they have hidden."

"I think the obvious is staring us in the face." David interjected. "We found an entrance into the city."

"But who knows where it leads? We need more information," Jonathan cautioned.

David replied, "Right, but I think this tunnel is the key to all of it. They are going to send troops out to search for the missing captives we rescued. What we need to do is post men at every single outlet that we can find. They will have orders to stay hidden from sight if possible and kill or capture anyone that exits the cavern. The advantage we have at this time is that they don't know we were in that cavern when they revealed the tunnel and their plan to us. We must not let them escape to fight us another day."

"It will be done." Joab looked at his officers. "Go and scout the land around the city walls. Post twenty men with ten archers at each cave entrance you find." Joab then added, "Stay hidden from sight and ambush anyone that exits from the cave. Orders are to kill if you must, capture if you are able."

"In the meantime, Jonathan and I are going to learn everything we can about this Citadel and tunnel." David and Jonathan headed towards the front of the tent and exited.

David walked quietly as he thought about the cave and tunnel into the city. This could change everything, but he needed time to plan and strategically exploit the tunnel. He needed more information about the other side of that tunnel.

The Dungeon Temple

Deep in the dungeon below Jebus, Vlulor and Flagor stirred as Ahmet walked down the corridor that came from the upper prison where he had made his rounds checking that all was secure. They guarded the inner sanctum where Tsalmaveth made his plans from the confines of his box that acted as a tether. Keeping the secret had been job number one. Ahmet was forbidden to speak to anyone about what he'd seen. If he did Tsalmaveth would read his thoughts and know. So, he compartmentalized this part of his life and the same for his life outside of the dungeon. He'd witnessed some gruesome things in the last month that gave him nightmares. But he'd wake in the morning and see his fire burning in the hearth, his wife and child sleeping with their bellies full of food that he'd been able to provide. He'd even bought Ramah some new clothes and shawls to wear to the market. He had a purse full of coins in a box under his bed. Life had improved even as the siege wore on outside the walls. It was enough to allow him to justify the unsavory profession he now found himself in. He wasn't proud of it, but he was proud of the life he'd finally provided for his wife.

Ahmet remembered the day he'd arrived home, late for dinner after being given the job of head jailer. Ramah was cross with him and quietly placed a warmed plate of gruel in front of him and sat down across the table and looked at him up and down. He slowly picked up the ladle and brought some to his mouth. He tasted the gruel and swallowed it laboriously. Then he looked at Ramah with a smile that said he had a secret.

"What is that smile about Ahmet. Out with it! Problems with my cooking now?"

He looked at her without saying a word. He pulled the coin purse, shook it twice and slid it across the table to her.

Ramah snatched up the purse and pulled the drawstring to allow it to open wide. "Where did you get this Ahmet? Were you gambling again? You promised no more gambling!"

He'd joyfully explained that their changed fortune was due to a promotion not from unsavory games of chance. The look of pride on her face was followed by an explanation that she thought this was too good to be true. He'd received a month's wages up front. A life-changing sum of money. That night they celebrated while Nathan and Ramah sang songs and ate their fill of stored food, knowing that they wouldn't go without it again. That had been the best night of his life.

The next day, as the siege began, he reported to the jail to assume his position. Lox met him there and led him down into the dungeon below and showed him the real work to be done. Half a dozen Israelites in a holding cell sat on the floor looking up at him with hallowed out expressions. His job was to keep this place a secret and personally feed and water these captives, making sure they stayed alive. Days went by, nights passed, and the cells began to fill with captives. From where, he couldn't figure since he knew that very little fighting had occurred in the few weeks of siege, but he didn't ask questions. Lox kept the pay coming periodically.

Soon he lost count of the numbers in the cells. Then he started to realize the numbers were dwindling. Day after day he saw that more were gone without explanation. He'd happened upon the answer when he realized he hadn't visited Vlulor and Flagor in weeks and decided to pay them a visit, hoping his absence hadn't caused the unintelligent creatures to forget him. Not only had they not forgotten him they seemed overjoyed when he appeared near their quarters where they stood guard. The screams and cries followed by the sinister laughter echoed from the temple and sent the pair of beasts running for cover. Moments later, Lox came out of the temple dragging three men behind him. Lox stopped short and looked at Ahmet.

"If you say a word of this to any soul, I'll find out. You'll wish you were never born after I'm done with you," he said sternly as he walked past him and the beasts, taking the men down a different hall than the direction of the holding cells near the prison.

The men he dragged behind him were bleeding from their mouths and had a blank look on their face. They were all wearing a black cloak with a hood, and he recognized a demeanor like the Shades he'd seen most recently, the day he was dragged to see Tsalmaveth and then promoted. These men were vacant, empty in every sense of the word; their souls bound, and dignity taken from them. They now served Tsalmaveth. As did he, though he was not like these men. He was free to choose, or at least he hoped that was the case. There were moments during the last month where his conscience would prick at his senses causing him to reevaluate.

He did not like the methods Lox employed on these men even though they were enemy combatants from outside the wall. It was cruel and inhumane, the things Lox did to them. To what end? More servants? More power? Or was it for some noble purpose that justified the means? These were the questions he would put out of his mind as soon as he remembered his family was now secure for the first time since he'd taken Ramah as a wife.

Ahmet put those questions out of his mind as he slowly walked up to the two beasts chained to the walls of the corridor that led to the temple. He heard a whimper and a ringing of the chains as one of the beasts, Vlulor, turned his head to look at him. They made no aggressive movements which made him less anxious that they would mistake him for an intruder.

"Hi Vlulor, it's me. Ahmet." He was aware that they were nearly blind and would need to smell him. Vlulor lumbered up to him and sniffed the air around Ahmet. Satisfied that Ahmet was a known person, the beast settled back on his haunches and exhaled a burst of air. It smelled putrid, likely from rotting teeth. In the dark lighting from only his torch he could see the sores on their skin and lesions forming. He was sure they had never been given a bath nor did they receive any medical treatment. They were just guards to Lox, not human, not worth caring for. He felt pity for them every time he saw them, and he resented Lox for treating them this way. Ahmet even bought bolts of fabric with his own money and hand stitched a loincloth for Flagor and a slip for Vlulor to cover up their nakedness.

Cautiously, he approached Vlulor and knelt beside her. The beast inhaled and exhaled slowly with a raspy sound. The cold damp air of the dungeon did this pitiful thing no favors.

Ahmet unwrapped a cloth he'd packed in a pouch on his waist. Inside were some healing items he'd pilfered from the prison storerooms such as, salves, poultices, clean cloths, etc. The lesion that looked the worst was on Vlulor's forearm and was festering something fierce. It was inflamed and red around the full areas spreading across the arm like veins.

As Ahmet reached for the arm, Vlulor pulled back and growled, followed by a slight whimper.

"Easy there girl, I just want to look at it. I've brought something that might help if you'll allow me." Ahmet said carefully as he reached for the arm again. After a moment of hesitation Vlulor allowed Ahmet to take a closer look at the lesion. It was clear that the skin was torn by constant itching, and it appeared that one of the scratches was infected and causing further irritation and discomfort. He had brought a medicinal salve in a clay jar that would help to sooth the skin and reduce the itching from infection. Maybe that would keep Vlulor from scratching at it.

Ahmet applied it liberally to the forearm and said, "You need to leave this alone Vlulor." Vlulor replied with a grunt from her nostrils and couldn't resist touching the potent salve that covered the skin, taking one of her three fingers and bringing with it a bit of the glistening compound.

"No Vlulor! Don't eat it!" but it was too late. Vlulor tasted the salve and immediately regretted it as she ran to her water bucket and lapped the water and spit it out on the floor. Ahmet laughed aloud at the sight. Vlulor used a blanket that Ahmet had brought her months ago to wipe her tongue off in a comical fashion. "I told you Vlulor. It's for your skin only."

Flagor was intrigued now and before Ahmet noticed the beast had grabbed the jar and began liberally applying it to his legs, arms, chest; grunting joyfully as the cool salve tingled on the skin as it soothed him.

"Flagor! That is hard to find! Don't waste it!" Ahmet said futilely as the empty jar fell to the ground at his feet, the clay shattering into many shards. Flagor sat back, clearly pleased with himself and Ahmet noticed a rare semblance of a smile come across Flagor's face as the beast calmly enjoyed the soothing properties of the medicine.

"Now look what you've done, now we don't have any for your sister to use." he said, gently scolding the beast as he picked up the pieces and put them into a cloth and wrapped it up. He'd have to pilfer some from the supply room later to bring.

Lox appeared from within the temple suddenly, "Ahmet, these beasts are not pets, they have one purpose and that is to guard. Cease this obsession with them. They are dangerous and I don't want your interference to temper that any further."

Ahmet, red-faced, bowed and apologized, "Apologies, my lord. I did not realize it was a problem."

Lox was over it, "You've done well with the tasks I've given you. Don't let yourself become too complacent with your station here. You'll serve Tsalmaveth and me only if you continue to do well, let it lapse, and you'll be right back where you were."

"Yes, my lord. I won't disappoint." Ahmet said, bowing to show respect.

It was then that a commotion came from the end of the corridor. Shades ran from within the temple and sprinted past Lox and Ahmet and disappeared into the dark.

Lox sounded frustrated, "Whatever could that be about?" he said, as he hurried after the Shades into the darkness. "Follow me Ahmet."

Ahmet hesitated for a moment as Vlulor and Flagor stirred, their hackles raised. "That is an order, Ahmet!" came Lox's voice from a distance. Ahmet took one step toward the candle-lit corridor and realized he'd never venture much past this area. What lay beyond was a mystery to him.

"Ahmet!" Lox yelled and Ahmet broke into a run after him, the candles flickering precariously as he rushed by.

Meanwhile, Inside the Citadel...

Thoros stood at the entrance to the stables listening as the guards told him about a fat taskmaster being killed. They had discovered it an hour ago and woke him in his chambers. He had slept far longer than normal, though he didn't even remember going to bed last night. Last he remembered he was going to check on the stables. Next thing Thoros knew he was being raised by some guards with urgent news of an escape.

Thoros was exasperated, "tell me how it is that twelve half-starved prisoners managed to kill the taskmaster and several guards? Has anyone started a search yet? Show me this tunnel, take me to the bodies."

The much smaller man was visibly intimidated to be put into the position of explaining things to the prince of Jebus, "Y-yes my prince," the guard responded.

Thoros was resisting the urge to let his temper explode. His father was critical of his hot temper, saying it was a sign of weakness to not have control of one's emotions. Apparently, there was a tunnel to the underside of the city that led to parts unknown, and no one had thought to tell the commander of Jebus about it. Heads would roll when he got to the bottom of this.

Thoros was taken aback as they led him through a storeroom and down a set of stairs that led underground. He had a feeling that he'd been here before but how could that be? "So, let me get this straight: We held Hebrew slaves, let them escape, and there is a tunnel that leads right into the fortress? And I'm just now hearing of it?"

"My Prince, I didn't think..."

Thoros was losing patience as he examined the dead taskmaster, "You didn't think? Tell me, did I or anyone else EVER give you the duty to think for yourself? Your duty was to watch over prisoners and guard this fortress!"

By the end of his tirade, he could feel the rage filling his head. "Get out of my sight this moment or I will make you disappear. When you reach your superior tell him to send three of his best warriors, I'll find these men myself! Hopefully before they tell all of Canaan about this tunnel."

Thoros knelt next to the taskmaster and noticed the precise fatal wounds and the brutal treatment of the head in particular. The face was no longer recognizable as human. Whoever killed the taskmaster made this one personal.

Unbelievable, right under our nose. The gods must be toying with me, Thoros thought as he stood and began pacing, his temper ready to crack any second.

Thoros shouted over his shoulder before the last soldier exited, "Tell them to be ready in ten minutes! There had better be a guard detail on this entrance and above from now on. And get someone to barricade the corridors that lead into the city!".

This was a nightmare. The fact that a tunnel existed was problematic enough, now he had several escapees who might find their way to the Israelite camp. A thought struck him; *what if they had help?* He thought about running up to his father to inform him, but time wouldn't allow for it.

Suddenly Lox appeared from a tunnel and stopped short. His demeanor said that if Thoros hadn't already seen him he would have slinked back to where he came from. Instead, he walked toward Thoros cautiously.

"Brother, I came as soon as I heard. What happened here?" Lox said.

"You tell me, Brother," he said sarcastically. "I should've smelled your odor on this. You want to explain all of this?" He motioned to the surroundings and for the first time realized Lox's little pet jailer was there also. More tunnels jutted off from the half circle room and he was beginning to feel as though he was being played the fool with all this secrecy beneath his feet and right under his nose all this time.

Lox feigned surprise and then commenced a long-drawn-out explanation about how this was only a recent discovery, and he was nearly ready to inform the council and the king of his fortuitous discovery.

Thoros cut him off in the middle of his monologue, "Lox! I don't care about your reasons. This is a major breach in our defenses, and we could likely be exposed to attacks from under our feet now!" He said this while gesturing wildly to the corpse of the taskmaster at his feet. "I'm going to my father now and I expect you to come this instant and explain everything. This secrecy is unacceptable, and I'll have you answer to the King for the exposure you brought on us."

Suddenly, Lox's eyes widened as he looked right past Thoros. "Baaldir?"

Thoros was perplexed. "What does Baaldir have to do with this?"

"Nathan!" Ahmet screamed as he rushed past Lox and Thoros.

Thoros turned around to find Baaldir stumbling through one of the doors with a boy on his shoulders. "Brother, help...me..." he said, voice trailing off, as he collapsed on the ground with the boy falling to the side. Ahmet was there to catch the boy while screaming a series of frantic pleas.

"Oh no, my boy. Nathan! Somebody, help him!" Ahmet said, tears flowing down his face.

Thoros rushed toward Baaldir and knelt down and cradled his head. He was bleeding from wounds and was barely conscious. "Baaldir, stay with me. Help is on the way. You there! Go and fetch the healers immediately. Have them meet us in the stables!" A guard took to the stairs and disappeared to carry out the order.

Lox walked over to Ahmet who cradled the boy. He grabbed his wrist and quietly held it between his thumb and forefinger. "The boy has lost a lot of blood, but his heart still beats ever so faintly. We need to get him up to the healers, and quickly. Stand aside Ahmet, let me carry him."

Ahmet's face was drawn and white as a ghost as he reluctantly stepped back and allowed Lox to pick the boy up. Thoros picked up young Baaldir and led the way up the stairs into the storeroom and out into the corridor that led to the stables. By the time they reached the far end of the stables the first healer made his way down from the palace carrying a bag of instruments. He immediately went to Baaldir and checked his pulse. Baaldir was still conscious but only just as he managed to say, "Nathan, save Nathan."

The healer looked at Thoros, "The young prince seems to be stable; he will need some rest and monitoring for the night."

"Go to the boy then" Thoros ordered. The healer hurriedly ran to the boy, Nathan.

"Please help him." Ahmet pled as the healer set to work assessing the wounds and checking his eyes.

"This boy is bad off, are you his father?" the healer asked.

"I am. His name is Nathan," Replied Ahmet.

"Carry this boy to the fortress and find a room with a table." The healer ordered two guards who looked on. Then he said to Ahmet, "He's lost a lot of blood, we must move rapidly if we are to save him. Follow me. There is no time to waste." The guards carried the boy, and Ahmet followed the healer as they disappeared into the fortress, leaving Lox and Thoros there with Baaldir who had fallen asleep.

Thoros was aghast, "I am going to find who did this and I will bring their head back on a pike! And YOU, Brother, will answer for your part in this. Take my brother up to the palace and ensure that someone is there to monitor him. If he dies, I will blame you, you understand me?"

Thoros shouted at three guards to follow him as he grabbed a sword and shield from one of the stalls and made his way back to the tunnel. To each man he handed a torch. Over his shoulder he yelled, "And get more men down in the tunnel to guard it. I want this sealed off!"

Thoros was fuming. Actually, he was more than fuming, he was hot as lava ready to explode. He would find these attackers and make them pay with their lives. He would not rest until he did.

CHAPTER 8

The Citadel Fortress, Jebus

L ox left Baaldir's room after the healers assured him that he would make a full recovery. However serious the wounds were, they were not life threatening, at least not at the moment. The concern would be if the wounds festered and became necrotic. It would take some down time for the wounds to heal and for now, they had sedated him.

Lox ducked into a side hallway and headed for the dungeon. He didn't want to be around when the King, Baaldir's mother, and Siv showed up to ask him questions. Questions he did not have answers for. This turn of events had mucked up his plans to fix it, he would need to find the underlying cause of it and clean it up. His charm on Thoros had worked the first time because he clearly did not remember the underground. But somehow those cursed Israelites had escaped and killed soldiers and the taskmaster in the process. That had brought Thoros barreling down the stairs wildly and he couldn't believe his rotten luck.

To make matters worse, Baaldir had somehow gotten attacked in the caverns. He recognized the work of daggers and had a sinking feeling that this was not the Israelites doing. He was also certain the escapees had help. No way they were in any condition to overtake the soldiers.

So, two things were true at the same time. One was that Baaldir and Ahmet's little runt, were attacked and almost killed by daggers in the tunnels that the Shades frequented to bring captured prisoners to the dungeon. This he knew from the door Baaldir had come through. Second, the prisoners had escaped with help; skilled help at that. *But from whom?* That was the question that nagged him as he made his way through his personal study into the tunnel that led into the bowels of the dungeon.

In a matter of minutes, he was walking past Vlulor and Flagor as they shrunk back into their respective spaces to avoid any punishment from him. He didn't like that Ahmet was so flippant around them. They were for one purpose and one purpose only. The moment they ceased to serve that purpose he would put them down as he would a dog or horse with an ailment. This was the way of things with owning animals.

A few short steps down a hallway and he was mounting the stairs that led into the temple to Yaldabaoth. He took two steps toward the altar and heard the familiar shuffling from all sides. Shades appeared all around him as he walked to the other side of the altar and retrieved the stone box from its hiding place. He removed the lid and out flowed Tsalmaveth. The smoke billowed and filled the area around the altar and began to form into a humanoid shape.

"Master, are you aware that Baaldir, son of King Adonizedek was attacked and nearly killed in the tunnels by your Shades?"

Lox looked around at the Shade who betrayed no emotion and noticed for the first time that there were three of the twelve missing.

"I was not. And I see that three of my Shades are missing." Tsalmaveth swirled around and wrapped his tendrils of smoke around the head of the nearest Shade.

"Where are my Shades?" he asked aloud as he read the mind of the closest Shade.

"Unbelievable. Lox, I expect you to find the underlying cause of this and find my Shades." Tsalmaveth said curtly.

"Yes, master, but what of Baaldir?"

"What of him? What do I care if a foolish boy is harmed walking around somewhere he ought not be?" Tsalmaveth said snidely.

Lox responded, "Harming him has brought undue attention to our operation here. We cannot afford..."

Tsalmaveth cut him off, "I'll will tell you when we cannot afford something. What you cannot afford is to fail me, Lox. If you say there is a mess, then clean it up. And clean it up fast!"

Lox bowed his head, "Yes Master. Apologies for being presumptuous with my concerns. You are above these trivial issues. There is another matter if I may..."

Tsalmaveth interjected, "This had better not be another presumption. Well, what is it?" Tsalmaveth was clearly losing any semblance of patience.

Lox thought for a moment about whether he ought to say anything at all but decided not saying anything would be worse.

"Sometime around the time our Shades attacked Baaldir there were also six soldiers, and a taskmaster killed at the convergence of the tunnels."

"And why is this important to me?" Tsalmaveth queried.

"Twelve of our rejects were with them and they are yet missing, Master."

Tsalmaveth was quiet for a moment and Lox imagined the facial expression he would make if he had a face instead of a smoke-filled shape of a head.

"Twelve near dead Israelites escaped and killed those men. I hardly think so. Who helped them?"

"That was my thought as well. Whoever did this made it personal, judging by the condition of the taskmaster. Our rejects wouldn't have had the strength nor the opportunity."

Tsalmaveth began to swirl around and came back to rest near the altar, "The obvious is staring us in the face. It was Israelites helping Israelites. Oh, this is just too good. The plan is moving forward faster than I thought."

Lox was baffled, what had he missed? Why was the fact that the Israelites knew of the tunnels a good thing?

"Master, I don't see how this is part of the plan. Surely the Israelites knowing about our tunnels is not a benefit to us?"

"On the contrary, Son of Cain. Those rejects you failed to fully turn are worth more to me now than before. "

Son of Cain, Lox thought. There was that name he hadn't heard in decades.

"We all have our part to play in the coming battles. First, I want you to find my missing Shades. Then I will tell you the next part of our plan." Saying this, the smoke that held Tsalmaveth in his form released and rapidly made for the stone box; once inside, closing the lid.

"Go and find them." Lox said forcefully to the Shades inside the temple as he walked from the temple and turned toward the fortress. He had some cleaning to do.

Meanwhile at the Israelite Camp...

Along with Joab, Jonathan and other officers, David sat in front of the men they had rescued the night before. All of them looked back at him with blank stares, almost looking through him. They had been through a great ordeal during their captivity inside Jebus. Though, none of them could talk about it since their tongues were no longer in their mouths. There was one of the twelve that still had a tongue but as of now he was still unconscious.

There had to be more.

David looked over his shoulder at Jonathan and Joab who sat there quietly. He swiveled on the stool and stood up to head towards the exit of the tent and the two men followed him out. Once outside, Joab excused himself to attend to other needs in the camp.

Jonathan had a solemn look on his face, "David, I know what you are thinking. But we can't..."

David cut him off. "How could you know what I'm thinking?"

Jonathan chuckled, "Because I've seen that look on your face before; Not one day ago, when we rescued them. But that was different. We were there already. What you're talking about is running blindly into a city filled with the enemy. We don't have the slightest idea where they are being held or if any are still alive."

David pondered this for a moment. Jonathan was not a timid warrior. Before David slayed Goliath, Jonathan had already made a name for himself in battle. When he was a boy of seventeen, Jonathan and his shield bearer scaled a cliffside to sneak up to a sleeping army of Philistines.

There were ten thousand.

Jonathan and his man went to work quietly slitting the throats of every commander in the encampment. Then they set fire to each tent. Once the army woke up and noticed that their camp was under attack, they went into a panic. With no enemy in sight and no commanders to direct them, they began to attack one another until only a few were left, which Jonathan easily dispatched. Before David had ever lifted a sword, Jonathan was already a legend among the people. For Jonathan to caution against a foolish mission meant a great deal to him, and it could not be easily dismissed.

"Brother, I know you are right. But we still need to find a way to exploit that tunnel. Right now, we have the element of surprise."

His mind began to run down all the resources and weapons he had by his side. In the several years he had been on the run from Saul, he had many men who had stuck by his side through thick and thin. Joab, his two brothers, and his lieutenant Uriah were a few of those men. He called them affectionately, his band of Mighty Men. Each one had proven their prowess in battle a thousand times and was just as loyal to him. All total he could think of thirty men that he felt would do anything he ordered and not deviate in the slightest. Twelve of these men had been with himself and Jonathan the other night in the cavern.

"Jonathan. Could I ask of you a small favor? Would you get word to as many of those men loyal to me that I need them to be ready at a moment's notice?"

"I will certainly do that brother, but I'm still advising against a rescue mission."

"Not a rescue mission. I'm going to end this siege and take this city. And maybe rescue a few unfortunate souls along the way." David smirked.

No sooner had he finished his statement than he heard a shofar blow in the distance. It came from the eastern side of the city. A moment later he heard another shofar, this time closer.

"What is that all about David? Have the Philistines come to engage?" Jonathan queried.

"Hard telling." David said reservedly. "Let's go and check it out."

Jonathan yelled towards the tent where Joab was just exiting. "Joab, have Uriah round up horses and meet us along the way. Signal for the camp to come alive and prepare for battle if it comes to that!"

Joab quickly delegated the order to Uriah and others and joined them as they ran up the path leading from camp, grabbing a spear and shield from a rack as he exited the center of the camp. A moment later David heard a chorus of shofars blaring through the encampment, signaling the soldiers to form up the battalion. David ran at a blinding pace towards where he had heard the first shofar blast. Jonathan, who was several years his senior, was nipping at his heals with Joab bringing up the rear close behind. He heard the shofar again. It sounded, now that they were away from camp, that it was clear on the other side of the city. Uriah was now gaining on them with three other horses in tow.

Uriah rode up to David and Jonathan who were sprinting, "Here are the horses, my lord. Any idea what is happening?"

"Not the faintest idea. Let's move quickly." David mounted his horse in a single hop, grabbed the reins and kicked the steed rapidly with his heels until it was at a full gallop towards whatever action was afoot. Minutes later, they came to the top of a bluff overlooking a rocky hillside and field that gradually rose to the walls in the distance. There, twenty men engaged in a struggle with a hulking giant and two other soldiers.

There were arrows in the giant's leg and shoulder but still he swung a massive sword towards the men who jabbed at him with spears, keeping him at a distance. The giant had a long shield on his left forearm that was full of arrows which he cleared with a single chopping motion from his sword.

They had nearly surrounded him after backing him against a large rock formation but with a sudden rush like a bull, the beastly giant was amid the smaller men where their spears were ineffective. He smashed his shield to the ground trapping three spears in the dirt. Lifting the shield, he swung his sword in a broadside sweeping motion. It connected with the face of one man and flung his lifeless body on top of two others. But by then the rest of the spearmen had recovered their position and began pressing him back to the boulders. The other two soldiers with him were ineffective as they were armed only with short swords and knives. The best they could do was continually parry away thrusts from the spearmen.

David wasted no time navigating the rocky hillside on his horse with Jonathan and others doing the same. In moments they were riding full tilt towards the raging giant who did not seem to have any intention of quitting his defense. David was by far in the lead and would reach the fray before any of them.

Joab, who was skilled with a spear, let out a shout as he hurled his projectile mid-gallop as they came into tossing range of the enemy. The spear flew like a blur towards the foe's head. However, just as it reached the giant, he threw up his shield and braced for the impact of the javelin. The spear hit the shield with a loud, *"THWACK ,"*and had such force that it made the giant stumble backwards a step. By that point David was among the spearmen riding at full gallop towards the giant's flank, standing atop the back of the horse.

One second later, David was flying towards the faltering giant, having vaulted himself from his steed. Just before the giant regained his footing David's entire body crashed into the shield causing all his force to transfer into the struggling man behind the shield. David's horse whinnied as it tried to stop and fell backwards away from the collision. Even as large as this man was, at eight cubits tall, the force was too great for him to withstand. He fell backwards into a heap as David rolled down beside him. As this happened Jonathan and Uriah came riding through yelping as they each dispatched the other two soldiers with slices and cuts to their faces and chests.

In seconds David was on his feet and rushed the stunned giant who was trying to get off the ground. Just as the giant sat up, David was there with a foot to his chest and a sword pointing at his massive neck. The remaining spearmen closed in, bringing their spear tips to within a foot of the giant's body.

"Yield beast!" David commanded with a growl. "Yield!"

The giant man, exhaled and through gritted teeth muttered, almost as a curse, "I YIELD."

Several of the men went to work binding the giant's wrists and body. Jonathan directed the men as to how to securely tie up such an overwhelmingly strong captive.

"Do not skimp on the rope. Use it all and take no chances," Jonathan ordered. The rest of the men went to work tending to the fallen kinsmen and helping the injured ones with bandages.

David knelt before the giant who was now lying on his side having his arms and wrists bound back to his ankles. He looked the giant in the eyes and noticed that, unlike Goliath whose eyes were black as night, his eyes were a stark blue. *This is very peculiar*, he thought.

He also noticed that the man did not avert his gaze as David looked him over. Six fingers on both hands and six toes on both feet. By the look of his armor, he was no regular mercenary as Goliath was; Goliath being the only giant he'd seen up close as this. And he wore a purple tunic which would normally signify royalty or a high-ranking advisor. This could be turning into quite the catch if his instincts were proven.

Walking up next to the giant, he reached down and removed the helm that covered the giant's head and as he did, he gasped. This man was the giant he'd seen arguing with the other one inside the cavern, he was sure of it. David had an internal dialogue going as he realized what finding this giant here meant.

Curses upon my reckless anger. I should have hidden that taskmaster with the other bodies. No doubt the whole city now knows we were there. Why did I have to make an example of him?

"Uriah, ride back to the camp and return with a cart and oxen. Go now soldier."

Uriah saluted and ran to his horse and mounted it on the run and tilted towards the camp.

"Better bring a large cart!" Joab yelled to the young man as the hoofs of his horse kicked up a cloud of dust from the parched ground.

CHAPTER 9

Baaldir's Dream

*T*he sky was dark and dreary as Baaldir ran through the streets bounding over crates and carriages and vaulting himself up onto the roof of a nearby mudbrick hovel. He had been running full speed for several minutes trying to put some distance between him and whatever those creatures were. They looked like men, but smoke billowed from the eye, ears, nose, and mouth as they chased him. The smoke was black as tar and smelled of sulfur and ash. They pursued him relentlessly and acted as if they were toying with him. He looked over his shoulder and one was there a few houses back, calmly walking atop the roofs as if it wasn't concerned that their prey was escaping. Far to his right was another who stood there like a statue, fire in its eyes, waiting to see which way he went. He jumped without thinking toward another roof and landed, tucking his body into a roll and came up on his feet in a dead sprint.

The next time he looked he noticed that the creature wasn't there any longer. In fact, the one to his right was nowhere to be seen. Maybe he'd lost them? A split second later he turned his head back toward the direction of his flight and felt his heart fall into the pit of his stomach as he slid to a stop in the middle of a roof. Standing before him were five black cloaked creatures, smoke pouring out of their body and filling the space below their feet. Something was familiar about their faces. He'd seen them before but couldn't quite put his finger on it. They made no move to attack him as they stood there emotionless, almost as if they knew there was nowhere for him to go.

Suddenly there was a great crashing sound in the sky as lightning flashed and thunder rolled across the hills surrounding Jebus. Big droplets of rain splatted against the roof as he looked for a way down. But as soon as he'd set his intention to run in one way or another there was a creature there to meet him. There was now a shadowy creature on all sides of him with two standing in front of him. He was frozen, unable to think up an escape plan as one of the *figures walked toward him, almost floating, hatred borne across the face. As it closed the distance its mouth full of smoke and cinder opened wide enough to swallow a horse and enveloped him in complete darkness.*

***

It was then that Baaldir awoke, drenched in sweat, in his own bed. The first thing he saw was his mother and father sitting at his side and he realized he'd been dreaming. He felt as though they were leagues away from him though as he tried to speak, fatigue still claiming a hold on him. The only thing he managed to say was, "Nathan?" before drifting off again.

———◆———

Inside the Citadel Fortress

Ahmet sat by his son's side in an anteroom on the lower level of the fortress as the healer and alchemist finished examining Nathan and his many critical wounds. Ramah sat on the other side, tears in her eyes and silently praying to her god. A few minutes passed by and a few soldiers from the prison he oversaw came carrying a litter. They were to transfer Nathan to the litter and carry him to their house where Ramah would care for him and clean his wounds daily. For now, Nathan seemed to be stable though his shallow breathing was a cause for concern from one of the healers. At this point it was up to the gods whether he pulled through, or so they said.

Ramah had come a few hours ago and angrily asked questions that he had no answers to. She'd demanded that Nathan be brought back to the house and that he would not be left in this dank room of despair, as she put it. The doctors thought it a bad idea to move him but agreed that his condition was so grave that it might be better for him to be in a familiar place. They'd mixed up poultices made of yarrow, horsetail, birds beak herbs, garlic, and other oils said to help stop bleeding and prevent the wound from festering.

The soldiers gently picked up the linen that Nathan lay on, unconscious and placed him on the litter and picked him up. One of the men was his friend Musa who lived just a few houses down. Musa was likely the only man he considered a friend as while growing up because Ahmet was bullied by other kids and reclusive as a result. Friends were few and far between for Ahmet even now. Ramah was close by, telling the men to be careful and not to move Nathan around too much.

They started their trek across the city toward their humble abode. His coin purse jingled as he walked, and he realized he hated the sound as he looked at his son lying there at death's door. He would give every piece of gold he could ever earn for him to live. He could only imagine the types that tried to kill him and young Baaldir. Thankfully for Nathan, Baaldir had been there and was able to carry him out. The question as to why they were down there in the first place had not been answered yet, but he meant to find out. The two boys were inseparable, and they likely found a way into the tunnels to explore and happened to have the poor luck of being there at the wrong time.

They turned onto his street and as they came into view of the house Ahmet could see Lox standing outside with an escort. He looked concerned as Nathan came by on the stretcher with Ramah and himself flanking him. Ramah opened the door and ushered the men inside while Ahmet stayed on the street. It appeared Lox had business with him but waited for the door to shut after Ahmet assured Ramah that he would be right there.

"How is the boy doing Ahmet?" Lox asked. Ahmet was surprised to hear genuine concern in the man's voice.

Ahmet shrugged and looked toward the ground, "The healers did all they could for him. It's up to him and the gods if they exist."

"I hope you know that I intend to bring those responsible to account for this. They will rue the day they attacked the young prince and your son."

Ahmet had only known Lox to be a conniving, scrupulous man in the time he'd know him, so he wasn't sure how to respond to him.

"My lord, I will relish in that revenge. Do we know who the assailants were?" Ahmet asked timidly.

Lox looked over his shoulder and motioned for the walls, "My suspicion is that the answer lies out there with those dogs of Israel." He said hatefully.

All the commotion and worry about Nathan and he hadn't even stopped to consider that the Israelites had been to blame for the attack. It made too much sense now and as it sank in his blood began to boil and he felt his sight narrow into a hazy red glow. Of course, it was those dirty Israelites, scourges of Canaan.

"Tend to your family Ahmet, and when you are ready come see me in the temple and we will plan our revenge on these Israelites. Together, we will make them pay." Lox said this as he started off toward the palace with his entourage.

"Yes, my lord," was all Ahmet could say.

Ahmet went inside as the men readied themselves to leave. He'd gotten Musa a promotion to help him with the prison and subsequent guarding of the tunnel. He'd shown great gratitude over the last several weeks.

Musa placed his hand on his shoulder and said, "Take all the time you need friend. We'll take care of things up there until you return."

"Thank you, Musa," Ahmet said sincerely as he let them out and closed the door behind him.

Ramah sat next to Nathan running her hand down his cheek and crying. She used a sponge to put water onto his lips. Nathan had shown no signs of life other than the occasional groan and very shallow breathing. From what he could tell the active bleeding had stemmed so he chose to have a little hope that Nathan would fight and recover. Sprinkled in between those thoughts, Ahmet entertained thoughts of revenge and what he would do to those that hurt his son. He looked at Ramah and felt pity for her that her only son lay here critically wounded, before trailing off into fantasies of impaling the men responsible for it all. One day he would find him, and then he would bring hell to his doorstep.

Ahmet had tried to take a nap while Ramah tended to Nathan, but he was wholly unsettled by the demons that haunted his mind. He sat up and put his feet on the ground. Nathan lay next to them on a cot, and he leaned over to check on the boy. Ramah had fallen asleep at his side and woke as he put his hand to Nathan's forehead. It felt hotter than normal, which was one of the things the doctor warned of.

Ramah whispered softly but urgently, almost as if she were also talking to herself. "Ahmet, I cannot lose Nathan. I cannot bear it. God knows I cannot bear it so He will restore him. I know it. He must." Tears flowed anew down her face and fell to the blanket that covered Nathan.

"Ramah, God does not exist. Put that thought from your mind. This would not have happened if He did, as devoted as you are."

Angrily in a forced whisper, Ramah snapped back. "How can you say that? Are you so cruel that you would take my faith away as sure as I might lose my only son? Get ahold of yourself Ahmet!"

Ahmet said nothing further as the hate in his heart turned to stone. If there was a God, he would shout at him and curse him. Ramah began to sob, and his first thought was to apologize as she had been through enough. His second, more dominant thought, was what Lox said to him hours before.

"Ramah, I love you, but I must go." he said as he pulled his cloak from the hook by the door.

"How can you leave us now? What's gotten into you Ahmet?" Ramah shouted sadly, tears choking her words.

"I need to take a walk to clear my head Ramah." he said as he opened the door to her sobs growing stronger. He pulled the door behind him and whispered under his breath, "I love you, Ramah. I love you, Nathan," as he pulled the hood over his head and started up the path toward the fortress. The further away he walked, the stronger the pull of the hatred grew until it was burning full and bright.

<hr />

The Palace Infirmary

Lox waited around the corner in a dark alcove as King Adonizedek and Frigg left Baaldir's room followed by the palace healers. Orvandil and Ide were also present. Only Ide saw him as they passed by, and he gave him a side glance and kept walking.

"Where is Lox in all this? I have questions for him." Frigg said to her husband as they walked toward their own quarters.

"As do I." King Adonizedek said quietly. "A series of tunnels right under our nose and I was never informed. What madness is at work here?"

They trailed off as they walked further down the corridor until they were out of sight. Lox did not delay in entering the room where Baaldir lay sleeping. He needed to move quickly to conceal the damage done to the cause in the last few hours. The worst thing that could happen was for Baaldir to awaken and spill the goods on what he saw down below. Even if Baaldir sounded crazy to everyone, it would still raise suspicion. He needed time; time to regroup and clean up the mess so that he could have plausible deniability. Tsalmaveth had suggested, in not so many words that he kill Baaldir. That, he would never do. But he would make sure he remained asleep and unable to bear witness to what he'd seen. He'd have to charm Thoros and probably the king and queen as well.

Lox had done everything that Tsalmaveth required flawlessly. Surely that counted for something. Surely, one miscalculation and instance of bad luck wouldn't harm his standing with Tsalmaveth. He would recover the plan and with it the boon of power he'd been promised.

Lox walked quietly up to Baaldir who slept soundly, his chest rising and falling. The strong boy would most definitely recover, thankfully. He never wanted to see any harm come to Baaldir or Thoros for that matter. Reaching into his pouch he produced a small clay bottle with a cork stopper. The cork had a thimble attached to it which Lox poured the liquid into until it was half-full. He leaned forward and poured the liquid into Baaldir's mouth and placed the cork back onto the bottle. That would keep him sleeping for at least a day or more. Hopefully, this would give him plenty of time to do what he needed to do.

Somehow, he needed to cover up or at least explain the existence of the tunnel to King Adonizedek. The problem was that blood had been spilled. And not just any blood, but royal blood. A cover up would be nearly impossible at this point. Therefore he needed to control the narrative and as a last resort he could charm everyone involved. The problem with using that tactic was that it could come unraveled the moment a contradiction arose, not to mention the cost in blood for such an extensive charm.

Lox had seen that firsthand with Thoros just today and it would be exponentially more complex to weave a charm on that many people, and he could not avoid the physical toll it would take on him. The charm for Thoros had required a modest amount of his own blood as the price. He could only imagine the cost of charming the entire royal court if it came to it.

Seeing that Baaldir was sleeping peacefully, he turned to exit. He needed to get moving on the cleanup and time was not on his side. He gave a final glance as he exited and watched the rise and fall of Baaldir's chest, showing that the boy was breathing steadily. Satisfied, he stepped into the corridor and was surprised to see Ide hovering about.

"We have a mess to clean up Ide. What reason would Tsalmaveth have for harming Baaldir? Lox said anxiously.

"Our master must have had a reason. Who are we..." Ide replied.

Lox cut him off abruptly, "He promised that he would not harm the royal family. He swore to me that he would allow them all to leave Jebus alive. That was the deal."

"He made as much of a promise to me Lox. All I'm saying is that if Tsalmaveth wants death he usually gets it. We'd be foolish to stand in his way, lest we become the bearer of his wrath."

"We don't need to stand in his way, but we ought to have guards stationed within and without the prince's chamber," Lox reasoned with Ide.

Feckless coward, Lox thought.

Ide acquiesced, and Lox knew he was sincere because Ide was a terrible liar even as conniving as he'd proven to be over the last few years leading up to the siege. "I will see to it. I will pull guards from the palace and station them about the entire floor.

"Very well. When you summon the guards, tell them they are not to leave the door without another guard being in place."

"It will be done, do not worry," Ide said.

Lox placed his free arm on Ide's shoulder near his neck, his thumb and forefinger lightly gripping his skinny neck, "I know it will, Tsalmaveth will be the least of your worries if Baaldir is harmed further." Ide swallowed hard and hurried down the corridor. Lox could hear him ordering a guard to stand post outside as he went to gather more men.

He looked back into the room at Baaldir, "I'm sorry this happened to you boy." He said to the prince as he urgently walked toward his private study not far from there, all the while trying to make sense of how all of his careful scheming and plotting had led to ruin in the course of one day. This was a reckless thing Tsalmaveth had done, and it flew in the face of all the clandestine plotting they'd done. Lox bore King Adonizedek and the royal family no ill will, and he'd even go as far as saying he thought of them fondly as his own family as well.

Reaching the room, he fished a key from his pouch and let himself in, shutting and locking the door behind him. His study was spacious, if a little cluttered by artifacts, scrolls and ancient tablets filled with cuneiform symbols and pictographs that he'd collected from the world over hoping to piece together the many mysteries that haunted his own existence. Many of them were sent to him from contacts that he'd made during his travels. Others he'd personally collected over the course of several hundred years.

Needing light, Lox lit a set of candles and brought it over to his desk which was littered from corner to corner with still more scrolls and artifacts. His intention was to find a little solitude in his refuge here to collect his thoughts and hopefully come up with a plan to get out of this predicament. But after only a few minutes, he became frustrated as one thought would stem into countless others until his mind was buzzing like a swarm of bees. Opening his eyes, Lox stood up abruptly and in doing so, knocked over a neatly stacked pyramid of scrolls on the corner of the desk. They quickly rolled from the desk onto the floor and scattered across the room in all directions.

Lox shook his head at his own clumsiness as he walked to the first scrolls and stooped to pick up dozens of scrolls, many of which he'd yet to open, from across the expanse of the floor. He brought an armful over to the desk and placed them there once again, careful to prop them against something to prevent them from rolling back onto the floor again. After a few more trips around the room he'd managed to clean up nearly all of the scrolls. Scanning the room, he saw a solitary scroll behind the leg of a shelf on the far end of the room. When he picked it up the brittle wax crumbled and fell to the floor, releasing the scroll from its seal. From what he could see of the remaining wax he recognized it as a correspondence from a contact in Egypt from the royal court there. Unrolling the scroll, a small piece of paper fell from the roll and flitted around for a moment until it came to rest on the floor at his feet.

What's this? Lox thought as he carefully picked it up and turned it over in his hands.

The piece of papyrus appeared to be partially burnt and was covered in a clear wax to preserve it. Bringing it over to the light to examine it further, his heart began to race as he saw a drawing depicting two figures, one of them looked like an ancient deity, and the other a woman. The drawing depicted the woman using an amulet to destroy the deity in a flash of light. The crude drawing had been recovered in his research over the last few decades and as near as he could tell, it was traceable to Egypt. The depiction must have been thousands of years old, drawn with red dye and preserved with a coating of wax over the paper. The amulet reminded him of one he'd possessed a thousand years ago. This couldn't be his amulet, of course, but the memory persisted, lost to time and with it, any fondness for the memory of his lost love, Astarte.

The papyrus correspondence that accompanied it told of a magical amulet that gave a local priestess, angelic powers. Lox was always searching for ancient and magical relics to enhance his power, and this one seemed all too familiar as his mind began to wander to events of his past. He could already do more than the average man as his upbringing had been anything but ordinary. Things like transmutation or shapeshifting came easily to him, as did the dark arts and spellcasting and charms which his late mother had taught him in a far-away land as a youngster, but these came with the cost of blood and wore off before too long of a time. His long-lost amulet gave him the power to change at will. It was like an amplifier of sorts that would enhance the power he already possessed within. Moreover, he wanted to avenge the murder of his mother by a far-off tribe of nomads on the Steppes of Gog and Magog more than three thousand years ago.

He was raised by her, without knowledge of his own origins, when as a young man, she was burned alive by the nomads. He had been on a hunt for days and coming home, he found his mother's remains and ashes inside their burned hovel.

Lox's life had been filled with tragedy from the brutal death of his mother at the hands of an ancient nomadic tribe to the kidnapping of or likely betrayal from his beloved, Astarte. He had scores to settle but no faces to settle them on. This had turned him into somewhat of a brooding and self-destructive man as he became a scoundrel that would take a toll on surrounding villages and homesteads. He would steal livestock, and raid granaries, acting more like a troll than a man. Lox carried on this way for several years and, had he never met Adonizedek on the road that day, he may have continued down that path and probably ended up dead by the sword at some point.

The thing about cave trolls, or acting as one, is that eventually men would muster enough force and come to stop the threat. Adonizedek had shown him how to harness the anger and focus it on other pursuits. He had become an architect, a politician, a diplomat, and a governor at certain times during his few hundred years with Adonizedek. Lox couldn't really say he loved anyone but if he thought about it, he could reason that he felt affection for Adonizedek and even his dolt of a son Thoros at times. He owed his continued existence to Adonizedek for showing him a new way to live, but his past always needled him, and he continually felt like he was standing on a ledge over a great chasm in the quiet moments.

Lox was snapped out of his reminiscence as he heard someone urgently rapping on the door.

"Lox, Lox, open up! Lox!" came a muffled voice through the door.

Lox shook himself and quickly gathered up the papyrus and picture, placing it inside a leather pouch on his person.

"I'm coming, this had better be good!" he shouted back as he turned the lock on the door and yanked it open where he was met at the door by Ide, who wore an urgent look on his weasel-like face.

"What is it, Ide?" Lox said curtly.

"The prince has been captured..." Ide said, face flushed white.

"Captured! How? I told you to have him guarded." Lox said furiously.

Panicked, Ide spoke quickly, "Not Baaldir, he is safe now. The crown prince, Thoros. He's been captured by Israelites."

Lox had to let that sink in for a moment longer to make certain he'd heard correctly.

"Captured? How could he...? When did he...? Who...?" Lox was having trouble speaking clearly, still not sure he'd heard Ide properly.

"I only know he's been captured; the king is summoning everyone to the Council to discuss it immediately. We must go now, Lox. Best not to keep the king waiting."

Lox was at a loss for words, feeling as though in one day, he'd lost control of decades and even centuries of planning and scheming.

How is it that my luck has turned so violently, he thought as he hurried after Ide.

Meanwhile...

Ahmet timidly entered the temple after passing by Vlulor and Flagor who were sound asleep as he quietly navigated around them, careful not to wake them or startle them. Lox had told him to come when he was ready, and he hadn't expected that to be this afternoon, but here he was walking forward as if under a spell drawing him to the temple. He'd started his walk intending just to walk and clear his head and somehow ended up in the dungeon hours later. His only son, Nathan, lay on his death bed, having been viciously attacked by Israelites. Ahmet wanted revenge, and something told him this was the road to realizing that vengeance. He muttered a curse as he summoned the will to step forward into the temple, alone for the first time.

Ahmet had never entered the temple without Lox around so as he walked forward, he began to shake with nervousness, pausing to check for his resolve that was barely hanging on. So far, no Shades had revealed themselves, which was a relief, because creatures gave him the creeps. Miraculously, he was able to walk into the Temple undetected and wasn't at all sure what to do next as he looked around at the many statues of powerful beings that lined the edges of this stone temple. Ahmet felt a chill go from his neck down to his toes as the cool damp, musty air seemed to thicken and grow colder. This further reinforced the trepidation he was feeling with each step forward.

The last time Ahmet was here was when Tsalmaveth had beckoned him into service many weeks ago. He'd been rewarded handsomely for playing his part in drawing attention from the dungeon and seeing to the dwindling numbers of captives which he personally fed daily. The remaining ones had been moved into an open cell just out of reach of Vlulor and Flagor. They would never try to escape since their fate would be to be eaten by them upon setting foot out of the cell. At one point he felt pity for them but now that his son was dying from the hands of ones like them, he burned with hatred toward the Israelites.

Ahmet wasn't sure what to do here in the temple now that he'd entered alone. He felt a low vibration in the air that emanated from the altar. The stone box which housed Tsalmaveth would be found on the far side of the altar in a secret compartment if he remembered correctly. It seemed to beckon him as he slowly approached, becoming more intense the closer to the altar as he crept.

He reached the altar and looked behind him, sensing a presence around him. Nobody was there, but he had an uneasy feeling that he was not at all alone. He searched with his hands around the side of the altar until he found a small lever which he pulled. Ahmet heard a slight popping sound as the secret door on the side swung open revealing the ancient stone box sitting there unassumingly.

Ahmet reached into the compartment and retrieved the stone box and set it on top of the altar. Slowly, he removed the stone lid and set it to the side. No tell-tale smoke exited the box and filled the room. *How could that be?* Ahmet thought as he panicked, thinking he'd made a mistake touching something he had no business touching.

A deep voice sounded from behind him near the statue of the serpent god and, once again, a chill ran up and down Ahmet's spine at hearing a voice say his name out loud.

"Ahmet. My friend, it's good that you've come." The voice said, almost welcoming.

Ahmet quickly turned around at the sound of Tsalmaveth's guttural voice behind him. As soon as the turned he saw the black figure of the Shadow of Death swaying back and forth in front of the statue. Ahmet was stupefied as Tsalmaveth continued.

"Why have you come here alone, Ahmet?" Tsalmaveth said, drawing out the first syllable of his name.

Ahmet nervously managed a few coherent words, "Prince Lox told me to come when I was ready."

"Ah he did, did he? And what are you ready for, Ahmet?" Tsalmaveth said inquisitively.

"My son, Nathan. He has been gravely wounded. He may not last the night. I cannot sit by and allow those responsible to go unpunished. I want revenge. I want justice."

"Revenge. What a sweet-sounding word. And what makes you think this is the place you'll find what you seek?" Tsalmaveth swirled around and came down in front of Ahmet, close enough to reach out and touch him.

Ahmet, trembling spoke as clearly as he was able, "I want to kill the Israelites who tried to kill my boy. You hate them also, and I'm aware that you possess great power."

Tsalmaveth scoffed, "I certainly have great power, but why would I give it to you? What will you give me in return?"

Ahmet hadn't thought that far ahead, he'd only just concluded during his aimless wandering that Tsalmaveth may be able to help him on this revenge quest.

"Give me the power to find and kill those responsible and I will be your servant for as long as you require it." Ahmet said this as sincerely as he could.

"Ha! Do you offer me loyalty? Why would I accept something that I already expect from you? No. If you want power, I'll need something more than a pledge of servitude. Let's see, what will I require?" Tsalmaveth tapped what would have passed for his chin, if he were solid in form, as if he was pondering something. Tsalmaveth flitted around the temple and from multiple angles looked at Ahmet, sizing him up.

Just then a wounded Shade limped into the temple carrying another on his shoulder and dragging another behind him. In his hand was a jagged, crudely made dagger that was covered in blood. The Shade dropped a dead creature at Tsalmaveth's feet and dragged another beside the other.

"What have we here?" Tsalmaveth said urgently as he reached forward and allowed his smokey fingers to trail into the ears, eyes, nose, and mouth of the living Shade. This was the way he extracted information since the Shade was unable to speak for lack of a tongue.

Tsalmaveth seemed to dig deeper and began to laugh as he saw whatever it was that intrigued him unfolding from hours before.

Tsalmaveth yelped excitedly as he released his hold on the dying Shade, "SUCH POWER! I never knew that the key was here within my grasp. After ten thousand years it's here, almost as if it is offering itself to me. I can hardly believe it."

Tsalmaveth flew up to the ceiling of the temple and swirled around violently, talking unintelligibly to himself in some language Ahmet had never heard, before settling down back to the ground in front of Ahmet.

"Do you want the power I can give? And are you willing to do something for me?" he asked without further explanation.

Ahmet nervously responded that he did, but was unsure of what was being proposed, then he looked around as he saw that other Shades had appeared and surrounded him.

"If you allow me use of your body for a day, I will give you the power you desire to kill the Israelites who are responsible. Will you consent Ahmet? I cannot enter a human body without consent. And it only lasts for one day. On the second day I return to my place here and you'll have your body back." Tsalmaveth loomed over him waiting for his response.

Ahmet wasn't so sure and hesitated. Why was he suddenly keen on inhabiting his body? What had he seen in that Shade's mind?

"Ahmet, there is no time to waste. Will you allow me to use your body for one day, after which I will surely reward you with more power than you can imagine?"

"But what about Prince Lox?" Ahmet asked. "Isn't he due to receive power from you?"

Tsalmaveth scoffed, "Forget about Lox, Ahmet. His role in my plan is changing as we speak. You will receive my power if you agree to my terms. Now, no more talk. What say you Ahmet? You need only say yes."

Ahmet inhaled deeply, "Yes," he spoke.

Tsalmaveth wasted no time as he poured his smokey tendrils into him. Ahmet screamed while Tsalmaveth laughed. Soon the two dueling sounds became a deep growl as Tsalmaveth took control of Ahmet. Moments later, Tsalmaveth spoke to the Shades using Ahmet's voice.

"The key is in this city. Bring the young prince to me!"

One by one the Shades sprinted from the room and disappeared. Ahmet was powerless to use his own body though he was conscious of everything all the same.

Tsalmaveth cackled in a low tone as he tried out the new legs, "I'm going to go and see an old friend of mine. The way he said the word friend told Ahmet that Tsalmaveth was anything but, as he picked up the stone box and exited into the corridor that led to the tunnels.

CHAPTER 10

The Council Chamber

T he late afternoon sun was shining in the corridor as Lox entered the council chamber to a raucous argument and heated discussion. Lox watched as King Adonizedek paced back and forth in the Council Chamber. Everyone who was anyone was gathered in the room discussing the capture of Thoros. The king was raging at the near murder of Baaldir and having just heard about the tunnel he was nonplussed and irate at the same time, his face contorted and quivering as he barked at those in the room. Lox could hardly focus as he thought about his next steps in covering this debacle up.

King Adonizedek asked the room, "Somebody tell me, how did Thoros get captured outside our walls?"

Ide cleared his throat. "It appears Thoros went through the tunnel under our walls late last night with three other soldiers. One soldier made it back apparently, a guard captain."

King Adonizedek appeared to be wrought with anger, "Now, I want to know is why wasn't I made aware of the stairs and tunnel in the caverns under MY city!!" His voice booming, "LOX, you've been curiously scarce today; I smell your odor on this, tell me what I should've known long ago!"

Lox shifted in his seat, having just sat down quietly hoping to escape detection, unaccustomed to King Adonizedek yelling at him.

Lox cleared his throat, "My king. Thoros and I both decided to find out more about the caverns before bringing it up. We had no way of knowing how the siege would fare. He and I were just discussing sending scouting parties out into the caverns to find a safe escape route when we came upon the murdered taskmaster. Baaldir stumbled in wounded with his friend moments later. Out of anger, Thoros took a few soldiers and rushed off into the cavern. There was no way to stop him, and I figured that Baaldir was the priority at that point."

This last statement was mostly true. Lox was genuinely concerned for Baaldir at that point, but he was also concerned for the detriment to his plans that the attack on Baaldir had caused. The fact that Lox already knew the layout of the tunnels was known only to himself and Thoros. His lie about them working together on securing an escape route would be rectified as soon as he could determine the details of the charm that he intended to place on those involved.

King Adonizedek narrowed his eyes at Lox and held his gaze for an uncomfortable amount of time. Lox internally squirmed and thought, *he knows I'm full of it. Keep calm and stick to it.*

King Adonizedek broke his gaze and turned to the others, "Where is this guard Captain that made it back without my son?"

Jarnsaxa offered, "He is waiting outside, shall I summon him into the chamber?"

King Adonizedek nodded and with an annoyed tone said, "Yes, let's hear from this man, his version of what happened."

The towering doors to the chamber opened to the hall outside the room. Several guards escorted a skinny middle-aged man through the entry as the doors shut behind them.

King Adonizedek led the questioning. One of the many attributes that he possessed was the ability to make nervous men at ease. In a calming tone he asked, "What is your name Captain?"

The captain was stiff and looked around the room as they escorted him to the head of the table. He seemed to take notice of the polite tone and slightly relaxed, dropping his tense shoulders a bit. Confidently, the captain said, "My name is Urim, my king."

"Urim, can you tell me how it is that you ended up with your prince and future king, Thoros, in the caverns?"

"My king, Prince Thoros ordered it so. We were searching for the escaped Hebrew slaves."

King Adonizedek's eyes widened. "Escaped Hebrew slaves? Is that so? I was not aware that we had captured any Hebrews as of yet. Lox, you are in charge of the prison, do you know anything about this?"

Lox feigned ignorance, "My Lord, this is the first I am hearing of it. We don't currently have any Hebrew slaves. How could we? This siege has been nothing but waiting so far." Lox had to think fast. His tactic would have to be to distort and deflect attention away from implicating him or his work in the dungeon.

"However, my King, we did use prisoners to open the tunnel that exits into the caverns. I ordered them returned to the cells in the prison, to which our soldiers clearly failed and got one of my jailers murdered for their failure. It is clear to me that these prisoners overpowered the guards and killed them to make their escape. For all we know they escaped back into the city and are drinking at a tavern."

The fact that these were all distortions of the truth made no difference now with no one to challenge the narrative. And Ide would never implicate himself in holding onto knowledge of it.

King Adonizedek turned to the man. "Urim? Were these prisoners Hebrew, or not?"

Lox noticed the man shoot him a nervous look which told him that the man realized he would be contradicting another Prince of Jebus.

Urim replied rapidly, "My king. I cannot be sure now that I have heard Prince Lox's words. Perhaps I assumed that they were Hebrew based on what I saw and heard down below. All I know for sure is that they killed the taskmaster and seven of my company are missing; those who were on hand to transport them. I brought two of my best men with me at the request of Prince Thoros."

Lox stared at Urim pensively. His experiments in the underground temple were secret. Not even King Adonizedek knew of it. Those that were now missing were subjects in his rituals and experiments. He'd made great strides carrying out the will of Tsalmaveth and he wasn't about to have this captain unravel it any further.

King Adonizedek continued, "tell me, soldier. When you and the prince went through the caverns, what did you find? Did you find the bodies of the soldiers? Were the caves traversable?"

Urim replied, "My King, we wandered much of the night. With only torches it was impossible to figure on any movements of the prisoners."

Lox watched as King Adonizedek contemplated this. It was a hard notion to think that they were able to make it out in their weakened state.

Urim continued, noticing the cue that the king wanted more information. "As for traversable, my King? It was difficult given Prince Thoros' imposing size. We spent more time trying to find ways around narrow passages so that by the time we found an exit we could not determine how to return. Our intent was to exit the cave and find a way to return to the city walls undetected above ground."

Lox ran through possible outcomes. The Hebrew forces seemed to have been alerted to the use of the caverns, Thoros' capture at a precise place proved this. Two possibilities existed for how they would know of the cavern tunnel exit. Since no man was alive who built the original tunnel and it had been unknown for several hundred years or so, the knowledge would likely be lost. Either the Hebrew slaves escaped by overpowering and possibly killing seven armed soldiers, or someone helped them escape. Either possibility seemed far-fetched, but he didn't see any other choices.

Lox decided he needed to deflect attention from the escapees. Thoros' capture was a pressing matter for King Adonizedek after all.

Lox interjected with a question, "Can you tell me, Urim, about the princes capture?" Lox could tell Urim was uneasy about answering.

"My Lord, I didn't see much of what happened."

"You were there, were you not?" Lox questioned abruptly. He needed to steer the focus onto this poor chap who was in the wrong place at the wrong time.

"I was, my Lord, but when the skirmish began, we were nearly surrounded except for the cave we had just exited from. Prince Thoros rushed forward to press the attack and I was cut off from him and the others."

Lox pressed Urim more. "You were cut off? How then did you come to escape?"

"My Lord, I was pressed by several of our enemy back towards the cave and there was no way for me to cut through them to reach the prince."

Lox held a stern gaze towards the withering soldier. "So, what you are telling us is that you ran. Like a coward, you ran."

Urim's face was overtaken with panic and fear. "I had no choice! There were nearly thirty soldiers. There was no way for me to aid Prince Thoros."

Lox roared. "Do NOT say his name like you were a friend. You are a coward. A traitor. I ought to throw you off the highest point of this tower, so you have plenty of time to think about it on the way to your death!"

Lox may have laid that on a bit thick, but it seemed like a productive way to deflect King Adonizedek's ire on this poor man rather than upon himself. What he didn't want was anyone poking around in the caverns and finding his project.

For now, the focus was on Thoros' capture and not the fact that there was a system of caverns underneath the city and surrounding lands. He would divert resources to guard the entrance to the caverns and hopefully keep the Shades held below.

Lox's accusation seemed to have the desired effect as the room erupted with murmurs and chatter.

Urim collapsed onto the floor, blubbering. "Please my Lord, I beg you. I had no choice. After I was cut off, my concern was making it back to tell you what had happened!"

King Adonizedek rose from his seat, towering over Lox and the rest of the Court. His voice boomed, "SILENCE!"

The room fell silent as King Adonizedek looked down on the guard captain, who by this point, was in a heap on the ground at his feet, sobbing uncontrollably. At the command, Urim ceased his outburst. Lox had backed away to his seat to allow the king to have the floor.

King Adonizedek pondered the young soldier for a moment. "On your feet soldier! You will answer my questions without the hysteria, in a way befitting your rank as Captain. Am I clear, Urim?"

At this command, Urim stood up and straightened his posture. "My King. I will do as ordered," he said.

"Now then, Urim. I would like you to simply answer my questions one by one, without any excuses or explanation." The king added, "Will you do that for me?"

King Adonizedek acted as if it were a suggestion or a request; It was anything but, and Lox could tell that Urim understood that fact.

"Yes, my King. I will." Urim exhaled.

"Good. Now, is it true that you were with the prince when he was attacked outside the caves?"

"Yes, my King."

"Is it also true that when you were separated from your prince that you did not aid him or try to rescue him?"

Urim shook his head, "My King. There was no way to reach him."

"I didn't ask if there was a way to reach him. I SIMPLY asked you; did you try?"

"I did not." Urim looked at the floor.

King Adonizedek continued. "Urim. Is it true that you escaped back into the cave to preserve your own life?"

"My king, that isn't why..."

King Adonizedek cut him off, "Do not try to explain. Are you standing here before me today, ALIVE, while my son, YOUR Prince and future King is captured and likely being tortured or killed?"

"I am alive my king. Once I was separated, I believed my duty was to return here with the news of what had happened."

"Urim. Is it true that the number one duty you have, and swore to uphold, was to serve and protect my family and I, even unto death?"

"It is true my king. I made that vow."

"Good. We understand each other now. Can you tell me the ONLY thing that was required of you when the prince was attacked? What was the ONLY duty that you ever had?"

"To serve and protect the prince, my king." Urim, on saying these words, could tell where this was going. Lox judged this to be the case given the further deflating of the man, Urim.

"To serve and protect. Even unto death. Does that mean, only if you can reach him?"

"No, my king," Urim said solemnly.

"Good. You understand the particularly important vow you made then. What am I to think now that you are standing in my Council Chamber explaining to me in detail what happened outside the caves, but my son, Prince Thoros, is captured and likely in jeopardy of losing his head? Why are you still alive? Is it because you did your duty Urim?"

"My king, it's true. I should have died trying to save the prince. Please have mercy on me. I have a young wife and child as well. Too young to be left a widow and fatherless."

"Urim, you said it yourself. You should have died. I suppose the only solace I can take from this is that your failure at least allowed for the news of his capture to reach us. Guards! Take this man to the prison. There he will await a trial."

Urim sank to his knees. His fate realized. "My king, I ask you for mercy" he pleaded as tears streamed down his face and wet the ground in front of him.

King Adonizedek stood and thought for what seemed like several minutes then addressed Urim as the guards closed in, "You had better pray that my son is returned to me alive. We will take up your case at a later time."

Urim tried one more plea but was cut off by several guards putting a gag around his mouth. As they dragged him away Urim wriggled free and tore the cloth from his face. "MY KING. I KNOW THE WAY BACK TO WHERE THE PRINCE WAS CAPTURED!"

The guards continued to drag the man as he yelled. "PLEASE MY KING!"

"STOP!" King Adonizedek ordered. "Bring the Captain back to me." The men dragged him back and threw him in a heap in front of the king, "Can you show us how to get through?"

"My king, I made markings on my way back. I'm certain I can find the way out again."

King Adonizedek pondered this for a moment. He looked at Lox who had an inquisitive look on his face. "Lox, what do you think of this?"

Lox shrugged, "I don't know truthfully. Can we trust the word of a coward? Maybe he means to try and escape. Why don't we send an emissary to the Israelites and inquire on Thoros' well-being?"

Secretly Lox winced, the last thing he needed just now was a god forsaken tour through the caverns.

Urim interjected, "No, my lord, I can show you." Clearly needing them to believe him.

Lox's mind was racing as King Adonizedek took a moment to think. Finally, the king knelt to the level of Urim and grabbed him by his breastplate, lifting him off the ground ever so slightly.

"Here is what I will do. I'm going to give you an opportunity to reclaim your honor. Show my men how to get through and maybe I'll let you go back to your family."

Lox was internally panicking. The only way to shut this man up would be to kill him. Of course he could kill him in his cell but that would raise more questions. No, he decided he needed deniability. A plan formed in his mind as he spoke to King Adonizedek.

"My king, I will accompany him to the exit and ensure that we can use it to rescue Thoros. Two guards to accompany him with me should be sufficient."

Adonizedek dropped the man in a heap on the floor and walked away, pushing a cedar door open so forcefully that it splintered at the frame.

"Lox! You'd better get to it! And somebody fix this blasted door!" King Adonizedek said over his shoulder as he exited the chamber.

Lox sat back in his seat and finally relaxed his shoulders as the room began to empty. He spoke to a nearby officer and ordered him to take Urim and have two soldiers bring him below and wait for him. They would be leaving soon to track Thoros' movements through the tunnels. He first planned to go and talk to Tsalmaveth in hopes that the being would see that rash actions were not the wisest path. All the work they'd done could end in failure if they were not cautious. He debated whether or not to show Tsalmaveth the scroll and burned parchment depicting the powerful amulet.

Once the chamber had emptied apart from the odd council member chatting in the recesses, he pulled the scroll from the pouch and unrolled it, holding the correspondence in one hand and burned pictograph in the other. Three words nearly made his heart jump from his chest. They read, *Seen in Memphis*. It was then that the details of a further plan began to grow as he pushed back from the seat and hurried off to speak with Tsalmaveth.

The Citadel Dungeon Temple

Lox watched from his secluded vantage as Tsalmaveth inexplicably entered Ahmet's body. He silently cursed as he watched his power evaporate as if it were never there. Tsalmaveth had used him. After freeing him from the stone box, Lox had swallowed up all the promises of power and revenge that Tsalmaveth spoke with his forked tongue.

In return, Lox had positioned the Shadow of Death to take control of Jebus, helped him capture and turn men into his own personal army of Shades, and built him not one, but two temples to the god that Tsalmaveth was beholden to. A god which had shown him no favor, nor had he ever seen his power. To Lox this was all a ruse, he believed none of it now that he watched Tsalmaveth renege on every promise he'd ever made to him. He now thought back to all of the times he'd suggested that Tsalmaveth use him as a vessel, only to be dismissed.

The memory of receiving the stone box from the Ark niggled at his mind as he heard the words: *Come forth and play your part, Son of Cain.* He cursed again silently at the thought. It appeared to him that he was the plaything of both sides of this struggle that he was only now beginning to understand.

Lox asked himself, *How could I have been so stupid?*

Not only had he not seen this coming, but the dead Shades, killed by Baaldir and Nathan, were none other than two of the five he'd captured after they had attacked Baaldir in the streets a year ago. He now felt responsible for the harm that had come to Baaldir.

Tsalmaveth was now pushing him aside, and the evil wretch had also tried to kill a member of the royal family when he'd fervently promised to free them once he'd taken control of the heights above Jebus. It followed that Tsalmaveth would promise one thing and then just as easily do the opposite if it served his desires.

That realization made him less angry that Ahmet had stepped in to take his place as Tsalmaveth's pet. Hatred began to burn within Lox for

Tsalmaveth while he also pitied Ahmet. Lox knew that Ahmet would get more than he bargained for and still have nothing to show for it.

In truth, Lox was thankful that he'd witnessed this in the temple. He'd been on his way to try to reason with Tsalmaveth and ask him to honor his promise to spare the royal family. Then, he was still under the impression that he'd be receiving a boon of power from the Shadow of Death. With that power, he'd be able to use it to finally exact revenge on the people that had killed his mother. The thought of this led him to painful memories of his mother and the hopelessness he felt during the search for her killers. Lox was beginning to feel that same hopeless feeling again as he was brought back to the present, hearing a loud cackle from Tsalmaveth who was ordering the Shades to find the Key and bring it to him. The next words made Lox's blood run cold as he heard Tsalmaveth order, "The Key is in the city! Bring the young prince to me!"

What is Tsalmaveth doing! I need to go to Baaldir now! Lox thought as he ducked back into a passageway and dodged the Shades who blew by him, not seeing him as their focus was singular. Lox tiptoed down the corridor after them careful not to be seen or heard. His mind swam with worst case scenarios.

What if I can't get to him in time? Lox worried.

What if I stop them? Then what? He worried further.

None of the solutions made any sense as he was determined to reach Baaldir before the Shades. They would have to sneak through the tunnel and up through the stables. Lox could use his path through the study to reach Baaldir first. Doing just that, Lox barreled through his study and didn't bother to lock the door.

As he approached the room, he was relieved to see several guards surrounding the room. They parted as he passed through and entered the room to see a sleeping Baaldir. Next to the bed was Siv, Baaldir's sister-in-law.

Siv turned to Lox as he entered, shocked that someone had burst in.

"Lox what are you...doing?" she said but stopped as she saw the horrified look on his face.

"There is no time, Siv. We need to get Baaldir to the palace above. It's not safe here."

"What are you saying? The healer said he needed to rest here for a few days and that moving him could injure him further." Siv protested as Lox stepped forward to the bedside.

It was then that they heard shouts and clamoring outside in the corridor.

Lox's eyes widened as he yelled, "Pick the boy up, we must go. If you want to live you must do as I say, now!"

Sounds of battle muffled by the door outside resounded. The door swung open as a terrified soldier entered. "We are under attack. Foul beasts!" he said weakly as he fell dead with a dagger in the small of his back.

Siv was on her feet and picked Baaldir up over her shoulder as Lox retrieved the dagger from the dead soldiers back. "We need to move, stay close to me." Lox shouted as he approached the hallway. Shouts from down the corridor rang as the clang of swords and screams of defeat echoed in between.

Lox turned to Siv, "No matter what happens you cannot allow Baaldir to fall into the hands of those beasts."

"What beasts? What are you going on about?" Siv said, confused.

Lox ignored her questions as he shuttled her and Baaldir toward the direction of the palace. "Go, Siv. You need to get him into the palace and under heavy guard. Do not stop until he is safe."

He did not wait for her to reply and instead ran down the corridor where the skirmish was taking place. Fortunately, the Shades had yet to progress up to the room and it appeared that Ide's preparation of guards had proven effective. He rounded a corner and saw six Shades locked in close battle with ten or so guards. They did not tire, and he could tell the guards were tiring rapidly as one after the other fell. He wasted no time jumping into the fray. His powerful slashes of the dagger proved deadly as he sliced the neck of one, and punched the face of another, crushing its face with his withering blow. With renewed energy the soldiers reengaged. The Shades, seeing that the tide had turned against them snarled as they disengaged and pulled their fallen Shades with them. Now the two groups were separated with Lox in the middle of the soldiers and Shades, towering over all of them.

"Tsalmaveth has broken his agreement with me. You have lost, Shades. Go back to where you came from and do not return. I will be your enemy from now on."

One of the Shades stepped forward and through a tongueless mouth spoke in the voice of Tsalmaveth, "Lox, you fool." He chuckled before continuing nonchalantly, "No matter, I will add you to the list of those who will die an agonizing death. You had better prepare yourself for my wrath you ungrateful whelp." With that, the Shades picked up their dead and retreated back towards the dungeon leaving Lox and the terrified guards there alone.

It occurred to Lox that if he wanted that power to see where his hated foes vanished to, he would have to take it from Tsalmaveth. And to do that he would need power, the kind of power he would find in Egypt. He would find the amulet, take it by force if he must and return to Jebus to confront Tsalmaveth. Naturally, a by-product of that would be to save Adonizedek's city and his dolt of a son Thoros from the Israelites. He would crush them under his heel and then nothing would stop him from finally taking revenge.

"Go see the prince and princess. Make sure they arrived in the palace and are safe." Lox said as he hurried off towards the tunnel that he had opened, allowing this calamity to form. Maybe he could collapse the tunnel and barricade it, then go to the prison and seal off the many entrances he'd built over the last decade or so. He wasn't sure if that would stop Tsalmaveth because he knew that the system of tunnels below the city likely led to other ways to enter. He only hoped that it would impede or slow their ability to act.

When he'd left the meeting an hour ago just after sunset, he'd intended to do as Adonizedek asked and go through the tunnels to obtain information as to the wellbeing of Thoros. Then he planned to kill Urim to silence him; after which, he would tell everyone that Urim had slipped away into the tunnel and fled. Lox wasn't sure whether he would need to even go that far, but decided he would use the tunnels to escape and abscond to Egypt.

When the Shades retreated, Lox rushed back to his private room and began to rummage through drawers and chests. He cursed himself for allowing his emotions to take over and drive him on as he'd attacked the Shades without thinking first. His care for the family of Adonizedek, along with his newfound hatred for Tsalmaveth, had spurred him on in a frenzy. He wantonly struck down several of the Shades that Tsalmaveth had sent to take Baaldir, and no doubt kill him afterwards. And to make matters worse, Tsalmaveth, being inside a body for the first time in years, was able to connect to each of his Shades and see and hear whatever they did. This was evident when one of the Shades spoke to Lox even though they had no tongue.

One thing was plain now and that was Lox needed to leave Jebus immediately before Tsalmaveth sent Shades after him if he hadn't already. After packing a light satchel with supplies, bread, a waterskin, and a small dagger he rushed from the room and down the corridor. The nightfall had made it easier to navigate the corridors and keep to the shadows.

He paused for a moment as he heard shouts from soldiers coming from the direction of the palace accompanied by marching footsteps, clearly mobilizing forces to protect the palace. Lox had debated staying and helping to guard Baaldir, but he was worried that staying may expose his involvement and knowledge of the existence of this threat to Jebus. And worse, it could entrap him in Jebus with a siege from one direction and Shades from another. Staying in Jebus would not change any of those circumstances nor could he single-handedly defend himself. He would have to trust that Bulwark, Jarnsaxa, and others could defend the boy and keep them all safe. Hopefully, they would cut off entry points and fortify the fortress now that they were aware of assassins within its walls.

This wasn't supposed to happen like this, Lox lamented to himself as he ran towards the tunnel. The words, *Seen in Memphis*, kept running through his mind as he ducked through an archway and cut across the stables, increasing his speed on the open ground.

I'll go to Memphis, find the amulet and take it, then I'll return to Jebus and save everyone. With it, I'll be just as powerful as Tsalmaveth if not more powerful.

Lox descended the stairs three at a time and reached the bottom where he found the coward Urim and two others waiting as ordered.

"Let's go. There is no time to waste." Lox ordered as they departed with Urim in the lead.

The Israelite Camp: earlier in the day

Thoros lay on his side, still bound from head to toe. For the entire day he had laid here with the only contact being from a boy coming to slop water into a ladle and give it to him in a messy and unproductive manner. *No food*, his stomach reminded him repeatedly.

However, they had removed the arrow from his thigh and bound it tightly with a dressing. Outside the camp he could hear all kinds of hustle and bustle but couldn't ascertain whether coming or going. During the night he tried yelling curses and profanities at the men that he couldn't see outside the tent he was kept in.

Early in the afternoon he'd tried appealing to the boy who gave him water. Realizing it was no use he decided to reserve his strength and energy. It was surprising to him that not one leader of these Hebrew had come to talk to him. They surely knew who they captured. He ran through several possibilities on what they could be planning for him. Everything from ransom to execution crossed his mind.

Just outside the tent he heard someone playing a lyre. He had to admit that it was soothing to him, and he rather enjoyed listening to the musician play and sing. For the entire day they had played off and on periodically.

Thoros listened as the musician strummed three chords repetitively as he built up to the melody and began to sing; his voice carried throughout the camp as everything else fell silent. Thoros imagined everyone stopping to listen to the very gifted musician as the prose was offered up in song:

***

Whoever dwells in the shelter of the Most High
will rest in the shadow of The Almighty.
I will say of the Lord, "He is my refuge and my fortress,
my God, in whom I trust."
Surely, he will save you from the fowler's snare and from the deadly pestilence.
He will cover you with his feathers, and under his wings you will find refuge; His faithfulness will be your shield and rampart.
You will not fear the terror of night, nor the arrow that flies by day, nor the pestilence that stalks in the darkness, nor the plague that destroys at midday.
A thousand may fall at your side, ten thousand at your right hand, but it will not come near you.
You will only observe with your eyes and see the punishment of the wicked.
If you say, "The Lord is my refuge," and you make the Most High your dwelling, no harm will overtake you, no disaster will come near your tent.
For he will command his angels concerning you to guard you in all your ways.

They will lift you up in their hands, so that you will not strike your foot against a stone.

You will tread on the lion and the cobra, and you will trample the great lion and the serpent.

"Because he loves me," says the Lord, "I will rescue him.

I will protect him, for he acknowledges my name.

He will call on me, and I will answer him.

I will be with him in trouble, I will deliver him and honor him.

With long life I will satisfy him and show him my salvation."

***

The last note rang out and as it drifted the whole camp had fallen completely silent. Thoros hadn't even realized that, during the song, he had closed his eyelids and was now drifting off to sleep.

No sooner had he allowed himself to succumb to sleep than he was awoken by a voice spoken in the common tongue of Canaan. From the corner of the tent Thoros heard a man say, "My name is David, son of Jesse. What can I call you?"

Thoros quickly opened his eyes to see a muscular and battle-hardened man sitting there holding the burlap hoodwink that had previously covered his sight. He sat cross-legged a few feet away from him. Thoros hadn't even heard the man walk into the tent.

As he focused on the man called David, Thoros recognized him as the boulder that had plowed him over outside the caves yesterday. He wasn't a large man. Rather average in size but muscled from head to toe with scars on his legs and arms and one on his right jawline. Upon his lap was a lyre.

Thoros figured a civil reply was best, "My name is Thoros, first son of Adonizedek, the King of Jebus."

CHAPTER 11

The Israelite Siege Camp

D avid sat inside the tent where the captured giant lay tied up. He had spent a full day letting this large man sit without food or water, mostly because he didn't want to risk untying him to allow for use of the oversized hands he possessed; and nobody wanted to go near him. He also hoped that it would make the man weaker and, as a result, more malleable. For the day, he sat outside the tent playing his lyre and singing his songs. He figured since the giant had noticeably quieted down that it may be time to make a first contact with him. He began by introducing himself as politely as he could muster.

David removed the hoodwink and realized the giant was sleeping. He sat quietly and said, "My name is David, Son of Jesse. What can I call you?"

The giant woke suddenly and looked around puzzled as he sized David up. David repeated the question now that he was awake and the man responded in kind, "My name is Thoros, son of Adonizedek, the King of Jebus."

Thoros continued, "I am wondering if you mean to starve me? I'm sure you are aware it has been nearly a whole day since you and I met last."

David was surprised at the civil tone of the giant, "It is not my intention, Thoros, to starve you. Simply put, I don't think it prudent to untie your hands. You are immensely powerful, and I won't risk another's life so that you can eat. You are obviously not a frothing monster, contrary to the opinions of my men, so I will ask of you a simple question."

Thoros nodded in affirmation and waited for the question.

David continued, "If I untie your hands from your ankles and allow you to sit in a more comfortable position, will you repay that kindness with harming me or, more importantly, anyone I send into this tent?"

Thoros replied, "You will not have to worry. I know what my situation is in this camp."

David feigned skepticism, "Do you know, fully? You should know that I have one hundred men surrounding this tent during the day and three hundred men on watch throughout the night. Any attempt to escape or so much as a scratch on one of my men and their orders are to run you through without so much as a second thought. Do you understand Thoros, son of Adonizedek?"

"I understand completely. Untie me enough to sit up and I will be grateful to you for it. Give me some venison to eat and I might just give you my birthright to the throne of Jebus." Thoros cracked a smile towards David.

David raised an eyebrow. Obviously, Thoros had studied their history with the reference to Jacob and Esau. He knew that many of the common people of Canaan were distantly descended from Esau's bloodline, so it didn't come as a surprise that its rulers knew the stories as well. David's ancestor, Abraham was a Canaanite once upon a time ago. Mount Moriah, where the fortress in Jebus was built, was the place to which Abraham went to sacrifice his son and was provided a ram instead. He wondered if Thoros knew about that tidbit.

"Here is what I will do, Thoros. I will untie your hands from your ankles and allow you to be tied to a post with use of your hands for meals. Your legs will remain tightly bound."

He stood up at the statement and walked over to the tent opening and waved to a few of his guards. They came running to him. At the order they were hopping into action and in moments Thoros was unfettered. Thoros was true to his word and allowed them to help him sit up.

The big man groaned as his limbs stretched out for the first time since his capture. It didn't seem like he'd have been able to attempt an escape anyhow because his legs were most assuredly numb. The men had him arduously scoot his body over towards the large timber post at the center of the tent. There they tied his body tightly and added rope to his legs. The giant, Thoros, now had full use of his arms and hands. The men worked quickly to get out of reach of the giant as he sat there with a subdued demeanor, arms limp at his side. After they had finished David stepped forward.

David ordered one of the men, "Bring this man some bread and some broth. Make it a double portion."

As they ran off to gather the food, he patiently waited a moment for Thoros to settle before asking a question, "What I want to know about is the nearly three hundred of my men you have held captive. Are they in good health Thoros?"

Thoros balked. "Ha! Do you mean to interrogate me? Do not waste your breath."

David volleyed, "Thoros, this is no interrogation. I have a legitimate question as to the wellbeing of my men. Are they in good health?"

Thoros softened a bit. "Three hundred? I cannot say that I'm aware of any captives. If for some reason they were within our walls they'd likely be under the supervision of my adopted brother. He's known for that sort of thing. I don't generally take captives myself. Not that we'd have had the opportunity. So far, your siege has been rather boring."

David turned that information over in his mind for a few moments, "Your adopted brother. What would his name be?"

Thoros responded freely, "Lox is his name now. He has had many other names that are long forgotten. Brother is a peculiar term for Lox. I suspect he is far older than my father, King Adonizedek."

Older than King Adonizedek? David wondered. He had heard tell that King Adonizedek was the oldest living man on earth dating back to before the time of Enoch. "How old is your father after all?"

Thoros thought for a moment. "To be truthful, I do not know exactly. Let it suffice that I am closer to your age than I am to his. I was born here in Jebus. My father has traveled the known world for multiple millennia."

David understood these mighty men of old had long lifespans, but he thought that most of the ones from Enoch's time had long since perished. Of course, many survived the great deluge that covered the known earth millennia ago but when they recovered there were no kingdoms for them to possess so they largely went into hiding. Without their strength of numbers, the population of average men exploded. Those that managed to forge a kingdom were worshipped as gods among men.

David's mind ran wild thinking of old stories and legends he'd heard around campfires while tending to his father's flock.

King Adonizedek must be an original progeny of the fallen ones to be that old. Prince Lox was older than that according to Prince Thoros, so what did that make Lox? David thought, as his mind continued to race with all manner of possibilities.

Several men came walking in with the food and laid it in front of Thoros.

Thoros did the best he could not to tear into the food as it was placed in front of him. As soon as the men were clear he started to voraciously tear into the bread. He swallowed it, barely chewing, and then downed a whole jug of water and then drank the broth from the bowl. David rose from his place on the ground. Thoros was busy gorging himself and didn't even look his way, his hunger turning him into a voracious animal running on instinct.

On the way out of the tent he instructed a dozen men to watch him every moment and when he had finished eating, they were to bind his arms and hands behind his back. He started to head towards the command tent then at the last moment decided to take a walk through the camp to think.

He didn't realize it anymore, but he had a compulsion when he was thinking and planning. His left hand caressed the five stones he always carried. The stones were worn smooth from years of polishing with just a thumb and forefinger, which were now just as calloused and weathered as the stones had been when David pulled them from the brook more than fifteen years ago.

As he walked, he noticed that everyone was gathering near the path that led away from the camp. No sooner had he rounded the bend than he heard Jonathan off to his side.

"Brother. Over here." Jonathan waved him over, "They are waiting for my father. He is coming with his elite guard. He must've heard about the capture of the giant and wanted to see for himself."

David was taken aback a little as his facial expression betrayed him. "It's not like him to travel from his royal villa these days, Jonathan; even more so that he didn't send any word beforehand."

"True enough David. Maybe that's why he brought his entire elite guard since arrangements were not made to have a detachment escort him to us."

Saul was the anointed king of Israel, and coincidentally, David's long-time adversary ever since the Prophet Samuel had anointed David as heir to the throne of Israel. Samuel, the prophet who spoke for God, had passed away about two years ago and another prophet had yet to come forward with the anointing. This left the kingdom in some kind of spiritual limbo that caused confusion and strife among the tribes. King Saul himself had grown increasingly troubled in spirit as the last two years waned. There were even rumors that he had gone to see a soothsayer in Moab. No one had proof but the rumors swirled, nonetheless. Witchcraft was fervently opposed by their laws and all witches within the territory of Israel had been put to death ages ago, or so it had been ordered.

David and Jonathan stood watch and after a little while, they saw the first glint of gold and bronze reflecting in the late-afternoon sunlight. It had been unseasonably hot these last few days as the drought of rain persisted, so as the horses trotted along, they kicked up quite the cloud of dust.

They were drawing ever closer as a bank of clouds moved in, giving everyone a break from the relentless rays. David turned to Jonathan and then to Uriah who was always nearby.

"Uriah! How about you bring a few horses around and gather a dozen men to ride with us to greet the king?"

Without a second thought Uriah was sprinting towards the makeshift livery across the other side of camp. David heard Uriah shouting orders as he ran at full speed. That boy would make a stupendous captain one day. All the men already respected him for his skill in battle and loyalty to him. For such a young man he had excelled greatly and risen to great heights in the army.

Not three minutes later he heard hooves and shouts as Uriah and a dozen men rode up with two horses in tow. Both David and Jonathan mounted theirs on the run and took the lead in a steady canter down the worn path towards the king and his guard. They formed up a double column as they rode to show more decorum as they approached. Jonathan rode at the head of the column beside David with Uriah directly at his rear.

Once King Saul and his guard were within a stone's throw, David signaled for the two columns to part and flank the roadway. David stopped and brought his horse to face the road as the others fell into rank beside him. Jonathan did the same. David held up his fist in a salute as the chariot carrying King Saul drew closer. The chariot slowed a bit as they approached.

David could now see King Saul dressed head to toe in his battle armor. He was an imposing figure even for a man of almost seventy. King Saul's deeds and renown in battle were well-known all-over Israel.

The king ordered the chariot to halt before David and Jonathan as they both dismounted and ran over to the gold-plated chariot. King Saul stepped down with the help of his son as they both embraced. It had been a long while since Jonathan and he had been in Saul's presence; not since they rode north over a year ago to press Damascus and other states to become vassals in trade and tribute.

"My son, Jonathan! You are stronger than ever I see. And do I detect a touch of gray in your beard. My word. This life has moved past in the blink of an eye."

Jonathan smiled. "It's so good to see you father. And yes, I do believe the gray hairs resemble you at this age."

Jonathan was forty-two years of age; around thirteen years David's senior. Though to look at him you'd think he was the same age as David.

King Saul turned to David who was waiting reverently at Jonathan's side, "And my esteemed son-in-law. I have heard countless tales of your victories. Your wife has grown tired of hearing them and wishes one day you would come home to her. Maybe bring me some more grandchildren to bounce at my knee!"

David and Saul shared an awkward embrace that was more out of courtesy and respect than any great feeling towards one another. King Saul held him in his grasp a little longer than David would have liked. He noticed the same smell of sulfur and rot emanating from King Saul, and it mixed with a perfume meant to mask the smell. It nearly made David wretch, but he was able to stave off the impulse.

David held no ill will against King Saul for the things he had done. Power corrupts even the most upright of men and King Saul was no exception to that rule. He had many opportunities to end King Saul's life and was indeed given permission by Elohim through the Prophet Samuel to do so. But still, he honored the anointed king and would not harm him. For that, Elohim had greatly blessed him even further in battle and in charisma with his men. David's time to rule would come. He had faith that Elohim would see to it. Once the greetings and niceties had been exchanged, King Saul once again mounted his chariot.

"We will follow behind you father, David and me. You should lead the procession into the camp," Jonathan offered.

David looked at Uriah. "I would have you and the rest bring up the rear as the guard passes by."

Uriah saluted and grabbed the reins on his horse; waiting to position himself till after the king passed through with David and Jonathan just behind. It was a short jaunt up the hill to where the camp sprawled out towards the city. Once there the king headed straight for the command tent. David hopped down and followed next to Jonathan into the tent.

Joab met them at the opening and bowed before the king and then beckoned everyone to come in. Joab greeted King Saul with all the respect he could muster. He was David's man, and everyone including King Saul knew it, but this was still the king of Israel.

"My king. This is a great surprise! We had not expected a visit from you. My heart is glad to see you looking so well. It has been years since we occupied a command tent together."

King Saul was no doubt aware of the loyalties of all the men who led his armies but still he maintained his regal composure. It was no secret that King Saul disliked Joab, but David held as much sway over the army as his own commander Abner.

"Quite true, young man. It has been many a year since my duties as king overtook my duties as a commander in battle."

King Saul shifted his weight to ease up on the gout that plagued his left leg. "I heard a rumor that we have captured a high-ranking warrior from Jebus? Is this true?" He turned to face David once again.

David's first thought was about figuring out who sent word to the king with this information in the last day, but he supposed it didn't really matter.

David motioned toward a tent, "It's true, he is high ranking; indeed, very high ranking. Would you like me to show you to the tent where he is held?"

King Saul nodded, "Well I did not journey in the hot sun to glimpse the outside of his tent, that much is true. Lead the way! Let us go to him."

The entourage walked briskly towards the tent where Thoros was being held. Jonathan walked next to David in front of the group. "Father seems to be in good spirits today brother. It's been a while since he has been jovial."

David smirked, "We can only hope it lasts."

King Saul had a history of mood swings ranging from uncontrolled sobbing to murderous rage. It had gotten worse as of late and more unpredictable. One minute he would be clapping along with music and the next he would be throwing spears at his dinner guests. David was the recipient of many of those episodes. He had not seen his wife Michelle in years, partly because every time David was allowed to come back to court after one of King Saul's episodes, it would spark another episode that ended with David fleeing for his life once again. David felt that it was best just to stay away and avoid the conflict altogether until the time came for him to succeed Saul as the king. He hadn't seen his own children for quite some time as they lived in King Saul's court.

David rolled his neck around trying to loosen a knot that had just now presented itself. It made him uneasy to have the king in the camp now. He would have to watch his back at every turn.

The entourage reached the tent after a few minutes of walking. Coming to the guards that encircled the tent he addressed his officer at the doorway.

David met the guard at the door, "Has the prisoner been secured as we discussed?"

The officer saluted, "My lord, it has been done as you ordered."

With that assurance, David beckoned three of the guards to enter the tent as he and the others followed behind. Once inside, David heard a gasp from several of the men who had traveled with King Saul, who was himself visibly surprised at the size of Thoros. Thoros sat upright with legs bound together and his body and arms bound to a large cedar post behind his back. Even sitting on the ground, the giant man was taller than most men aside from King Saul who was the tallest of the Israelites. Thoros sat there calmly without blinking as the group took turns looking him over.

"My word! He is a big fellow!" King Saul exclaimed. "It had been nearly twenty years since I saw a giant last and lo and behold, David, you have for a second time, brought one to our feet. Well done."

It was good to have the congratulations of the king, but he knew that it could turn in an instant, "My king, thank you for the congratulations. Were it not for my brother Jonathan and my men we would not have been able to take him. This man here is a prince of Jebus, Thoros."

King Saul chuckled. "David, ever the modest man. They will sing songs of your feats back in Hebron for certain once word of this capture makes it back to their ears. I wonder, what is to be done with him?"

David explained, "My king, we have many captives inside the walls of Jebus. They are not well treated by the information we have. I would take this giant and ransom him for the return of those men. He is not just a giant after all, but a prince of Jebus."

In a booming voice that shook the tent, Thoros exclaimed in Hebrew. "King Saul, I presume?"

"Oh! He speaks; And in our tongue no less." Saul smirked. "Might I ask your name Prince?"

"Thoros is my name. I am the son of Adonizedek, the king of Jebus and surrounding territory which your people have unjustly taken from us." Thoros said calmly, not breaking his gaze with the king.

Saul looked stern as he folded his arms together, "We are very simply taking what we need to provide and protect our people. Your great city sits in the middle of our land and is a conduit for the Philistines to move through our land at will. If that were not the case, we would not bother to expend our treasure on your city-state."

"We have lived in relative peace with your nation for nearly five hundred years even as you destroy our allies and murder my family members." Thoros retorted curtly.

"Relative peace is a good description. We have seen your forces augment the Philistines for more than 100 years. As for your family members, I know not who you speak of."

Thoros took and deep breath, "My cousin's name was Goliath of Gath. Your general, David, killed him nearly fifteen years past. My uncle's name was Og of Bashan. He was the ruler of Jericho nearly 400 years ago when your Joshua beheaded him and his entire court. Women and children and even livestock were not spared. Still more have been killed at countless other outposts. Our support of the Philistines is in response to your continued attacks. They are and have been our only ally in the region for some time now. I will not apologize for supporting the only force that counters your threat."

"And that is why we will see this through to the end." King Saul began to pace,

"We've been given this land by the Most-High God. His hand is the one you speak of when you lament the loss of your land and family. Do you know of Him, our one true God? You cannot stand against Him."

Thoros balked, "I know of Him. My father, King Adonizedek, worships him along with Asherah, Baal, and others. I will confess that I even wonder at times whether any of the others have left us behind with the way your people have sliced through Canaan. Although recently, I would give most of the credit to the man standing beside you."

Thoros shot a look at David. "What is it that they say in the streets? Saul has killed his thousands; But David has killed his tens of thousands."

King Saul grimaced noticeably as Thoros finished the popular chant that was often sung by the throngs of adoring common folk. The more David won victories for Israel, the more it was sung. It was no secret that Saul hated that chant, and the Prince of Jebus had recited it in perfect Hebrew.

Thoros, seeing the reaction, pressed further still. "Saul, the king of Israel; replaced by a shepherd boy. Some even say he is already the king because your people love him more than you. It is clear to me that this is true. I have eyes and ears everywhere."

David rolled his eyes and stepped forward, "Alright that will be enough, why don't we retire to the command tent and discuss what to do with our oversized pot stirrer? Guards! Put a gag on this man. Now."

But King Saul was not finished. Thoros' words had dug into his thinly placed skin all too easily, as was a common occurrence these last few years. He lunged forward and began to punch Thoros in the face as savagely as he could; his rings cutting and bruising.

"You will die! Do you hear me, Prince? I will have your head!" King Saul screamed. Jonathan and David both pulled the raging king from the restrained prisoner. He kicked Thoros as they dragged him out of the tent.

David slapped his forehead in frustration as Thoros spat a mouthful of blood to his side and began to laugh aloud. As they ushered the king away, Thoros' booming laughter could be heard throughout the camp as the king was taken to the command-tent to be attended to by his healers.

Everyone stood there stunned and David repeated his order, "Somebody go into that tent and gag that man. I don't want to hear a sound coming from that tent! Hoodwink him and double the restraints!"

"So much for the jovial mood," Jonathan said defeatedly, as they stood outside the command tent. Inside they could hear King Saul yelling and crying all at once. "I just wish I had thought about what Thoros might say to my father. We should have gagged that giant from the start."

Jonathan gazed stoically at the city that lay before the camp. "On second thought, I don't think it would have mattered. His mind is constantly tormented. If it wasn't this, it would have been another thing that flipped his disposition."

David threw his hands up, "Well one thing I know brother, is that we had better find a way to bring this siege to an end and save the men who are captured. I hate to say this, and please don't take this as a slight, but with your father here now this whole ordeal had become more complicated." David dropped his shoulders forward and slouched against a post nearby.

Jonathan shifted his stance and leaned against a wagon as the camp began to calm from the excitement. King Saul was no longer screaming and Thoros had quieted. "No offense taken. I understand what you are saying, and I agree. It would have been better had he not come to the camp at all."

An officer walked up and saluted the two men before turning to Jonathan, "My Prince," the officer said with a slight bow, "The King has finally calmed and has asked that you enter and speak with him."

Jonathan nodded and followed the officer to the tent. Over his shoulder he said, "I'll come find you after I speak with father."

David walked away from the tent and busied himself practicing his sling, setting up stones against a berm and knocking them down one by one, using smaller stones from the ground. Soon, he was lost in contemplation, wondering just how he was going to win this siege.

Inside the King's tent...

Once inside, Jonathan saw that the tent had been made into a bed chamber instead of a command tent. At the back of the tent his father sat on a cot and had his back leaned against a table that had been turned on its side. He was sipping some sort of tea, no doubt to calm him down and had buried himself under a mountain of blankets. The smell of incense was heavy in the air.

"Come forward to me if you would." King Saul beckoned Jonathan.

Jonathan stepped forward quietly and knelt at his father's side, studying his face for a moment and noticing that his father's skin was grey, and face withdrawn. His hair was tangled and disheveled.

"Tell me son, what would you do for you sworn brother David in order to save his life?"

"Father, there is nothing I would not do to save his life if it were in my power to do it." Jonathan said assuredly.

"Good to hear my son, listen closely to me then as I tell you exactly what you must do to save your brother's life."

Later that evening...

Night had fallen as David prepared a fire in a secluded part of the camp. David stared at the flames licking the dry air as Jonathan repeated what King Saul had said to him.

"He actually said that?" David asked as Jonathan paced back and forth.

"Brother, I had to agree to it before I left the tent. He said your life would be spared if I agreed to execute Thoros at noon tomorrow in front of the city walls."

"That is ludicrous! Right now, we have a Prince in captivity and can use him for all manner of ransom or negotiation purposes and he wants to kill him? That would seal the fate of those men still in captivity inside. Not only that, but it will also strengthen their resolve to withstand our siege. It may even embolden them to make moves they normally wouldn't make! You can't seriously be thinking of following through with this can you?"

"I said I agreed to it, I haven't decided if I will go through with it. In his condition a refusal would've broken his mind further. He is unwell brother. His mind is being attacked constantly. Who knows if he will even remember this tomorrow?"

Jonathan stopped pacing and squatted to the ground and used a stick to draw shapes in the dirt, something he did when he was trying to make sense of things; much like David's own quirk with the brook stones in his pouch.

"So why hasn't he had me taken captive then? He had to know you would come to me and tell me. We have no secrets between us for better than fifteen years now." David picked up a few pebbles and flung them at a tree branch.

"As I said, his mind is twisted. He struggles to hold it together when these episodes happen. It wouldn't surprise me if his rationale was to keep you free because it would cause dissent in the camp. You have more supporters here than he does now, but he could flip and send guards to detain you any minute. We need to decide what to do quickly. It is now after dusk, and the Sabbath has begun. We should be finding a Shabbat dinner to go to."

"There! That is your out. You cannot execute this man on the Holy Sabbath! Even if Saul could obtain permission from High Priest Eleazar, it would take many days to do so. Meanwhile, I will take some men with me and go through the cavern into the city and attempt to free the captives inside."

"Even if that foolhardy plan could work, how are you going to get around the fact that your mission will take place on the Sabbath? You will be breaking the law, being a professional warrior, no?"

David thought for a moment then replied, "War is not one of the things that the Law restricts, technically. But I take your point that my work consists of waging war so I will make a simple promise before God that I will not kill a single soul nor will the men who accompany me, unless our own lives be in danger of being lost. I need only seven men. As for the rescue, there is no other time or way to do it. It must be now. I will ask for the priests to offer a lamb sacrifice on my behalf after I have returned. But I believe this is a just cause and that the Lord is with me. Besides, we may fight in order to save lives. And that is precisely what I'll be attempting to do."

Jonathan mulled it over for a few moments before replying, "Well at the very least, my refusal to do it on the Sabbath will buy a day for you and maybe, just maybe, my father will come to his senses in that timeframe. "

"Brother, do me a favor after I go? Could you inform Joab and Uriah to secretly have my men leave this camp under darkness and head to the hills of Ephraim. My warriors, The Gibborim are already there. After I make the escape with the captives I will need to run."

As he asked this, he was glad he listened to his intuition and divided his personal cavalry from the main force. They were all his sworn men to the last and he may just need them. A few hundred were now waiting in the pastures and fields near his ancestral home. After he finished his mission, whether successful or not, he decided he would not be caught off guard by Saul. The king was unpredictable, and David had come to realize that if something happened more than once, it was very likely that it would happen again. The king would most assuredly attempt to kill him again.

Jonathan nodded, "Of course brother, I will make sure this is done. It seems our paths will diverge once again."

David embraced his brother in a hug to rival a bear. "It seems so, but it all works out for good. Always has. Take care of yourself brother."

With that David turned and jogged back towards the camp leaving Jonathan looking in the opposite direction. He had to get moving, his plan wasn't working the way he wanted but he was adapting. Not being able to kill unless in self-defense would be a challenge and would certainly change the type of men he would need for this raid. As he entered the main camp, he saw a man to his left who was exactly the kind of man he needed.

"Jeroboam, I need to speak with you in private please," David said as he looked back in the direction of the king's tent.

The Cavern Tunnels

Lox followed behind Urim closely as they made their way towards the cave opening where Thoros had been captured. It had taken them two hours of wandering the caves to finally get on the right path. Urim was a blubbering fool apologizing profusely every moment of the way, "Sorry, my Lord. I know the way. I promise. Sorry." he would exclaim over and over and over.

I can't kill him yet, Lox thought, only half-joking. He hadn't decided whether to kill him or not but was weighing the option of killing him slowly and painfully, or suddenly and brutal-like. He hadn't yet decided on that either. But as he reasoned through the possible outcomes, Lox decided that he would indeed kill Urim purely for the fun of it, if only to shut up Urim's incessant chatter.

Just as soon as this idiot finds the way out, Lox thought as he cursed under his breath. All the while, Urim did his best to make sure anyone in the caverns heard them coming. He might do better to lead the way himself and just kill this fool right now. The truth be told, he expected this to take a while, as he already knew the way out, but what he didn't know was if he was going to run into thirty or so Israelites when he exited otherwise, he would've lost them hours ago. He needed them to act as his personal shield and planned to send them out to ensure it was safe for him to exit. Stumbling around with torches in a dark and damp cavern system was not exactly a science. *If only Urim would shut his mouth,* he thought. But he never did.

Urim talked about everything from his love of baking pastries in his relaxation time to his children misbehaving, of which Lox was interested in for a brief moment.

"My son, he likes to steal things from other family members..." Urim lamented.

To which Lox replied, "Good lad that. Sounds like he has promise."

Of course, it went right over the dolt's thick head, and he kept blathering on and on.

Lox busied himself with planning his next move. His transgression against Tsalmaveth had made him paranoid that Shades would certainly be lurking around every corner waiting for them to make a wrong turn. So far this had not been the case, but he was still vigilant.

His anger toward Tsalmaveth stewed as they navigated the caverns. The shadow being had made promises to spare Adonizedek and his family. He'd also promised to give Lox a boon of power for his efforts, power that would allow him the knowledge and ability to seek out and destroy his ancient enemies, wherever they may be. Instead, he'd watched that little twerp Ahmet allow Tsalmaveth into his body and heard Tsalmaveth all but tell Ahmet that Lox himself was used up goods. Lox had long suspected that Tsalmaveth had no intention of making good on said promise but was stringing him along.

Lox didn't know whether he would find what he was looking for in Egypt, but he resolved to at least check it out. Best case, he would obtain a powerful amulet. Worst case, he would return empty handed. Should this amulet prove to be the power he sought, he would use it to take the power from Tsalmaveth and trap the Shadow of Death inside the amulet.

Then Lox could use the relic to finally seek out and destroy the people that murdered his mother so long ago.

After another hour of useless one-sided chatter, they finally reached the exit where Thoros was captured. Urim stopped and for the first time in forever said nothing. He just stared out into the pitch-black midnight sky.

On spears at the opening were the heads of his fellow comrades who had been slain during the skirmish, facing inward as an ominous warning. Torches were lit near them, illuminating their sullen expressions.

Lox, never one to miss an opportunity to jab, spoke first this time, "Just think Urim, had you done your duty you'd probably have joined your fellow soldiers."

Lox moved towards the opening then stopped and turned, "All of you, go out first. I'll wait until the area is secured." He felt a little uneasy, wondering if those mouth breathing Shades had been ordered to track him through these caverns, but he reasoned that he had better make sure he was not walking into a company of soldiers outside the caves either.

The small entourage and Urim hesitated for a moment but realized the alternative was to disobey and certainly die, most likely in a gruesome fashion.

One by one they exited. After a little while the soldiers returned to give the signal to Lox. But Urim was missing.

"Did no one see where Urim went?" Lox seethed.

"My lord we all went separate directions to scout for the enemy. We were all going to meet back in ten minutes. It seems all clear for us to exit safely."

"That dirty little vermin." Lox said under his breath. He had counted on intimidation to keep Urim in sight. Now he had no doubt seen an opportunity and taken it to escape with his life. He had to admit that he underestimated the little coward, which made him laugh. If he'd intended on going back to Jebus he would be paying Urim's family a visit, especially his kleptomaniac son. He might even spare the boy and mentor him.

"My lord, what about the prince? Shouldn't we try to rescue him?"

"Well, that would be suicide, so no. Besides, my brother has been in worse and survived. He will figure something out. I have other plans."

Upon saying this, he took his dagger out and cut the throat of the first guard, the second took off running. Lox was much faster with the knife as it sailed through the air and lodged itself in the man's shoulders just below the neck. The man dropped to the ground dead. Lox walked over and drew the knife from the back and wiped it off on the guard's clothes and then tucked it back into the sheath on his belt. He looked around for Urim for a few minutes but assumed that the coward had run off into the night, so he gave up the search and returned to his true mission as he jaunted up and over a berm and disappeared into the night.

Outside the Israelite Camp...

David crept up behind the soldier hiding from the men below.

"Don't move a muscle," he said quietly, pressing a blade against his back. Jeroboam came forward and threw his forearm around and locked over the soldier's throat in a chokehold.

"I think we have ourselves a deserter Jeroboam. Turn him around slowly."

David leaned against a boulder; one leg resting on the other, eating an apple.

"Would you care for an apple?" David said, producing another large apple. He held it forward to the man who looked it up and down and shook his head in refusal.

"It's not a trick; I assure you." David leaned forward and held it closer to the man, who finally relented and hurriedly grabbed the apple from David and began to devour it.

David rose and offered his hand in a greeting gesture, "My name is David and you and I are going to be friends."

He watched as the man before him finished the apple in an instant. The man reluctantly gripped his hand and seemed to relax a little.

"What's your name?" David asked.

"Urim. I live inside Jebus."

"Well, Urim, we heard that you are deserter according to the big man dressed in black and purple robes. Is that true?"

"He was going to kill me!" he shouted as Jeroboam cuffed a hand over his mouth to silence him.

"Urim. My friend. I need you to please be quiet. Can you be quiet while we talk?"

Urim nodded and Jeroboam pulled his hand away from his mouth.

"This man; who is he?" David asked.

"He is named Lox; a Prince of Jebus." Urim said timidly.

Another prince? It seems like every prince in Jebus is out for a stroll these days, David thought and noted that this was the man Thoros had told him of during their brief conversation. *Just what are Lox's plans,* he thought as he looked Urim up and down.

Urim shrugged. "I was with his brother a day ago at this very place where he was taken captive, although I was not involved in the battle. Regrettably, I hid away and fled back through the caves."

"And you are here now a day later with another prince. Why? To free his brother?"

Urim shook his head, David's calm demeanor had disarmed the nervous deserter, "I was ordered to lead him through the caves to reclaim my honor. Or so they told me. But I was sure I would have died by Prince Lox's hand the instant we left the caves. I don't know what he was planning truthfully."

This man would tell me anything I demanded; that is clear. His mouth leaks information like a sieve, David thought, careful not to betray a smirk that had started to form.

"Fortunately for you that you did Urim; otherwise, you'd have been in the same condition as those men, and we wouldn't be having this nice chat."

He motioned to the heads on the spears which now were accompanied by two palace guard's corpses littering the ground.

Urim groaned. "Oh! I should have died. Now my family will pay for my foolish...!" Jeroboam put his hand back over Urim's mouth again. David waited patiently with arms crossed until Urim signaled with his eyes that he understood why his mouth was covered again. He looked at Jeroboam and nodded. The hand was removed again allowing the nervous deserter to speak again.

Urim continued at a lower volume, "I can never return, they will kill me for certain if I show up in the city without another prince a second time. They'll kill my family too."

David pressed, "This Lox fellow; does he plan to try and liberate his brother?"

Urim responded enthusiastically, "At first, I had thought that was the plan. But you never know with Lox."

David cocked his head sideways, "I heard him say he had other plans. Do you have any ideas?"

"None that I know. But whatever it is you can be sure that it involves lies or deceit. Pure evil comes out of that man. That is the truth of it. I've heard from others of the screams they hear coming from the prison, a place that the prince frequents. For a brief time I was assigned to feed the prisoners once a day, that was until my friend Ahmet reassigned me to guard the work details and patrol the grounds outside the prison, promoting me to captain."

David just let him speak, a plan was beginning to form in his mind as Urim finished his thoughts.

After what seemed a long silence, David rose and walked across a series of boulders to have a look at the surrounding land. After a minute he jumped back down and came face to face with him.

David placed a hand on the man's shoulder. "Urim. We are going to go into the city, and you are going to help us. Understood?"

By the expression on Urim's face David could tell that he wasn't too sure, "You are concerned for your family, right? If you help us into the city, then you can go retrieve your family and escape with them, we'll allow them to leave safely ahead of us taking the city."

Urim groaned, "You don't understand. I can never return, not now. The king only spared my life because I knew the way back to where Prince Thoros was captured. If I return without another prince for a second time, he will not only execute me on sight, but he will likely cast my family out of the city and that would be as good as death in this drought and famine we are in. Not to mention the full-on siege outside the walls."

David let him go on for a moment before interjecting, "What if I could offer your family safety? Would you be willing to help us then?"

"Help? How could I be of help to you? I hold no authority or possess any skills that would aid you. I would just be walking into my execution."

"I wouldn't need anything from you except information once we get inside. You may depart from our company and go to your family then. No doubt you know the layout of the city, or the prison perhaps. What if you could show us the way and we'll take it from there? All we want is to rescue our comrades from captivity."

"I am no traitor, why should I help you? If I do, what's to say you won't kill me and then find some way to open the gates, allowing your army to enter Jebus and slaughter everyone. I've heard the tales of other cities. None left alive, buildings burned, and cattle slaughtered."

"Our reputation being what it is, do you think we will fail to take Jebus if you don't give us what we want?" David said firmly before adding, "I am giving you my word that I will not harm you and your family if you help us as I am requiring. It is your choice, Urim. Help us or die here and now, not knowing what became of your family. Do you understand?" David pressed a dagger to Urim's throat, the fact that David was sworn to not kill this day was unknown to Urim. Behind Urim, Jeroboam and the others smiled wildly noticing the ruse at play.

Urim dropped his shoulders and reluctantly agreed, "I am at your service, just please honor your word and allow me to go once you've entered the city."

"Splendid!" David said with a wide grin. "You've chosen wisely Urim. Men, let's get a move on!"

CHAPTER 12

The Caverns, Below Jebus

D avid and Jeroboam spoke in a low whisper crouched behind a large rock formation above the entrance to the staircase where they had slain the guards and rescued their countrymen two days ago.

"I can hardly believe that there is a tunnel that was built way down here. Who would've built this?"

"Hard to say." David said quietly. "The city of Jebus has been built upon countless times, our ancestor Abraham lived here in the time of Melchizedek and I'm sure that Melchizedek wasn't the first ruler. It wouldn't surprise me if each time the new inhabitants just built on top of the old ruins."

David assumed that this was probably the most any living person knew about the origin of the tunnel. He peered from the hiding place to view the, now well-lit, area at the entrance to the tunnel. From what he could see there were half a dozen guards standing posts. Each had a horn in one hand and a spear in the other. No doubt that was for the purpose of sending a very noisy signal down the tunnel into the city stables, which most definitely held more guards or soldiers. That was the unknown.

Urim had confidently told them, the stables were at the far end of the Citadel tower. From there it was a short distance to the lower chamber beneath the temple where the Israelite men were being held. The problem was that the distance between the stable and the temple was a courtyard expanse that they used to house supplies and materials. It was in full view of the wall and the entrance to the Citadel was just to the south. In daylight they would be very exposed, but they had no choice.

King Saul coming into camp had been a very unfortunate event. He knew that the king was always an upsetting word away from snapping and the giant captive they held had done the damage. David now wished that he would have killed the giant prince the day they captured him, but he wanted so badly to use him to ransom for the prisoners. And if he succeeded in this rescue attempt, he would again be a fugitive. Most of his life since he entered the court had been as a fugitive. It shouldn't have been a surprise at this point. There would be no lasting peace in his life until King Saul passed, and his reign was through.

David pushed those thoughts from his mind and forced himself to think only of the rescue plans. Being the Sabbath until sundown the next day, he needed to be able to accomplish this without shedding blood. The very fact that they were attempting this was skirting the edge of the Law, but he reasoned it was a necessary bending of the rules. Rescuing kinsmen on the Sabbath seemed a good reason to bend the law which said that no work could be performed on the Sabbath. The fact that he was a warrior by profession and his work was indeed war was generally excused in times of war. Going and looking for a fight was where he personally felt guilt in not keeping the Sabbath. He did not want to violate it but he also could not stay in that camp while King Saul made foolish decisions that would cost the lives of the men he knew were somewhere behind those walls being mistreated and tortured. For this reason, he felt justified in attempting this rescue.

By his estimate it was early morning, a couple of hours before sunrise. It had taken them several hours to traverse the cavern. They had made a camp further back where they could get some rest before proceeding to enter Jebus via the tunnels. Down here in the dark it was easy for one who was unaccustomed to the darkness to lose sense of time and direction, so he had decided to try and keep it simple. He had one lantern with oil in it to light the way and it served to keep them feeling as though the darkness was not swallowing them whole. David could see in the dark well enough after his eyes adjusted to the extremely limited light that guided their way. He was familiar with many parts of this cavern system. Even still, this part was unknown to him, and he wouldn't rely solely on his eyes to help him make his way to the tunnel.

David and Jeroboam inched their way back into the darkness of the cavern.

"Jeroboam, how far is your range?" David said, referring to how far he could sling a stone accurately.

Most skilled slingers could send a stone at a target twenty cubits away with deadly force. A particularly skilled slinger could even cause the stone to hit broadside and stun a target long enough to close the distance and subdue it. That is how David was able to kill Goliath as the stone that dropped him was a stunning blow that knocked him unconscious. David then used Goliath's own sword to remove his head.

Jeroboam studied the distance, knowing what he was asking. "Twenty cubits on flat terrain; but we have the elevation advantage, so I'd say at least thirty cubits. If I were to throw from here, the stone would just about make it to the first of the guards. The others are similar in range, give or take a cubit or two."

David contemplated this for a moment, "We have seven of us, in addition to Urim. There are six guards. The biggest threat is that one of them can blow the horn. If that happens, we can surely escape into the darkness, but our rescue will be impossible afterwards."

"We could station ourselves, two by two around the perimeter, and when you give the signal, we will take them down." Jeroboam suggested.

It was as good a plan as any. They could not kill on the Sabbath otherwise he would've brought archers and ended this quickly and assuredly. But for stealth work, these were the sort of men he needed. Shepherds like him, they had spent their lives in the hills of Ephraim fending off wolves and lions and bears; and fighting beside him against the enemies of Israel for years on end.

"Very well, go inform the others and make ready. Tell two of your men to prepare to rush in and stop any of the guards from blowing those horns should one of our stones miss the mark. Complete silence is needed. I'll wait here for you. Be swift."

Jeroboam nodded, saluted, and made his way towards the camp, careful to only uncover the lantern when he was out of the line of sight of the tunnel and the guards.

The campsite was only a few minutes away, deeper into the caves, so it shouldn't be long. While David waited, he thought over the plan and tried to predict what would happen once they entered the tunnel that led up to the city. He made it a habit to come up with as many scenarios as possible so that he could spend less time deciding when the action was taking place. This had served him well and allowed for him to be the victor in many battles over the years. Captured generals and kings had wondered at his ability to see a battle unfolding and meet it with simultaneous counteraction.

He then tried to think about what he would do should one of the guards blow his horn, thus signaling whoever was at the end of the tunnel. All of the options he could think of resulted in bloodshed. "My Lord, give me courage and make my sling accurate."

David prayed as he decided failure was not an option as he closed his eyes and focused on his prayer for a few moments longer in silence. He could hear soft footsteps approaching from behind. That would be his entourage coming to begin the operation. David looked over his shoulder briefly to make sure he was correct and seeing Jeroboam, he returned his gaze to the tunnel which was their only way into the city.

He stood there stoically, contemplating the next moves, as all of them except Jeroboam left to take their place around the perimeter. In the darkness he couldn't see if they were in place yet due to the many rock formations, but he knew there were several points with which to conceal them while still having a clean shot. He would just have to trust that they would be in place once he gave the signal because there would be no return. Jeroboam stood ready, stone-faced, sling in his left hand with a stone in place. He had forgotten that Jeroboam was left-handed. It was rare for a slinger, but he certainly had proven that it was not an impediment to him or others. In truth, David thought that Jeroboam was better with a sling than he was. He estimated that the time had passed and gave Jeroboam a look. Jeroboam began to twirl his sling at his side, one foot forward.

David began to twirl his sling and placed his left foot forward, the opposite of Jeroboam. As his sling gained velocity, he chose a point above the guards to send the signal stone. The moment he found it he sent the stone hurtling with blinding speed.

A split second passed, then a resounding, *"CRACK!"* echoed across the cavern.

Jeroboam's stone was already one its way as the signal sounded out. The guards looked up, stood dumbfounded for a moment, then became rigid as they looked to cavern ahead.

Just as one man made a slight motion to raise the horn, a stone hit him broadside in the head sending him falling in a heap. Jeroboam's target would have a splitting headache in a couple of hours.

David released a second stone towards the first guard, seconds after the signal. It easily found its mark and the guard collapsed just as Jeroboam's had. They both loaded another stone and rushed forward from hiding. So far four of the six guards had fallen.

Two had missed. The two furthest away from them.

David saw Jeroboam's men rushing forward towards the two guards who were just about to blow their horns. David and Jeroboam both let their stones go free simultaneously as they continued to close in. One stone hit the hand of one of the guards causing him to drop the horn abruptly. The other hit him on his body with great force causing him to double over. Jeroboam and another were on him immediately and wrestled him to the ground in a chokehold and after a moment of struggle the man was subdued and unconscious.

The last guard was nearly to the tunnel when one of the slingers launched himself and tackled the man, who was just barely blowing his horn at his lips. The force of the blow from this caused the man to exhale suddenly, making a dull sound that would never carry from the ram's horn. They hit the ground with a thud and began to struggle mightily. At this point, David was in the tunnel entrance. He grabbed a spear and pointed it toward the guard who was on his back trying to fend off the blows.

"Stop your struggle man. You've been beaten." David said quietly. The guard stopped and yielded. But Jeroboam's man pulled his blow too late, and it fell square on the jaw of the guard, knocking him unconscious.

The other men had already dragged the other men to the side and began binding their wrists behind their backs and then binding them all together so they would not be able to move should they awake. The horns were broken and thrown into the darkness of the cavern.

The first part of this crazy rescue was a success but so much laid ahead that could not be planned. David knelt at the mouth of the tunnel and waited for each man to join him.

"Very well done. All of you." He said proudly before scanning the room looking for their party guest, Urim.

After a short search, David found Urim, who was huddled behind a boulder awaiting the outcome. He knelt down beside the man and asked, "What can we expect next?"

"When we make it through the tunnel, we will enter a small chamber that is used for storage. It may have been cleared out since I left, and I would expect guards to be posted inside the room and without," Urim explained nervously.

David pondered this for a few moments trying to visualize the scenario. This was about as perilous as it could get, he surmised. The only way in was through this tunnel and they would no doubt be outnumbered with only slings to defend themselves with. What they needed was applied force using stealth. Maybe a ruse?

David looked at the man up and down and asked, "Urim. You mentioned that you are a captain?"

Not sure why David had asked the question he turned his head slightly and replied slowly, "I am. I oversee the prison and the surrounding areas under the fortress. I am still low-ranking in the palace guard, as it were. Why do you ask?"

"I have an idea that only you can help us with," David said as he picked up a spear, placed the tip on the ground and stomped on it until it broke from the shaft. He relayed the plan quietly to Urim and the others as he tested his new non-lethal staff. Jeroboam and others took this as a queue and did the same and soon they were all armed with staves.

After David had finished explaining the plan, Urim's face was flushed white. David said not another word as he retrieved the worn stones he'd slung at the guards and placed them back safely in his pouch.

The Dungeon Temple

Ahmet had lost all control of his body as he became host to Tsalmaveth for one night until the sunrise of the following day. Almost as soon as the shadow-being entered his body, Tsalmaveth started to laugh and celebrate. Ahmet could hear him speaking in his mind, but almost as if Tsalmaveth were next to him speaking audibly. It was a bit disorienting at first.

"So much room Ahmet, this will do. Oh yes, this will do. Now, let's go for a stroll. I have some important people to visit tonight."

With that, Tsalmaveth began to move Ahmet's legs and arms, rather clumsily at first but soon found the equilibrium and walked more assuredly. His first direction took him into the caverns and after a series of turns in the dark with no light he came to an exit. Outside the walls, less than a kilometer, they passed by two dead Jebusite guards on the ground and two with their heads on spears. Ahmet recognized these as palace guards.

What in the world are we out here for, he thought.

"You'll see Ahmet. In just a little while," Tsalmaveth said knowingly as he turned down the path heading to the southern end of Jebus. The Israelite camp in the distance lit by only fires as the sun had now set. It was pitch dark as Tsalmaveth walked with Ahmet.

How will we enter the camp undetected? Ahmet thought curiously.

"We will stay in the shadows. They'll never see us coming." Tsalmaveth reassured him.

Sure enough, they walked into the camp under total darkness, past guards, and tents full of boisterous laughter and music. It was as if no one perceived them as they headed straight to the center of camp. Coming to the center he darted into the space between two tents and circled around the back of the biggest one. He carefully lifted a flap and peered into the tent. Sitting on a makeshift throne was a kingly looking figure, draped in gold and purple cloth, upon his head sat a crown. And from the looks of it the man was sleeping while sitting up.

"That poor soul is Saul. King of the Israelites. One of my favorite triumphs."

Ahmet had no clue what that meant, and he wondered how Tsalmaveth knew he was there in this camp.

"I have eyes everywhere Ahmet. Besides, I can sense when someone I've touched has drawn close." Tsalmaveth gloated. "My plan is working Ahmet. You'll love what happens next." With that a tongue of smoke exited Ahmet and flitted around and seeped through the flap and into the tent. Ahmet watched through a slit as the smoke nonchalantly made its way along the edge of the tent toward the sleeping king. The smoke gradually made its way up the armrest of the throne and crawled up the king's arm, barely visible to anyone who might look upon King Saul. As the smoke reached the king's shoulder it formed into a set of hands with long slender fingers. Using them, the smoke penetrated the ears and entered the mind of King Saul. King Saul's eyes shot open, but he was unable to speak or cry out. All at once Ahmet could tell Tsalmaveth was gaining information from the king just as he had from his Shades back in the temple.

"Oh my! This is just too good. I must find him. I have a score to settle. We just have a few more stops to make in this camp and things will start to happen."

Tsalmaveth released the king's mind and rapidly retreated to Ahmet. King Saul shrieked in horror as several guards came running. It was then that Tsalmaveth took a few steps back and looked toward the city. "Lox, you fool." He whispered and went back to watching the Israelite camp. Ahmet was unsure what his reference to Lox was about.

"Bring my son and that upstart to me at once!" Saul shouted irately.

Tsalmaveth snickered as they tiptoed away from the king's tent and circled the middle of camp to the opposite side. And started to exit the way they'd come in.

First, Tsalmaveth entered another tent and sitting before him was a bound and gagged Thoros, Prince of Jebus. A rumble of thunder began to roll in from the distant hills. For the first time in months, Ahmet felt a tiny rain drop hit his cheek as they ducked into the tent.

The Israelite Camp

Jonathan stood before his father, King Saul, and waited for him to respond. A moment ago, he had informed his father that he would not be executing Thoros on account that it was the Holy Sabbath, and he could not and would not disobey the commandment to keep it holy. His father sat silent for much longer than was usual and it became an awkward sort of silence as he sat there breathing in and out while staring past him.

After another minute he finally spoke, "No matter son, I've sent my royal guard to arrest David before I had them bring you here, we will postpone the execution until tomorrow at noon. Then you will carry it out." The whole time he did not look at him, but rather, looked right through him.

Knowing that David had already gone to the caves he knew it was a matter of time until the guards returned with news that he was nowhere to be found so he might as well try and reason with him while he could.

"Father, you know that this prisoner is valuable and could be used in several ways to help us and our cause. Killing him will serve none of our purposes. I know you see that."

"Nonsense son, killing him will serve my purpose fine. If you don't, I will kill David for your disobedience," Saul said with a deadpan stare, his face hard as a stone.

"Why do you now want to kill David yet again? You have come to terms that he will be the king when you are gone. At least that was what you had said when you asked him to come home and help us beat back the Philistines yet again. Which he did without a second thought."

Jonathan was exasperated. This was never ending, and it was because his father was sick. Everyone knew it; King Saul knew it as well, which made him even more vicious.

Saul sat silently, his eyes narrowed and fiery.

Jonathan continued, "David loves you father. He could have killed you twice and he didn't. He even had Elohim's blessing to do it according to Samuel, yet he would not do it. This fixation must be due to whatever ailment you are suffering from. You are not getting any better or younger for that matter. And David is the heir to the throne.

"I have not accepted that David is the heir!" Saul raged throwing a goblet of water to the ground at Jonathan's feet. "Samuel is dead, and another prophet has yet to show himself. Until such a time that Elohim speaks directly to me, you will be my heir! And David will die!"

Jonathan tried a different angle, "Do you love me as your son, father?"

"What kind of a question is that for my son and heir to ask of me?"

"Would you kill me father?"

"Why would I kill you, Jonathan?"

"If you want to kill David it will be with a spear through my chest! I will not raise a hand against you, but I will not allow you to kill David. Doing so will mean my death father. You cannot have one without the other I can promise you that."

"Don't you see that he has usurped your crown son?"

Jonathan was incredulous, "My crown? It is not my crown father. Nor is it your crown! It belongs to The Most-High God. He crowns the rulers of this world and draws the boundaries of the nations. It is His WILL that David should rule instead of me, your firstborn son."

"Nonsense son! Pure nonsense. I was made king by the Lord, which is true. But the people chose me from among them and gave me hereditary rights to have a successor for all time! This is your right son. It's my right!"

"Father, you will not kill David and place me on the throne. His death will mean my death that much I can promise you. Why can't you see that your mind has been poisoned with malicious thoughts because of your illness? What happened to the father and king who honored the Lord in everything and when he made a mistake, he owned up to it and changed his direction? Is this man gone; replaced by this hateful and power-hungry man sitting before me?"

Jonathan had said his peace to his father. He would say no more. He didn't bow or perform any of the customs when exiting the royal tent. He just turned and walked out. As he walked, he heard his father begin to sob. For a second, he thought maybe he had made a difference; made him see the error of his ways. But he knew better. As he left the tent, he bumped into the royal guards returning hastily. The look on their faces told him everything. David had gone from the camp. He kept walking. From behind he could hear the shouting in the tent coming from his father.

Saul screeched, "Detain him! Now! Put my son in chains and let us see what this usurper, David will do about it!"

Jonathan quickened his pace, trying to get away from the line of sight of the tent. But it was too late.

"Prince Jonathan! Stop!" A guard said running up behind him, swords in hand.

The guards pleaded, "Please my lord. The king has ordered me. Stop, please?"

Jonathan stopped and took a deep breath allowing the guard to catch up to him. "I'll follow you to where I am to be detained. There's no need for weapons."

Off to his left he saw Joab and Uriah peering through the slit in a tent. Each gave him a gesture saying they were already preparing as he was led away to be imprisoned. Everyone jumped a little as they heard the unfamiliar thunder roll in the distance. It had been several months since the last rainfall, and they were certainly due.

The Israelite Camp

Thoros sat in silence and darkness. King Saul had ordered a hoodwink to be placed on his head and it was dreadfully hot. Nary a soul had entered the tent in more time than he could remember. He thought about the reaction King Saul had when he prodded him earlier. That man was on a razor edge in his mind; that was plain to see. But part of him thought that he might have prodded a little too far. He had intended to agitate his enemy, not break his mind. A man with a sickened mind was liable to do anything.

From his tent he could hear the screams of King Saul. The rage was tangible in the air, like a dust cloud. For a minute he began to think maybe he had sealed his fate. Saul wanted to kill him, and he was powerless now to stop anything from happening. His father had warned him to control his temper, and he rarely listened and now his mouth may have proved his father correct.

As Thoros sat there thinking, he heard the rustle of the tent flap open and quiet footsteps walk towards him. Then it was silent. He could hear someone breathing not a cubit away from his cheek. The smell of dried blood and rotting teeth filtered through the burlap. He strained to see through the small holes in the fabric but there wasn't enough light in the tent to make out any features.

"Well? What is it you wanted?" He finally asked the mystery guest.

It was then that Thoros heard footsteps running around behind him toward the back of the tent. Then he heard what sounded like the cloth from the side of the tent lift and drop back down with a light rustle. His mystery guest was gone. Voices carried through and drew nearer to the entrance.

"Right this way prince. I'm very sorry to have to do this. Your father ordered it."

"Do not trouble yourself. I do not hold it against you. Do what you must."

With the lantern light coming through he could just make out that Jonathan was led through the entrance to the tent where Thoros was being kept. One man set to work tying his legs tight while the other tied his hand and wrists together. The guard looked him in the eye as he tied the bonds.

Curious, he thought to himself. Most guards would not look at a prince or any man of high rank in the eye.

"Can we bring you anything my lord prince?" The other asked.

"Some water for me and the big man across the tent." the man said.

"Right away." As they withdrew quickly.

One of them returned shortly. The one that had tied his hands.

"Lord Prince. Here is the water you asked for," He offered.

"I am in no need. Give what you have to the Prince of Jebus please."

The man nodded and walked over to the giant man. He removed his hoodwink and tipped the pitcher to give him water. He saw for the first time the man who was sitting across the tent from him, bound with ropes. It was Jonathan, son of King Saul. This was interesting indeed.

Thoros guzzled the whole pitcher down without any rest to breathe. He coughed and choked as he swallowed too hastily and breathed in a little water. The guard stepped back quickly. Once Thoros had calmed he nodded at the man signaling he was satisfied.

Returning to Jonathan the man knelt and said something so quietly that he could barely make it out, but Thoros was certain he heard the name David.

"I can't say I'm surprised that he has men with the King," Thoros said wondrously.

The soldier retorted, "Make no mistake, my allegiance is with the king. I intend to protect him from himself. David is to be king after Saul. That is the will of the Elohim." The dutiful soldier said as he adjusted the knots on Jonathan's wrist to make it looser and easier to slip. Without further conversation the soldier left through the front and was gone from sight.

Thoros couldn't help but chuckle.

"Should've had them hoodwink you again, prince. What is so funny?"

Thoros chuckled again after getting a response. "I'm marveling at the fact that a Hebrew prince, heir to the king, is sitting in my tent with me in the same condition as me."

"David is the heir. And I am his sworn brother." Jonathan said nothing more.

"And where is David now?"

Jonathan sat silent, stoically gazing past Thoros. Thoros didn't expect an answer. They both looked up at the top of the tent as the wind began to blow ahead of a storm moving across the valley. Wind whipped the flaps of the tent, creating a dissonant rhythm that lightly pushed and pulled on the structure of the tent.

"Looks like badly needed rain," Jonathan said, changing the subject. The way he said it was sarcastic, implying that the benefit of this rain was to the city of Jebus, and not that of the Israelites who had used this drought as an opportunity to lay siege.

⬦

The Palace

King Adonizedek stood on the dais overlooking the courtyard. Sitting atop the Citadel he could see for miles and miles during the day. From here he could practically look right down into the Israelite camp. There, his son was being held captive; the result of the brash arrogance and hubris that Thoros was known for. Lox had left with the coward captain Urim to try and see if a recovery was possible.

There had been no word from the guards, and he was starting to doubt that Lox would do what he said he would do and return his son to him. Lox was a peculiar sort that he had come to rely on and mistrust at the same time, if that were possible. On one hand, he loved Lox as he would a son. On the other he feared Lox for the mysterious knowledge and power he possessed, and for Lox's boundless ambition. Truthfully, Lox was far older than him. How much older, he had no idea, though his maturity was more like that of a young adult.

Lox had never told him the whole story of his origin, but he knew only that it was brutal and unforgiving. When he brought Lox into his house initially, he intended on using his powers to rule Canaan, but several years after Lox's arrival the Israelites made their first attempts at conquering the land. He had sent Lox as an emissary to his half-brother Ville, known as Og of Bashan, who ruled Jericho which was the mightiest city in the southern region of Canaan. His task was to convince King Og to join him in his coming campaign to bring all of Canaan under the rule of one king. From there he had dreams of an empire stretching to the furthest oceans.

As fate would have it, Jericho was the next city in the path of the Israelite army. The story of conquest, if you believed it, was well known. No survivors were spared, apart from a lone woman and her son who had helped give information to the Israelite leader at that time. Using some unknown spell, Lox apparently transformed himself into a crow and escaped with his life, bringing with him the tale of Ville's death.

From there Lox fled to Philistia and succeeded in making allies. The scourge of the Philistines on the Israelites was credited to Lox and his persuasive tongue, as well as the uprisings in Damascus and other city-states under the supervision of Israel. Lox had put his skills at manipulation and scheming to skillful use in keeping the Israelites occupied as they put down revolts and defended themselves from constant invasion.

Adonizedek had the practice of worshipping all gods equally including the god of the Israelites. Their god's power was undeniable, and he felt it only right that homage be paid with animal sacrifices. He didn't know if this god, appreciated it or even knew of these sacrifices but nonetheless he persisted in the practice. He acknowledged that the horde of Israelites outside his gates was a likely testament to the standing he had with Elohim.

For a moment he allowed himself to contemplate his own death and that of those he cared for. He knew how other Israelite foes had fared after defeat and he decided at once that his story would not end that way. He made a silent vow as he looked at the encampment outside his walls. He would live regardless of whatever the will of Elohim was. Of that he was certain. He would sacrifice his right eye to ensure it if he had to.

Just then, from the dais he saw a crack of lightning many miles in the distance, a storm was brewing. If it weren't for his knowledge of omens and signs, he would welcome a deluge, but he couldn't ignore it. The rain was desperately needed, but he felt a sense of foreboding that made itself known with another lightning strike just as the thought escaped into the ether.

CHAPTER 13

Below The Citadel Fortress

David motioned in the dimly lit tunnel for everyone to stop while he tapped the man on the shoulder, "Okay Urim. This is the moment."

Urim was sweating profusely. His skin looked pale. "I don't think this is a good plan. What if they already know I'm with you?"

"There is no way they could know that. You know what to tell them. Besides it's only a distraction. We just need to get past them. We will be ready if things go south. Just act natural." As David said this, he silently hoped that Urim's version of natural would be something approaching normal.

Urim exhaled and held his empty lungs for quite a few seconds. Until his body involuntarily forced him to breathe in deeply. "Very well. I will do it." He said, mustering up what little confidence he could find.

David crept forward in a crouch and peered around the bend to the room that lay beyond the end of the tunnel. It was illuminated dimly with braziers and torches at a large doorway that was guarded by four men with spears. No horns or drums to speak of.

This is good , David thought, *this means that once these guards are dealt with, we will likely be in the clear.* He looked at Urim and motioned him forward.

To his credit Urim did not hesitate. Though he walked forward timidly at first, he quickly straightened his posture and walked with purpose like an officer on a mission would do.

In a matter of seconds, he heard the first guard shout, "Halt! Who goes there?"

"It's Urim!" one of the other guards exclaimed.

"Musa. It's good to see you." Urim said to an officer. "I'm in a hurry. I was given an order and separated from the prince to rush back here. Only,

I got lost in the caves. I need to get to the King as quickly as possible. I have important tidings for him from his son. Time is of the essence."

Urim really was a good actor. He was very convincing as he spoke to the guards, "Go right ahead Urim. You'll need to go through the city though. The access through the stable has been barricaded. Apologies my friend." Musa motioned him past.

David was listening intently. His heart raced when he heard the guard direct him to the city. They needed to go through the stables. He hadn't found an opportunity to take out the guards yet and so far, this wasn't going the way he hoped. Urim was to lead them away somehow so they could get into a position to subdue them when they returned.

Not good, David thought.

"Ah! Musa, I NEED to get to the King quicker. I am carrying orders from Prince Lox himself. I am going to need you all to help me remove the barricade to the stables. It will take too long to traverse the city to the Citadel summit."

Urim pleaded with his friend, "You can barricade it after I pass. Let's go everyone. No more time to waste. Prince Lox will be coming at any moment, and you don't want to explain to him why you delayed me."

Musa took a moment, "Okay Urim. We will help you. And I'm glad to see you looking well, my friend. We were all very concerned for you. You know how rumors spread. They said you were a traitor, but I did not believe it."

Urim replied quickly. "It was all a misunderstanding. Thankfully, the king gave me an opportunity to prove myself. Anyhow, I really need to get moving. Prince Lox is not the type to be kept waiting.

Musa motioned to the other guards, and they all turned and marched in the direction of the stables.

Perfect! David thought.

He wasted no time advancing forward as soon as the men were out of sight. David motioned Jeroboam to slowly follow the guard's direction towards the stable. He waited for the other men to pass then he ran up quietly to the front.

At the end of a short hallway was another running right and left. He stopped, not sure which way to go. After a few moments he heard Urim in the distance. They went to the right and crept slowly as the sound grew louder. Just before they reached the stable entrance, he saw a stack of crates and building materials along the wall to the left. This would make a good hiding spot until the guards returned to their post at the distant tunnel entrance.

There was an extraordinarily little amount of light, which was considered an advantage to their stealth movement. He motioned to Jeroboam and the others to take up a position out of sight of any passersby. There they waited for Urim, and the others removed the crates and other materials that made up a hastily made barricade. They must've barricaded this off because of the proximity to the Citadel Tower once they realized the tunnel posed a threat to the city.

"Musa. Many thanks friend." Urim said as he passed through and headed through the stables.

David knew this was the moment to strike and he didn't have to tell Jeroboam and the others his plan. The guard's backs were turned and there was little chance they'd be able to escape or fight back effectively. He readied his staff, and the others did the same, having followed his lead in making a staff of their own using the spear shafts of the guards below. There was bound to be some noise, and he didn't want to bring more guards down upon them. The best that David could tell, there was no one else apart from these four men. He motioned to Jeroboam and the others that he wanted them to take the other guards. They understood and began to creep forward steadily. It was like they were of one mind moving forward like a pride of lions that had chanced upon a stray sheep. David and these men of his were well acquainted with the stalking habits of lions as they positioned themselves as the hunters surrounding their quarry. Quietly, they fanned out and rapidly closed the distance between the guards who were oblivious to their presence.

David reached the man called Musa first who turned just in time to see the butt-end of a staff crash against his skull. Musa barely let out a word before he collapsed into a heap at David's feet. The decision to remove his helm had proved to be a painful mistake.

Jeroboam jumped to the top of a crate and used it to simultaneously vault himself through the air into a spinning back kick that connected with the next victim's face with such force that it caused spittle and blood to fly into the air as the man fell to the ground. The guard made a loud noise that passed for a startled whimper, his chin taking the brunt of the damage as he fell in a heap on the floor, unconscious. Jeroboam landed on his feet and swung his staff low toward the nearest guard, sweeping his legs out from under him. Disoriented from the fall the guard was unable to recover his bearings as another of Jeroboam's men cracked his forehead with the butt end of his staff. Three down, the last guard standing attempted to run but was cut off by the rest of the group. The guard seemed to understand that there was no hope of escape and dropped his shoulders in surrender.

David walked calmly and said in the common tongue, "If you make a sound, you'll join your comrades."

David looked at the men on the floor and then looked at Jeroboam. His choice to use these exceptionally talented men had proved a good one. Jeroboam and his band were known everywhere for their stealth and skill with a sling and staff. Fellow shepherds like himself; they had spent many nights guarding their flocks from lions and other predators. In those moments where a predator threatened their flock a shepherd would become the stalker. He would scale a tree or hop across boulders with ease and, as quiet as a leaf falling to the ground, descend upon the predator turned prey.

"Hide them behind the crates. Bind and gag them." David whispered and lifted Musa, Urim's friend, up from under his armpits and quickly dragged him behind crates.

David began to tear strips of cloth from Musa's cloak, binding his arms and legs. He finished with a gag and used a burlap sack as a blind. Once the others had finished David motioned for them to begin opening the passage up again, crate by crate, until the opening was just large enough to walk through. With any luck they would have some freed captives to bring back through in a short while.

As they moved into the next area, light from scuttles overhead beamed through, making sight difficult for a few seconds as his eyes adjusted to the change in light. The dank and dark cave and fire-lit chambers were a stark difference from natural light from the sun.

There were doors on both sides. This must be some sort of quarters for servants he thought as he pressed forward to the end of the corridor and found a wooden door slightly ajar. To call it a door was an understatement. This door was three times his height and weighed as much as he did.

Surprisingly, the cedar door swung easily upon the well-oiled iron barrel hinges, a recent upgrade to former copper and bronze hinges that wore down so easily under the weight. David had used them in his own home as well; made by a local blacksmith.

They made their way carefully, not knowing what lay behind each door. As they passed through, they found another hall running perpendicular to the one they just exited. To the right seemed like a dead-end so they went left. This was going to be more difficult than he'd expected.

Urim, unsurprisingly, was nowhere to be found. Best case, he was going to retrieve his family. Worst case he was alerting the powers that be in Jebus to their intrusion. Either way they needed to move and move quickly. He'd gotten a rundown from Urim earlier on the layout of the prison and how to get there so it didn't matter if he was there or not. This, of course, depended on the accuracy of the information given by Urim.

David whispered, "There is no time to waste. From here to the moment that we return to the tunnel we will need to move decisively."

They rounded the corner and came to a large arched opening. To the right was a door that he imagined led out into the city. To the left were the stables, which were absolutely the largest he had ever seen. Hundreds of stalls lined both sides as he realized this was going to take longer to bring injured and malnourished prisoner escapees through afterward.

David began to run faster as they made their way through the stables, forcing himself only to focus on the goal at hand. His mind was trained from years of battle and survival to always pick up details in his surroundings. In this case the task at hand was singular.

He kept reminding himself, *We need to get in. Get out. No time for planning. No time for strategy, just running.* In this case they could not waste time strategizing and over-thinking. The only thing they would do is act and react from here on out.

In less than a minute they had covered the ground to the other end of the stable and came to a large stone-arched passage where the concourse of other halls streamed into a half-circle atrium. David wasted no time looking around and veered sharply to the left and through a door that was supposed to lead to a prison if Urim's directions were accurate.

It was a gradual downward grade that seemed to get steeper as they went, and the lighting was less than adequate. He could feel a change in air flow also as they descended the ramp down into the prison quarter. He was suddenly concerned as he began to realize the peril of pushing, pulling, dragging, or carrying sick and weakened men up this grade at a steady pace would be nigh on impossible.

The passage seemed to curve around 180 degrees as they gradually spiraled down. Just as they reached the bottom it opened into a rather large square room with a barred gate just ahead. There was a guard asleep at the door with his chair reclined on the back two legs.

He must have the keys, David reasoned as he swept his foot under the chair leg and planted his elbow at the man's throat.

The man was startled as he fell and the force of landing with David on his throat caused the man to lose his wind. This was long enough for David to hit a crushing blow to the side of his head which knocked him as unconscious as he was when they found him. David searched the man's belt to find the keys and quickly opened the door.

Once inside the prison quarters, he scanned around as quickly as he could. There didn't seem to be many in here now, so he grabbed a torch and took the looking in each cell one at a time. The hall was rather long and lined on both sides, so each man took a torch and began searching. After a thorough search, every man returned to the beginning. It was clear to all that there were no Israelite prisoners in this cell block. Jeroboam went straight ahead to the first cell and shined a light into an empty cell. In the dim light he saw something on the floor.

"We need to open this door!" Jeroboam exclaimed as David rushed forward with the jailer's keys. The door was locked from the other side of the bars inside the cell. *Very odd,* David thought.

Jeroboam stepped forward as the door swung away and ran to the center where he moved a thin linen sheet covered in dust from the floor revealing a metal grate. He signaled for another to help, and they pried and pulled at the grate until finally, it creaked loose with a sudden scraping noise. He shined a light down into the hole and descended a steep staircase into a chamber below. As the others filed in, the light from the torches lit up the space and they suddenly realized they had entered a hallway that disappeared into darkness at the edge of the torchlight.

"Follow me." David said. He didn't need to order it at this point. The single-minded movement of the men with him reminded him of a beehive as they plunged forward into the dark hallway. After twenty paces the hall made a hard right turn and carried forward another twenty paces where they came to a cross-section of halls.

David paused for a moment, *Right or left?* he thought. Realizing there was no way to know, he decided to turn right. The hall seemed to go on forever and he silently hoped that there were not any confusing turns to get lost by on their way out. So far it had been easy to remember.

As he said this another crossing appeared. This required a choice of right or left as well. He stood still for a moment to listen and motioned for the others to still their movement. He needed to hear what lay ahead in the pitch black as he began to focus on breathing slowly and long to still his heartbeat.

The others looked on as he trained his ear into the darkness. For a long while there was not a sound apart from a faint movement of stale air. Not enough to freshen the air in the hallways but enough to keep it from being toxic to a short-term occupant like themselves. David certainly could not see how being down here for an extended period would be healthy. He thought of the men captured and tortured down in these depths for months on end. Would any of them still live? Would they be worse off than the wretches they rescued in the caverns? Suddenly he heard what sounded like a faint wail or cry to his right and his mind was made up. Right, it was.

He plunged ahead into the black not waiting to check if any others in the party had heard the same. He felt the ground begin to incline slightly under his feet as they proceeded up into what appeared to be another chamber.

Inside the chamber he saw a row of cells that lined the far wall. It was too dark to see into them from where he stood so he crept closer. As the light began to illuminate the foreground, David suddenly heard a rustle of chains to the right and left and what appeared to be too large dark figures standing up. No sooner had he noticed them, than the figures lurched forward at them. They all retreated just in time for the two creatures to come to the end of the thick chains and jerk backwards from the force.

Maws frothing, they tried to reach out for David who stood well out of reach of the wild beasts. He stood there like a sentry as the other men instinctively withdrew to a safer distance away. One of the men threw a torch at the figures and when it hit the ground before them, a shower of sparks and embers flashed. The two figures recoiled at this for only a moment and resumed their fruitless advance. David furled his brow and tried to see just what manner of creatures stood before them.

Something tells me these are more dangerous than an average lion or wolf, he thought as he calmly withdrew two smooth stones and a leather sling from his pouch. David knew one of them to be the very stone that had knocked Goliath unconscious years before as a boy of thirteen. His life had changed so much since then. The stone was worn smooth and polished from years of friction by his weathered fingertips. That stone was for thinking, not throwing. It had killed once, long ago in his defining battle with Goliath and now became a sort of talisman for him. Quickly he dropped the stone into his pouch and selected another before stepping forward with his sling.

It was hard to see the creatures, and they were so large that not a single torch would illuminate the whole of them well enough to see details. As he drew in a breath, he placed the stone into his sling and pulled it tight across his body, turning the stone in the sling in such a way that it would hit a target using the flat side of the stone, doing less trauma while packing near the same punch. David had perfected this technique during multiple hours of boredom while guarding his father's sheep in the fields. He could even hit a target on the other side of a tree with lethal force using a side arm release that made the stone curve its path around the tree, the spin on the stone controlling how tightly the arc formed between him and the target.

At close range and in tight quarters such as this he decided to use a simple overhand release using his legs to spin and transfer his momentum to the stone as it flew from the sling. Standing square with the beasts he took two steps back, stepped forward on his left foot and simultaneously twirled the stone. David increased the speed of the sling while his right foot swung forward and sent him into spin that sent the sling over his shoulder. The moment his left foot came around and touched down, his finger released the tether, sending the stone hurtling through the dank air. The stone found its mark even in the dim lighting of the torches with a loud thud!

Suddenly one of them jerked back, stumbling clumsily as the stone hit it right in the middle of the forehead, and fell to the ground prone and was incapacitated. The other beast, enraged by the intruders, suddenly dropped onto his knuckles, and used all four limbs to run to his fallen companion. It was jarring to see a beast such as this act in such a human way as it checked over the unconscious one with great concern.

A boisterous yowl erupted from the beast as it looked directly at David, knowing he was the cause. The beast shot David a fiery look and tried to pull at the chains that kept it from tearing David to bits. David calmly sent a second stone which found its mark on the side of the skull and, all at once, the room was quiet as the second beast collapsed on top of the other. Raspy breathing was the only sign that the creatures were still living.

Each of the men stood awestruck at what had just happened in the dark dungeon. David stored his sling away and walked boldly up to the sleeping giants and retrieved his stones and placed them back in the pouch.

The rest of the men with Jeroboam cautiously crept forward toward the beasts and for the first time they could see that these beasts were similar to human shape. If not for the peculiar details of only having three webbed fingers and toes and only one eye at the center of their forehead, their bodies were shaped in proportion to man. However, their facial features were slightly distorted in an inhuman way, and they were at least three times the height of an average man. From what David could tell one of them was female and the other one male.

Each lay unconscious bleeding from the head due to a well-placed impossible blow from a stone. They were both breathing very heavily, and one even began to snore a bit as they lay there on top of one another. David noticed the scars on the bodies as well as what appeared to be a flesh-eating fungus on the skin and for a moment felt pity for them.

These poor beasts down here chained up. How cruel must their master be? David thought empathetically.

"We need to move." David whispered as he stepped over the giant's bodies. Approaching the cells, he could see that there were men in there as he cautiously moved towards one of the gates to the closest cell. The first thing he realized was that there was no barred gate on the cell. And that it was completely open to walk in and out. There was no need for one, due to the presence of the beasts chained up just outside. Anyone trying to escape would be torn to pieces and likely eaten. As the light reached the faces of the men who lay in the cell, David's heart sunk in noticing how few there were. Not even a dozen lay broken and nearly catatonic on the damp stone floor of the cell.

David entered and knelt beside one of the men. His face was covered in blood and mangled from abuse; the tongue was torn out in a vicious manner and, from the looks of it, both eyes were gouged out from their sockets and a terrible scar had formed across the neck. It appeared to have been cut with a knife and allowed to heal. A quick look around revealed several men who were no longer living. They had been mutilated beyond recognition. Some of them scarcely looked like men any longer.

David stood up and quickly walked out of the cell.

"How many?" He said to the group.

After a moment, a reply returned. "Seventeen, but only eleven are alive. Six are dead."

David paced a moment or two as he processed the idea that nearly all of the captives, he expected to find were either dead or missing. A mixture of rage and sorrow welled up and he quickly tamped it back down. There was no time for either. He expected to find three-hundred or so and instead he'd found eleven.

Jeroboam was searching around the immediate area and had gone just out of sight when he yelled back to the group, "You're going to want to see this!"

David silently hoped Jeroboam had found more survivors as the whole group went in the direction of his voice. Not twenty paces more, and they were ascending a set of wide stairs into a large room with pillars lining the outer walls: twelve in all. Each one had a different angelic being painted on it.

They were painted to look fierce and terrifying, each one having the head of a different bird, animal or beast. At the center of the room was a brazen altar covered in ash, and at the extreme end of the room stood a statue of what appeared to be a Canaanite deity of some sort, though David couldn't really figure out which one.

It had the head of a lion and the body of a serpent that was wound around a pedestal made of marble. The creature had what appeared to be a dozen wings of various lengths and texture, and four arms complete with razor sharp claws attached to what passed for a torso. David had never seen anything like this before in all of Canaan. The colors of the wings were gradients of all the colors found in a rainbow and the head, complete with flowing mane, was solid gold.

The others walked about the room, forgetting about the task at hand for a moment. David heard Jeroboam whisper in an urgent tone, "My lord. You need to see this."

David hurried over to where Jeroboam was as the others joined him. At the foot of the statue pedestal was a set of words written in Hebrew characters which said: 'TSALMAVETH.'

"Death's Shadow," David offered as he traced the characters right to left with his forefinger.

David not only realized that the words were written in dried blood, but also that the word had been traced over the top of the same word repeatedly. There may be dozens of traced layers of blood on this stone. Some of it appeared to be freshly dried within the last few days as he used his fingernail to flake off little flecks from the characters.

David noticed a strange sensation standing near to the altar and it felt as though the statue of the ugly winged serpent lion was staring at him. He walked around until he stood between the winged creature and the altar and noticed a stone box sitting open at the base. He picked up the lid and examined it closely and noticed the strange language and symbols on it. A slight chill ran up and down his spine causing him to snap out of his thoughts and refocus on the task at hand. There were numerous conversations happening simultaneously in the dank temple as the men searched around awestruck.

David placed the lid back on the ground and stood up, abruptly walking away from the altar, giving the box a final glance as he turned towards the door. He had a passing thought that he needed to take the box and learn more about it but decided that he shouldn't.

"Gather up those that are alive. Carry them if need be. We must move quickly," David ordered.

Reaching the open cell, David was relieved that the two beasts were still unconscious and did not appear to be at all lucid. Nearly half of the survivors were able to stand, and Jeroboam began to lead them out of the cell. The others would need a shoulder to stay on their feet as they were clearly starving, their faces withdrawn and pale from the lack of sunlight, too weak to move unaided.

Once all the survivors were on their feet, David began to lead the group with a torch in hand. They stepped around the two one-eyed giants and left them behind in the dark. The group walked through the tunnel with as much haste as eleven near-dead escaped prisoners could manage. It was a tedious walk, but the halls were spacious enough to allow for the able-bodied men to walk next to the more decrepit ones.

David walked forward cautiously; half-thinking of the winged lion serpent looming in the darkness behind them.

As they neared the grand stairs that led into the strange temple, David paused for a moment and stared into the darkness ahead of his torchlight. David was visibly curious to explore that room more, and Jeroboam could tell, by the way David paused and slightly leaned toward the temple.

"My lord. There is nothing there for us now. We must keep going. Time is not on our side."

David snapped out of his gaze and abruptly turned right towards the exit without saying a word. But that word 'TSALMAVETH' went through his mind as he tried to mull it over even as it began to haunt him, causing him to draw further away. David had spent many years in the dark without a single ounce of dread or fear, but this moment he had a fleeting thought that he did not want to go back into the cavern. Rather, he would go back to that temple and face down whatever evil created such an aberration in his mind. He knew it would be pointless. It was only a graven image of lesser gods. None would match his God who was Lord of all Creation.

Suddenly David realized he wanted to kill Lox. It came into his mind as an opposing thought to his previous thought of the power of Elohim.

That thought smacked him a bit. He had never entertained a thought to murder a specific person; not even Saul when Elohim told him in a dream that he could without penalty.

David had killed countless men. Ended bloodlines for all time while he slipped and wallowed in blood and bodies, engaged in a righteous bloodlust. Though, it never was personally connected to a desire to kill, but rather a survival of the fittest during the ugly torrent of chaos, called war.

David had made warfare an art form. He could anticipate an opponent's movement based on his any number of factors and could sit atop a horse and guide his men to exploit an armies' weakness. David was the best at killing, but he did not enjoy it. He reasoned it as a necessary action to save his country and protect his loved ones. He did what was necessary and never apologized for it.

However, David would enjoy killing Lox. David realized he now intended on killing Lox in order to reclaim the dignity that Lox had stolen from these hundreds of men.

He felt a pang of guilt and conviction as his mind fantasized about the details of this murder. *This is not like you, David,* he told himself as the group walked on.

Suddenly, another thought invaded his mind. *When I finally catch up with Lox, I will have fire and pitch waiting to melt his body limb by limb.*

David retorted internally. *I am no murderer. I will trust God to bring justice.* The internal dialogue kept harassing him with every step he took.

You were made for killing, David. Killing Lox is a righteous act. David thought this, and it unnerved him how it simultaneously felt as if he was arguing with himself and a completely different person at the same time. A chill ran up his spine as his arm hair stood on end.

I'm not sure who you are, but you don't know me very well. I put my trust in Elohim alone.

The voice in his mind cackled maniacally. *David. I am you, and you are me. Soon you will see...murderer. Give into your hatred. You cannot escape me.*

NO! David responded. *I am not ruled by my emotions. Lox is the murderer, not me.*

David was now certain that something had gotten ahold of him and was invading his thoughts. His mind flitted to the image of the stone box at the altar and the dark energy he felt. When he held it, he hadn't recognized the energy as anything tangible.

Be gone from me, evil one. You have no hold on me. I am the anointed future king of Israel. None can stand against Elohim.

The voice in his head cackled deeply yet again. *Keep telling yourself that. One day you'll see. One day you'll allow your true nature to be shown to the world, as it should be. On that day you and I will rule the entire world and bring death upon every soul. Soon, the effect of my essence will wear off and you'll think you are free of my influence. But David, you and I have unfinished business. I'll be seeing you and yours very soon. I am everywhere. When you lay your head down at night, I'll be there. When you ride into battle, I'll be there. When you celebrate the birth of your son, I'll be there. You cannot escape your own Shadow. Murderer.*

David was totally unaware, as he lost himself in his thoughts, that from the depths of the halls came the roar of waking giants who were now feverishly trying to free themselves from the bonds that held them in the prison.

CHAPTER 14

The Citadel Fortress

There was little else that Ahmet could do as he walked under the control of Tsalmaveth. They had reentered the fortress via the tunnels after paying a visit to the Israelite camp where he'd watched Tsalmaveth torment the King who he'd called Saul, visit some poor souls who looked as though they had been tortured, and finally they entered a tent that held Prince Thoros, bound and hoodwinked. They had come with a hairs breadth of his face before retreating at the sound of someone entering.

How on earth did the Prince end up in captivity? he wondered, before remembering that in all the turmoil with Nathan and Baaldir that the prince had run off into the caverns to search for the assailants. It would appear that had not gone as planned for the prince.

Thinking again of the way Tsalmaveth had tortured King Saul with just a little bit of his essence, it made him wonder at the power of the Shadow of Death and he was starting to think that maybe he did possess the power and desire to give Ahmet the revenge he sought. Of course, he still wasn't sure how that could be accomplished.

Tsalmaveth, sensing Ahmet's thoughts replied within, "Don't you worry about that big lout, Prince Thoros. I have special plans for him."

Tsalmaveth changed subjects to his current thought, "So, you like the power and you want it for keeps? Well, in order for you to access my power you'll need to go through two rituals. One is like the ones you've witnessed from time to time. The other must take place no more than three days later for the effect to be permanent. Come to me when you are ready. Make sure you are ready because there will be no way to turn back. Consider this to be a sampling of the power I can give you."

Ahmet shuddered at the detailed explanation that followed a mere thought from himself, *Can I trust Tsalmaveth?*

"Can you trust anyone?" Tsalmaveth replied to his thought.

Ahmet now spoke audibly. The voice in his head too real to have an internal dialogue with and appeared to passersby to be talking to himself, "I trust my wife. Though she doesn't trust me."

"She doesn't trust you Ahmet. Why is that?" Tsalmaveth hissed calmly.

"She often complains I say one thing and do the opposite." Ahmet lamented.

Tsalmaveth chuckled, "spoken like every mediocre man in history. I suppose you agree with her. You aren't trustworthy, are you Ahmet?"

Ahmet started to protest but realized he was drawing stares from people, so he just said hushed, "No, that is not true."

"No? Well from where I'm sitting, I wonder if you really are a good fit for the power I'm offering. Can you be trusted Ahmet?"

Suddenly the tables had turned, and it was Ahmet making his case to Tsalmaveth.

"Tell me what I have to do to prove my loyalty, Master." Ahmet said suddenly, lowering his voice toward the latter part of his plea.

"Come to me when you are ready Ahmet, and not until then. I need men of substance Ahmet. Are you such a man?"

Ahmet wanted nothing more than to be sure of his answer but shakily said, "I am Master. You will see."

Tsalmaveth said nothing more as they approached the lower level of the fortress, just outside the palace where they had taken Baaldir the other evening. The sun was beginning to rise, though it was still the wee hours of the morning, as he was stopped by a squad of guards lined up outside the room.

Ahmet could feel Tsalmaveth stirring as they met the obstacle. Using his lips Tsalmaveth spoke to the guards and waved his hands in an array that seemed to be a spell of its own. The words spoken were not of the common language and Ahmet imagined a people deep within the earth speaking in such a way. Chills ran through him as Tsalmaveth spoke toward the men while making various hand motions.

When he finished the guards simply looked past him as if they'd never seen him in the first place. Ahmet walked through the guards and into the room completely invisible to them. How was this possible?

"YOU did that Ahmet, not me. I just gave you the words. This is but a taste of the power I can offer you. Now, let us see what this young man can offer us. If I'm right this one is the key I've been searching for."

Tsalmaveth was talking about a sleeping Baaldir who was soundly unconscious and recovering from many wounds. This boy, the prince, was a friend of Nathan, and they had been together down in the caverns. The only reason Nathan made it out was because of this boy here.

"Relax Ahmet, I'm not going to hurt him. I just need a bit of his blood to test my theory." Tsalmaveth said as Ahmet realized he was holding onto a small dagger that he hadn't remembered carrying.

Ahmet relented and allowed Tsalmaveth to reach for Baaldir's arm and using the dagger made a shallow cut in the palm of his hand. Blood began to pool as it slowly filled Baaldir's palm. Out of Ahmet's mouth came a tongue of smoke that wound its way down to the boy's hand. The smoke inter-mixed with the blood for only a second and hastily retreated. Tsalmaveth was on the verge of having a fit as he spit and scowled.

"This is the wrong one, there must have been a mistake. I was so sure but now...This one's blood is foul to taste! Of course! Baaldir must be a Guardian..." Tsalmaveth suddenly stopped, and Ahmet imagined the being pondering some fact that had just presented itself.

"It was the other boy! It must have been!" Tsalmaveth exclaimed.

Nathan, Ahmet thought to himself.

"Yes. Yes. Yes. Your boy Ahmet. It was his blood on that dagger which explains why I was drawn to you. I will go to him at once."

Ahmet, hearing this and suddenly realizing that Nathan was in the sight of Tsalmaveth yelled aloud, "No! Leave my son out of this."

Tsalmaveth, not caring one bit, started to leave the room, one foot in front of the other until he suddenly stopped short of the doorway.

"What is this? Do you dare to struggle with me? Surely you know that you have no choice, mortal. Besides, I only need a bit of his blood for my purposes." He started to walk again, only this time Ahmet fought harder for control.

"My Son is not to be touched!" Ahmet shouted, dagger in hand. He pulled at his arms and swung his body around and stumbled back into the room, all the while fighting the pull of Tsalmaveth who was shouting vulgar insults and curses. Tsalmaveth made Ahmet punch himself and threw him against the wall next to Baaldir's bed, knocking over a stand that held a pitcher and bowl for washing, sending it flying and clanging on the floor. All the while making a loud enough noise that it would surely be heard in the halls.

Tsalmaveth finally took control of Ahmet once again and hurriedly stood, knowing that the noise would alert the dazed guards just outside. He snuck behind the door just as it burst open, and several guards piled into the room shouting for the prince.

"Young prince, we are here. What is it?" Seeing him asleep they were puzzled by the origin of the noise, noticing the out of place furniture and instruments. Tsalmaveth wasted no time sneaking past the guards and out into the hall. He heard a guard take note of the blood on the prince's palm as they began to search the room. Two more steps and Tsalmaveth froze.

"No! Not yet! I should have one more hour! Curses!" he shouted as Ahmet hit his knees, palms flat on the ground. Suddenly the smoke that contained the Shadow of Death exited from every orifice without fanfare leaving Ahmet heaving and coughing in the hallway. Tsalmaveth's test run had ended as the first glint of morning sun shown on his face through a narrow passage.

Ahmet, having control of his body finally, could only think of one thing. Nathan. He had to get to him, and they needed to leave the city at once.

The guards behind him, hearing the coughing fit shouted, "You there! STOP! At once!" as Ahmet pulled himself to his feet and started running, dropping the dagger on the ground. The guards were in hot pursuit shouting all the way.

"Get him! Don't let him escape!" one yelled.

While another shouted, "Protect the prince!"

"That was the jailer, what was his name? Ahmet! That's it. Someone, run and alert our captain!" another shouted to a subordinate.

Ahmet wasted no time running from the fortress and into the city. He ducked and dodged and dove through alley ways and over carts and under barricades. After a few maneuvers he found a place to hide as the guards ran by shouting all the way.

The first thing he cared about was getting home to Ramah and Nathan. Ahmet tried to order his thoughts as he made his way through the upper city, down a steep grade to the lower city where his home was located. It had taken him far too long to cross the city, trying to stay in the shadows and not be seen in the open. He needed to get his wife and child out of Jebus in any way possible. They could go to a cousin's farm in Moab until they could figure out where to go.

He rounded a corner that led to his doorstep and stopped short. Soldiers were walking briskly toward his direction from the other end of his street. He quickly ducked back around the corner and pressed his back and shoulders against the wall of the mud brick hovel. His house was three doors down. He waited for a moment hoping they would pass by, and then peaked around the corner. His heart skipped a beat, and a cold chill ran up his spine as he realized the group of soldiers were at his door demanding that the occupants open up for them. They pounded on the door very rapidly and yelled from without.

"Open up, in the name of the King! Open this door!" one of them yelled, rapping violently on the door once again.

He heard his wife Ramah open the door and with tears in her small voice said, "What is it, can't you see I'm grieving?"

"I have orders to search this home for the traitor Ahmet. Please step aside." They didn't wait for her to comply as they pushed by her and filed into the house from the street.

Ahmet panicked as he racked his mind trying to come up with a solution; a plan to get him and his family out of this predicament. The soldiers did not stay long, the one room hovel providing no hiding places. Two of them came out and quickly walked in the direction they'd come from. The other two came out. Ramah met them at the door, seeing them out.

"If your husband returns home, it would be wise that you come and find us. It will not go well for you if you aid a traitor." After finishing the threat, they turned and walked in his direction.

Ahmet scampered back into the small alleyway and saw a stack of crates and pile of refuse. He backed into the hidden alley and behind the crates just as the two soldiers walked past. He moved across the alley to get a better view of the street but as he did, he bumped into a poorly stored stack of buckets. Time seemed to slow to a crawl as he watched the buckets fall to the ground.

Ahmet swore under his breath and cursed his clumsiness, and he attempted to stop the fall. He recovered all but one bucket as it tumbled to the ground. It was amazing how loud something could be at the most inconvenient time. He froze in place hoping that the pursuers hadn't heard his racket. Unfortunately, his run of bad luck continued as the two soldiers came back cautiously looking down the alleyway. They walked directly toward him. His back was at a dead end and there was no way to escape.

"You, there! Stop!" one soldier ordered.

Without thinking, Ahmet slammed into the crates and pushed with all his might. The crates toppled over and slammed into the soldiers. He vaulted over them as they lost their footing and fell under the weight of the crates. He turned left and went back the way he'd come. He needed to find somewhere to hide. His pursuers recovered much faster than he'd hoped and soon gave chase after him.

Ahmet darted in and out of alley ways and blindly turned down streets. All sense of direction and reason left him as he focused solely on putting some distance between them. He could hear shouts behind him but paid them no mind. He looked back just long enough to see one of the soldiers had rounded the corner some way down the street.

Ahmet turned to continue running and was stopped suddenly as he ran directly into a brick wall and fell backwards sprawling out onto the ground. Though, as he looked up from the ground, he realized that it wasn't a wall, it was Bulwark, the palace stonemason. The soldier that was pursuing him ran up out of breath. Bulwark looked down at Ahmet and drilled him with piercing eyes.

"I've found your traitor, soldier." He said as the man grabbed Ahmet by the armpit and forced him to stand. "Take him to the king."

Three more soldiers appeared and bound Ahmet's hands in front of him and tied a lead-rope around his neck. They marched right past Ahmet's home as he craned his neck to look. He'd hoped to see his wife so at least she'd know what became of him. He feared he would never see her or Nathan again as they pushed him onto an oxen cart and headed back toward the Citadel.

Out of the corner of his eye he saw large man in a brown unassuming cloak with a large hood pulled over his head to hide the face. The man waited for them to pass and then made his way down the street and was out of sight as he rounded the bend. None of the soldiers paid any mind, almost as if they could not see him.

His heart sank as he heard wails coming up from the direction of his home. It sounded like Ramah. His fear was confirmed when one of the soldiers explained to the other, "Did you see the boy? I imagine he had just now crossed over. Poor soul." They were oblivious to the fact that they were dragging the boy's father away at that very moment. Either that or they didn't care.

Ahmet burned with rage and sorrow all at once. This wasn't supposed to be his life, and he didn't know how, but he was going to make someone suffer for killing his only son. Tsalmaveth's words echoed in his mind as he was overcome with grief on his way to the fortress prison. His son Nathan was most likely dead, and all Ahmet had left was rage.

The Dungeon Tunnels

At first David didn't hear Jeroboam calling out to him. As his hearing returned to him, David shook his head and looked about in confusion. It was then that David realized that he was kneeling on both knees and had his palms on the ground.

"How long have I been like this?" David asked.

Jeroboam looked puzzled. "Only a few moments my lord. You worried me a bit. What was that all about?"

David shrugged, "I'm not sure. I never had that happen before. I feel as though I just climbed out of a deep pit."

"Might I suggest we climb out of this deep pit?" One of the others suggested urgently as a chorus of roars reached towards them from within.

David stood up quickly and listened to the sounds in the direction of the temple. *The Cursed Temple,* David thought as he heard the roars echoing down the halls.

"Alright let's move!" David shouted as the roars seemed to come closer each time he heard them.

They were not far from the set of stairs they came down in the upper prison chambers as they doubled their pace. Many of the men threw a weakened man over their shoulder and dug in with their legs to quicken their retreat. It wasn't too far now.

As David thought this, he wondered why they weren't there yet. Every step seemed like walking through muck. Maybe it was just his imagination, but the hall seemed to get longer and longer the more they advanced. Step after step they ran, but no staircase. The roars grew louder and louder as David stopped to look at his surroundings. Is it possible that they took a wrong turn somewhere?

"Where were we when I blacked out?" David asked.

Jeroboam quickly answered. "At a fork in the corridor."

David realized all at once that they had gone the wrong way. How? He didn't remember seeing another hall converging on the one they had entered.

It didn't matter. A roar in the depths of the dungeon made its way to them and he realized they sounded too close. Could those monsters have freed themselves? Or was it something else lurking in the darkness that they'd awakened by their presence?

David suddenly realized their situation, "We can't go back! We need to keep moving and hope to find another way out."

David moved to the front once again with a renewed energy. He ran and ran down the corridor, every step unsure in the dark as his torch only had enough light to illuminate a few feet around him. "Stay close! The torches are running low!"

Each man ran with purpose, dragging those along that couldn't move rapidly. They suddenly came to a group of cells on both sides of the corridor. Jeroboam shined a torch into them, and he realized what they'd stumbled upon. Looking back at him were their countrymen except that they didn't look normal. Sure, the rest they'd rescued were in rough shape, but these men looked empty. They all stood like statues, more than three-hundred packed into the cells with standing room only. Not even one blinked and their eyes were as black as night. They barely breathed and had no facial expression.

David sprang into action, "Give me the keys! Quickly!" He said while snapping his fingers impatiently.

Someone produced the keys, and he proceeded to try key after key in the lock; none worked. David was just about to look for something to try to pry the cell door open when a high-pitched shrieking roar echoed down the corridor to them. At the same moment as the screech a set of hands reached through the bar and grabbed David by his collar. The arms pulled him close as the man on the other side attempted to bite him on the face. All at once the entire row of cells erupted into a cacophony of shrieks and screams as arms protruded from every set of bars. David managed to pry the hands from his clothes and pushed them out of reach.

"David, we need to go! Now!" Jeroboam exclaimed.

Frustrated, David pounded on the ground with his fists, "They've all been changed, these are no longer men here."

Jeroboam was frustrated also, but he was focused on the approaching roars, "We need to get out of here! And now!"

Seeing the sense in what he was saying, David snapped out of his rigor. The roars echoed again, further impressing the need to get a move on. The others had already left and headed up the corridor, deeper into the unknown dungeon.

Jeroboam and David quickly caught up to them. The corridor was long and straight and seemed to stretch on forever even though they could only see five cubits in front of them. The roars echoed again seemed to be closer than before. They needed to find a way out.

David took three more steps and almost ran face first into a massive door made of metal. It stood twice the height of him and from what he could see it had no handles apart from one set of bars at the top, rigged with some sort of mechanism.

"I need someone to hoist me up!" The roars and shrieks were close now; the beasts were in the same hallway and closing fast. Judging by the noise they were not having any trouble running in the darkness.

Two men knelt and helped David climb upon their shoulders. He reached up for what looked like a handle that, if he pulled down on it, would release the bolts that held the door shut. It was just out of his reach as he strained to put even one finger on it.

"Higher!" David shouted as the two below strained to give him more reach. He now had his hand on the lever and yanked down on it. It didn't budge.

"David! Hurry!" Jeroboam shouted.

"It won't move! I can't turn the lever!"

"Try pushing it upward instead of downward!"

Of course. Upward, David thought, as he pushed the lever upward and was upset at how easily it had moved. But he was relieved as soon as he heard the bolts release from the frame of the door. He was lowered at a speed that was more like being dropped and was barely caught before he landed.

"Let's go!" as they all placed their fingers on the edge of the door and pulled. It had to be made of solid iron because it took four of them to pull the door open enough to move past. Once on the other side they helped the others through. Torches lined the corridor which led to the stairwell.

"We can't close the door." Someone shouted.

"Leave it, we have to go." David said.

At least he could see better now. The giant beasts were gaining on them by the second and being able to see greatly helped their chances. The first one to reach the top shouted down, "Another door!" someone shouted.

David came to the landing and was thankful to realize this door, while large, was much lighter and not quite as tall. It had a lever at the top and bottom and appeared to open inward. "Turn the levers! Top and bottom." David shouted, using his intuition to guess the way to open the door.

He heard the beasts down the at the bottom of the stairs. They were pulling the large door open much easier than several men had.

"They're coming! Open the door!" As two men turned the levers the bolts released, and the door opened inward. The men fell through the door one by one and once all had made it, they closed the door behind them. But no lock could be found on the door. No handle, no lever, no bolts. How would they lock this door?

David and the others found themselves in a civilized room full of trinkets, weapons, and artifacts. If the situation weren't as dire, he would have cared to peruse and explore the contents. David instead began to move furniture and whatever he could in front of the door. Others followed suit and in a matter of moments there was a pile of furniture and statues in front of the door.

"That won't hold them long." Jeroboam said as the beasts slammed against the door. The pile shifted ever so slightly. "That won't hold them for long!" Jeroboam yelled again, more urgently.

"Let's not wait to find out. Everyone needs to move quickly. We have no idea where we are, but we will have to adapt." David opened the door across the room and peered out through what appeared to be a hallway. I was clear from what he could tell. And they might yet be able to make it back before the guard changed over at dusk as Urim had said.

The giants on the other side raged and slammed their bodies against the door again, and again. Each time they moved the pile another increment closer to being able to pass through and devour the intruders.

David waited not a moment longer thinking about what to do. He had to act now and worry about the next hurdle. If they stayed any longer in this room the giants would kill them or attract soldiers from the racket that they were making in trying to get at them. He exited into the hall and went right; instinct told him to head back in the general direction of the prison in hopes of finding a familiar part of this labyrinth.

Jeroboam brought up the rear, coaxing along the survivors that could walk on their own. The others either carried men over their shoulder or helped them walk. Many of them, in addition to being muted and starved, were blinded and missing fingers and toes. David wondered how any of them would survive the trek through the cavern.

David's instinct was right, as they came to the very same interchange that would lead them to the prison or to the stables where they would exit. He went left and continued down the set of turns that he was surprised he remembered after the tumult they had experienced. David began to quietly think that this might succeed as he passed through the door to the stables.

All at once, his heart sank into his stomach because in the center of the stables stood Urim, next to Musa and twenty guards all with spears at the ready. Musa had a bandage on his head and looked at David with fiery hatred. The other guards held another man bound at the wrists and a hoodwink over his face, head hanging low. Musa held a rope that tied the two together and cinched it up.

"You've really made a mess for yourself, Ahmet." Musa said to the hoodwinked man. "What were you thinking?" he added.

Jeroboam and the others trailed in a few seconds after and the disappointment on their faces could be felt in the air. The survivors, as before, showed zero emotions. Then a shout came from behind.

"Move to the center!" As guards came in from behind and forced them all to move towards Urim and the others.

"I knew he couldn't be trusted." Jeroboam said aloud as David looked on in disgust at Urim who said nothing. David was mostly disgusted with himself, because he realized he was so headstrong about this mission that he put his trust in someone who he could not vouch for. He should have expected no less from Urim. David had a tough time blaming the man for trying to save his own skin. He was certain that once Urim was caught, he'd spilled the beans on their plans and whereabouts without so much as a thought of secret evasion.

Musa scowled at David as the men moved toward them and forced the other captive to kneel as they all waited for something.

David was trying to figure out a plan. He and the men were so close to the caverns. He looked around at the guards that surrounded them and quickly counted. Near thirty. Too many for seven of them to subdue. They would take out more than half he was sure of it, and his men would fight without any convincing. But David couldn't be reckless with their lives or those of the survivors who were oblivious and near catatonic. Any skirmish would surely mean the death of many of their rescued countrymen.

"We killed no one. All we want is our men back. They need medical help and food and water. Let them all go, and I will come with you peacefully."

Musa mulled it over for a moment. "No deal." He motioned to his bandaged head. David could see this was not going anywhere. Jeroboam wanted to fight; he could tell. As did the others, as they surveyed the condition of their own countrymen who were imprisoned here.

"Jeroboam, I am sorry for getting you into this," David apologized.

"My lord, this is what we do. No need to apologize. To follow you is our great honor," Jeroboam graciously offered; his teeth gritted in hatred for their captors.

The guards had circled around them and kept a far distance from them. Were they waiting for something? He couldn't tell. But it was clear that they were not going to make an escape as they were surrounded by men with spears. Jeroboam came and stood next to David, the spears shifting as he moved cautiously.

"What's the plan then?" he asked.

David chuckled. "Plan? Do you any ideas?" Jeroboam looked on and fell silent, clearly hoping that a plan existed. David had nothing that could save their skin. There was a rustle of activity from behind at the stable entrance.

"On your knees!" Musa ordered. David and the others slowly knelt and turned their heads to see several giants walking through the door to the stables. This was what the wait was for. He'd heard tales of giants on the heights above Jebus but never had he expected to see so many together.

"All hail, Adonizedek, King and Supreme Commander of the armies of Jebus!" one of the giants yelled in a booming voice that echoed and bounced around the massive building. The few horses that occupied the stalls whinnied and snorted at the sudden burst of noise as the soldiers surrounding them snapped to attention, body erect and spear upright.

They parted as one of the giants walked forward; King Adonizedek with his purple and gold tunic. He wore no crown but instead wore a hood over his head and he carried a long spear made of ash as a staff. His face appeared to be weathered from many years, but he didn't look old. If anything, it appeared wizened and stoic. He carried himself as a warrior would from the look of his gait. David detected a slight limp in his left leg, maybe from gout or an old injury. It didn't seem to hamper his stride though but was just the kind of thing David had learned to notice. Strength was not lacking in this old king.

The king crouched down in front of David and brought himself to within a few cubits of him. He noticed that King Adonizedek still maintained a distance and a posture that would allow for swift defense if needed. David didn't flatter himself in thinking the king was threatened by him in this circumstance, but he was a warrior through and through, that was plain.

"The mighty David of Israel." He said in flawless Hebrew before rising and turning to walk away from the circle.

A man of few words, David thought.

"Take them to the prison. Give them food and water." King Adonizedek ordered as he strode away with his detachment before adding over his shoulder, "I will deal with the traitor Ahmet later."

At once, the circle closed around the men as they were ordered to rise. The group began a procession back through the halls which now looked familiar to David.

He could see King Adonizedek and his men walking ahead of them for a moment before they disappeared down another hallway. When they passed it, there was no sight of the king. The other man looked defeated by the way his shoulders slouched, as he walked at the head in between Musa and Urim. They were nearing the interchange where they would be led to the left down to the prison again. As they entered the corridor to the prison and started down the grade, they heard a blood curdling scream from below at the prison entrance.

The group stopped and Musa ordered six men to run ahead and find out what the commotion was. They ran down and around the slight curve. No sooner had they disappeared than they heard a high-pitched roar accompanied by a low growl that reverberated down the hall. Five men came running back with looks of horror on their faces.

One was yelling, "RUN! RUN! RUN!" as he clawed to stay ahead of his comrades.

Before anyone could react, two beasts from below in the darkened dungeon came rushing around the bend dragging the sixth man, or what was left of him. They flung him around, using him as a bludgeon, hitting a few, before pouncing into the mass of men.

The hoodwinked man was the first to be hit by the giant's swing. He was flung against the wall nearby and fell to the ground with a thud. The hood fell off as he slowly stood up and mustered a few words that made no sense.

"Vlulor! Flagor! Stop! It's me!" the man screamed as the giant picked him up and pummeled him with a fist and threw him to the side like a rag doll. As he landed in a heap he was impaled by a broken chair through his stomach. This man whether alive or dead, was now unconscious.

The beast turned his rage onto the next. By this time, each giant beast had been cut and slashed, but it didn't seem to make a difference. The chaos was thick in the air as each man turned to run for his own life. The looks of fear had turned each man into a scurrying rat, compared to the pair of monsters who began to grab whoever they could with their long reach.

David, in the chaos, had managed to muster a few of his men. The rest were either cut off or had run with the other soldiers. Most of the men they had rescued had been lost. At this point there was no telling how many, if any, still lived. But they had managed to put some distance between the giants who were finishing off those that were not lucky enough to escape the carnage.

He had picked up a sword and shield from the ground and he saw that the three men with him had managed to grab what they could. One had a spear. The other two had a sword each.

Where was Jeroboam? David did a quick scan for him and feared the worst of not seeing him. They stopped at the interchange before heading back to the stables once again and David waited for a few moments. He could barely hear but it sounded like the giants below had quieted and he couldn't decide if that was a good thing.

Just as he was about to give up, he saw a man limping up the ramp with another on his arm. Behind him were two others carrying a man apiece on their shoulders. As they neared, he saw Jeroboam, bloodied but no worse for the wear. He was helping one of the captives walk, or they were helping him. Either way, they were supporting each other's weight.

The other two seemed no worse with only cuts and scrapes. One carried himself like he had a broken rib or two. David and the others rushed forward to help them as he took his outer garment off and tore strips of fabric from it. The others were not in the best shape, but they could still move well enough. He motioned for the two that had escaped with him to grab Jeroboam and the others and help them along.

"Let's move." David said. He waited for them to exit down the hall to the stables before he followed. He heard a roar in the distance and knew they didn't have very long.

As they entered the stables, he felt the pace quicken. The only way to survive was to make it to the caves. Though, in their current condition, survival was in doubt.

A set of roars and screams coming from the beasts echoed through the stable. They were close now and it was plain that they were not going to make it.

"Keep going!" he ordered.

David started to lag and allowed the men to put some distance between him and them, hoping that none would look back and see him. When sufficient distance had come between them he stopped completely in the center of the long and wide corridor with stables on each side. David still had a sword and shield and he had his sling. The group by this point was over fifty yards away from him, nearly to the end of the stables when one of the beasts, covered in blood and entrails burst through the doors, frothing at the maw. For whatever reason, only one of the beasts had pursued them.

David counted it a blessing that he may only have to face one of these mindless giants at a time; two would've been tricky.

"Keep going! I need to buy you some time. Keep going!" He repeated. "That's an order!"

"David, no!" Jeroboam protested, starting to return to him.

"Jeroboam! Go! Save as many as you can." David yelled, not looking back as the beast closed the distance.

Jeroboam, seeing the beast hurtling down the open stable, saluted David before turning and fleeing with the other men carrying the captives on their shoulders.

There was not a single thing they could do since he was so far away, and the beast was hurling itself at him at a blinding speed. David didn't have the luxury to look back at his men as they fled. Instead, he focused on the attacker. Dropping his shield, David grabbed a stone and placed it in his sling. He needed to wait till they were within kill distance.

He assumed a defensive stance and dug his left toe into the dirt a bit. The key to accuracy and power was in use of his whole body, not just the speed of the swing. He swung the sling in front of his body in a figure eight motion, calm and steady. It was surprisingly difficult to judge the target due to the uniquely uneven way of running, almost a hop and crawl at the same time, upright for a few steps, then on both hands and feet the next.

As soon as he found his target, he effortlessly increased the speed of his swing and let a stone fly. The first stone hit it in the throat, and it appeared to hurt enough to slow it, but it was still moving ahead. He loaded and fired another stone and missed. Another and another failed to find its mark with any effect. Each stone was only a few seconds apart from the former. David had one final stone, the smooth one that he kept for himself. Without time to think he loaded into the sling and prepared to throw. He had only about five seconds before he would need to grab his sword and shield for close combat.

David calmed himself and began to swing in the same figure eight motion in front of him. One rotation. Two rotations. And on the third he accelerated and let the stone fly with an overhand motion. It flew with great speed and smacked into the single eye of the giant, causing it to fall backwards, grabbing at its face and stopping its advance, being visibly in pain. The beast knelt on the ground at this point trying to remove the stone from the eye with little success; blood began to stream onto the dirt from the laceration the stone caused.

David wasted no time. He grabbed up the weapons and charged with a battle cry and guttural scream that came from deep down. This seemed to surprise the giant a bit who shrieked and backed up in a defensive posture, temporarily forgetting its grave injury. David rushed forward as he could tell the giant's eyesight was impaired now but the beast didn't seem to rely on its eyesight in the first place, being from a dark and dreary dungeon where it had resided for its life. Instead the giant smelled the air as one would a cooking aroma.

Catching David's scent, the giant swiped at him with surprising accuracy. David rolled to the left and ran as fast as he could around the back side of the giant. The giant turned to meet him, using his peaked sense of hearing to locate him once again.

Again, the beast adeptly reached for David and was able to grab the shield, pummeling it with its fists before deciding to relieve David of it, tossing it across the stables like a toy disc.

David changed tactics as his bones ached from the barrage. He would circle around and try to find a way inside to damage the beast. After a few tries and evasions from the attack of the beast, David backed up a few cubits and then rushed in wildly, sliding on the dirt beneath the foe. As he slid under and through, he sliced one of the hamstrings deeply, causing the giant to fall to one knee and cry out in pain. It could no longer stand as its powerful leg had been disabled. David stood behind and kicked the kneeling giant in between his shoulders causing the giant to fall forward onto his forearms; then, stepped around rapidly to the side and, in one fell swoop, severed the head from its shoulders.

As his sword followed through, the massive frame of the giant slumped over and fell unceremoniously to the sandy ground. Walking over to the giant's head, which was a good distance from the body, he knelt to pick it up to look at the single eye in the center of the forehead.

What form of human beast is this? David thought before nearly dropping the head as black smoke billowed from the mouth, ears and eye of the head. The smoke dispersed almost immediately and dissapeared into the ether. He remembered seeing something of the sort back when he'd slew Goliath and now it felt familiar as he felt a shiver through his spine, remembering the words of the being that spoke to him down below. *You cannot escape you own Shadow. Murderer.*

Are these two instances related? David wondered, as he looked back to where Jeroboam and others had been and noticed they were no longer there. Suddenly he was aware of a presence behind him that was not there before. As he turned, he heard applause coming from behind.

"The mighty David of Israel." King Adonizedek chuckled.

David had no time to reply, as he saw King Adonizedek standing over the body of the beheaded monster. David was about to turn back and run toward the cavern as a club from an unseen assailant met his skull.

———◇———

Meanwhile below...

Ahmet fell in and out of consciousness, barely understanding that he was being carried, however clumsily. A moment passed and he opened his eyes, recognizing the female beast, Vlulor. He muttered her name weakly before passing out again from the stabbing pain.

Sometime later, he woke to Vlulor holding him as a mother would an infant. Her rank breath filled his nostrils, causing him to feel nauseous. Ahmet could tell he was dying as he became aware of his grave injuries at the hands of the beasts. As he craned his neck, he managed to determine that she had brought him to the lair just outside the temple entrance.

"Vlulor, put me down." he said weakly, barely able to speak. Vlulor grunted and shook her head before looking at him expectantly. Ahmet cursed his luck as the beast chose this moment to require politeness. He'd worked with both of them to be more amiable when asking for things and had even taught them a hand signal that meant 'Please'. This was confirmed as the giant clumsily mimed the word with her three-clawed hands.

"Please, Vlulor." He breathlessly pleaded.

This time she complied and gently placed him on the ground. It was then that he became more aware of the painful nature of his injuries and that his life was waning with each passing second. Vlulor nudged him awake once again, the look of grave concern on her face for a moment. Her attention was drawn to a noise down the corridor and Vlulor became tense as she bounded on all fours to the edge of her lair. Seconds later Vlulor stood up and ran into the darkness towards whatever sound she heard, roaring and grunting all the way.

The lair fell quiet as Ahmet was left alone. *What a sad ending to a tragic life,* Ahmet thought as he cycled in and out of lucid thoughts and visions of his wife and son Nathan.

Nathan...Ramah..., he thought as he reached out for their visage only to have it replaced by black smoke and disappear.

Come to me Ahmet...Come to the altar, a voice said in a low growl, almost a whisper.

Ahmet couldn't grasp the words long enough to respond before he fell towards oblivion once again.

This time, he was jolted awake by the sound of Ramah's voice. *Ahmet, please. Go to the altar, it is the only way to restore your family to you. Go! Don't delay!*

"Ramah," Ahmet said audibly as he reached for her and rolled over to his stomach. Her visage stood several paces away and every time he pulled himself toward her, the visage would move to a place a little further away.

Ramah kept encouraging him. *Keep going Ahmet, you must reach the altar. Your blood is the Key to your salvation. Give Tsalmaveth your blood.*

"Ramah, the pain. Its...too...much...I...can't", Ahmet cried as he started to lose himself again.

Wake up father! Wake up! Suddenly, the voice of a boy filled Ahmet's mind.

Nathan? Nathan! Ahmet opened his eyes once again to see his son standing next to Ramah, just out of reach.

You have to fight father. If you want to avenge me, you must fight. Come to the altar, father.

With renewed energy, Ahmet crawled on his stomach; blood leaving a smeared trail behind him.

Just a little further, he told himself, as the pain returned through a wave of nausea.

That's it, father, keep fighting. Nathan coaxed Ahmet on with each pull.

Ahmet was in so much pain that he nearly passed out several times more; but each time, Nathan and Ramah were there to encourage him.

Just a little further, Ahmet thought as he reached out for his family.

Nathan...Ramah...help me, he thought, pulling himself closer to the altar.

Finally, Ahmet crawled up a set of stairs into the temple where he'd witnessed the rituals time and again in secret and in the course of his duties as Lox's lackey. This was his only hope now. His son Nathan was dead and, not only his love for his family, but his desire for revenge had given him the strength to crawl here to this place.

Ahmet kept thinking about Ramah standing at the door, only steps away from him, as the soldiers told her of his alleged treachery. It was not Ahmet, but Tsalmaveth who had actually been the one to commit the act, and it seemed like some kind of cruel joke that he was crawling toward the entity that he had just been relieved of hours before, at sunrise.

Ahmet thought about hearing the guards talking about the boy in the house who had just passed away. He had failed Nathan and Ramah yet again; it was too much to bear.

As he came upon the brazen altar, he looked at the stone at its base and saw the word TSALMAVETH traced in dried blood. Twelve Shades dressed in black cloaks appeared from their hiding places behind the angelic statues. They surrounded him as he crawled up to the altar.

Ahmet cried out with as much fervor as he could muster, "Oh Luminous God who commands Darkness and Light. Your servant is here, in need of your salvation!"

Ahmet had witnessed the ritual a dozen times, but he was just guessing at the words as the waves of pain started dissipating and a cold numbness washed over him. He'd never really taken the time to memorize the words. His only hope was that his plea would be answered regardless.

Ahmet managed to pull the lever under the altar that opened a door. Inside was where the stone box was kept, but upon opening it, he realized the box was gone.

It's...not...here, Ahmet thought, all hope fleeing at that moment. He needed Tsalmaveth, to save him.

The Shade at the head of the altar stood there stoically as a roar of laughter came from behind it in the direction of the image of Yaldabaoth.

Tsalmaveth swirled about in his incorporeal humanoid form, shouting with glee. "And here he is, just as planned! Well Ahmet, what do you have to say to me?"

Ahmet pleaded, making up words as they came to him, "I am here of my own free will, to offer up my life to you, to use as you see fit. Make me your

Shadow. Let me live in death to serve you for eternity when you come to rule the earth and all men."

He used his own blood to trace the word on the stone. Ahmet struggled to speak as he mumbled the words, his strength waning with each second that passed.

"I give my whole being to you," Ahmet said weakly before sitting back against the altar, waiting for something to happen.

But nothing happened. There was no help on the way. No salvation. Ahmet drew in a deep syncopated breath, and as he exhaled, he knew he would die. Death was the common thread that connected all men.

I'm sorry Ramah. I'm so sorry Nathan. I tried. Darkness filled his eyes as he drifted off into final oblivion. No visions, no lights, no afterlife waited for him on the other side.

Ahmet, the tragic soul, who could not get out of his own way, exhaled one final raspy breath that trailed off into an abrupt silence.

<hr />

Later that day...

For six hours, Ahmet's cold body lay. Surrounding him were the twelve Shades, standing like statues all the while. A pulsing frequency cycled in and out from the center of the room, too low for the average man to discern.

"The time has come. His body is ready for me." Tsalmaveth said triumphantly as he swirled around above the altar, smoke filling the room by way of the walls and hanging low on the floor. The smoke wormed its way like fingers across the floor toward the center of the room. Three Shades picked up Ahmet's cold body and placed it atop the altar and returned to their stations.

The room began to tremble in a low discordant frequency, and Ahmet's lifeless body began to contort and convulse until his body went straight as a timber.

Ahmet's body began to levitate until he was floating above the brazen altar, and the room filled with a choking black smoke that twirled like a dancing dervish, around the altar. Once all the smoke had collected into the whirlwind, a pair of arms grasped Ahmet and stood his rigor-mortised body on its feet, while a faceless creature's head protruded from the smoke.

The rumble began to rise in frequency until it became a fevered pitch of a throbbing heartbeat about to burst from the strain. The room began to quake with the vibration, and dust began to fall. Just as the room seemed like it was going to come apart at the seams, the figure opened its vacuous mouth, and a long tail of smoke came out in the shape of a long, forked tongue. It extended itself toward Ahmet's body and entered his nostrils. Ahmet's eyes popped open as wide as they could without leaving his skull entirely. He was suddenly aware that he was alive, evidenced by the searing pain that ripped through his body like a torrent and settled into his bones like a hot pitch. This experience was nothing like the possession that had taken place just yesterday. This wasn't a possession; it was an indwelling. Tsalmaveth was moving in and taking up the space in every part of his body.

The tongue of smoke continued to enter his body, now through his eyes, ears, throat and by any means necessary. It gathered speed, as the smoke twirled in a tighter spiral, until it centered into a single column above Ahmet and focused the tendrils on his throat.

Through bloodshot eyes, Ahmet watched in horror as the smoke instantly entered his body like a punch in the gut. He couldn't breathe as the space within him filled from the top of his head to the tips of his toes. Ahmet felt the sensation of another body within his own trying to make room for itself, as his own limbs began to flex one by one, then going stiff again. Then, searing heat entered his body and burned its way through his bones until it felt as though he would spontaneously combust. Ahmet's only thought now was that he wanted it to end. He wished he would die right here and now and be done with this torture.

"Oh, the plans I have for you, human," a voice within burst forth in a low guttural tone. Ahmet could only scream. In his mind he intended it to sound like a scream of agony but all he heard was sinister laughter.

His feet came to rest on the cold stone floor at the foot of the brazen altar; the pain had all but subsided now, and he couldn't quite figure out if he was in his own body or just barely hanging on to it from the outside. It was a peculiar feeling.

A voice spoke into his mind. "You are mine now, you are now Tsalmaveth."

As soon as Ahmet heard the voice he fainted and fell to the temple floor in a heap. He was just barely hanging on to consciousness as he muttered words he had never thought.

"I have become Death's Shadow. I am Tsalmaveth."

And then he fell into the abyss of darkness.

CHAPTER 15

The Israelite Siege Camp

I t was well into the late evening when the guards came into the tent carrying bread and water. Sabbath had ended according to Jonathan, and he explained that they would bring in more food and drink.

Finally, Thoros thought.

Earlier in the day, the guards had come into the tent and rearranged the bonds so that his hands were in front of his body. Thoros couldn't move very far but at least when they handed him a loaf of bread, he could manage to reach his own mouth. He'd give a left leg for a skin of wine, but he was happy to have the water they provided.

Thoros was so thirsty he could drain the whole sea if given an opportunity. He silently chuckled at his over-exaggerations. A few days sitting on his rump with his hands bound behind him had apparently caused him to think in sensational terms.

The guards had been in a few times during the day, mostly to check on Jonathan, who sat across from him. He noticed that their apprehension with him being nearby had subsided a bit; at least to the point where they didn't shake in fear or move erratically about the tent.

A few moments later, Joab entered the tent and walked over to Jonathan. He knelt and spoke in hushed tones. They were only a couple of feet away, but he couldn't make out many words. Thoros was curious what they were up to. With the little information he had Thoros was able to deduce that much of the camp was on David's side, including Jonathan.

Apparently, Joab the commander was as well. That spelled rebellion in every language of the twenty he could speak. This David fellow must be quite the leader for King Saul's own son to be in league with him. That, or King Saul was simply a terrible leader. In any case, they had no trouble conquering the whole of Canaan which, to Thoros, meant they were against King Saul for another reason. He had heard rumors of King

Saul's mental frailness and disobedience to his own god. This had been on display yesterday when he'd been so easily turned inside out by a helpless man tied up at his feet. They really did put a lot of trust in this god of theirs.

Rightly so, he supposed it had served them well by all accounts. Thoros strained harder as he saw Jonathan nodding his head in agreement to what Joab was saying.

Thoros couldn't make out the whole of it, but it sounded as if Joab had said, "We are ready."

Ready for what? Thoros thought, as they continued their conversation, he ran through the possibilities: *Ready for his execution? Ready to take the city? Ready to overthrow King Saul?* He couldn't really pinpoint the meaning.

There was the fact that Jonathan, son of King Saul was a prisoner of his father's, and that Jonathan was indeed loyal to David as the future king of Israel. Though Jonathan didn't seem like the type to commit treason against his own father. At least not from the limited conversation they had with each other over the last day since Jonathan was confined here.

What was plain to Thoros was that the commander of the Israelite forces was taking the time to discuss plans with someone who was on the outs with the King of Israel. This meant that the most likely options of topic were either Thoros' execution or their eventual treason against King Saul.

If they were ready to take the city, then his execution was imminent. If they were ready to attempt an overthrow of King Saul, then his execution would also be imminent, if they failed. Of course, he could be completely off base with his conjecture and deductions.

From what Thoros gathered in eavesdropping on the conversation, it seemed that Jonathan was not keen on his father's order to kill their captive, but he couldn't be sure. He assumed Jonathan's aversion to it was tied to David. But where was David? He was chief commander over all the armies of Israel throughout Canaan, yet he hadn't shown himself since the other day when King Saul had lost his temper.

Thoros remembered David talking about using him to ransom the prisoners, and then King Saul threatened to kill him after an ill-advised prodding. *That was a mistake,* he thought. Had he known how thin King Saul's skin was, when he jabbed him with his words, Thoros would have chosen a different tactic. He now wondered what kind of things he set in motion with this mistake. *My father always told me my mouth would land me in trouble one day,* Thoros thought before turning his attention on the current state of affairs.

With no sign of David for an entire day, and King Saul's own son tied up like a prisoner of war, it can only meant one thing, as Thoros reasoned it; *David was on the outs with King Saul as well. If I had to guess, I would say that David was no longer in the camp,* Thoros marveled at how he was able to make so many deductions from the words "we are ready." However, the realization of what those words meant overshadowed his own pride.

"Excuse me commander." Thoros chimed in. *Let's see if I'm as smart as I fancy myself,* he thought as he interrupted the pair's conversation.

Joab turned and looked at him and said nothing. The look on the Commander's face showed him that he was waiting for Thoros to make his statement.

"I would like to speak with David. Would you kindly request him to come and talk with me? I have something important to tell him."

Joab glanced to the tent entrance and said, "If you have something to tell him, you can tell me."

"What I have to say is for David, and David alone," Thoros added. The reaction he received was what he had hoped for.

"Again. Tell me," Joab repeated.

I was correct, David is no longer in the camp, Thoros thought, not taking time to pat himself on the back, figuratively. David not being in the camp meant that the presence of Jonathan as a captive was in relation to David leaving the camp. The question was whether it had anything to do with him. He also wondered what David was now up to as he thought of the caverns and that blasted tunnel that Lox had failed to reveal to anyone.

"I'll wait for David." He looked away signaling that he was done with his request, and Joab went back to talking to Jonathan.

Jonathan shook his head in disbelief as Joab relayed more information. "He's gone mad," Jonathan said a little too loud as Joab cautioned him to speak in a lower volume. Thoros could see he wasn't getting any more out of Joab; not that he gained anything much from his few words anyhow. Thoros assumed that Jonathan only meant King Saul's mental state.

The pair continued their hushed conversation for a few minutes longer until Joab arose to leave, giving him a glance as he passed by to exit the tent. Jonathan sat there with his head leaned back on the tent post, looking up at the canvas roof. It had begun to rain briefly, for the first time in what seemed like months, and the water droplets smacked the parched canvas with a loud popping sound.

Thoros was a believer in omens. There was no thunder or lightning so far, which meant that the attention of the gods was favorable. A light soaking rain began for the next several minutes. He could see small streams of water running under the tent before being absorbed into the cracked earth that resembled the scales on a lizard's back.

He decided this meant good things, so he leaned forward slightly and with a softer voice said, "Finally some rain to fill the cisterns..."

Jonathan didn't look his way but simply said, "It's been a long hot season."

Thoros replied, "I remember one year where not a single drop of rain fell in Canaan. It was the year before your people invaded with your armies. The major cities had barely recovered their grain stores."

He said this knowing how connected talking about the weather was to omens and predictions. It could have been seen as a warning to ready themselves for the coming Hebrew invasion; the benefit of hindsight being what it was. Perhaps he should have asked Skald to cast the bones and tell him of his impending capture.

Thoros laughed at himself. *Ah! Who am I kidding? Skald would have spun me a riddle about fish walking on land or something.* It was then that the words of Skald made their circle back to him. *I see a Prince in captivity,* he recalled, now realizing he may need to rethink his outlook on things should he somehow find a way out of this. Skald knew things and Thoros didn't know how, but that crazy old coot somehow had the pulse of things.

The rain began to fall harder and harder and another thought came to mind regarding how connected the weather was to the Hebrew god acting. Stories about the Great Flood millennia ago had roots in the god of Israel and the near East.

The key to knowing what to see in the rain was determined by the wind, thunder, lightning, the conditions before the rain, the intensity of the downpour and for how long. For instance, a light soaking rain that sustained for a whole morning was seen as a good omen in most every way. The priests would cast bones and ask questions during this time and report what the gods were saying. If the rain lasted for days or weeks on end, however, it was seen as an omen for terrible things coming such as famine, in which case, preparations were made. The absence of rain for a long drought, would be considered a punishment from the gods which would require sacrifice and blood to propitiate the wrath. If a sudden rainstorm popped up with thunder and lightning it would be seen as a message or warning from the gods not to do something or, in some cases, to do something. He chuckled at the mental distortion of this and occasionally wondered what, if any, real implication the weather had on their fates. Of course, he didn't wonder enough to do away with the superstition of it altogether.

Just as he began to think of the situation at hand, he saw a flash of light and a loud cracking sound. This was followed by a rolling thunder that lasted for what seemed like several minutes. Multiple flashes could be seen, accompanied by thunder rolling across the landscape from further away. He learned as a boy that the time between the flash and the thunder told him how many leagues away the worst part of the storm was from him. It seemed now that he was in the worst part of it.

The storm clouds had darkened the skies to the point that the lighting in the tent was insufficient with the lanterns. As the wind blew it caused the flaps of the tent to rise and fall and the tethers strained under the force of the gale. Hopefully, the tent would hold up in what seemed to be a fast-moving storm.

Jonathan looked his way finally. Thoros credited him as a handsome man in his own right, with gray hair running through his beard and hair. Even sitting down, he could see that he was lean and muscled like a warrior accustomed to swift movement in battle. He had heard stories of Jonathan even before David appeared in the conversation at state meetings.

"Is it true you and your shield bearer climbed a cliff and killed one thousand sleeping Philistines?" Thoros asked.

"Ten." Jonathan said.

Thoros blinked at him, not understanding.

"Ten thousand died that night. Most by their own hands in the chaos." Jonathan clarified.

Thoros was actually impressed. He was a legendary warrior himself, but he never could have imagined that an enemy of this caliber would be tied up as a captive in the same tent.

"Many ran off the cliff and fell to their deaths in the darkness and confusion. I helped along as many as I was able." He said in a sort of, matter of fact, type way.

"I heard from the Philistines that they believed an entire army was attacking from the panic you and your man caused."

Thoros loved to hear stories of defeat from the mouths of those defeated. A man learns a lot from defeat.

Thoros continued. "Tell me prince, did you ever expect to be placed under arrest by your own father."

Jonathan stared blankly. Then replied flatly, "It was only a matter of time I suppose."

"Why is David no longer in the camp?" Thoros decided to get to the crux of his questioning.

Jonathan betrayed surprise and smiled. "What makes you think he isn't in the camp?"

"Come now. I know a pair of brothers such as you would never allow the other to be tied up and held as captive if the other were still around. He is gone. The question is where?"

"Wouldn't you like to know? For the sake of argument and realizing we are both likely to die tomorrow let it suffice to say that David is doing what he feels he must do."

Thoros grimaced. *Tomorrow then?*

This was not the response he wanted to hear, but at least he could stop wondering. He could tell that the rain had subsided, the thunder rolling in from far away, quieter now. Thoros and Jonathan both bantered back and forth for several hours sharing war stories. Thoros was surprised to hear Jonathan corroborate many of his own versions of the stories he'd heard tell in the court and around the city for years. If circumstances were different, he may have liked to form a friendship with the man and even train with him. Thoros had the idea that he could learn a lot from a man such as this.

It was well past midnight before they decided to try and get some sleep. It was very dimly lit inside the tent from the lantern at the entrance. No sooner had Thoros shut his eyes, than he could hear a commotion out in the camp. Something was happening. Jonathan looked about, and his eyes were drawn to the side of the tent behind Thoros.

Thoros tried to crane his neck to see what he was looking at but couldn't quite make out what Jonathan was seeing. But the look on Prince Jonathan's face was wide-eyed and urgent.

"What are you doing?" Jonathan said excitedly as a figure limped across Thoros' peripheral. He could smell the sulfur and unwashed stench coming from the man, resembling the mystery visitor they'd had the night before. The shadowy figure produced a strip of leather and wrapped it around Jonathan's neck from behind the tent post and began to squeeze and choke him. Thoros saw panic fill the eyes of Jonathan as his face began to turn purple. Jonathan was bound and there was nothing he could do to defend himself as the assailant unemotionally squeezed the life out of him.

Suddenly, Jonathan's hands were freed, and he forcibly stood up even as his ankles were bound; apparently the guards had deliberately done a poor job at tying him up. He grabbed at the hands of his attacker and finding no purchase decided to throw his body forward causing the attacker to lose grip on the strap as Jonathan hurtled forward and nearly fell into Thoros' lap.

The attacker dove wildly onto Jonathan and they began to struggle at Thoros' feet. Jonathan was now on his back deflecting blows from the frothing attacker who surprisingly made extraordinarily little noise apart from heavy breathing and the occasional grunting sound. The look on his face was filled with rage, almost a type of hunger, fueled by madness. The attacker grabbed Jonathan's hands and bit down on the side of his wrist, pulling a chunk of skin from the forearm.

Jonathan grimaced in pain but continued to try and land blows on the attacker from his back, even as blood ran down his arms from the bite wound. His ankles had somehow come untied in the struggle and he was able to free his right leg from the restraints, allowing him to bring his knees between the attacker. Then he placed his right forearm against the man's collar and his left hand gripped his black sleeve. In one fluid motion he kicked his right leg up and over his opponent and pulled down on the sleeve. The man flipped right into Thoros' lap with a dull thud, losing his wind as he tried to regain the advantage. Jonathan, with his other foot tangled in the rope, was too slow to capitalize on this reversal and the man began to scamper from Thoros' lap. Thoros acted without thinking, as the attacker was halted by a large hand grabbing at his cloak tightly, stopping him cold.

Thoros pulled the man toward him with his hands, bound together at the wrists, and managed to throw his arms up and around the man. It looked as though a man was hugging a child. Thoros squeezed the man harder than he had ever squeezed anything. He felt a struggle for a while until he heard bones cracking in the torso causing the man to inhale quickly. The man struggled for a moment longer but in the grasp of Thoros, it was no use. After a long minute, the man fell limp, and the struggle ended. Thoros realized he was holding his breath as well and it was all he could do to exhale and release the lifeless man from his deadly embrace.

The man fell to the side of him, thoroughly crushed and expired. The adrenaline, coursing through his veins, gave him a rush of strength. He hadn't killed a man in a close struggle like this in a very long time and Thoros suddenly realized he had the strength to free himself as he twisted his wrists in opposite directions causing the ropes to stretch enough to slip his bonds, the adrenaline ran through his veins like lightning. Once his hands were free, he was able to break the ropes that tied his torso to the tent post. Thoros made short work of the ankle bonds and quickly rose. Jonathan was still recovering from being choked and bitten and in a matter of seconds Thoros was free.

He took a single step towards the exit and realized he was falling. It wasn't until his face planted into the newly muddied ground that he realized both of his legs were totally asleep due to sitting on his rump for days. The searing tingle began to creep down each leg as ample supplies of blood rushed through. He suddenly felt like the world was spinning as the adrenaline began to dissipate into the extremities of his legs. All he could do was roll to his back and begin to sit up. He would crawl if he had to. His stomach sank as he was met with a sword to his gullet.

"Not another movement or I'll run you through," Joab said as he pressed in. Thoros relaxed his tense posture showing that he was not intending on fighting; not that he could anyhow. Seconds later, a half dozen of Joab's men were surrounding Thoros. Joab went to check on Jonathan, who was just now rising to his feet. Jonathan had torn a cloth from his cloak and wrapped his forearm and was gently rubbing his neck which had pronounced ligature marks from being strangled; heavy bruising would surely follow. Joab turned the dead man over and visibly reacted to what he saw, stepping back a pace or two in shock.

"This is one of the men that David and you rescued, Jonathan." Joab shouted and then quickly hushed himself. Jonathan knelt and got a closer look at the man who, in the dim light, looked more like a creature than a man. Outside they could hear shouts and screams and chaos.

Joab seemed as though he was putting a riddle together that he was now moments from solving. "There have been attacks tonight as soon as night fell. That storm hit and during it hundreds were killed or maimed. Not a single culprit has been caught. Apart from this one," he said, motioning to the dead man at their feet.

Joab added, "The attacks are still ongoing without any ability for us to predict. They are like shadows, only visible with light at your back. As soon as you shine a torch they are gone. There must be hundreds of them."

Jonathan replied with a raspy voice, "He came out of nowhere, this was one of the ones that had his tongue removed. Where are the rest of the men?"

Joab shrugged, "All gone except this one. The rest of the twelve we rescued are nowhere to be found. We had begun to investigate when all hell broke loose. The panic alone caused many injuries and death. My first thought was to come here and check on you, Jonathan."

Thoros' legs were starting to tingle in a painful way as he could feel the blood returning to them. He listened as Jonathan and Joab talked. The men that Lox had tortured had attacked their own people. He could hardly begin to believe it, but as he thought about it more, he had seen stranger things come from some of Lox's schemes. Lox seemed to be plagued by unintended consequences of the things he set in motion; it could be that this was but one example.

Thoros had a tough time thinking this was his plan all along but without Lox here to divulge it he could only guess using what he saw. In any case, this man that attacked was clearly in a different state of mind. The rotten smell that overwhelmed the room was a different curiosity altogether.

"I don't suppose we can get the dead man out of here?" Thoros asked rather bluntly, the smell of sulfur on the body near him causing him to wretch.

Joab didn't seem to notice the smell, or if he did, he didn't show it. He took two steps around the side and stood just out of arm's reach of Thoros. Joab began to size him up from the expression on his face. It was notable that they hadn't bothered to tie him back up yet, but rather, several guards stood nearby in an aggressive posture, pointing their spears at the small of his back. As he lay there on his stomach, Thoros thought that maybe they were trying to find stronger bonds since he had defeated the ropes a few moments ago.

Joab, without saying a word to Thoros, motioned for two guards to pick up the deceased attacker and remove him from the tent. He then turned his attention to Thoros.

"And WHAT is your part in this?" Joab jabbed at Thoros who appeared nonplussed at the accusation.

Jonathan spoke up, "Joab, this man is the reason I am unharmed. His actions just now saved my life."

"Well, we aren't taking any chances. I need to go check on your father and try and bring some order out there. I'm leaving a few guards here to watch this tent. I'll be back before too long, and we can discuss what to do about our other problem." As he left, the guards helped Thoros sit up and get out of the mud that had formed by the storm runoff. Joab bowed to Jonathan and quickly left with several men following close behind.

Other problem? Thoros guessed that was related to David and King Saul and whatever role he played in this whole debacle. For now, he was left untied, which was a welcome thing after more than two days of captivity. Not two minutes later Joab came running back into the tent in a frenzied panic. No guards were with him.

"My prince, did this giant really save your life as you say?" Joab asked hastily as Jonathan confirmed with a nod. He was confused at the quick entrance and subsequent question.

Joab took a few seconds, clearly torn between decisions. Finally, he went over to the back of the tent and, using his sword sliced the canvas wall from top to bottom. He ran back over to Thoros.

"How are your legs, can you walk?" he asked.

Thoros, hesitated then answered, "I can walk."

"Then go!" He motioned to the newly made door, "Don't wait! King Saul and his men are on the way to kill you. They think this was your own doing, but David would want me to repay you for saving Jonathan's life tonight."

Thoros was dumbfounded at this turn of events. He was not one to look the gift horse in the mouth, so he rose to one knee and, crouching low, walked to the back of the tent and ducked through the opening that the Commander had opened.

"Do not stop until you are far away from this camp. If you are caught, I will deny any involvement. If you enter the city, I will not guarantee your safety when we take it from you. Consider your good deed repaid."

"Thank you" was all Thoros could think to say as he turned and bounded through the dark camp.

As he ran, he could hear Joab shouting, "He's gone! He must have escaped!" He didn't look back to see if any pursued him, but he assumed they had.

The wet ground from the evening rain left tracks that any imbecile could follow. He needed to find a way to lose them. He ran to the edge of the camp and was surprised that he hadn't seen a single person. They must've all run to the center of the camp fearing being exposed to whatever attacks were coming. All the better he supposed. He looked at Jebus and the scant fires burning throughout the city and quickly decided that he would indeed try to reenter the city. Thoros could climb the walls easily enough and he knew them well.

It was about a twenty min walk to the main gate up a main road, but decided not to take the main road, figuring that whoever pursued him would assume he went towards the city. Instead, he chose a tougher route through and over boulders and uneven ground. He had the thought that maybe this would cover his tracks better if anything. It was rather dark with very little light showing through an overcast sky, so he had to take care not to stumble and slip. The last thing Thoros needed was to injure himself and get caught as a result.

As Thoros leapt over a boulder he came to an area where he saw catapults and other contraptions jutting up into the sky. From cover, he spied on the camp and determined that this must be the siege engine camp. He suddenly realized that this would usually be under heavy guard but as he entered, he saw not a single soul; only a few smoldering, low-burning fires with several tents ran down the row for fifty yards or so.

Thoros crept up to one of the tents and peered in. What he saw made him wretch for a second time tonight. The whole tent was covered top to bottom in blood and human body parts though no single bodies were recognizable as such. He quickly withdrew and tripped over a pile of wood and nearly fell into a bed of coals from a dying campfire. Luckily, he was able to recover his balance and went quickly to the next tent. This time he was ready for it and discovered that, like the first, the inhabitants had been brutally killed and from the look of it, eaten.

Was this from lions or bears maybe? Another thought crossed his mind, but he realized he'd rather that it be lions or bears.

The next few tents were the same. Not a single soul was alive in this small camp. He realized he was spending too much time on this and decided he had better vacate before King Saul's men came here and tried to blame this atrocity on him also. Then it dawned on him that an opportunity was presented to him just now. He went to the middle of the camp and found several casks of oil which they used to ignite projectiles that were soon to be hurled into the city proper of Jebus. One by one he doused each siege weapon with oil. Then, he made a torch and lit each one on fire.

Thoros retreated from the blaze and admired his handiwork and felt somewhat guilty that he had repaid Joab's deed with destroying every siege weapon the Israelites had, but when he thought about how much time that may buy his father and people of Jebus, he felt satisfied. The Israelites would have to spend days and even weeks on end collecting and hewing wood to build new weapons.

Thoros would need to move quicker now that he had basically lit a beacon for the Israelite army to come right to him. The wall wasn't far now but as he rounded a bend in a narrow path a rather pungent odor made its way into his nostril. This made his hair stand up on his neck as he realized that this was a familiar smell from earlier.

He looked up into the sky for a solitary moment, and through flashes of lighting he could see the clouds above roiling about, ready to let loose their ocean of water at any moment. The darkness was tempered only by the fire of the siegeworks that had already began to die down as the wood fuel quickly burned.

Thoros was hardly able to see if anything came near and his heart began to race when he saw a dark figure move in his peripheral. He quickened his pace as he saw the wall looming ahead, not more than five hundred cubits away. Thoros stopped short and gasped audibly, being startled as three figures appeared on the trail ahead of him. Thoros changed into a defensive stance and picked up a rock that sat nearby, not taking his eyes off the figures before him. The wind picked up from behind and he smelled rotted flesh and feces. From behind he heard a chorus of heavy breathing almost as soon as the smell arrived.

Thoros didn't have to look to know he was surrounded. These were Lox's pets. His own experiment from deep in his lair and from what he could tell these beasts had no loyalty to him, being the brother of Lox. They probably had no loyalty to Lox either. They were about one purpose now...death.

Resigned to do battle with however many of these creatures presented themselves, Thoros let out a roar that shook the boulders around him. He rushed in quickly to close the distance between them and him. The three before him stood their ground in an almost stoic fashion, betraying neither fear nor anxiety toward their impending doom. A flash of lightning lit up the dark area like daylight as he was able to see the contorted looks on the creature's faces, unfazed by the rain that was just now beginning to resume, pelting the ground with great velocity.

The space between them closed quickly as Thoros raised his bludgeon to strike. Bringing the first stone down toward the frozen statue before him, his focus was on the middle one. But as he followed through his blow caught only wind and he nearly fell face first into the dirt. The three men were no longer in front of him. Then all at once he was set upon by several of them. They began biting and tearing and landing blows upon him. He fought back ferociously but every time he hit one another was on him. Thoros pulled one from his back and threw the creature to the side while kicking another in the torso, sending it flying.

Soon It seemed like he was buried in them to the point that he would eventually be overcome. They did not seem to tire, and they felt no pain. But he knew they could be killed. Just an hour ago he had strangled one in the tent where he was held captive.

With one last effort Thoros stood to his feet and grabbed the head and neck of the closest one and twisted with all his might. The beast fell limp and fell to the ground motionless. The others seemed to have backed off to a safer distance and then began charging in at random only to be repelled by Thoros' blows. They were lightning quick, and he was injured in several places from head to toe either from blows or daggers and Thoros' neck was pulsing noticeably from a large gash.

Thoros could feel the hopelessness of this struggle as his strength began to ebb away the moment a dagger planted itself in his chest. He became dizzy and fell to one knee and was able to catch his fall before he was lost. Taking this as their queue the horde closed in at once to finish the kill.

Just as he expected the onslaught, the sun began to show through the storm clouds as the skies began to clear from the southeast. It was at that moment that he heard a horrific horn blast up on the hillside behind. It sounded like the shofar but with a distorted type of chortle added to it, almost as if it came from the throat. It gave him chills to hear it sound. Three blasts of the horn sounded in quick succession.

Following the horn, the attack never came, and suddenly all was silent as he felt the rain subside. Far to the east the sun began to rise causing the sky to glow redder with the passing moment. Every attacker had fled the battle at the sound of the horn. Thoros looked around at the ground on which he had just fought. With the light increasing every second he could see blood. His blood. Lots of it. Too much of it, running down the slight incline of the path like a miniature stream.

Where Thoros was kneeling, a pool had formed and continued to grow slowly as it overcame the sandy ground's ability to absorb the liquid. He knew he was gravely wounded. He had to get to the gates of the city if he was to be saved.

Thoros forced his will to stand up and began to stumble forward toward a wall that, being only five-hundred cubits away might as well have been five-hundred leagues. The distance was too great. As he lumbered forward, he caught a glint of bronze in his eye to his left. He paid it no mind because he had focused all his will into making another step after each step.

Thoros could see the wall, seemingly no closer than when he began moments ago. He could hear his own heartbeat, and he knew that he would die before he ever reached that wall. This knowledge was the second to last thing he thought about as he lost his footing and fell to the ground unconscious. The image of Siv flashed before his eyes standing there with his children, and Baaldir with Vithas accompanied by his mother and father. Just before he closed his eyes to die, he heard a chorus of voices from some direction that didn't matter.

Interlude

Before the conquest of Canaan, 1473 B.C.

M oses climbed, and climbed, over rocks to the summit of Mount Nebo. At the ripe old age of one-hundred and twenty, Moses had only moderate difficulty negotiating the steep grade and challenging climb. Moses was healthy and spry for his age even if his body looked worn down and wrinkled.

In his conversations with Elohim, he'd learned that due to his one instance of disobedience not long ago, he would never bring the nation of Israel into Canaan. Instead, the much younger Joshua would take the mantle from him. Joshua had already been prepared for this day, though Moses couldn't help feeling a little regret that he had not been able to say goodbye to his student who was now nearing sixty years of age.

The disobedience seemed like a trivial matter when it happened. To quench the Israelites thirst in the desert, Elohim had commanded him to speak to a large rock to make water flow from it. Instead, he'd consulted with Aaron, who suggested using his staff to strike the rock instead.

Striking the rock, water gushed forth as it split in half to the rejoicing roar of the Israelite people. The Lord told him to speak to the rock, but Moses and Aaron, being wise in their own eyes, used the rod to show Elohim's power.

Now that years had passed, he understood what that little detail meant. Elohim required anyone who led His favored people in this war waged against the darkness, to obey, in even the smallest detail, without fail or hesitation. His disobedience was tantamount to the leader of Israel saying to the Lord, 'I don't trust you.' Thus, he would not be allowed to step foot into the land of his ancestor, Abraham. It would instead fall to the younger generation of leaders.

That very morning, Michael had appeared to him with instructions.

"Climb to the summit at Pisgah because your time has come. No one can see the place where you will die. On your way place the stone box into the Ark and close it. There it will stay until the appointed time."

He'd obeyed the order as he started his trek in the wee hours of the morning. The Israelite camp was still asleep when he entered the tent that housed the Ark of The Covenant, carrying the stone box to the inner room of the tent. This marked the first time the box housing this evil had been in the presence of the Ark, and thus the presence of The Most High god, Elohim.

One month ago, Aaron had died at Mount Hor and Aaron's son Eleazar, had taken the High Priest mantle from his father that day, and with it the stewardship of this box, which was always kept in a back room of the Tabernacle tent compound. It was concealed within a wooden chest for transport as they wandered the desert for forty years. No man apart from Aaron and Moses had even held the stone box without the close supervision of one of them. The power and influence it had on men was otherworldly. Even Aaron had momentary lapses of judgment in dealing with the artifact. Moses thought back to the brazen calf that the Israelites made while Moses was away on Mount Sinai receiving the Ten Commandments. Upon returning from the Mountain he saw Aaron and the people worshiping the golden calf and he smashed the first set of commandments out of anger. Elohim graciously gave him another set which were put into the Ark for safekeeping. Moses also had trouble resisting the influence and it was a constant battle within him even when he was away from it. After so many years, he'd mastered the feeling, and it now did not bother him.

Eleazar was sleeping at this hour just outside the tent where his Levite priests made their residence. Moses couldn't help but wonder if the reason for placing it in the Ark was to spare the younger generation from the box's influence.

Only Moses was permitted into the tent without a Levite present, and no one save Moses, and the High Priest were allowed into the Holy of Holies unless transporting the Ark, so anyone who may have seen Moses walking into the tent would think nothing of it as it was an almost daily occurrence.

As Moses carried the box, he felt the vibration increase and the heat became nearly unbearable, almost like grabbing a handle of a cooking pan when it had sat on the fire too long. He picked up his pace as he fumbled his fingers around trying not to let any one of them stay in contact with the box surface too long. He placed the box on the floor and watched the vibration move the box ever so slightly.

The Ark had only been opened on a few occasions. It was built about a year after their exodus from Egypt. The first time opening it was to place the stone tablet containing the Ten Commandments, written by Elohim's own hand. The second was to place a bowl of manna into the Ark to remind them that God provided food in the desert these forty years. The third time was to place Aaron's rod inside to preserve the integrity of the almond sprouts that miraculously grew from it, signifying that Aaron and his line would be priests in the House of the Lord forever. The lid was called the 'Mercy Seat', and it weighed quite a bit more than it appeared.

He had to push it to the side just enough to allow the box to pass through. Working quickly, he picked up the stone box and placed it into the Ark, nearly dropping it as his fingertips screamed with searing pain.

As he sealed it up again, he realized how quiet things suddenly were. The dissonant hum of the stone box, and evil it held, dissipated with the closing of the Ark. He had become desensitized to the hum over the years, and it was only when he closed the Ark that he heard what true silence felt like. The trek up to Mount Nebo from the incredibly low plains near the Dead Sea was no small task. The Dead Sea sat well below sea level so that to look at the land of Canaan would be like looking at a range of mountains. As he climbed the mountain, he began to see that the land of Canaan was a plateau that stretched as far as the eye could see. It undulated with hills and valleys and had rivers and bodies of water bigger than any inland lake he had ever seen.

A tear fell upon his cheek as he gazed over the bordering Jordan River that flowed to the ocean. A vast green, lush, fertile plain stretched out before him, and he could see hills and mountains far in the distance. This was as far as he would go but he was grateful to have the chance to at least see it after forty years in the desert. This had been his life for eighty years and everything he'd done had been for this moment.

He stood there for several minutes looking out over the land that was promised to his people. He could see the city of Jericho sitting far below. That would be their next move and would serve as the corridor through which the nation of Israel would move into their new home. The details of it were not known to him and he suspected that Joshua and Eleazer would know very soon the steps they must take.

Moses felt the cool breeze on his face as the sun began to rise behind him. He felt the warmth on his back that wrapped around him like an embrace. The world began to spin in his head as he lay on the ground. Though his body was not tired or frail he knew this was the moment of his death, and a new beginning. The wind began to blow and soon picked up speed in a gale that spun around the summit where he lay. As Moses drew in one deep breath, he knew it would be his last. He held it for just a moment and then exhaled slowly, his breath trailing off until it could not be heard but by the keenest of ears. There he died at the age one-hundred and twenty years.

Moses' body was lifted from the ground by the gale that swirled faster and faster around the mountain. His body began to spin with the momentum of the wind. A low hum arose from the ground as dirt and stones were picked up in the whirlwind causing it to turn a solid gray and brown color. It spun for a few more seconds and then as quickly as it had come it dissipated and disappeared altogether, the stones and dirt falling to the ground. Moses' body was not among the things that returned to the mountaintop.

CHAPTER 16

The Valley of Elah, 1025 B.C.

Fifteen Years Ago

Revelry ensued after the complete route of the Philistine army and looting of the Philistine camp. They passed around gold, weapons, and armor as well as fine robes and other garments worth many thousands of shekels. In their panic to flee, the Philistines had left behind horses, livestock, food, wine, and their slaves as well. Very few of the Philistines escaped the pursuing Israelite's spears and swords as they scattered across the countryside to escape.

David and his older brothers: Eliab, Abinadab, and Shammah stood before King Saul in a crowded royal tent with thousands of soldiers surrounding. Each one of his brothers held a piece of Goliath's armor while David stood in front of them holding Goliath's sword. Two other men, acquaintances of Eliab, stood to the side holding the ends of a canvas. Upon this canvas was the head of Goliath. Everyone gasped in wonder as the two men walked and laid the giant's head at King Saul's feet and retreated behind David and Eliab as the cheers resumed.

King Saul lifted his right hand as he beamed, signaling that he would speak. Like a retreating wave from the beach sand, the camp fell silent as King Saul stood from his chair.

King Saul spoke loudly enough for a good part of the camp to hear him, "Today the Lord has delivered our enemies into our hands. And to show His power it was at the hands of this thirteen-year-old boy you see standing before us!"

Shouts and chants arose again as he gestured to an unassuming David standing before him. He raised his hand once more to quiet the crowd. "Tonight, we will feast, and tomorrow we will take the news of our total victory home with us! But first, I would like to offer David his choice of spoils from the route of our enemies. I know I promised a wife, but we will have to revisit that at another time when he is older and has established his own house. As promised, his family will be exempt from annual taxes for the following seven years. What say you David, son of Jesse? What will you choose for your spoils."

David, yet unaccustomed to having all eyes on him bowed lightly and spoke, "Good King Saul, I would not know what to choose from these spoils so I will just keep the armor of Goliath as a token. This was not my victory, but the Lord's. All glory and honor belong to Him. I was just the vessel He used, my king."

"Well said young man! Well said!" King Saul exclaimed before addressing the crowd once more, "Eat and drink tonight, tomorrow we will disband and go back home to tend our fields and our families!"

Saul turned to David and placed his hands upon his shoulders, "When you have come of age, come, and see me. In the meantime, I will send tutors to train you in the use of weapons and tactics. Be well young lad."

Young David nodded shyly as he and his brothers turned and disappeared into the crowd of cheering men. King Saul lifted the head of Goliath, which must have weighed twenty pounds, and placed it next to his chair at his feet. Tomorrow, he would have someone take it and boil it down and would keep the skull as a trophy to parade in front of the Philistines the next time they inevitably reared their ugly heads.

King Saul looked out over the camp as the crowd broke off to continue their festivities and then went back to the head of Goliath at his feet. He was very tired as the area around his camp grew silent and soon nodded off to sleep in the chair.

King Saul slept soundly, unaware that as he slept, a tendril of black smoke, almost too small to see with the naked eye, wormed its way out of the ear of the gruesome head of Goliath. The black smoke playfully danced through the air toward the sleeping king and upon reaching him, the smoke entered the left ear gently at first, but as it went deeper it rapidly entered his body and soon disappeared from sight.

King Saul awoke suddenly in terror, his mind reeling from a nightmare and he now felt like someone had placed a burden on his shoulders. "My Lord has abandoned me," he thought suddenly as his eyes narrowed. His nightmare had only just begun as distant chants of "David! David! David!" could be heard.

The Citadel Fortress: 1010 B.C.

Baaldir awoke suddenly as the storm outside the fortress raged. He was weakened more than he knew as he tried to lift his head from the pillow and immediately collapsed back onto it, looking up at the ceiling. His hand stung and he looked at it, noticing the small gash with dried blood on it. It looked very fresh. Just then, the door swung open and in walked his mother and father.

The lightning crashed outside as they carried lanterns into the room and seeing him awake, they cried out in surprise.

"My son! You are awake!" Frigg said, overjoyed.

"Mother, where am I?" Baaldir asked.

King Adonizedek knelt next to him, beaming. He answered for her, "You have been resting for the last day or so Baaldir. You were badly hurt in some caves below the city."

The recollection suddenly returned to Baaldir as he tried to sit up rapidly. "Nathan! Where is Nathan?"

Frigg pressed down gently on his shoulders and cautioned him to stay in bed and told him that the sutures would pull and cause him to bleed again.

"Where. Is. Nathan?" Baaldir asked urgently.

King Adonizedek, wearing a somber look, shook his head at Baaldir confirming that the worst possible outcome had happened.

"Oh! It was my fault! I shouldn't have forced him down there with me. We witnessed Israelites attacking and got separated and lost. I finally found him, and he was under attack from three dark figures. They weren't men Father. Rather they were demons. I'm sure of it. I fought them but it was too late, Nathan had been gravely wounded, and I tried. I tried!" Baaldir was rambling now as tears welled up in his eyes. His mother pulled him in close and he wailed in grief at losing his closest friend.

"I know you tried dear; I know." Frigg said, trying to comfort the now inconsolable Baaldir.

King Adonizedek sat there stoically, absorbing the light that Baaldir had shed on the happenings below. Anyone seeing him would see a man lost in contemplation. He finally shouted to the guards outside, "Bring something to carry my son. I need him moved into the palace proper where he will be safer and cared for."

With that, his father rose from the bedside, "Son, I'm very happy that you are on the mend, and I am very sorry at the loss of your friend. Though I didn't know him, your mother told me you were close like brothers. We are here for you son." He placed his hand on Frigg's shoulder and said, "I need to check on the siege defense and talk with officers. I'll see you in the palace."

Baaldir laid his head back with a tear welling up on the corner of his eye. It soon ran down toward his ear. "Mother, I...I...I'm sorry. I need to see Nathan's parents. I need to apologize to them."

"My dear son, you cannot blame yourself. It was not you who did the violence. And from what I've heard, you tried valiantly to defend him and get him to safety. Nathan was fortunate to have a friend so close that he would risk his life to save him. Not many grown men can ever claim to have even one friend such as this."

Baaldir's mind was reeling from all of the memories of the cavern flooding back in. "Mother, those creatures. They were the ones who attacked me in the streets a year ago. Only, they were completely changed. What happened to them?"

"Baaldir, our minds can play tricks on us sometimes. Especially in a dangerous situation like you and Nathan were in."

"But I am sure of it. I saw the face of one of them clear as day before..." Baaldir trailed off lost in fearful contemplation. He looked at his mother with tears flowing now and said, "Before... I killed him. Mother, I had to. I had no choice."

Frigg scooped up Baaldir in an embrace and hugged him tightly. "My son, I'm so sorry that you had to do a thing like that. Now it is my turn to apologize to you. Your father and I wanted a different life for you. We wanted you to enjoy your boyhood. I am sorry that we did not protect you as we should have." She held him close and rocked him as she used to when he was a younger child.

For several minutes, they both cried until finally no more tears came out. For several more minutes they just sat in silence.

Baaldir finally broke the silence. "Mother, I have been having dreams. One's similar to fathers. Dreams of the end of the world, dreams of the city and those creatures descending upon us. The worst thing is, I try to do something about it, but I keep getting thrown back. I always end up right back in a world without any color and it feels as real as the world we are sitting in right now."

Frigg studied Baaldir quizzically. "Tell me your dream Baaldir, I am listening. Leave no detail out, even the most mundane."

Baaldir sat upright and swung his legs over the edge of the bed slowly, wincing with pain, and began to tell her everything in detail.

<hr/>

Outside the Walls of Jebus

"Commander! Over here. I found the giant!" a soldier yelled. Joab ran up on the group of his men that had surrounded the giant and burst through. The man lay on the ground bleeding and from what he could tell, not breathing.

"Is he alive?" Joab asked hurriedly splashing through puddles of water as the storm had temporarily subsided.

One of the men checked his pulse and put as ear to his chest and above his face.

"Only just." said the man. "He won't be before too long."

Joab motioned to several of the men. "Do what you can to stop the bleeding."

Then to several others, "Go to the siege camp and grab anything we can use to make a litter to carry this man." They hesitated, "Go now! Quickly!" The men ran off to conduct the orders.

"He's lost a lot of blood Commander. I don't know what good we can do."

Joab shrugged, "Do what you can. We need him alive."

As the chaos fell into full swing during the storm, madness and hysteria soon followed. Hundreds or maybe even thousands were murdered and many more badly injured in the bedlam that followed. This had set into motion a mad series of events including King Saul mobilizing his entire guard to scour the countryside for Thoros. It was thoroughly surprising that they hadn't found him being so close to the siege camp which was now demolished by fire; no doubt the work of Thoros or maybe the creatures that had killed the men in the camp. The timing of the fire suggested Thoros being the culprit. He cursed his own poor judgement and realized the siege weapons may as well been set ablaze by his own hand. He couldn't blame the prince of Jebus, after all, for doing what was necessary to preserve their city. The fall of Jebus and its heights on Mount Moriah was inevitable but it would now require considerable labor and the expense of providing food for a standing army.

Joab had a bad feeling about David and his mission to free the prisoners inside the city, having heard no word. He had to assume he was either captive as well, or worse. The latter made him shudder as he refused to believe it. David was a man that possessed the ability to be swallowed alone by a horde of Philistines and somehow come out on top of the heap victorious. He was just uneasy about the swiftness and reckless severity of the decisions that were being made at this point by all involved.

King Saul, as sick as he was, should not have joined this siege especially since the death of the prophet Samuel. The king was cut off from Elohim, and desperate. This was on full display in the day's past but who can tell an anointed king who has lost Elohim's favor that he should lay low?

Below the Citadel Fortress

Tsalmaveth, using Ahmet's body, returned to the caverns with streams of Shades running by him to find refuge in the darkness as the sunrise began. Today, seizing the opportunity during the storm, had been the first strike on Elohim's chosen people. His desire for death and destruction was a thirst that he'd not often been free to slake which had made this time plotting with Lox a nearly unbearable task. He needed to bind himself to this host and soon. Tsalmaveth could feel his power waning as the day wore on.

Once he'd entered Ahmet's body, he felt invincible and wasted no time opening the cells and sending his Shades out into the siege camp using the tunnels under Jebus. But he was soon reminded that he was only a guest in this body, not the owner. Not yet. Tsalmaveth had three nights to perform the ritual, or he would be expelled once again and bound to the stone box he'd been imprisoned for many millennia.

Lox had tried to convince him to enter his body, and that had been tempting. But he had other plans for Lox and that included his master, Yaldabaoth.

Ahmet would do just fine. And that boy of his, Nathan, may just be the key to everything. It just so happened that Ahmet believed him to be dead which Tsalmaveth could use to manipulate this man into binding himself to him. He was yet unsure if Nathan was indeed dead, it would be a pity if so, seeing as all that power would be wasted, though if he managed to obtain some of The Key's blood it may work just as well.

Once this body belonged to him, his power would be sustained, and he would bring this city and all of Israel to its knees. The last night he had borrowed Ahmet's body and visited his plants in the Israelite camp. They had started the attack almost as soon as the indwelling ritual was performed, and he had permanent control of Ahmet, using the twelve 'rejects' as Lox called them as an advance force hidden within the Israelite camp. He'd activated them on his last foray into the camp where he found Thoros captured and helpless. Tsalmaveth was now linked to the 'rejects' telepathically, so they acted at the speed of his thought. Unfortunately, the big lout Thoros had foiled the plan to kill Jonathan, son of the king and close brother of his real target, David. In return he had sent his Shades to exact his revenge on Thoros. That idiot was likely no more, he snickered to himself. A lot of good it did him to kill one of his Shades.

Ever since David defeated Goliath on the field of battle years past, Tsalmaveth had waited and waited for his time. Saul, taking the head of Goliath as a trophy, was unaware that it functioned as a talisman of sorts that was connected to Tsalmaveth, giving him foresight into the actions of the Israelites and David in particular. That fact had been unknown to Tsalmaveth before Goliath's death, and he let it serve as a consolation prize in his unfortunate defeat.

Goliath had been his first hope to escape the prison he so rarely could leave over the last several millennia. He'd managed to perform the binding ritual with Goliath hoping to achieve his goal of severing his connection with Azrael, the Angel of Death. This did not work, so for forty days he taunted Israel at the head of the Philistine army, searching for a strategy, until finally a teenage boy by the name of David had presented himself and accepted the challenge. Lox had been in the ranks with other dignitaries observing from a hillside a safe distance away, holding the stone box. He'd tried to destroy the box once he was bound to Goliath, but it was not destructible by natural means, nor any supernatural power that he possessed. Therefore, as soon as the head was severed from Goliath and his life lost, Tsalmaveth was catapulted back to the stone box with such a force that it sent Lox flying several cubits as he held the box. That was when he ordered Lox to take him deep under the city of Jebus to allow him to rebuild and plan.

Using the head of Goliath, now a skull that Saul brought everywhere with him, he was able to use a trace amount of his essence to torment Saul and cause him to go mad, and in turn disobey Elohim. Tsalmaveth spat as he thought of the name of his captor. He hated lots of things, but nothing burned in him hotter than his hatred for Elohim. One day, when he was free of his bonds, he would cover the entire world in his Shadow and destroy it all. To do that, he would need to bring an old acquaintance back from his own purgatory. Yaldabaoth was far more powerful than himself and he dared say that he could rival Elohim and his heavenly hosts if given the right set of circumstances and a kingdom on the earth with which to wage war.

With these in his thoughts, Tsalmaveth entered the intercourse where the different doors ran off into the darkness of the caverns underneath the city of Jebus. As his hand ran along the hewn stone that lined the corridor, Tsalmaveth could feel his grip loosening on Ahmet just enough to allow the man some ability to control his body during the daytime hours while he rested and restored his power. Until the binding ritual, he would feel fatigue after using Ahmet's body. As the sun began to set this afternoon, Tsalmaveth would have full control once again. During the daytime, as he remembered Goliath, he was only in partial control. Though Goliath retained his power and strength as he waged war on the Israelites, even after the binding ritual.

This time, however, he believed he had found a way to give him some more agency during the day under the sun. He and Lox had researched high and low, reading scrolls from the Far East and beyond.

As he entered the newly made temple he found a place to sit and grabbed a piece of glass that was hanging on the wall. He had to hurry so that he'd have time to speak with Ahmet before going dormant for the day.

Suddenly a confused thought from Ahmet echoed. "What? Where am I?" Tsalmaveth sat Ahmet on a stool and prepared to converse with his new hopeful. Through Ahmet's face muscles, a sardonic smile, crooked and depraved, became visible on his face.

<hr />

Outside the gates of Jebus

Joab and his men carried the wounded Thoros on a massive litter that carried his nearly lifeless fifty-stone body. It took ten men to carry him softly enough so as not to mortally aggravate the man's injuries. Why he was going to this length to save him he couldn't quite figure, but his instinct told him that David's life may hang in the balance with the fate of this royal giant. That is what he and Jonathan discussed back in the tent before the inexplicable attacks began throughout the camp. The likelihood that David was not successful in his quest grew by the hour. He should've been back earlier in the day and here it was the very next morning.

Joab kept pressing forward. They were so close to the walls of Jebus that they could see the men on top of them. There was no telling if the men could see them as well, but he assumed they could as they slowly carried Thoros up and over the rocky terrain outside Jebus. He had decided, given that they could not return to camp with Thoros, and they had little chance of saving him if they took him elsewhere, to take him to the gates of Jebus where they would hope to gain access as emissaries. Perhaps he could find out what had happened to David in the process.

Joab was staunchly loyal to David, which was why he felt this was the best path forward. David wanted Thoros alive, and he wanted to save those captured inside, so this hairbrained move was precisely the type of thing he would do in this circumstance. It wasn't as hairbrained as entering a city through a cave and infiltrating a prison to bring back up to three-hundred captives, which was nearly impossible for the average man, not that David was an average man by any stretch. Maybe this plan to save Thoros by delivering himself into the hands of his enemy wasn't so crazy after all.

By now the men on the wall were aware of their presence as they walked the length of the wall at a safe distance, out of range of the archers. The main gate was not far now, only a few hundred cubits more, and then they would raise a flag to signal the men in the tower before approaching.

As they rounded the last bend Joab's heart sank as he saw the gold glint of King Saul's guards traveling up the main road with chariots and on horseback. No doubt the king was among them as he never went anywhere without them close by. His paranoia wouldn't permit it. This was just the kind of thing Joab was concerned about when he made this choice. Now he would have to defy King Saul, making him a traitor, in order to carry it out.

Joab resigned himself to the fact and accepted it as something that was not in his control. The only thing he could do was make sure Thoros survived long enough to save David. The rest would have to happen as it no doubt would.

"Pick up your pace men!" Joab commanded "We must move within range of the archers."

The men obeyed by doubling their pace. They also knew their fates were sealed. When he had chosen them, he'd made sure they were fiercely loyal to David. After he let Thoros free at the camp he figured he had better see to David's order to have all men loyal to him exit the camp and head for the hills to wait for him. They were to use the search for the giant as their cover to slip away on horseback.

He took a dozen men with him to feign searching for Thoros when he saw the flames coming from the siege camp. That was fortunate for the giant as it led Joab and his men straight to his location in time enough for them to attempt to save him. They now turned straight on with the main gate and began to march forward, hoisting the giant up on their shoulders.

Saul and his guard were bringing up the rear, now only a few hundred cubits away and closing fast. They felt the ground rumble beneath their feet as they moved well within range of the archers on the walls of Jebus.

Thankfully, no one had fired a shot toward them as they walked, likely because they could see the giant being held up on top of the litter. With King Saul at their back they continued double quick towards the wall, and he could now hear shouts coming from the king's guard as they came to a halt just out of range from the archers. It became eerily quiet, and he could now hear Saul's shrill voice booming over the expanse.

"Joab, you will cease this instant!" King Saul screamed. "Stop your advance and place our enemy down on the ground. Do it now or I will be forced to strike you all down!"

Joab kept walking despite the threat. Soon after he heard an arrow whirr past his head and stick into the ground ahead of him.

"Joab, that was a warning! Force my hand and I will unleash a rain of arrows on you and your men," King Saul threatened again. "Stop at once!"

Joab signaled to stop briefly. Maybe he could try to reason with the king. "My king, I cannot stop. This man has saved your son's life just last night. I will deliver him to Jebus as repayment. He is gravely wounded by the same creatures that attacked our camp last night. Without medicine and a healer, he will die." Joab shouted this loud enough for those on the walls to hear as well. He waited a moment for a response.

Hearing none, he signaled for his men to march forward toward the gates. The next sound he heard was another arrow. This time it found its mark in Joab's left calf. He grunted with pain as he now limped along awkwardly, still trying to carry his share of the weight.

"We need to move faster!" Joab screamed, doing his best to not allow the pain in his leg to slow the march down.

They were now only forty yards or so away from the gate. The walls loomed overhead as another volley of arrows came soon after. This time two men fell off to the side, mortally wounded as the weight of the giant seemed to increase suddenly with two less men to bear the load.

At this point it was all they could do to maintain the pace and hold up Thoros' litter as they closed in on the gates, now out of effective range of King Saul's archers. Just then a volley of arrows from the wall rained down behind them toward the king and his guard. Joab looked back and saw several guardsmen fall. Apparently, Saul had misjudged the range of Jebus's archers atop their forty-foot walls which were on higher ground than King Saul to begin with.

King Saul screamed, "After them! Do not allow them to reach that gate alive."

The king's guard commander signaled for his left column to advance. They were reluctant since so much distance was now between them and Joab's men and Jebus's archers had the advantage on range.

"Go now! Or you won't have to worry about their archers. I'll kill you myself!"

With that threat King Saul's men surged forward unenthusiastically. At the same moment, the heavy gates of Jebus cracked open enough for two columns of men to march out with spear and shield. One column to the left and one to the right swiftly marched to the flanks of Joab and his men. Then the Jebusite infantry wheeled about behind them, locking shields and lowering their spears toward the oncoming soldiers.

This was enough to strike fear into the exposed men who had already lost a few men on their advance to archers. They did not have the stomach for an ill-advised advance on bad ground. One by one, they slowed and then they turned tail and retreated. The soldiers from Jebus stood firm not giving chase. As Joab and his men limped through the gate the two columns detached and quickly marched back through the gate.

King Saul, enraged, screamed with spittle flying from his contorted mouth, "Turn back! Kill them all! Your king demands it!"

But it was to no avail. Joab and his men continued through the gates of Jebus. At that point King Saul was despondent. He hurled insults at his officers and threats at his fleeing guard. Joab could still hear his king's pitiful screams as the gates closed behind them. He ordered his men to lower Thoros to the ground and step away, at which point several soldiers of Jebus picked up Thoros, placed him in a wagon and though he could not see the cart through all of the commotion, he soon heard it carry the prince away, deeper into the city.

An officer ordered some of his men to disarm the Israelites and then to function as an escort for Joab and his men as they were beckoned to sit on a wagon pulled by oxen. Joab would need a healer to remove the arrow from his calf. In a matter of moments, they were being pulled through the city and up a steep incline. Joab craned his neck backward and looked up. They were being taken up and into the infamous Citadel Fortress.

<hr />

Atop the city walls, Jebus

Adonizedek peered through a parapet at the southernmost gate. Quizzically, he stared at the smoke rising from the direction of the Israelite camp and wondered what that could be about. Black smoke usually meant that something was fully engulfed and being fueled rapidly. Gray smoke typically meant slow burning smolder and white smoke generally meant that the fire was extinguished and no longer fueled.

This fire, despite the steady rain, was burning hot and fast. Adonizedek studied the horizon in the early morning light as the clouds broke, giving way to the sun. Suddenly he heard a horrendous horn sound in the distance, southeast of the wall a bit.

"REEEEEEEEE!   REEEEEEEEEEEEE! REEEEEEEEEEEEEEEEEEEEEEEEE!" it sounded with both high and low notes, almost sounding like the screech of a dreaded dragon he'd glimpsed once as a little boy in a far off lost land.

Adonizedek looked at his men. "Was that one of ours?" he said, looking at several officers for any answers.

"My king, that was not ours. But it sounded like a retreat to me."

"Is there fighting happening down our eastern wall?" Adonizedek turned to walk in the direction of the sound.

"No my King. It has been all quiet. We saw the fire in the Israelite camp, and I wonder if that horn came from whoever is fighting there?" The officer opined and then waited for the king to answer.

"Perhaps, I am going to check the stables and will be returning to the palace by way of them. Keep me posted of any change in situation. Something is in motion, and I don't like being in the dark."

"My king, we will see to it and will bring you news straight away." The officers present saluted and bowed as Adonizedek exited down a set of stairs, an entourage of guards close behind. As he started towards the stables, the guards surrounded him and escorted him. It was a twenty-minute walk to the stables, and he needed some time to think. His mind was troubled by the events that seemed out of his control.

Adonizedek lamented his families latest hardships, *Thoros is captured, Lox missing in action, and Baaldir is aid up with injuries sustained in a cavern that I never knew existed underneath my own city.* That was much of the reason he needed to check on the stables and see to it that Bulwark and his men closed off the tunnel before any other unexplained things happened. Baaldir had given him information that he lacked when he told him that the missing slaves were freed by Israelites who had found and exploited the tunnels. David, who he now had in captivity, was no doubt the mastermind of the operation. Until Baaldir awoke and shed light on what happened to him he was under the assumption that David and his men were responsible for the harm to Baaldir and the death of his friend, Nathan.

Adonizedek thought as he walked, *Baaldir mentioned creatures that looked like men but were not men, but demons. Baaldir also remembered seeing David and his band kill the guards and taskmaster two days ago. The two must be linked but how?*

Just then he remembered that last night, hours before that scoundrel Ahmet had attacked Baaldir, that he had heard reports from Siv that the guards and Lox were involved in a skirmish with some assailants that met the description of the creatures that Baaldir described. Lox had left to pursue them and then, according to the guards, left with Urim and an entourage to find the tunnel layout and bring back any information about Thoros that they could find. The captain, Urim, was the only one who had returned, and he was being held in the fortress, having survived the attack from the one-eyed beasts. He would be kept there until he spoke about what he knew. So far, his only words had been to warn of the Israelites coming through the city and not a word about the whereabouts of Lox.

It troubled him that Lox was involved in all of these happenings, and he had his suspicions about the supposed prisoners that Lox claimed were not slaves. He and Lox had disagreed time and again over the issue of slavery and he knew that Lox was the type to do things and then ask for forgiveness later.

I can smell your hand in this Lox. When you return, we will have to settle this once and for all. Adonizedek resolved. Lox would have some explaining to do.

Somehow, Lox and the tunnels were connected. The tunnels, in turn, were connected to the mysterious creatures that Baaldir described, and the Israelites, led by David had penetrated the fortress and nearly escaped back into the tunnels. What's more, one out of two of the giants, that Lox apparently kept, was still at large. He dreaded to think what would happen if the beast entered the city and began to lay waste to unsuspecting citizens. Adonizedek supposed he should be thankful to his prisoner, David, that he'd dealt with one single-handedly. That was impressive to Adonizedek. He only knew of a handful of his men who would fare as well, himself being one.

When David awoke from his knock on the head, Adonizedek would be there to question him about the whereabouts of his son. Surely, the mighty David knew details, and Adonizedek would wager anything that Thoros' capture was directly connected to the deeds of the Israelite hero.

After about ten minutes of walking he reached the halfway point to the stable. Up from behind him came a runner shouting. "My king, My king! Your presence is needed back at the wall. News of your son, Your Majesty."

"I will be there straight away." Adonizedek said as he took off running back the way they had just come from.

It only took a few minutes to return to the top of the wall and looked out toward the sandy ramp that led up to the gates. His heart skipped a beat, and his jaw dropped as he saw several Israelite soldiers stop less than one hundred cubits away holding a massive body above their shoulders.

"My son...is he...," Adonizedek said, fearing the worst. Another one hundred cubits behind the ones carrying Thoros, he saw King Saul shouting at the men and shooting arrows at them.

King Saul is attacking his own men. But why? Adonizedek thought.

"The man below says he is alive and needs medical attention. They have just asked to enter into the city."

"Let them in and return fire on those Israelites at the back. I don't want my son to be hit by their arrows."

"My King, it could be a trap..." an officer said.

Adonizedek cut him off and snapped back, "I don't care! You will send men out to retrieve my son this instant! Do not make me order it a third time!"

"It will be done!" The officer saluted and ran off hurriedly. Moments later, a company of infantry marched out of the gate as it opened and formed a shield in between King Saul and the Israelites carrying Thoros.

All the while, King Saul raged as his own soldiers retreated from him, paying no heed to his orders and threats.

Adonizedek rushed from the wall and made his way to the gate. When he reached them, they had already placed Thoros on a cart and were readying themselves to transport him.

Thoros. My son... Adonizedek thought, as he walked right past everyone and sat on the cart. "Get him to the healers now!" he shouted as the oxen surged forward and raced away from the south gate.

Below the Fortress

Ahmet awoke with a fit of coughing as his eyes opened in the very dimly lit room. He sat on a stool and as he woke, he realized he had not a clue as to where he was or how he got there. He vaguely remembered the pummeling he took from Vlulor and Flagor but much past that, was a foggy memory. He saw flashes of the temple and altar but couldn't put his finger on why. He slowly got to his feet and did a quick turn about the stall and realized he had bedded down in the stable.

"Wake up Ahmet," he heard a man's voice say.

Startled, Ahmet turned to where the voice had registered and saw nothing but a very large piece of dusty sandglass hanging on the wall. Ahmet walked timidly over to the glass and wiped the dust from it with his hand and backed away quickly after being startled by what he saw. Ahmet started to say something like a question, but no words would exit past his lips.

"We need to have a talk, you and I, Ahmet, You've slept the entire waking day. It is nearly nightfall again." the voice said, and Ahmet realized then that it was coming from his own lips as though he was saying it. Except, he was hearing it as though it was coming from the glass.

Ahmet walked up to the glass again, wiped it clean with his sleeve, and peered into it. He had no frame of reference to describe what or who he was seeing in the looking glass. The person in the glass held a shape of a man that resembled himself with lean muscular limbs and torso. However, the skin was jet black. The man's face was like no face Ahmet had seen apart from the resemblance to his own reflection. Sure, there were eyes, a nose, and lips, but the man had pointy ears, and his eyes were an infinite void, and Ahmet felt as though holding their gaze too long would swallow him into an uninhabited abyss. In an instant, Ahmet was aware that before him stood Tsalmaveth, The Shadow of Death.

"Who are you?" Tsalmaveth said.

The way Tsalmaveth said it, Ahmet understood somehow that he should already know the answer. What was he really asking? Ahmet started to say something like his name.

Tsalmaveth shook his head and softly said, "That is what you are called by people who don't matter now. WHO are you?"

Ahmet involuntarily blurted out the name "Tsalmaveth." The words shook him as he said it. It surprised him to hear his voice utter the Hebrew words. He had a sinking feeling in his gut but at the same time felt strength course through his limbs. Before him stood Tsalmaveth, who now lived inside his body. And he was now Tsalmaveth also.

"That's right Ahmet, you are my Shadow. Why am I here?"

Ahmet didn't understand, "Why are you here? I don't know."

"Come on Ahmet, you know the answer." Tsalmaveth leaned forward toward the glass and Ahmet could smell sulfur coming from his mouth as he breathed close to the glass.

The answer came to him automatically, "To usher in the kingdom of Yaldabaoth."

"Right you are!" Tsalmaveth said with a clap of hands that startled Ahmet. "I knew you were a smart one!"

Ahmet couldn't tell if he was serious or not. Something told him that only halfway serious was the answer to that question. "What do you want from me?"

"To do everything I command without fail." Tsalmaveth said curtly and followed with a threat, "If you don't, I will make you kill your wife and child with your own hands."

Ahmet winced at those words and started to say "I would never..." until he vaguely remembered a guard mentioning that Nathan had died just that day. Anger welled up in him followed by deep despair as he changed his reply, "My son..." Ahmet choked on the next words before spitting them out suddenly, "is dead."

Tsalmaveth drew an incredulous look at Ahmet and rushed forward into the glass, causing Ahmet to recoil in horror as his black tongue flicked menacingly. "A pity, Ahmet. Don't forget part of our agreement was that you'd get your revenge."

Tsalmaveth stepped back and appeared to relax as he raised his hand. When he raised his hand Ahmet's hand raised with it. Tsalmaveth raised the other hand and Ahmet's raised with it yet again. Then he dropped them suddenly and Ahmet's dropped to his side.

"You see Ahmet, you are mine. That is the deal you made for your life. When you've done what I've asked, you have my word that I'll leave you to live your life. But do not for a second think you can resist without consequence. Who are you Ahmet?"

Ahmet said simply, "Tsalmaveth." And he knew that he was, completely.

"That's right Ahmet, you are my Shadow, and we have work to do. Come and see the world we will make." Ahmet's mind went blurry as he felt the Shadow inside him take over. A moment later Ahmet was standing back in a black room with a candle in the center of it that he'd been in the night before, completely cut off from the world.

On the road to Egypt

Lox stopped for a moment to catch his breath. For the entire day he had run at a pace that would undoubtedly bury a normal man. His longer than average stride made covering large distances fairly easy for him, though the blisters on his feet reminded him that his body, while superhuman, was not impervious to the damage traveling on foot could do to a man.

Through the night as he ran, he'd look over his shoulder expecting Shades to ambush him at every turn but as the sun rose his current worry subsided only to be replaced by a fresh one. Now his worry was that King Adonizedek, and company were woefully unprepared for the enemy they were about to face in Tsalmaveth. The army of Shades he'd helped make back when he naively thought the Shadow of Death would honor their deal, was about to swarm over Jebus and Lox would not be there to stand in the way.

Lox felt guilt in leaving Jebus. However, he was left with little choice in the matter, and he doubted that his being there would benefit Baaldir or Adonizedek. In fact, staying would only draw the ire of the court as his role in this would be revealed eventually. Staying would be stupid, put plainly. He'd be a fool not to think that the very old and wise Adonizedek would not already be placing his dealings under scrutiny. If he were still there, he'd likely be slapped in chains and sent to prison.

Retrieving the amulet, if it existed, could potentially give him the power to return and save the day in Jebus. He would just have to hope they could resist and hold out until he could return. Baaldir would be safe within the palace as long as Siv did as he said and stationed substantial amounts of guards and limited the entrance and exit points with the palace. His hope was that Tsalmaveth, as reckless as he'd proven to be, would find it difficult to enter and do him any harm.

Lox was fuming over the renege of his deal with Tsalmaveth. He'd only worked with the entity because it was foisted upon him so many years ago in Goliath's Hall. For all he knew, this was part of the plan all along and he resented being treated like a plaything by the gods. Not only would he oppose Tsalmaveth if he gained the amulet's power, but he would also oppose the god of the Israelites. He would oppose any god or entity that stood in the way of his long-sought revenge on those that murdered his mother so coldly millennia ago.

Lox sat on a rock under a dead tree, watching the sun set. By his estimate, he'd covered half the distance to Memphis. His feet, and the blisters that had formed confirmed this fact. As he sat there, he went through his pack and pulled out a bandage and salve which he applied to his feet before standing up to continue his journey. If this weren't so urgent he would stop to make camp for the night, but he certainly could not sleep knowing that the amulet was nearing his grasp the more leagues he covered. Blisters or not, he would make it there by tomorrow evening and track the amulet down, take it, kill if he must, and then return to Jebus to save the people he'd come to know as family. When he defeated Tsalmaveth, he would shove him back in the stone box and send it to the bottom of the ocean, never to be seen again.

CHAPTER 17

The Citadel Fortress

David opened his eyes to a blinding light and immediately closed them. Behind his eyelids he saw green floating orbs in front of an orange backdrop. He brought his hand up to cover his eyes and stopped midway as a strange tension tugged at his wrists. He only slightly opened his right eye; the left felt like it was under pressure and caused a dull ache when he tried to open it. David tried to raise the other hand and realized that it too was disabled due to a tugging sensation.

He finally opened one eye to see a brightly lit room with the blinding morning sun splashing in through the window. David's whole body ached from his head to his toes but mostly his head as he closed his eyes again. He realized the tugging on his arms and legs were due to ropes binding them to the cot he was laying upon.

"He awakes!" someone shouted from somewhere on the other side of the oaken door as he heard several footsteps running to and from.

In a few moments he heard more footsteps coming down what appeared to be a hall. His right eye open, he began to crane his neck back and forth to try and see who was entering. He managed to pull himself up to his elbows as far as the bonds would allow him to and this gave him a little more of a vantage of the room he occupied. Stone walls, thatched roof, and one window in which the sun spilled over right onto his cot making it difficult for his eyes to adjust.

He had been taken prisoner after a battle with a one-eyed giant bent on devouring him and his comrades, though he could not remember the battle entirely. The only thing he remembered seeing was Adonizedek across the stables as he blacked out. The cause of the blackout was apparent now in the inability to open his left eye and a pounding headache.

A few moments later the door opened, and two guards came in followed by a man carrying a tray who walked over to the side of the bed and set the tray down. Silently he mixed herbs in a mortar adding willow bark, feverfew leaves, coriander seeds, rosemary, and several other herbs and began to work on them to turn them into a fine powder. He then placed them in a small piece of cheesecloth and tied the ends to make a pouch. Placing the pouch in a cup, he poured boiling water over it and swirled the cup. After a minute of swirling, he set the cup down and proceeded to untie David's hands and feet from their bonds.

"Drink this tea. For the headache and swelling." The man said as he transferred the cup to another tray and exited the room without another word; the guards followed and locked the door from the other side.

David tried to sit up in bed but suddenly felt a sense of vertigo and sunk back into the straw mattress, his head spinning wildly.

Okay, slower this time, he thought as he waited for the last of the spinning to subside.

Opening his eyes, he decided to pull himself up against the headboard of the bed. This he accomplished without incident and took to surveying the room from a sitting position as he sipped on the tea the man had made. The taste was bearable though he could tell this tea was more for medicine than leisure. It was slightly bitter and smelled like body odor, so he decided to down the tea quickly. David turned on the bed and let his bare feet fall to the cold stone floor and trained his ear toward the only door into the room.

Silence. His mind was foggy on recent events, no doubt a side-effect of the head injury and it was difficult to focus his hearing on the goings on outside his little room.

David's bed was basic and comfortable enough; a cot with a straw-filled mattress. No other furniture was kept in this room, apart from a chair, as the size of the room would no doubt feel crowded with any type of chest or table. He decided to try to stand up slowly and as David gained his balance he reached up toward the ceiling, locked his hands together and stretched upward while leaning backward to stretch his back and hips. Feeling the blood rushing to his legs, he instantly felt better.

The tea for the headache was working fast, and as David took a few steps toward the door, he felt almost normal again to the point that he was able to slightly open the swollen eye. He began a series of deeper stretches and exercises, as was his morning ritual, which ranged from long stretches with focused breathing to body weight exercises that built endurance. After ten minutes or so, he felt energized and his head was clearer than before, though still had no lasting memory of the events in the stable. Only fragments presented themselves.

David worried about Jeroboam and the others. Hopefully, they made it out to the caves and found their way back to camp. He dropped to the ground and began a set of push-ups, slow on the way down and explosive on the way back up to start the repetition over. He had only finished half a dozen before he heard the key engaged in his door as it swung open. Two guards walked in and beckoned him to rise. As he stood the guards parted as King Adonizedek entered, wearing a sullen expression.

King Adonizedek looked at David up and down before walking to one end of the room and turning back around. "I see you are no worse for wear after the blow to your head?" The king turned around and took a seat in the chair which was too small for a man of his stature.

David was puzzled, "I'm going to need the recipe for that tea your healer gave me." This he said after realizing that, apart from the shiner on his eye and bruised head, he was feeling rather normal.

King Adonizedek smiled lightly and shook his head in the affirmative. The giant king sat back with the wooden chair creaking under him and pulled one leg up onto the other knee. Then he leaned forward, but didn't speak while he studied David, who was beginning to feel a little uncomfortable. David started to tap his foot and shifted his weight as they sized each other up.

David broke the silence. "Did my men escape or have they been captured as well?"

King Adonizedek shrugged, placing his hands out in front of him with palms facing up before bringing them together and folding his hands together. "Your men were not captured, nor did I send anyone to chase after them. Once we captured you, the mighty David, there didn't seem a reason to pursue them. Rest assured that will be the last time they use that tunnel. I will be collapsing it for good in the coming days."

David took a seat on the edge of the cot. "King Adonizedek, to what do I owe the privilege of a visit from the king of Jebus himself?"

King Adonizedek let his leg drop to the ground and then leaned forward with his forearms resting on the knees. "I wanted to see the man who all of Canaan fears to ascertain what type of man you are. Are you dangerous, reckless even? Or are you someone altogether different?"

David didn't understand the direction King Adonizedek was headed. The king continued with another question. "When you captured my son, Thoros, why didn't you kill him? Was it for ransom?"

"Among other things," David said. "I had the opportunity to speak with your son not two days ago and found him to be more than, well let's say, a one-eyed giant bent on destruction. My whole childhood, I heard of the sons of Anak and the times before Noah and the Great Flood. Ravenous beasts that devoured everything. Your late family member, Goliath, did that perception much credit. Thoros, I judged to be worth more alive than dead."

King Adonizedek nodded, "Goliath was not one for civilized living, his only purpose was to swing a sword. You should know that those under my roof do not believe the sword is the only way to live, me included. But make no mistake, we understand the language of the sword quite well."

David thought about this for a moment. He'd always been intrigued by the times before the Flood. He had spent many nights watching his father's flocks thinking about the fallen Watcher's and the battle of the Archangels.

This was his first opportunity to ever converse with someone connected to these events by only a few generations. The stories he heard around the campfire were thousands of years old.

"King Adonizedek, you say you don't live by the sword, yet you help the Philistines at every turn. And there is the matter of the hundreds of my former kinsmen beneath your city, who I have seen with my own eyes. They are locked up in cages like animals. Hundreds of men were stolen in the dark of night and mistreated and maimed by your own adopted son, Lox. They were transformed into ravenous creatures that I can no longer call my kinsmen. They would've killed us had they not been penned into cells and they are right beneath your own feet, Your Majesty."

King Adonizedek seemed surprised by this revelation. "I had no knowledge of the goings on in our prison. That has largely been Lox's domain as far as I was concerned. I had no idea the extent to which he'd been imprisoning those poor souls. You say hundreds?"

"Hundreds, King Adonizedek. Kept in cells with standing room only, no food or water or latrine buckets. I attempted to free them but was attacked by them, which revealed to me that they were beyond help. I had to leave them behind to escape those one-eyed beasts."

King Adonizedek mulled David's words over in his mind for a moment. "I do not make it a practice to mistreat servants, and I abhor slavery. Lox is occasionally misguided, and he is also conveniently missing. I will have to investigate these claims you've made and if Lox returns, I will deal with him if the claims are proven. You have my word."

"The way Lox killed his escort outside the caves the other day would suggest that he does not intend to return. He seems to have fled the siege and left you all to perish."

Adonizedek silently weighed David's words again. He was clearly surprised by the revelation that Lox had fled and killed his escort, and that David had witnessed it.

David continued, "I spared your son, but if I am not there in that camp, he will be dead by sunset. King Saul is there and has other plans for your son." David let that settle for a moment, but Adonizedek cocked his head to one side and then stood.

"You will need to follow me and my guards." With that, the king walked out of the room, leaving David standing there.

The guards beckoned David to follow them, which he did. He spilled out into an open-air walkway covered by a canvas awning overhead. The midday sun beat down on it, but it kept the area quite shaded. There were several soldiers surrounding him at this point and someone lightly pushed him forward, so he began to walk in the middle of the escort. To where, he couldn't tell. Adonizedek had hastily left and was nowhere to be seen.

The guards led him up a steep incline into a staircase ascending to a dais that overlooked the compound below. As he rounded the corner he gasped. Before him was an expansive garden surrounded by a marble atrium with five floors shooting up to the sky. He was astounded to say the least but was shook out of it as the soldier beckoned him to move forward with another light shove from behind.

They walked through the garden and over to the east side of the atrium and entered a large room with lots of windows. For a second time David was dumbstruck. There before him stood Joab, as a healer put the finishing touch on a set of sutures on Joab's left leg. Several others, which David recognized as Joab's personal guard, sat over to the side drinking from a skin and passing a bowl of fruit between them.

David turned and saw King Adonizedek crouching low resting his elbows on his legs; his hands folded in front of him. He remained crouched so that he was only slightly taller than David. Joab was now standing on his own with the aid of a wooden crutch and wore a sullen expression.

"How did you come by these wounds Joab; by whose hand?" David inquired of Joab as he crossed over to meet him in brotherly embrace. For the first time he saw a table that supported an unconscious Thoros as healers were just finishing repairing wounds and stopping the bleeding.

"King Saul, my lord," was all Joab said and became sullen once again.

David was surprised on one hand and not surprised on the other hand. "I don't mean to interrogate you cousin, but there are just so many questions. Who did this to the prince? Was this Saul's work as well?"

Joab shook his head side to side and looked over toward Thoros. "We found him like this outside the city. Unfortunately, the attackers fled just before we came upon him. Someone sounded a battle horn to retreat. Which is how we were signaled to his location. We were the only Israelites in the vicinity as near as I can tell, though Saul had an entire battalion out looking for him after he made his escape."

"How did he escape?" David pressed.

Joab explained. "I let him go before Saul could kill him last night while we were under attack from within the camp. At minimum, a hundred had been murdered in cold blood. Our entire siege engine encampment was killed, as it turns out. It was set fire to after the attacks, I'm guessing by Thoros' hand though I doubt he had anything to do with the loss of men. Anyhow, the tent holding him, and Jonathan was attacked, and the prince saved your brother's life, killing the attacker. Therefore, to repay his act, I let him go free. When Saul sent his guard to kill Thoros on sight, I took my men to mount our own search."

"Who was the attacker? Philistine?" David wondered now if the Philistines had finally decided to honor the alliance with Jebus and attack.

Joab replied, "Not Philistine, but Hebrew; except, not Hebrew any longer. It was one of the catatonic men you brought back from the tunnels. He had turned into a frothing beast, and we found him dead on top of Thoros' lap, crushed to death. When the attacks started, we were beset from all sides in the wee hours of the morning, a few hours before sunrise."

David's first thought went to Jeroboam who had taken the surviving captives into the caverns. He had so many questions, but he decided not to ask any more of Joab. David looked at the table where Thoros lay unconscious, shallow breaths were the only evidence that he was still living. He tried to fathom that Thoros had saved the life of someone dear to him.

Over in the corner, near the king, sat a very tall woman with curly blonde hair and olive skin and striking features, even as she was stricken with grief and sobbing. The woman sat with her legs crossed and rocked back and forth. Two children, who looked to be the age of seven or eight clung to her.

Another woman stood next to her trying to console her. He could only guess that this woman was Thoros' wife and the older woman with her bore a striking resemblance. Maybe a mother or sister? He noted that even sitting on the ground they were nearly as tall as him. He had never seen a female giantess before and to be honest this was the first time he had ever seen one convey human emotions.

The world he knew told him that giants were an abomination, that they were unnatural, and one should always be weary of them. They could be on your side one moment and ripping you apart limb from limb the next. His entire mind was plagued by a dissonance that pulled him to the edge of what he knew to be the truth. Here sat a grieving wife, a concerned father, a wounded prince clinging to life by a thread, and here sat his close friend and ally Joab and his men who had by all accounts been given medical treatment and were not being held captive.

David couldn't escape the notion that he had gotten a few things wrong as his perception of who these people were shifted. There was a marked difference between these giants and the two one-eyed giants he had faced in the stables and in the underground lair. He noticed that like himself they had features proportional to a regular human. In this way he now began to see them as human instead of the monsters that all Israelites hated with passion. They had a nearly four-hundred-year history of killing giants throughout Canaan. Most of their cities were once ruled by the overthrown giant men of renown that were in legends as far back as five thousand years.

David looked over towards Thoros who still had no signs of life apart from shallow breaths. He cautiously took a step or two toward the table where the prince lay and checked to see what the reaction to this was in the room. The guards began to move forward but stopped their advance when Adonizedek held up his hand and signaled them to stand down.

David walked up to the foot of the table and surveyed the wounds that ran up and down Thoros' body. They looked like terrible bite marks and vicious scratches where the flesh was ripped and torn almost to the bone from his legs to his torso. He also saw multiple clean stab wounds from a dagger by the look of it; one on his left side and one just below the collarbone looked to be the most grave of his wounds being so close to vital organs.

On the table were many surgical instruments that he had heard of but never actually seen. The healers that worked on Thoros clearly were skilled beyond any that Israel possessed, evidenced by the fact that the sutures on his numerous wounds were extremely clean, and it appeared that the wounds would heal with little scarring should he survive. David recounted the many times he had sewn his own wounds up with a bone needle and loose threads from his clothes. He could easily remember by looking at the ugly scars left by his handiwork.

One of the healers was busy mixing up a large batch of poultice with a mortar and pestle. He now recognized him as the healer who had made the tea a short while ago. The man finished and started to work packing the poultice gently onto each wound and covering it with some type of leaves while the other two sewed the last of the gashes on his lower thigh.

On the table next to him was a short, jagged dagger. It appeared reasonably well-made though the handle was a crude carving of a lion-headed humanoid with the lower torso of a snake that's tail curled into a spiral. The tail appeared like it was intended to fit around a wrist when grasped on the hilt.

David pointed to the dagger and asked, "May I see that dagger?"

The man hesitated but Adonizedek chimed in, "Let him see it. This man will not harm anyone here."

How and why Adonizedek trusted him he wasn't sure, but he wasn't about to question it as he reached for the dagger. David picked it up and held it up into the light to try and study the blade of the dagger and found that it had symbols etched into one side of the blade. He couldn't quite make out the inscribed symbols in this dim candle and torch lighting, so he walked over toward the only window in room and held it up into the late afternoon sun, which was just beginning to set.

David turned the blade in his hand, feeling its weight and realizing the wrist wrapping hilt was quite comfortable on his forearm, as he turned the blade, he gasped and nearly dropped the blade out of the window but recovered it barely. Slowly, he brought the blade up and turned it to the other side of the blade and spoke in a whisper, the word *TSALMAVETH*, which was a Hebrew word for an agent of death. It had many other symbols on it that he did not recognize. The word was the same he had seen in the underground temple. Death's Shadow loomed over him in his mind.

Deep in The Caverns

Jeroboam ducked through a narrow opening and hid behind a large boulder. He had been cut off from the others when the inexplicable attack came. For all he knew, the rest of his men had perished or were separated and just as lost as he was. He ripped a long piece of fabric from his tunic and wrapped it just above a large gash in his leg and then checked his body blindly to see if any other injuries were present. Finding none, he slowed his breath and listened.

The passage he'd squeezed through was barely big enough for him and he was a small man compared to the average of his day. There was no light as he felt around the edges to find another exit, to no avail. The reality of his situation set in once he realized that he might be safe here from whatever those creatures were, but he would die if he couldn't find a way to the surface.

A shiver crept up his spine as he now realized how cold it was. He focused on his breathing instead. Deep inhales, slow exhales; allowing his lungs to empty then holding that for a few seconds before repeating. He tried as hard as he could to think only of the breath he was taking. After what could have been several minutes, he finally settled, and his body temperature adapted to the cool dampness of his tomb.

He listened for several minutes and heard nothing. He had lost track of time and had no way of knowing how to find the surface. He had no light, no weapons apart from his sling that he'd taken off one of the dead guards during their escape from Jebus and that wouldn't do much good without seeing his target. He had some water in a skin at his side so that gave him a bit of hope because it would help him survive a few days if he stretched it out. He seriously doubted one of those creatures could find his little den through that tiny opening, so he decided he'd be better off staying here for a time to rest and then figure out what to do from there. All was silent for the moment with the only sound, the occasional drip of water somewhere in the cavern.

Jeroboam shut his eyes but didn't sleep. To shut the eyes in the darkest cavern he'd ever been in seemed a little futile, but he kept them closed anyhow hoping that he'd somehow find inspiration that would lead him out of this dire situation.

He wondered if David had perished in the stables, but he didn't want to doubt his good friend and future king. David had a knack for surviving any situation no matter how sticky. He wondered where his men were and if they had survived.

Jeroboam thought about the events of the last few hours. They had been moving deeper into the cavern trying to find their way back the way they had come with the wounded and emaciated countrymen they had rescued, which had already taken them most of a whole day he estimated. None of them could walk on their own when they started out and it was laborious to help them along every step in unsure surrounds. That was until he noticed a change in the one who was using his shoulder when the man's heart began to beat faster, and his stride strengthened. He thought nothing of it except he was glad to be able to move slightly faster and more sure-footed. The others ahead of him seemed to be moving better as well so he plowed on ahead, thinking nothing of it and just glad to finally be moving more rapidly.

Jeroboam hadn't noticed until it was too late that his group had become spaced too far apart where he couldn't see any other torches through the winding caverns. Then the inexplicable happened. The man at his side collapsed to the ground suddenly and began convulsing and foaming at the mouth. He'd never seen anything like it. Then the man started to wail, his body contorting into unnatural shapes, and he soon realized he heard the same from the rest of the party ahead as he knelt beside the poor man and tried to steady him as he shook. '

The shaking subsided and Jeroboam called ahead to his men and received no response. That's when he felt a searing pain in his upper leg; flesh tearing and parting from the rest of the tissue. The man who moments ago was near death was tearing at him with ferocious anger, intent on cleaving his flesh from the bone with teeth alone. It was all Jeroboam could do to pull the man from his leg, and he resorted to repeated blows on the skull to get his leg free. Then it was a scramble to find footing as the man, turned beast, advanced again; this time with a hateful disposition intent on killing him. Without thinking he took the torch, still in his left hand and swung it wildly toward the man. It connected on the side of the man's cheek and exploded with flying embers. The man fell to the ground either dead or unconscious, his face severely burned and still holding embers on the skin.

Remarkably the torch wasn't fully extinguished, but it wouldn't last long without more fuel. He tore off pieces of his tunic and quickly wrapped a few pieces on the top and blew at the embers to help them ignite the fabric. This would burn for a few minutes at most, but it was better than no light. He took a quick look at the man who lay there, not breathing. The skin was pale, face gaunt, and the fingers and limbs were just skin and bones. With no more time to waste he plunged into the dark again to find his men.

Only a few moments later he was attacked again. The man lunged at Jeroboam with the same ferocity as the last attacker. Jeroboam instinctively dropped low to the ground and the man nearly ran over the top of him. Jeroboam drove his legs forward into the man and he was taken from his feet and slammed into the wall of jagged stone. The man slid down to the ground, clearly stunned and Jeroboam separated himself from the man before he could recover and picked up his torch and ran further into the dark, not stopping to make sure he was on the correct path. He only wanted to put distance between that beast and himself as he heard a deep-throated scream behind him and figured the creature was now headed his way. So he started to dart in and out of openings, up and over boulders with no thought as to the correct path to the ground level.

By now, Jeroboam's torch was reduced to glowing embers and barely lit the way in front of him. He decided he had better find a place to hide if he could. After a few minutes he'd found this little cave through an opening barely as wide as his torso which he shimmied through. It was nearly the length of his body, so he had to inch his way through until he came to the opening on the other side and spilled out onto the floor. He'd kept his torch, barely glowing, and quickly used the waning light to see if there was any other way out but realized he was at the bottom of a small naturally occurring shaft. Perhaps if he climbed, he might find an opening?

Jeroboam had torn off more pieces of fabric, attempting to ignite the torch, but it was too late, and the last ember flickered out leaving him with no light and no way to see an escape route. It was at that moment he heard a shriek just outside the crevasse he had climbed through. How had they found him so easily and so quickly? He couldn't see what was on the other side, but he could hear the creature begin the laborious transit from there to here. With no time to think and even less eyesight to climb safely, Jeroboam stood and grabbed blindly upward until he found a handhold and began his blind climb upward to wherever it might lead. He estimated that he'd climbed several cubits when he heard the creature bursting through into the opening below with a loud and shrill scream. He'd never heard anything more bone chilling.

Jeroboam kept climbing, however slowly, since he could only guess where the next handhold would be. He could hear the man below jumping and trying to reach him. Then he heard another shriek coming from below as another one barreled through the opening. These men turned beast used to be his kinsmen. Now they were something twisted and vile bent on killing and maiming.

He kept climbing, one grasp at a time. Somehow, they could see him, he couldn't fathom how since he could barely make out a hand in front of his face. Suddenly he felt a hand dig into his heel.

Jeroboam panicked, *They're climbing! Not good!*

The creature yanked and pulled at him, trying to break his grasp on the stone above so he would fall to his demise. Fortunately, Jeroboam had found a firm grasp which he hung from as the creature pulled and pulled, trying to climb up and over him. He began to kick blindly until he felt his foot connect to the head of his attacker. The creature roared as his grasp was broken and he fell below. Not wasting any time, he climbed to wherever he was going. Moments later he found an outcropping that jutted out over his head. He pulled himself wholly onto the ledge and lay there trying to still his heartbeat and catch his breath.

The heavy breathing below intensified as he realized they were rapidly climbing again. He had nowhere to go, at least from his limited sight. He prepared to defend himself in the next moment when those creatures reached his summit.

"Elohim, defend me against this evil." He prayed fervently.

He heard one reach up over the ledge and started to kick wildly in the direction of the noise. His foot found a jaw which he repeatedly kicked until the creature fell backward. But he heard another and another climbing. How many were there?

"Elohim defend Me!!" he shouted into the darkness.

The creatures reached him at that very moment they began to pull them self over the edge. He thrashed, kicked, and punched as they began to descend upon him. He would lose this fight at any moment, and he prepared to meet his end.

"DEFEND ME ALMIGHTY ELOHIM!" He shouted into the darkness as his fist connected with the side of a face.

The moment he finished his final plea when all hope was lost, and he started to surrender to his fate, the ground began to shake. The creatures suddenly stopped as the ground above opened, and a sliver of light began to shine directly on them. For the first time he could see his attackers; their twisted faces contorted with rage and malice. The blinding light came through and they raised their hands to cover their faces. One by one they turned their bodies and jumped over the ledge as rocks began to fall. They disappeared below and likely ran back into the cave where they had come from screeching all the way.

Jeroboam laid back as the quake subsided and let his eyes adjust to the light coming through bathing his body. After just a few moments he was able to completely open his eyes and sat up, pulling himself up against the walls. Assessing his wounds, he was relieved that he only received some cuts and scratches, and the bite wound would heal though he needed to clean it. Nothing that would cause lasting harm to him. Satisfied that he was not mortally wounded he picked himself up and looked about the fissure that had opened just now, before his eyes. It was a somewhat long climb to the surface but one he was glad to make.

When he finally reached the surface and pulled himself up to safety he rolled away from the edge and just lay there again letting the early morning sun sooth his skin. It felt wonderful to be in the land of the living again. He surveyed his location as he stood and figured out that he was close to the Israelite camp judging by the proximity to the distant walls of Jebus. He'd need to make haste to get back and warn the camp of what he'd experienced.

CHAPTER 18

The Palace Infirmary

David stood only feet away from King Adonizedek in the corner of the room where Thoros lay recovering on a stone table. The wounds were all tended to and according to the doctors if the fever broke by the next morning, he may have a shot at living. Siv sat across the room next to Thoros, stroking his hair and kissing him on his forehead, hoping to see a sign of life, willing him to survive.

King Adonizedek turned and walked across the room and stopped at the door. He glanced to his right and said, "Walk with me, David?" and then turned and exited the room, spear in hand.

David, not sure if this was a request or not, decided he'd better humor him and hurried along to catch up. King Adonizedek's stride was quite a bit longer, nearly double his height, so he walked considerably slower alongside David as they descended the stairs to the garden level. The word garden was an understatement as he gawked at the massive tree that grew from the middle of it. Every kind of fruit known to man was here in this garden. They walked for a while, still the giant king said nothing. The overcast skies cast a grey hue on the buildings as a cool breeze from the west rolled in just as they reached the dais at the furthest end of the garden. From there they could see the Israelite army encampment sprawled on the hills south of the city.

"Standing here, looking down on the earth one gets the sense that they're untouchable; here, above it all." King Adonizedek said knowingly, "I believed that until fourteen hours ago when your men brought my son through the gates on a litter."

Without a word, King Adonizedek turned and walked toward the center of the garden underneath the large tree. He sat on a bench and beckoned David to sit on the one across from him. He reached up and pulled his purple cowl down and then leaned down and placed his forearms on his knees, fingers intertwined, his spear resting on his left shoulder.

He drilled David with his stark blue eyes and then said, "And here I find myself in a conundrum. The men responsible for saving my son's life are also our greatest enemies."

David mulled this statement over and said, "We only do what is right at the time. When we captured him, it would've been alright to kill him, at least from our perspective. Just as you had the opportunity to kill me when you captured me in the stables. Once the determination is made that a man is worth more alive than dead it isn't a far leap to taking actions like Joab took this morning."

King Adonizedek nodded affirmatively. "You must be aware that your man Joab is on shaky ground with your King?"

David shrugged nonchalantly, "Joab made his choice, as did I when I stayed behind to face that beast in the stables while my men escaped. We do what we must especially when there is no one else to do it."

David had thought a lot about this, and his men all knew that they had a choice to be loyal to him or to King Saul, or both. He would never usurp the king in this way; though he had recently spread secretive instructions for his solidly loyal men to abandon the camp and sneak away to his cavalry encampment in the hills of Ephraim, these instructions were up to each man to decide their own path. His only exception to following his orders was in the heat of battle and matters of tactics; these kinds of orders were to be followed without discussion or failure. In any case, David estimated that at most, a thousand would heed his call. Not enough to challenge King Saul if it came to it but enough to give him mobility around the land and ward off other enemies as he made his getaway from the king's murderous contempt.

He had grown to dislike the man who had been his mentor who had brought him into the palace and treated him as a son. Still, he prayed for King Saul daily that he would see sense and soften his heart toward him and toward Elohim. The more King Saul's mind went toward hatred of David the further separated he was from Elohim. He knew this would end in calamity the very first time King Saul welcomed him back after David had spared him, only to throw a very well-placed spear at David at his return banquet. Had it not been for his own awareness he wouldn't have been able to dodge the spear. He eventually came back into good graces with King Saul for a second time but this time he would not embrace Saul as he did before. Instead, he kept him at arm's length, knowing that if something happens once it will most assuredly happen a second time. This second relapse in their relations served as a proof positive reason for the cynicism.

"I am on the outs with King Saul as well, for refusal to execute your son."

"But he is your king, and Thoros is the enemy."

"And now King Saul is my enemy, once again. See how quickly these things change? I would have killed Thoros in the heat of battle without blinking. But to execute a high value prince because of a petty insult defies all logic. I expect the men loyal to me to question motives and to never follow anything that goes against our moral code. I expect them to choose to do what's right. My men know this and are encouraged to exercise free will to choose their path. They follow my orders when it comes to military operations but when it comes to their own path, they must choose for themselves."

David straightened his posture and brought his right ankle up onto his left knee and continued, "When I was on the run years back, the first time King Saul exiled me, I received a word from God through our prophet that I had full blessing to take up arms against King Saul and kill him to take the throne. I even had a dream where the Most High came to me and told me the very same. This would've been easy for me to do, and I had Divine permission, but I didn't feel right about touching a hair on the head of Elohim's anointed king, even if I was the heir. Do you see what I'm getting at?"

Adonizedek cocked his head to the side and then straightened his head, "I suppose the easiest and most obvious path is not always the right path. I admire your take on this though I don't share the sentiment of free will. I prefer my men to do as I say without question."

"Had Elohim commanded me to kill King Saul I would have done it without question, but he gave me a choice and my choice not to kill him gave the king a chance at redemption. Who am I to be the arbiter in the struggle between The Most High and His anointed king? In any case, the refusal to kill Thoros this very morning in front of your gates led to where we are now, you and I talking amiably rather than watching me swing from a noose."

"It is as you say David. I am only looking to understand why a renowned warrior such as you made the choices that you made. I had a hunch about you, and I see that I am proven correct that you are a man of integrity and good character. I have decided to spare your life and those of your men."

"Good king, this is more than I expected as I am under no expectation that I have a say in these matters now."

"Well put, and a very stoic sentiment. We only control what is ours to control. The rest is up to the gods." Adonizedek sat back and propped his leg up on his other knee, mimicking David, appearing more relaxed.

David looked about and noticed two ravens sitting on a middle branch in the tree next to them. Adonizedek looked up and smiled, "Ah! Hugin and Munin have returned." With a wave of his spear the ravens floated down and assumed a place on his shoulders. He raised his right arm and the one on the right walked down to his forearm. He pulled his arm over with the raven and it began to squawk and almost seemed to be speaking to the king.

Adonizedek raised his arm again and the bird scurried back to its place on his right shoulder. He raised his left arm in the same way and the bird followed the same process. Once again, Adonizedek listened to the bird talk to him, as one would a messenger, then he beckoned it back to his shoulder.

His demeanor grew solemn as he rose from his seat, donned his hood, and walked away. He left David sitting there alone. Adonizedek hastily walked over the edge of the garden and peered out toward the Israelite camp. David slowly walked up behind him and joined him on the balcony.

David audibly gasped, the Israelite encampment which was pristine moments ago was completely ablaze, flames reaching a hundred feet into the air; smoke traveled into the air and blanketed the ground for what seemed like miles. Calamity had struck his army, or what used to be his army. The consequence of having a king who was demented was evident. All he could do was watch as the camp burned. The first siege of Jebus had ended in defeat for Israel.

Outside the Israelite Camp

Jeroboam crawled to the top of a ridge and looked down onto the Israelite camp below. A few hours ago, he'd climbed out of the caves and started to head towards the camp. As he came up onto a ridge, he saw black smoke rising. It took him a few hundred steps to reach a bluff that gave him a good vantage of the camp below. His jaw dropped as he saw that the camp had all but been destroyed and looked to be hastily abandoned.

Moving as quickly as his sore legs would allow, he made his way down towards the camp and surveyed the destruction. The camp was deserted and there were men dead to his left and right. The whole army had fled after what appeared to be a vicious attack. The center of the camp was smoldering with black smoke reaching high into the late morning sky as the sun approached its zenith.

Jeroboam walked carefully, stopping to check if any were alive. Who had done this? Surely the soldiers in the city hadn't left their walls. He kept thinking of the creatures he had just escaped and wondered if they were related events. This certainly fit the chaos which he knew only in the darkness of the caves he had just escaped with his life. Just as Jeroboam was about to turn away, he noticed a hand reaching up out of a pile of debris toward him. He lifted a heavy wagon wheel off the injured man. That's when he realized it was Uriah.

"Uriah! It's Jeroboam. I'm here to help." Jeroboam knelt next to him and gave him some water from his leather waterskin. Uriah drank voraciously until he choked a bit and began to cough. Jeroboam withdrew the skin and placed his hand on Uriah's shoulder. The young man looked terrible.

Jeroboam asked, "Are you injured Uriah?"

Speaking for the first time, Uriah answered, "I think my leg is broken," as he winced with pain trying to lean forward and feel his leg.

"I'll do what I can to brace your leg. I'll need to build a litter to get you out of here. Do you know what happened here?"

Uriah shook his head in disbelief as he began to explain the events of the last day. They had indeed been attacked by the very same type of creatures last night. Hundreds were slaughtered by the attackers, and then hundreds more were slaughtered in the ensuing pandemonium. Confusion set in and men started attacking one another. Uriah had been pinned beneath the wagon as it tipped over.

"Where is King Saul, and the prince Jonathan?" Jeroboam asked.

Uriah gestured in a confused manner, "Couldn't say, perhaps they fled with what was left of the forces. It's been quiet for several hours. I tried yelling for help, but nobody was around until you showed up. Thank Adonai you did. I had given up hope."

Uriah tried to sit up straighter, and he yelled out in pain with the movement of his right leg. "Definitely broken," he said, exasperated.

"Didn't you leave with David? Where is he?" Uriah questioned.

Jeroboam was at a loss. He looked Uriah in the eye and then hung his head toward his feet. There was a long silence as they both pondered the consequences of the last few days' events and actions. David was likely dead after sacrificing himself to help them all escape. The mighty army of Israel had crumbled from within in less than two days. King Saul was mad and there was no telling what he would do next and worst of all, there were Israelite men, turned into monsters, terrorizing the underground and the outskirts of Jebus.

Jeroboam rummaged through the rubble and debris and ran about the camp grabbing tent posts and canvas. He found a knife and cut strips from one of the pieces and then punctured a series of eyelets in the second canvas. He then laid them on top of the canvas and set to work tying the strips of canvas through the eyelets and around the posts. Working as quickly as he could, he tied a dozen on each side.

This will have to do, he thought, as he flipped the makeshift litter over.

It took him a while to make one suitable to carry the weight of a grown man and he searched the camp nearby for water, food, and any supplies that may help them out. By the time he finished it was late afternoon. The nights were long this time of year, so he figured he had only one or two hours of light left at most. How far could they go in the dark? The reality of it was he dreaded being out and exposed when the night came. The last thought made him shudder to think of his ordeal last night into the early morning. He couldn't help but associate them with the darkness now.

"Okay Uriah. I need to get you onto this."

Jeroboam stood up and looked around. "We need to move. I'll try to be careful, but it will be painful. We can't stay here after dark. I fear those creatures will return and I don't want to press my luck with them again."

He reached under Uriah's armpits and pulled upward and scooted him over onto the litter. Uriah screamed in agony and nearly passed out cold. Jeroboam stooped over him to check his splint and once satisfied he pulled him sideways the rest of the way onto the litter. Uriah was groaning with every little movement. He waited for a few minutes and gave Uriah some water and some bread he'd found. He ate a little himself as he thought over their options. This would have been easier with a horse because, with it, they would move much faster, but they had no such luck this evening.

With precious little daylight left there was no more time to waste as he threw his waterskin and Uriah's satchel over his shoulder and picked up the lead ends and began to drag the litter toward the edge of camp. He stopped abruptly and grabbed a length of heavy rope. He used it to fashion a sort of sling the ran across his shoulders and over his upper arms to allow him to lift the litter using his whole body. With that modification he was able to pick up the pace. He would need to stick to the roads since the terrain was too rocky and uneven to drag Uriah over.

Pulling Uriah, Jeroboam soon came to the main road where a left would head south into Israel while a right would lead to the gates of Jebus. He estimated he had very little daylight left, and he dreaded the thought of being left exposed out here with those creatures. His theory after seeing them react to sunlight and Uriah's account of the attacks led him to believe they operated at night and preferred to stay out of the light. This realization that he could not risk a left turn and a few day's journey to their home unsettled him and filled him with consternation. Jeroboam could hardly believe it himself as he realized his feet had chosen to take the path toward Jebus as the sun began its descent over the hills of Ephraim.

"Elohim Defend Me," he said quietly as the walls of Jebus appeared, looming over him. He prayed that he'd made the right choice. He feared that no matter the choice he and Uriah were doomed.

Better the enemy you know than the one you don't, he reasoned to himself. When Jeroboam had come close enough to the gates, he yelled at the guards above who no doubt had seen him approaching.

"My name is Jeroboam, and this man is Uriah. He needs medical help! Please allow us to enter. We will surrender to you."

A few moments passed as he saw a flurry of activity above; several men ran to and from the post at the gate. He was just about to turn away to get out of range of the archers should they decide to go the other direction with his plea for help. Just as he took a step the gates hissed and creaked. The doors slowly opened inward, and several soldiers exited and lined the road. One beckoned him to walk forward, and he did cautiously, not wanting to walk into a trap. As he passed the soldiers, they stared at him emotionlessly. Passing through the gates, the soldiers to the outside began to follow behind. Once all had returned to the courtyard the doors creaked shut and with a thud the beam was lowered into its cradle.

Moments later, a flat cart appeared being pulled by an ox with a man using a whip to coax it forward. Two soldiers grabbed Uriah's litter and lifted him up onto the cart. They gestured to him to sit on the end of the cart. Once he complied, they signaled to the man to carry them on into the city. They walked at a steady pace through the streets that had come alive in celebration that the Israelites had fled just as the drought had ended.

◆◇◆

South of Jebus, on the road to Hebron

Jonathan rode as fast as his horse would take him to the rear of the fleeing Israelite army. Each soldier looked as if they had just experienced the most horrifying ordeal ever. Jonathan couldn't blame them after the night they all had. He did his best to keep order, but the throng of men went awry almost as soon as he straightened them out. He shouted at the men to keep ranks; they would straighten their columns for a moment, he'd move to the next company and do the same. By the time he'd straightened out that company the one before was in disarray again. It was an exercise in futility. This had been the case for the demoralized army of Israel for the last day or so since they fled with their tails tucked.

His father's caravan had long outdistanced the main army several hours ago and they were likely already back to Hebron. His father was in no condition to give orders nor strategize the next moves now that they had been horrifically outdone by what seemed like a demon army. He didn't know what they were, all he knew was they used to be his own countrymen. They had been turned into something else altogether and he could not explain what he'd seen.

Jonathan witnessed the man come in and try to kill him in the tent when Thoros, the prince of Jebus had saved him. The man's eyes were transformed into a black abyss as if his soul had been replaced by another being. There was no humanity in those eyes. He shuddered to think of it. Those flesh and blood demons had brought the mighty army of Israel to their knees and stolen from them a most assured victory at Jebus. He'd spent the entire night trying to hold back the chaos. What's more, he had learned of Joab's disobedience to Saul at the gates of Jebus where he had defied him and walked, toting an impossibly wounded prince Thoros right up the gates of Jebus and handed themselves over.

There was more going on here that he just couldn't fathom now. Jonathan felt as though everything was out of his control at this moment and would somehow not be in his control for some time. That possibility irked him because Jonathan was used to being in control, stoic and reserved. The past few days had tested him to the breaking point after the finding of the captives in the caves, witnessing his father's inexplicable rage and mental decline, then having to choose between his own father and king and his blood brother David who he'd sworn to protect. He'd even saved and released a giant-sized prince to roam the camp during that chaos. He doubted that any of this was due to the prince, but he had his suspicions that the siege camp burning was the work of such a man. Three days and all hell had broken loose and his whole life seemed to hang in the balance. His whole country seemed like it was falling right before his eyes, and he could do nothing to stave off the disaster.

Jonathan wondered about his brother, David. Somehow, he knew David was still alive, which gave him hope. David had always been a rock steady ally and friend. They had bled in battle, mended each other's wounds, and saved each other in battle countless times. He could not ask for a better friend who'd stuck to him closer than a brother. The fact that their paths had now diverged again troubled him, but this would now be the third time in five years that David had fallen out of favor with his father. He had hoped that David would return, and he'd be able to see his brother again. He looked to the hills in the west and wondered how many of David's "Mighty Men", as David called them, had escaped. There were at least a thousand among the ranks. There was no telling how many of them took heed of their plan to ask them to exit the camp and leave King Saul's army.

That was another thing he wrestled with as he plotted to help David maintain his safety and position against King Saul's will. He meant his father no harm, but he truly believed David was the best leader for Israel. Even the late prophet Samuel had spoken of David as the anointed successor to the throne of Israel. His father was tormented to no end in his mind, and he assumed the only thing that his father had any semblance of control over was his throne and the keeping of the crown that went with it.

His father was consumed by it now that he felt Elohim had deserted him, which he had indeed. It was his own disobedience and hubris that had brought this judgment on him, not any work of man. Certainly not David, who was thrust into this life after being just a lowly shepherd as a boy. He pitied his father, but he did not love him as a son would. He respected him and even feared him, but he found it impossible to love the man or the king because they had become one and the same. Jonathan remembered his youth when his father was humble and followed The Most High's will in everything, but he now considered it a long-lost memory that often surfaced to remind him that man was gone for some time now.

Jonathan reached the end of the trail of men about an hour later. A few mounted officers hung back to round up any stragglers. He approached one of them and said, "Ride to the front and let them know it's my order to make camp. We are three hours from dusk."

The rider left instantly and disappeared over the rise to carry out his order. Jonathan wheeled about on his horse and galloped away from the rear and retraced their travel for about a mile. He rode back to the top of a hill that jutted upward several dozen feet higher than the road below. To the north he could just barely see the spire of the Citadel Fortress rising above the plain on Mount Moriah. He said a prayer to the Almighty God that he'd see his brother again before returning to the column of their defeated army. The sun was beginning to set to the west which meant that the last of the army would be coming in after dark. Jonathan would stay with them and be the last one into camp. For the second night he hoped they'd be safe from the terror that had attacked them outside of Jebus.

CHAPTER 19

Memphis, Egypt

L ox crouched behind a row of shanty houses and tried his best to make himself inconspicuous. It was near sunset and many of the workers were returning from their labor in the fields along the Nile. This was the place where his informant had spotted it, and he was anxious to begin his search. But he needed the cover of darkness to do so. The shanty town was basically a mix of wooden lean-to and mud brick homes covered by thatch roofs. The condition of squalor was palpable as the wind shifted and brought the smell of the latrines nearby to his nostrils. He wasn't squeamish by any stretch, but he couldn't wait to be able to move about.

Lox briefly let his mind wander to thinking about Jebus and the siege. He wondered how Thoros would fare, and he realized he cared a little more than was usual about what happened to Adonizedek, who had shown him the favor and treated him like a member of the family in the middle of a very trying period of his long life. Even Thoros, his adopted brother, managed a bit of passing sympathy from him as he thought about his plight.

The only way now was to regain his power, and his destiny would be in his hands once again. All the work he'd done these last years was on the edge of being ruined by the ill-fated siege and the unpredictability of a certain shadow being who could not stick to the plan. Still, all was not lost. If he could obtain the amulet he would go back and attempt a rescue to ensure that Adonizedek and his family were not swept up as casualties in his quest. That was always a worry of his which was why he'd insisted on Tsalmaveth's promise to spare them.

Tsalmaveth's divergence from the plan had set every contingent plan ablaze. Lox silently cursed and spat on the ground at Tsalmaveth's inability to be patient and wait for their plan to work. It irked Lox to no end when he thought about all of the wasted effort stretching over several decades. Things such as gathering the Philistines and turning them on the Israelites only to have Tsalmaveth contract with Goliath to be his vessel and then lose to a fifteen-year-old shepherd boy. When he'd returned to Jebus at the behest of Adonizedek he'd secretively built a very expensive temple and tunnel network away from the prying eyes of the Court. He'd used Adonizedek's trust in him to siphon off tax income to fund the materials and laborers, all of which he'd killed after their work was completed to avoid talk of it. Had he not happened upon the parchment by accident a few days ago, telling him of this amulet he may never have known. And now he wondered if this amulet was the one he'd lost so many hundreds of years back along with his lost love who was murdered and burned as a witch. That opened up a whole separate set of emotions ranging from anger to despair.

As he waited, he began to think of his lost love, Astarte's laughter and her blue eyes. Her blonde hair and olive skin was not unlike Siv who reminded him so much of her. Their curly hair, skin color, and eyes were so alike that he had trouble looking at Siv in the palace and felt what he could describe as shame at the thought of it as she walked by. Her perfume wafting about the halls even reminded him of Astarte. Siv was widely regarded as the most beautiful of creatures in all of Canaan.

Astarte was more beautiful in the way she swayed her hips when she walked. Her sense of humor and wit was even more appealing to a man such as him. She had fire in her eyes and would never take no for an answer from anyone when she desired something. But she had been cruelly taken from him so many years ago. She was dead, lost to the ages. He'd given her his amulet to wear for a ruse. So, with her went his power and doomed him to stay in his human form for all time. He could of course use blood magic spells to transform but it was hard to do and frowned upon by nearly everyone, and it lasted for only twenty-four hours. With the amulet he could change into anything at will, without blood magic. It was given to him by an old crone long ago and now he held a small hope that this amulet was the very same one.

Lox had even begun to age because of the missing amulet, which kept him youthful in addition to giving him immense power to transform into any creature, known or unknown to man. He finally snapped out of his stupor as his attention was drawn back to the amulet he sought.

He couldn't really see the entire street in which he hid himself, but he could hear people walking by on their way home from the day's labor. A sort of bustling energy found its way to him as Lox began to feel a bit restless waiting. He tried to busy himself by drawing a map of the city, as he knew it, in the dirt with his finger. He would do well to have a good recollection of it when he escaped.

In the distance he heard several small bells ringing in a sort of rhythmic fashion. One by one they sounded very faint at first but as it grew closer, he could hear the bells more clearly. Lox could hear an extremely low chant coming from the same direction and he wasn't sure what he was hearing, thinking for a second that he might poke his head out and try and catch a glimpse. He thought better of it seeing as it was still light enough that anyone seeing him might raise an alarm. He hunkered down and allowed the procession to come closer.

The chant was a mixture of low and high tones sung in harmony. It was very soothing and at the same time he felt slightly uneasy. The musical tone was coming from one person he determined, maybe the leader of the procession? Lox was astounded to hear two separate notes coming from one set of lungs. No words were being sung that he could tell. It grew louder and louder as it approached his hiding place in a deserted alley. Finally, Lox's curiosity boiled over and completely overtook his sense of self preservation.

Lox slowly rose and crouched behind the crates and barrels of useless forgotten wares and attempted a look at the procession as it began to pass by. He saw a man dressed in a gold tunic holding a bell in each hand. Bells hung from his tunic and ears. He had tambourines around his wrists, elbows, and ankles. Lox thought the man looked ridiculous, but the sound coming from his lungs was mesmerizing. He then saw several gold-clad soldiers marching in neat columns, four across and six deep, as they passed, he saw a palanquin carried just behind them with guards in purple and gold lining the sides of it.

The palanquin itself was gold and ornamented with jewels of all shapes and sizes. Rubies, emeralds, diamonds, topaz, and blue sapphire adorned the images of a bull, an eagle, a man, and a lion decorating each corner of the palanquin which was covered by a finely embroidered veil of silk. Behind the palanquin followed another column of twenty-four men in white tunics with gold laurels on their heads. They each carried a silver staff bearing a jasper and ruby star on it that looked a little ostentatious.

His blood ran cold as he gazed upon familiar symbols, recalling the frighteningly overwhelming presence of those beings outside the Ark in Goliath's throne room. This had to be a coincidence.

Another question came to mind, why would a royal be down here in the commoner dwelling at the end of the day no less? It made no sense. The men at the back looked like some sort of priests he figured. As the palanquin passed closer to his hiding place, the wind began to stir a bit and with it carried a fragrance that pulled him back down behind the crates.

Lox never underestimated his sense of smell to recall memories and the jasmine and black fig perfume with a hint of honey and citrus had done just that. One thing he now knew was that he must follow this procession. By now the sun was setting and certain portions of the street were dark and deserted after the procession went by. At this point Lox didn't really care if anyone saw him. He listened to the procession moving away into the distant city and decided to try and follow. As he entered the street, he saw that not a soul was around.

Where are all the people? Lox thought as he looked around at the deserted streets. It was peculiar that no residents were on their stoop watching the procession when, moments before, he could hear countless feet busying themselves on their way to their homes. But after the procession not a soul could be found. No windows with lights in them. All shuttered as if no one was home or a storm was brewing. It made him uneasy but at least he could now walk a little more freely. Lox decided he would stay close to alleys whenever possible so he could hide if need be.

He stopped periodically and listened for the bells and singing which he could barely hear in the distance, so he quickened his pace, hoping to catch up. He soon came to a crossroad where he listened for a moment before turning right, hearing a bell ring. After a hundred yards, Lox found an alleyway to hide in for a moment.

The sound was coming from just around the bend and he needed to be able to think for a moment and find out what was going on. He climbed up onto the roof and tried to walk to the edge where he knew it was solid; the last thing he needed was to fall through into someone's home. After skipping over a few narrow alleys and homes he could finally see it; a massive temple with a huge statue in front of it. He was astonished to see that it was nearly the same as his own temple. Every single detail was the same apart from the fact that his was underneath the city.

He hadn't imagined one ever existing of this size anywhere in the world. His god had a small and devoted following or so he thought. But here was an opulent example of a temple to the god Yaldabaoth, the creator and rightful god of this world. According to Tsalmaveth, the god that the Hebrews worshipped was a pretender to the throne. All the symbols he saw on the procession made sense now. He remembered seeing the heads of animals on the two scary beings that day in Goliath's Hall, as the Ark was opened, and he came into possession of the stone box containing Tsalmaveth. These seemed to be a play on the very same creatures that had ripped apart and dismembered the unknowing slaves that fateful day.

The only thing Lox could reason was that this must be the center for religion. He realized he only knew a part of the inner workings of this religion even as he'd had contact with Yaldabaoth through his agent Tsalmaveth, whom he'd all but left behind in Jebus. Had it been that long since he'd been to Memphis? He thought a moment about it and realized it had been before Jericho that he was here. In the last few hundred years, Yaldabaoth had gained many followers to be able to build such a massive temple.

A throng of people were in front of the temple, chanting and cheering, as the procession made its way up to the high steps of the temple. Lox needed to get close enough to see, so he jumped down onto the street and ran the rest of the way, taking a left just before the main avenue. He ran along rows of market stalls, until he came to a long alleyway that headed straight for the temple thinking that it must be a supply road for the temple compound which, by the size of it, housed thousands of people who served in the temple and surrounding area.

Lox came to an unmanned gate, no doubt due to the festivities. He easily scaled the gate and landed on the other side to find a good-sized yard with pens of livestock, chickens, and a granary that was bursting full. He quickly had a thought of the starving citizens in Jebus and wondered if an un-walled city such as Memphis would even stand a chance if even half the Hebrew army marched on it. These idiots had no idea how posh their life was here in this city that sat upon the fertile Nile River.

Lox crept around in the shadow of the waning light from the sun and found a vantage that held a view of the front of the temple from the side. He could see the palanquin at the bottom of the stairs, and it looked like the occupant was no longer in it, but instead he saw the procession reaching the top of the stairs. Lox couldn't see the occupant of the palanquin because they were surrounded by the priests that had followed behind. A long moment of silence passed before the procession fully reached the top. The soldiers had stayed below to protect the entrance to the temple should anyone try and enter by way of the stairs. Lox could feel the tension in the air as the throng of people looked on expectantly.

The entourage of priests stood at the foot of the huge statue of Yaldabaoth and one by one pricked their thumbs and rubbed their blood at the foot of it. After each had done so, the woman from the palanquin finally revealed herself to the crowd.

She walked forward, as a booming voice, the one who had been singing with the bells in front of the procession, proclaimed, "Behold, The Queen of the Earth! Wife and Servant to Yaldabaoth! All hail, Yaldabaoth!"

As he made this proclamation the woman stepped forward. She was covered head to toe in gold and jewels. Her shawl, woven with fine strands of gold and silk, glinted in the remaining sunlight. Lox could not see her face or any skin for that matter but then he saw it...the amulet; a black onyx in the center with every single gemstone found on earth surrounding it in a perfect circle. It was all set in a gold sun that seemed to radiate its own light.

*My amulet. After so many years...*Lox thought, beginning to salivate. This was indeed his lost amulet, strung around the neck of the masked woman.

Lox's jaw dropped as she walked forward to the edge of the stairs; he could see that she was transforming. This was the first time he'd seen this amulet at work in over seven hundred years and he could feel it pulling at him. No doubt the energy of the amulet could sense his own familiar essence.

The woman removed the golden shawl that covered her body and let it fall from her shoulders revealing a gold tunic that accentuated her shapely figure. She raised her arms and simultaneously revealed a set of sprawling wings that protruded from her back. They were black as night, which was a complement to her golden wardrobe. The wings stretched out to an expanse that nearly covered the front of the dais that she and the priests stood upon, the work of the amulet, no doubt. Her transformation was not complete though.

She began to grow rapidly as the sun behind her began to set. She grew until she was the same size as the statue to her right. For the first time Lox realized the seat next to the statue of Yaldabaoth, who sat atop a throne made of gold, a snake wrapped around his body to the bottom of the throne with two rubies for its eyes. She turned and strode to the right side of the statue and began to address the throng of stunned people.

"People of the Nile; I will now speak for the God, Yaldabaoth. Hear me!" she proclaimed as the crowd fell completely silent.

In a powerful voice, she spoke to the crowd that had gathered at the foot of the Temple. "Your God, Yaldabaoth, has decided to swallow the sun and bring darkness upon you! He has allowed Death's Shadow to enter this land and cleanse it of all who have disobeyed him."

The sun began to set directly behind the temple as she finished the statement. As shrieks of terror arose from corners of the crowd, pleas for mercy were shouted in anguish from around the entire compound.

"But do not fear! Yaldabaoth has given me a message. He has heard your plea and has decided that not a single man, woman, or child will die this night if you prepare your home with the blood of a goat over the door lentil!"

The woman's voice amplified as she shouted this decree, and her wings pointed upwards just as the last of the sun set behind the temple. The light in the compound was waning now. Shouts of praise echoed about.

"Praise him, our merciful Yaldabaoth!" shouted the priests in unison.

The same was echoed by the throng of people below! Over and over, they chanted, until the last of the light was gone.

"Go now! And prepare your home. If you obey you will see the sun in the morning, do it not and I cannot tell you what will happen to you." she proclaimed as she stood and bounded over to her original place.

She looked more like a dark shadow now with the very dim light from the fire that burned within the temple. A few torches had appeared in the crowd as it dispersed. Gradually, she returned to her normal size. The wings folded up and disappeared from her back as some of the priest aided her in donning her shawl and veil once again. They led her into the temple and disappeared.

Lox was stunned. Not in all his years had he seen someone command common people with such a show of power. Even Adonizedek, in all his glory, was not able to produce such a display, apart from the instinctual abilities he possessed to see the truth or the lie in someone's character, along with the astounding wisdom that Adonizedek used to grow in influence. He was a natural born leader. But this was a surpassing ability Lox had never even dreamt of. Lox suddenly felt inadequate, which angered him. She had commanded the superstitions of the people to compel them into worship and she had used his amulet to do it. He hated to admit it, but she may have used the amulet more effectively than he ever did.

I need to focus, Lox thought. At long last he was within just a few yards of the object of his desire. Then the thought crossed his mind: *Of which object; the woman or the amulet?*

The Palace Garden

King Adonizedek stood next to David as the Israelite camp burned. The smoke had turned from a black to a gray hue which told him the fuel for the fire was nearly spent. His ravens had told him that the Israelites fled the siege after King Saul's attempt at stopping Joab. What's more, there were more survivors that showed up at the gates just moments ago.

David placed his hands upon the railing and leaned in with his head hung low. "It would seem your city has been saved." The disappointment was evident.

King Adonizedek, not wanting to gloat, said, "For now, you may be correct. Though my fear is that whatever calamity befell your armies may come to visit us. I've seen too many things over the years to feel secure in this victory."

"Those men in your dungeons are no longer my kinsmen, I can tell you that much. They were completely transformed by whatever methods Lox used on them. Those are the very sort that attacked our camp and almost killed Thoros. That is plain to see. Something has awakened them and mobilized them." David said, matter-of-factly.

King Adonizedek turned these words over in his mind for a moment. He had learned to listen first and speak slowly. "I need more information; we must go to the dungeons and ascertain if what you say is correct but first, I need to reveal something else to you. If you would follow me back to where your men are?"

They turned and walked the short distance back across the garden to the side room where Thoros lay unconscious, and his man Joab and company were recovering. As they approached the guards opened the door wide. Adonizedek motioned for David to enter ahead of him. He watched as David went through the door and stopped short. Clearly, he was shocked that yet more of his men had found their way into the city by way of the front gate.

David shouted, "Jeroboam! You made it out? What of the rest of the men?"

Jeroboam hung his head low and shook his head in such a way that told David that no one else made it out.

David crouched low and drew an imaginary drawing on the stone floor with his forefinger. "I feel I owe you an apology for leading you into that foolish mission."

King Adonizedek made a mental note of the humility that David displayed. It was not often that a man with power over others would admit when they had erred. He was starting to believe that David was someone with whom he could possibly trust. Not many men or women in the world could be described with that distinction. He wasn't quite ready to say he would trust him but the other part of his dream, which he'd withheld from the Council begged him to consider the possibility that this man could be the one he'd been searching for. After all, there was the rune reading from Skald to consider as he remembered the part about an enemy becoming an ally.

Adonizedek was lost in contemplation for a moment. *Could this be a fulfilled prophecy after all?* He thought.

King Adonizedek walked over to Thoros while David was catching up with Jeroboam and the other younger man who was now on the mend with a splint on his leg, lightly sedated but conscious. He placed his hand on the shin of his son who lay there in a dream state as his chest rose and fell slowly. He never could have imagined these events if he tried. His son lay here, life in the balance, as likely to die before his time as he was to survive. He prayed a silent prayer to whatever god may be listening. As his utterance traveled into the ether, he noticed that David and his men were now on their knees in a circle, those that could kneel. He listened in as David spoke with head bowed:

"Blessed are you O God. In thee, O Lord, do I put my trust; Let me never be ashamed and deliver me in thy righteousness.

Bow down thine ear to me; deliver me speedily and be thou my strong rock, for a house of defense to save me.

For thou are my rock and fortress; therefore, thy name's sake leads me and guides me.

Pull me out of the net that they laid privily for me, for thou art my strength. Into thine hand I commit my spirit.

Thou hast redeemed me, O Lord, God of Truth. Have mercy upon us O Lord, for we are in trouble.

Our eyes are consumed by grief in our soul and in our belly. But we trust in you O Lord for Thou art our God.

Our lives are in your hands.

Deliver us from the hands of our enemies and from them that persecute us. Make your face shine upon thy servants.

Save us for thy mercy's sake. For the Lord preserves the faithful, and plentifully rewards the proud doer.

Be of good courage, and he shall strengthen your heart, all ye that hope in the Lord."

Never had King Adonizedek heard such a contrite prayer. He had heard stories and whispers about the warrior poet named David. He quietly walked over to David as they finished praying and began to stand again. David turned and looked up at him with red eyes, his cheeks wet with tears. Joab and Jeroboam wiped tears away from their faces as well as their spirits seemed to be lifted.

King Adonizedek simply said, "My son Thoros…"

David looked up to the king and then over to Thoros. He said, "Your son will live, that prayer was for him as well. You will see the power of Elohim firsthand."

King Adonizedek didn't know what to think but somehow that gave him comfort to hear David so sure of his own God. He walked back over to Thoros and looked at Siv who sat by his side. She had been next to him the entire day and had not left to eat or drink. Her countenance was shattered as she visibly wept. Siv was a loyal wife and mother, and her beauty surpassed all creatures. Even in this chaotic situation she still somehow managed to exude beauty through the tears.

There was a knock at the door as the guards opened it. In walked his wife leading Magni and Thrud, his twin grandchildren. Following them was his own son Baaldir, who was nursing injuries himself and walking laboriously for a boy of fourteen, and his youngest son, Vithas. They were just on the other side of adolescence and ready to be evaluated as men in the coming years.

Baaldir, who had awoken this morning, was very skilled in combat and sport as well as possessing a sharp intellect and he had just been through a harrowing ordeal below the city. Vithas on the other hand was shy and not at all like his brothers. He was competent with his martial abilities but no comparison to Baaldir would be accurate as Vithas preferred to study tomes and manuscripts. He was a thinker which was a valuable characteristic to possess. In this way he thought Vithas took most after him. He would make a good leader one day.

Baaldir looked up to his older brother and would copy him and his fighting style and even practiced Thoros' mannerisms much to the annoyance of his older brother. Baaldir was a daredevil to say the least; he would jump from a roof and leap over a speeding cart. Until three nights ago, it appeared that nothing could harm him; he never seemed to get hurt even when he fell from a great height. Baaldir had climbed the ash tree in the garden many times and nearly fell on his head many more times. No amount of chiding from his mother would slow him or humble him, it seemed. His uncle Lox was a constant influence on his daredevil antics. Lox enjoyed great entertainment out of goading Baaldir into another feat of daring, almost as if Lox was trying to see if something would succeed in killing him eventually.

King Adonizedek embraced his sons and his grandsons as they gathered around Thoros' bed where he lay unconscious, oblivious to the gathering of loved ones around him. He prayed a silent prayer to David's God and asked Him for mercy for his son.

What could it hurt? he thought. They still had a temple to the Israelite God from the time of Melchizedek near the spring of Gihon at the foot of Mount Moriah. If Thoros pulled through he may just revive it once again and burn sacrifices to Elohim.

Siv visibly warmed as her sons embraced her and stayed close as she assured them that their father would recover. She stood up and leaned over

Thoros and kissed his lips as a tear fell from her cheek onto his. She looked at Adonizedek and said, "I will take the boys to their beds for the night my lord and then I'll return."

King Adonizedek nodded and urged her to stay in her room and get some rest also, but she shook her head and replied that she wouldn't be able to sleep with Thoros in this state. With that she put her hands upon her sons' shoulders and led them from the room. Baaldir and Vithas assumed seats next to Thoros and their mother, Frigg.

David came over to Adonizedek. He spoke in a faint voice, "Good king, my men have some information that you need to hear. Could we talk outside?"

King Adonizedek nodded and asked David and his men to lead the way. Once outside they were able to speak more freely. David motioned to Jeroboam, "Would you please recount your experience inside the caverns?"

Jeroboam went ahead to explain what he'd seen and heard including how he escaped miraculously through a fissure that opened during a localized earthquake. It was curious that the quake was not felt anywhere else in the region. It truly sounded like an act of Elohim to David and he uttered a few words of praise as Jeroboam finished the tale.

King Adonizedek was stunned, the way Jeroboam told of his harrowing escape and coming up upon the scene at the former Israelite camp it was clear that a larger force than a few twisted souls had attacked. He decided he needed to send men down and see these dungeons firsthand, but he feared he already knew the answer to that question that raged through his mind. They had likely traded one enemy for another.

The Palace Infirmary

Baaldir sat in the room next to his brother who he'd just seen for the first time since being attacked in the tunnels below the city. He was still trying to wrap his mind around the enemy Israelites, whom he'd seen murder those guards several days before, sitting and conversing with his father and others as though they were friends. Had so much changed in three days, he wondered? There was no sight of Lox and for some reason he faintly remembered seeing him on the edge of consciousness shortly after the doctors saved his life, but he'd not had the opportunity to ask his father about it. Something didn't add up though and his brain was still foggy from the restless sleep he'd had over the last few nights. The dreams plagued him fiercely and he wasn't sure why he'd been stricken with them, but a lingering irritation persisted. It was similar to an annoying sliver in the hand that shouldn't hurt as badly for something so small, yet it had wormed its way into his psyche and consumed his waking thoughts, as well as during sleep.

Baaldir balanced this with his grief in losing Nathan, his very closest friend who was like a brother to him. The last time his mother had informed him, she'd heard from some guards that Nathan had likely passed on last night from his many fatal injuries. It had been a stroke of luck that Baaldir had survived and recovered to the extent that he had so quickly. For the last day or so he'd wrestled with his emotions and tried his best to master them, but upon the realization that Nathan was no more, he'd collapsed in his mother's lap and sobbed for many hours until no more tears would come. He'd wished and prayed to the gods that he could go back and try again to save him.

Alas, that was not to be. Now all he was left with was reality.

This reality consisted of so many things that it was hard to make sense of them, so he'd done his best to organize them. First, he was alive and recovering. This was obviously a good thing. Secondly, his brother Thoros had been captured, released, attacked by creatures outside the walls, and then been saved by his captors and brought here. His wounds were likely due to the very same creatures that attacked him and Nathan. Thirdly and most horrid, Nathan was killed by those shadow figures in the tunnels. As he choked back tears, he realized he needed to find out more about them but didn't know where to start. His mother and father would never allow him to venture back down there to seek answers so he would either need to sneak away when he'd recovered, or he'd need to find the answers elsewhere. Lastly, across from him sat Israelites who all looked to be professional warriors. The one who seemed to lead him was the famed warrior called David and he'd seen his deadly skill just days before.

Baaldir watched his father, David, and another short and stout Israelite converse outside in the courtyard just far enough away from the door to muffle most of the hushed conversation. From the looks of it, the stout man seemed to have firsthand knowledge as he recounted a harrowing ordeal. David would hush the man gently as he became louder and then retracted into a low whisper for a few sentences only to gradually elevate his voice almost as if the story could only be told properly this way. He was unsure of what the man said fully but from what he could tell he had been below in the caverns as well and had experienced an attack of some sort and just barely made it out alive.

Baaldir was unaware as they spoke that his head had peeked through the door while trying to hear more of the conversation. Adonizedek shot him a knowing glance and Baaldir quickly retracted and crossed the room to a chair that sat next to a window. As he sat, he saw an object sitting on the windowsill. He realized it was an oddly shaped dagger which he curiously picked up, turning it over in front of his face. What he saw on his blade made him shudder as a cold chill ran up his spine and made the hair on his neck bristle. His education had taught him the Hebrew characters and what he read almost made him drop the blade at his feet. On the blade was the very same word or name he'd seen on the daggers that those Shades held on to the rooftops in his dream. Tsalmaveth was the word. The Shadow of Death had tried to take his brother's life and had killed his friend.

Memphis, Egypt: The Temple of Yaldabaoth

Lox crept up on the open arched door to the inner part of the compound carefully so he wouldn't trip or knock over an unseen crate in the darkness. Only moments before, he had watched the high priestess use the power of the amulet resulting in hundreds of local people now huddled in their hovels, fearing death, and praying to Yaldabaoth for mercy.

Feeling his way through the night, Lox came to a narrow stone ramp toward the back of the temple that led up to what appeared to be a balcony overlooking the western part of the city. The stones to his right were a shear face that rose thirty feet or so to the main temple.

He decided to risk the exposed walk upward, seeing no one around; even so, he crouched low as he ascended the steep ramp. There was no rail or parapet to his left which made the climb a little too precarious for his liking, but Lox focused his steps upward, one at a time until he reached the balcony. There was a second set of stairs leading upward at the rear of the balcony and as he reached the summit, Lox crouched low and peeked up onto what appeared to be a rather large landing that led to an oversized doorway into the temple.

Due to darkness of the evening hour, Lox couldn't see to the right or left very far but after a few moments he determined that nobody was outside with him on the landing. It made his hair stand on end, in the eerie silence, and he decided it was because of his expectation that he'd have to fight at some point.

This has been too easy so far, Lox thought.

Focusing his eyes to look at the structure, he was able to make out the silhouette of the temple. It appeared to have a long patio that ran down both sides with the temple roof being supported by numerous columns. Lox decided to go left and walk the patio towards the front of the temple where he hoped to find an interior building. He also needed to find an escape route since the front was guarded by soldiers.

Walking along he was able to look out over the sleepy city of Memphis and see the Nile River shimmer, every so often, in the scarce moonlight. Turning his attention to the temple, he saw that the building itself was more for opulent show than usefulness. The massive roof was supported by columns in a gridded pattern where he could walk through the middle to the other side. There was no accessible area aside from a series of long corridors running up and down and side to side between the columns that were slightly wider than his arm span. His choice was to walk out in the open or walk under the canopy between the rows of columns. He chose the latter since it provided him with an option to hide behind if someone came. It occurred to him that someone else could hide just as easily. Still, he sidestepped into the first row and walked until he reached what looked like the middle, before turning his head toward the front where he had last seen his prize.

Lox was mesmerized by the perfect rows of columns that he passed between and found himself looking upward at the sheer height of the canopy. He was not watching his steps when suddenly, Lox lost his balance and began tumbling down a very steep set of stairs, for what seemed like an eternity, bumping, and scraping each elbow, knee, and finally his head on the stone as he came to rest on his back.

Lox laid there for a few moments as the world turned about like a wobbling top, and as he tried to sit up, he found that there was a force weighing on his head that kept him from accomplishing the simple act. Instead of trying to sit up again, he lay there for a few moments more until the spinning subsided. He slowly began to sit up and felt the back of his head and his fingers came away bloodied.

Curses, he thought as he checked the rest of his body and determined that was the worst of it. No broken bones or major wounds could be noticed, aside from a throbbing headache due to the head injury.

It was too dimly lit to make out anything meaningful, so he figured the best course was to try and go back up to the top and search more but as he stood, an involuntary groan escaped, betraying the fact that he had indeed fallen harder than he first assessed. His ankle was throbbing, and he could tell that he had likely cracked a rib as his breathing became slightly more labored. He removed his outer tunic and used a knife to cut long strips of fabric; these he used to wrap around his torso tightly which gave some relief. Sitting on the steps he used a strip of the tunic to wrap his foot and ankle in the same manner. Standing again, Lox evaluated his weight on the injured ankle and, though it tinged with pain, it was bearable enough to walk. Looking up the many stairs he had just fallen, he decided to explore this tunnel and hallway since he was already there, maybe it would turn out to be a serendipitous fall. There was dim lighting from a few oil sconces here and there. This would have to suffice. He resolved himself to it and lumbered down the narrow passage towards what he hoped was the amulet he desired.

CHAPTER 20

The Lower City, Jebus

Amidst music and revelry, Ahmet came up into the ward where most of the soldiers and their families lived. Apparently, there were ancient tunnels underneath the city that could be accessed from the caves via the underground spring that fed the Gihon Spring in the Kidron Valley, which supplied water to the whole of Jerusalem. In this way, he and the Shades could enter the city in a multitude of different areas through culverts and cisterns. There was little doubt that the rulers of Jebus would be closing down the tunnel near the stables and would have that area under heavy guard, so entry into the city was not possible that way.

The city was in a state of celebration as the Israelites had turned their tail and run. The rains began again the night before and continued steadily through the day, leaving muddy streets throughout Jebus. Children laughed and played in the puddles, while prayers and rejoicing to their many gods could be heard all over the city.

Tsalmaveth had been silent for the last day. He had told him that his services would be needed soon to move the plan forward but hadn't elaborated. Tsalmaveth was scant on details, preferring to just instruct him in the moment rather than rely on him to carry orders out.

Ahmet didn't complain, he was still dealing with the bargain he'd made and learning to live with it. At least it seemed like he was able to exercise some amount of freedom during the day. He was afraid to push it, but it seemed like Tsalmaveth was mostly dormant during the day and more active at dusk. Which made sense when he thought about the Shadow of Death. Every day the sun sets, dead for the night. Every morning it was reborn again. As he thought about this, he realized he'd traveled through a shadow to another twenty feet away. This bewildered him at first until he looked down at the street again and noticed a shadow from a large building. Instantly, he was standing in the shadow. Repeatedly he bounced from shadow to shadow in the deserted part of the city. Up to roof tops and back down the street. This was unexpected.

Ahmet heard Tsalmaveth in his mind, "If you like that little trick, just wait until you bind yourself to me. You have no idea what power awaits you Ahmet."

Ahmet's eyes widened as he thought about what that could possibly mean before shaking his head side to side to refocus on his purpose for wanting to come up to the city proper. He wanted to see his wife for the first time since Nathan had died and he'd been arrested a day ago. She would no doubt be distraught given the visit from the palace guard and riddled with grief at the loss of their son. Ahmet choked back tears at the thought of it and he couldn't wait to see her and tell her he was alright and hold her again. Now more than ever, she would need him, though he wasn't so sure Tsalmaveth would allow him to stay with her. He'd asked Tsalmaveth for permission to go during the day while The Shadow of Death was somewhat dormant. Surprisingly Tsalmaveth had actually agreed, though not without crudely mentioning that it was a vain pursuit.

Ahmet had decided to use one of the tunnels to bring him close to his doorstep. He came up through a cistern in an alleyway just around the corner from his home and began to slowly make his way to it. The streets were quiet as the sun went down on yet another day. He walked up to his home and tried the door and realized it was locked, and nobody seemed to be home.

Ahmet searched the top of one of the window lentils to find a key that he'd hidden years ago. He'd lost his somehow in the last few days. Turning the key and stepping inside he'd nearly dropped the key when he realized the one room house was unoccupied. He fumbled to catch it and recovered it before it dropped to the ground. The waning light made it hard to see around but there was just enough light left for him to see that she had left in a hurry, taking only clothing and linens. On the primitive wooden table that sat in the corner was a handwritten letter. His wife could write well for a woman of low birth. He couldn't write very well but he could read most things.

The letter said:

"Ahmet. I fled to a safe place away from the city with the help of a friend. It is not safe here in Jebus and had to leave hastily, fearing that you had been killed. I hope the rumors were not true and this letter finds you alive. I will see you again if Elohim is willing.

Always yours,

Ramah"

Ahmet started to shake with anger and panic mixed with an anxiety that caused him to hyper-ventilate as he was unable to breathe. He collapsed on the floor and began to sob, tears falling to the floor and smearing the charcoal script on the message that his wife had left him. Tsalmaveth began to rage within him, seizing control over his body.

Tsalmaveth screamed, "Curses! Where is the body? What rotten luck. We will have to find them before it's all lost!"

Ahmet, still reeling from reading the letter, didn't seem to notice the comments about the body. Instead his thoughts became scattered as Tsalmaveth ransacked and destroyed everything in sight with the modest home, piece by piece. As he kicked a chair it shattered against the hearth, breaking chunks of the mud brick mantle and sending wood splinters flying in all directions.

"No. She wouldn't have just got up and left. There has to be more to it. What friend? Maybe she was trying to tell me something?"

"She left you, Ahmet." Tsalmaveth said mockingly, as he punched the table, shattering his fist and the table simultaneously, blood running from his knuckles as the table collapsed. "She left you and took the Key with her."

No, she wouldn't have left unless she thought she was in danger. And I can't blame her for that. I just wish I could've seen her and tried to stop her. Ahmet thought this as he heard himself begin to chuckle.

"Well now I can't use that threat of having you kill them so there's that." Tsalmaveth said, stating the obvious.

Ahmet was nonplussed, "is that supposed to make me feel better that my wife is in the wind, going where only God knows? Not only have I lost a son, but now I've lost my wife."

"She left you, Ahmet. Your wife couldn't even wait a day for you to return or for news of your status to reach her." Tsalmaveth's chuckling turned into boisterous laughter. "And she's taken the Key with her so now I'm really starting to get angry. It's like He is toying with me! I can smell that cursed aura all over this dwelling!"

"She wouldn't have!" Ahmet said as he felt control of his body returning. He was singularly focused on Ramah and totally missed the statements from Tsalmaveth.

"There must be something else I'm not seeing; she must've been forced to leave so suddenly." he said audibly as he slumped onto the floor next to what used to be a bed. Ahmet's hand rested on a chest that had tipped over and the contents sprawled on the floor. This was a keepsake chest that Ramah would keep things in, only taking them out on occasion to look at them and tell Nathan about what they meant to her.

Sorrow filled him as he picked up a golden hair pin that he'd scrimped and saved for and given to her the day after Nathan was born. She only wore it around the house but would never wear it in public, not wanting to attract attention. Instead she would pull it out and tell Nathan about it once a year and wear it while she cooked and mended clothes, placing it away again the same evening.

Tsalmaveth sighed in his head again, "Ahmet, you really need to focus on what's in front of you. I have indwelt your body, by your own choice, you'll soon have all my powers at your beck and call, and you will be immortal so long as I am here. Your wife and child will be a memory that you'll think back on as the eons pass you by. Think of the things you'll do in a thousand lifetimes. This is only a small portion Ahmet."

"What good is all of that without Ramah and my son Nathan?" Ahmet retorted.

Tsalmaveth sighed, "Ahmet, Ahmet. You have to stop. The reality is that the only way you can avenge your son and hope to see your wife again is to do exactly as I say. We need to find your son's body. His blood is the only way you'll ever have what you desire Ahmet."

Ahmet was incredulous as he finally came around to Tsalmaveth's comments, "My son's blood? I told you he was not to be touched. What could he possibly do for you? Is this why you saved me? To use me to get to my son? You agreed to let me come here for what, to get to my son?"

Tsalmaveth scoffed, "Careful Ahmet, you are forgetting your place here. Obstinance will not be tolerated."

He then continued, "I told you Nathan was the Key, and I'm telling you for a second time though the first time you overreacted as you are about to do now, leading you to be arrested for attacking Baaldir. I also told you I only needed a little of his blood. I would not have harmed him so long as I got what I needed. There would have been no need to harm him, Ahmet. A few drops of blood are all I will need."

Ahmet interjected, "I still don't understand why a common boy such as my son is the key to your plans?"

Tsalmaveth growled low in frustration and annoyance, "His blood is the Key to raising my master and friend, Yaldabaoth. Once he is freed from his prison, we will be able to bring back your son and locate your wife and you'll be reunited. Your son, as it happens, is dead and not by my hands, Ahmet. You have already forgotten that it was those dirty Israelites who killed your son in their desire for power and conquest. For this you attack me, even as I've given you a second chance. Don't forget, you were as good as dead when that beast carried you to the temple door. You should be falling on your knees thanking me, Ahmet. Instead, you question my motives?"

Ahmet hung his head, "You're right, Master. I forgot myself for a moment."

"You most certainly did, Ahmet. Who killed your son and caused your wife to flee in fear, Ahmet?" Tsalmaveth prodded.

"The Israelites did." Ahmet said, kissing his teeth.

"You have two more days and then you must complete the ritual. Once that is complete, it will unlock my full power for you to use. No man will be a match for you then." Tsalmaveth encouraged.

"Why wait two days, Master. Tell me what I have to do."

"Patience, Ahmet. If you completed the ritual right now your body would not be able to handle it. By the third day your body will have acclimated to my power enough to make it through the ritual."

Ahmet exhaled, "What will we do in the meantime. The Israelites have fled and are getting farther away with each passing hour."

Tsalmaveth chortled ominously, "Tonight my Shades will be sent to pay their fleeing army a visit. In the meantime, you and I will pay Adonizedek a visit and see if we can learn anything from that royal brat, Baaldir."

Memphis, Egypt: Below the Temple of Yaldabaoth

Lox rounded a corner and looked down a dimly lit corridor. At the end was a well-lit room with light shining through a partially closed door. All sense told him that, even though what he was looking at may be in that room, it was a bad idea to enter without knowing what lay ahead. He had long since abandoned his sense and plowed onward. The walk to the room was much shorter than he had estimated.

Upon reaching the door he stayed close to the shadows as he peered through the door. Inside, the room was indeed well-lit, compared to the corridor torch light. Lox decided to try his luck and slowly pushed the door open as silently as possible. Accomplishing this, he crept through the door into an expansive room that housed a luxurious chaise, and pillows accompanied by dozens of gold candelabras and incense burners. The smell of lavender was heavy in the air as he stepped forward onto a plush rug that was made from the finest threads. He saw no one or any sign of recent occupants here in this room so he pressed forward and crouched low as he came to a door that was divided by a veil. The shear fabric parted easily as he made his way through the doorway. Again, the room was well-lit and was uninhabited.

His luck ran out as he crossed the room and noticed another hallway to his right. Carefully, Lox looked around the corner and realized at the end of this hallway was a door and outside the door stood two guards, too far to make a run at. He thought about doubling back but the treasure he sought was through that door; he felt it deep in his gut that he had to find a way into that room.

Lox scanned the room for a hiding place and settled on a pile of blankets and pillows across the room, and carefully hid underneath them by placing them in such a way as to hide his form, leaving an area open for his eyes as he faced the direction of the hall. Once satisfied that he was well-hidden, Lox screamed a blood curdling howl that carried little further than the room he was in; the walls and floors were covered with fabrics that deadened the noise. However, it carried far enough. He heard the guards rush forward, their light armor made of woven reeds making the only noise as they stepped onto the plush rug. They scanned the room and moved to the next room.

As soon as they were out of sight, Lox threw the blankets off him and sprinted toward the door. There was no telling how far they'd search before returning to their post. He reached for the door, and as he touched the lever, he heard music. Trying the door, the lever turned easily, and the door opened without force. As Lox opened it, the sound of the music grew louder.

A rhythmic combination of harps, lutes, drums, and some type of wind instrument droned on like a steady heartbeat. There was no more time to use caution, so he stepped through and shut the door behind him.

Before him lay an opulent room filled with people in various states of intoxication and undress. The room was dimly lit and from what he could tell not a soul was even aware that he was there witnessing this debauchery in a sober state. It reminded him of his days in Babylon many years past.

Lox slowly advanced, tiptoeing over passed-out drunkards that littered the center of the room. At the other side, another door came into view. Light showed through the bottom. He tried the door. *Locked.*

Lox turned and scanned the room again and instinctively dove behind a nearby couch just as the two guards from before entered the room. They made a bee line straight for his end of the room, neither distracted by the scene. Lox could see a ring of keys hanging from the second guard's belt. As the guards reached the door, they scanned the room behind them. One of them spoke in a low whisper just barely audible to anyone else. The other nodded agreeably as he tried the lever handle on the door. Finding it locked, they turned to head back to their original post outside of the room.

Lox moved without thinking, possessed by his desire to find the amulet as he grabbed a tall bronze candlestick and rushed the first guard recklessly. The guard turned just as the base of the candlestick connected with his skull. It made a dull crunching sound, dropping the man to the ground like a ton of bricks. As if to accentuate the attack, the music abruptly stopped, and he heard a panic set into the room. Whatever trance had held these people unawares had broken the moment the music stopped.

The second guard tripped backwards and fell toward the ground. He scrambled to find his sword and clumsily drew it from the scabbard, but Lox was over him instantly. With a violent blow to his head with the same candlestick, he fell limp at Lox's feet.

The guests at this feast were now screaming and falling all over each other. Lox knelt next to the second unconscious guard and pulled the ring of keys from his belt. Luckily there were only three keys in the ring, he found the right one on the second try and turned the key. Trying the lever, the door popped open toward him, and he let it swing wide. The guests in attendance were nearly evacuated by the time he opened the door. The pandemonium would be headed back into the temple. He knew he had to move fast now; the panic would surely bring more guards, and he had minutes at best to get in and make his escape.

As Lox stepped through the doorway, he entered a brightly lit bed chamber filled with pillows and cushions. Not unlike the rooms before, but this room had a more delicate touch to it. A looking glass stood on a stand in the far corner, and a bureau with perfumes and brushes and jewelry sat next to it. He cautiously walked over towards the bureau and picked up the hairbrush and palmed through the jewelry. None of the necklaces looked anything like that amulet.

Lox remembered he didn't have much time; the guards would be raised any moment now and he would be trapped if he didn't hurry. With more conviction he ransacked the drawers and opened a wardrobe, tossing dresses and tunics to the ground, finding nothing.

Lox ran over to the bed, tipped the featherdown mattress up and looked underneath; again finding nothing. He was about to give up and make a run to escape when he noticed a faint light coming through a crack in the stone wall. Running his fingers over the crack he could feel that it was a doorway hidden from plain sight, and it was open.

All he had to do was pull the door open with his fingertips. It swung freely and stopped when it bumped against the bed frame. The light from the other side was the full moon in the clear night sky. He started to walk forward and then ran back to pull the door shut behind him. As he shut it tightly it latched. Maybe when the guards came, they would see the empty room and assume the intruder had already left. In any case, he was now trapped in what appeared to be a lush garden, so he moved forward through the vines and trellised fruit. He reached a small pool of cool water and just about fainted as he saw the woman who was bathing there.

Lox involuntarily fell to his knees and his heart sank into the ground dumbfounded and unable to form his next thought. He knelt there with both palms flat on the ground, staring at her face, not really seeing her nakedness. The woman turned toward him and the amulet around her neck shimmered in the intense moonlight. Fixated on her, Lox didn't hear the guards coming up behind him.

They must've known that there was only one place to go and within seconds he was surrounded. A guard moved to spear him in the back and the woman leapt forward.

"No! Take him alive!" She quickly ran from the pool and covered her body. The guards heeded her order and quickly bound Lox's hands behind him. He couldn't have resisted if he'd wanted to. They pulled him to his feet and began to forcibly drag him away. All he could do was mumble her name, "Astarte."

Beneath the City of Jebus

Tsalmaveth busied himself with thoughts and plans as Ahmet took his new body below once again to gather his Shades. He could only express himself during the daylight hours for short periods as it drained his power, causing him to have to give Ahmet control back while it built back up. This was the annoying part of inhabiting a new vessel because at night he had unlimited use of the vessel and his own powers. Once the binding ritual was completed, he would be able to take complete control over Ahmet if he wished. This part, Ahmet was unaware of. He chuckled to himself as he thought about the daftness of his new vessel. Ahmet's grief made him so malleable.

One thing he was puzzled about when they'd visited Ahmet's abode was that not only was his wife gone and his son's body gone, but he could not sense death anywhere in the room. As the Shadow of Death he was able to sense death everywhere he went. If someone had died, he not only would know it but would be apprised to the method and circumstances surrounding it. Azrael, the Angel of Death, had visited Ahmet's home but had not taken anybody's life force away. This was the confusing thing, he could sense death itself but not the death of Nathan, his Key. This filled him with a sinister vein of hope, though he would never share this knowledge with his vessel, Ahmet.

Ahmet walked into the new temple far below the city of Jebus. Over the last day his horde of Shades had turned this beautiful temple to Yaldabaoth into a glorious tribute to the god, complete with statues and altar. It resembled the one Lox had built in the dungeon but was much more opulent and, more importantly, was hidden away from whatever prying eyes or accidental wanderers might visit. Standing like statues around the edges of the chamber were all of his Shades, nearly three hundred of them. All of them catatonically staring onward with an ever so slight sway of the body which was not visible to a normal person.

Chained up in the corner near the tunnel that led to the dungeon was the last remaining beast, Vlulor. The beast had cried for an entire day after realizing that its mate had not returned but had since calmed down and was sleeping at the moment, replete with snoring and flatulence.

Ahmet walked over and knelt near Vlulor and stroked her face to which the massive cyclops cooed and snuggled up to Ahmet, drawing him into an embrace while comatose to the world.

Once he was in total control of the vessel, Tsalmaveth would put an end to this irresponsible coddling of a beast of burden who needed to be ready to do its job and guard the temple from intruders. Soon, Ahmet would be too busy working on his plan to even feed the beast.

Two more days and the binding ritual would be complete, giving him the ability to make his move. First, he would find Baaldir, through Adonizedek if needed, and then he would use him to find The Key. Tonight he would make a move toward fulfilling his quest that he'd been on for thousands of years since Yaldabaoth had freed him from his bond to Azrael.

CHAPTER 21

The Dungeon Below the Citadel

David descended the stairs into the dungeon, followed by Jeroboam, Joab, Bulwark, and Jarnsaxa. There was an air of anticipation present as they rounded the first corner that led to the temple that David had found. As they came into view, they stopped short. The room was completely empty. The alcoves that housed the statues were empty. The outline where the altar sat was the only clue that something had been there. Even the stone with the Hebrew characters was missing.

"I don't understand, where could it have gone? It was all here just days ago." David said, puzzled.

Jeroboam was stunned as well, having seen it himself, "The question now is who or what moved it and to where?"

Jarnsaxa looked around and walked up to where the statue of the god had been and said, "I never knew this room existed. Admittedly, I rarely ever come down to the dungeons."

David paced the room and looked for clues, anything that might show him something telling. He pulled himself up onto the alcove where the angelic statues were just days ago and looked down toward the former place of the altar. Nothing seemed to jump out at David as he shifted his stance and began to prepare himself to jump back to the ground a few cubits below. Just then, his foot clanked against something and he looked down and found a hammer and chisel lying next to the column. David picked it up and looked it over.

"I've found something." He said as he jumped down to their level. He handed the tools to Jarnsaxa who after looking them over, handed them to Bulwark.

Bulwark was a master stonemason. He tossed them from hand to hand and checked the weight and balance of them. "These are not like the tools we use. The handle is made from a different type of wood than the tools we make here. These could be from Tyre or Egypt even."

David took in this information of the mason's tools of unknown origin in a room that just yesterday was a temple to a foreign god. Lox had built this temple over the years, and he had twisted his countrymen into monsters in this very room. If the temple was not here anymore then it most certainly would be set up elsewhere. But where? He now knew that this wasn't the doing of a local mason thanks to Bulwark's assessment. He remembered hearing the masons in the caverns days ago. When he found the tunnel into the city, they had transformed that into a fully functioning room with stone walls and floors and archways for doors. Doors. That was it. A sudden revelation came as he threw his hands up.

"I know where they relocated the temple." David said. "We will need the torches. Bulwark have you closed up the tunnel stairs yet?"

Bulwark shook his head to the negative and explained that he was planning to do so this very day.

"That is a good thing in this case, we need to go there and see if my hunch is correct." David offered.

A short walk found them back up in the familiar corridor that led toward the stables and the entrance to the tunnel. They all followed David as he led the way to the stairs that descended into the world underneath Jebus.

"I remembered seeing a room that had been restored by masons just outside the tunnel. It had nine doors in a half-circle. We came at it from above the first time and left through a random door to escape the caverns then." David explained as he took the first steps down the long staircase. Jarnsaxa and Bulwark followed close behind having to duck to walk through the tunnel.

"Fascinating!" Bulwark exclaimed as he examined the stone archway, and the tunnel stairs carved right from the stone. "This must date back many thousands of years. Even before King Adonizedek was born."

That was interesting to David, he knew of history back to the time of Enoch, but he couldn't fathom the peoples before, apart from his own ancestor's connection to the region. He'd always thought of the Adam and Eve story as a symbolic representation of mankind rather than an actual man and woman in the Garden of Eden. He knew that Jebus had roots back to the times of Noah. Was Bulwark saying that Adonizedek was born before the times of Noah? Pulling that thread, he then reasoned that Lox, who was older than Adonizedek according to Thoros, had to be older than Enoch himself? Was he a Nephilim? Or something else altogether? Those questions would have to wait to be answered later.

They descended into a short tunnel that leveled off and then exited into the spacious room where David had first encountered the captive Israelites. Sure enough, there were the doors. Each now fitted with a torch holder on each side. The question now was which door led to their query? Not a soul was visible down here now, whereas before there were clearly masons chipping and chiseling somewhere deeper into the underground. They hadn't thought to go deeper and explore, not that they would have when they came upon the captive Israelites.

Logically he assumed the work he'd heard came from the furthermost tunnels. It seemed like directionally the other tunnels led either towards the city or toward the exits near the place formerly occupied by Saul's forces. He knelt on the ground and studied the stone floor that had been carved and noticed small grooves in the ground, likely from repeated dragging of stones. They led for the furthest door to his right. Just as he suspected.

"This way." He said, not waiting for anyone to follow, as he walked directly toward the tunnel. He grabbed a second torch and disappeared down the dark passage.

Jeroboam hesitated; he'd only just come out of the caves with his limbs barely intact. He was not keen on tempting that fate again, but David was ever the bold leader, so he mustered up the courage and chased behind David but added, in a low whisper, "We need to move quietly and be ready to leave quickly."

Jarnsaxa and Bulwark followed close behind ducking down and crouching through the narrow passageway. David looked back as he reached a fork where one led upward, and one led downward to the right. Logic told him the place they sought would be deeper rather than closer to the surface, so he veered right down a shallow grade.

The tunnel had widened considerably at this point and the taller members of the party were able to stand upright. It seemed to go for several hundred cubits but was hard to gauge in the dim light with no point of reference. David took to counting his steps as soon as he'd taken the fork to the right. So far, one hundred paces. He noticed an alcove or two on either side of the tunnel carved deep enough to store supplies. These must've been a refuge at some point below the surface. David remembered hearing stories of men needing to find shelter from fire that fell from the heavens. This seemed like the type of place that would be safe from anything going on up on ground level. He noted that they were yet empty so clearly not being used now for this purpose.

No sooner than he reached the end of the path than he heard noise coming from around the corner. He quickly doubled back and motioned for everyone to do the same quietly. He found an alcove with Jeroboam and rolled the torch in the dirt. Jarnsaxa and Bulwark each found an alcove to hide deep inside as they also disappeared. Darkness enveloped them as they waited for whatever was coming back their way. He saw a man carrying a torch walk by. The man wore a black cloak with a hood and was followed by no less than three hundred other gruesome looking men, silent and expressionless, their lips black with black veins meandered across their cheeks like a map of a river system on one of the many maps he was accustomed to consulting.

They smelled of sulfur and rotting flesh, which triggered his memory of Saul the day he came into the camp. The man was the only one carrying a torch so as he went further away the darkness crept back in. Thankfully, none had seen them. The last one passed by, and he waited for a moment before pulling the torches up and used a flint to spark the pitch once more. It sputtered and took a bit to overcome the dust and dirt and moisture from the hasty dousing of the flame, but it finally ignited, and he was able to light the second torch. Jarnsaxa came out and crept up to David crouching low.

"Who was that?" She said, not concealing the fact that she was disturbed by what she had just witnessed.

"I don't know but those were the beasts I encountered in the caves yesterday." Jeroboam whispered. "We need to get out of here. That may only be a fraction of them and we've just barely escaped being detected. There were hundreds in the prison the other day."

David contemplated what Jeroboam said. On one hand he was curious to know the location of the temple and see just what they were up to, but he decided that this encounter was proof enough that they had gone the right way and found the lair of this evil demon, Tsalmaveth. He also took note when someone as fearless as Jeroboam suggested caution. That could not be taken lightly.

"Okay, time to go. Let's get back to the surface. It'll be night soon If it isn't already." He only hoped that as they went back toward the exit that they didn't run into any of those beasts that may have stayed behind.

Thankfully, his worry proved baseless as they emptied out into the stone room with the nine doors. They wasted no time ascending to the ground level. Jarnsaxa ordered a nearby officer to triple the guard and barricade the door to the tunnel. No one was to come through from either side.

The worry now would be whether the city could be accessed elsewhere through sewers and such. But they had no way of knowing. Bulwark suggested that they go to Adonizedek with this information and then suggested they prepare to close off the Citadel fortress from the rest of the city, he would find a way to collapse this tunnel for good this very night. Jarnsaxa agreed and stopped some other officers and relayed their new orders.

Each one set off to gather up troops to defend the palace. The sight of those black cloaked beasts had lit a fire underneath each of them. Bulwark excused himself and went to see to the preparations himself. Jarnsaxa would escort David and Jeroboam back to the palace. An Israelite walking unescorted in Jebus would attract the wrong kind of attention.

He led them back up the stairs and ramp that led into the heart of the fortress. It was late in the evening already, so they resolved to see Adonizedek at first light and inform him of what they found. They would have to hope that their preparation was enough. Jarnsaxa left them at a vacant room, next to Thoros', and turned to head back to the fortress gates to mobilize his archers and see if Bulwark needed any help.

David offered to help in anyway needed but Jarnsaxa declined, "Get some rest, I'll collect you at first light to council with the king." David shut the door and looked at his men. Not one would sleep until he filled them in on the findings down below.

Meanwhile...

Baaldir followed behind, making sure that Bulwark and the Israelites didn't see him. He stood in the room at the bottom of the stairs trying to figure out where they'd gone. Soon he realized they must have gone to the far-right doorway judging by the fresh footprints in the dust, ones that could only be made by someone with the large stature of Bulwark.

He crept up on the long winding path and could hear some light commotion come from deeper within. He decided to quickly double back to the outer room and found a place to hide. No sooner had he ducked behind a pile of stones, left by the masons, than a man exited calmly followed by hundreds of those same creatures dressed in black cloaks. Their faces were twisted with black veins running through their skin, eyes dead, but filled with hatred.

Baaldir suppressed an urge to gasp as he felt a cold chill run from the back of his head down through his toes as his temples began to throb due to the blood running from his brain. He nearly lost consciousness but was able to take some deep breaths to regain his composure. He peered up over the top of the stones, what little Baaldir dared, and saw that the horde of shadowy figures were walking deeper into the tunnels where he had encountered them a few days past with Nathan. As the hundreds of them steadily filed into the caverns he steeled his nerves. He needed to find out more about this enemy if he was ever going to be able to avenge his brother and his friend, Nathan.

As the last one disappeared into the cavern, Baaldir decided that he would follow them, as foolhardy as this seemed to him, as he worked up the nerve to go. *You have to, for Nathan, and for Thoros.*

Baaldir checked his belongings: he had a dagger, his short sword, and a small skin with water in it. This would have to do as he grabbed a torch from the walls and drew his sword, forcing one foot in front of the other. Baaldir figured he should be able to trace the footprints in the dirt of the cavern tunnels. He was confident in the bearings of the tunnel after Nathan and him had spent so much time exploring. For this reason, he slowed his pace, telling himself to give the creatures plenty of time to move ahead of him. His steps would need to be deliberate and quiet as a mouse because if he alerted them to his presence, he would be dead before he had the chance to regret this decision.

Israelite Camp: On the Road to Hebron

Jonathan warmed himself by a fire outside his tent. The hour was late, and he had only just made his way into camp in the early hours of the morning. It had been dark for several hours already as the last of the men made their way into camp, thoroughly depleted of energy. The defeated Israelite forces lumbered along the six-league journey that under normal circumstances would take a day or so by foot. In this case, they had only managed a third of that distance. Not far enough away from the place of their undoing by any means. He had hoped to be within a short ride from Hebron by now.

He tore off a piece of his bread and slowly chewed as he pondered the events of the last few days. Three or four days ago they were on the cusp of possessing the final city in Canaan. Now they were a ragtag horde of defeated farmers and shepherds. The mighty Hebrew army so thoroughly defeated by unexplainable events, was but a shadow of what it was only a few days ago.

Jonathan suddenly realized how exhausted he was and went into his tent to lay down on the mat he'd rolled out. No sooner had he laid his head on the ground than he was asleep. No dreams came as he fell into a deep sleep. Hours passed and suddenly he awoke to the blast of a shofar across the camp. Scrambling to his feet he peered outside and into a camp ablaze in the pitch-black night. He heard screams and blood curdling cries from all around him. Also, at some point the rain had begun to fall again and had soaked the entire camp as thunder rolled off into the distance.

Grabbing his sword and shield, he ran toward the edge of camp until he heard screams to his right. He veered right and ran into a fleeing soldier with the most frightening look of terror on his face. The man ran by him without a glance and kept running until he disappeared into the darkness. Moments later a figure appeared from where the man had come from, dripping wet with rain and blood running from his mouth.

As the figure walked into the light, he realized it was a man, alert and ready to do battle. The man wore a long black cloak, his face gaunt and bent on destruction. Jonathan's destruction. He crouched low, circling Jonathan, holding a jagged dagger with blood already wetting it; the only expression on its face one of hatred. Jonathan moved with him, shifting his stance to allow him to parry a blow should the creature rush him. Suddenly, the man was upon him and crashed into his shield. Jonathan was forced backwards as his heels dug in. Halting the advance he pushed back and used his shield to redirect him away as he came downward with a slash of his sword. He found only air as the man swiftly recovered and advanced toward his flank.

Stepping into Jonathan's space, it began slashing and stabbing toward the torso. Jonathan side stepped and parried several attacks and dodged others, but he was beginning to tire, and he could see that his foe had not even begun to lose his energy. His only hope was to somehow get him onto the ground. It was much too quick for conventional combat. It was then that he decided it was time for a change in tactics as it was apparent that this would be won or lost in close quarters.

Jonathan threw his shield to the side and drew his dagger in his left hand with his sword in the right. He shifted his stance to favor his stronger side and began to circle the foe. The man lunged at him as he side-stepped and came down with a slash toward the shoulder and just barely missed. They traded attempts and Jonathan parried each one keeping his feet moving, circling trying to find an inside path to the vital organs. The assailant would lunge and slash wildly and retreat before the blow from Jonathan could land. He wondered if all of their enemies in this attack were this fast. It certainly didn't help that the ground was sopping wet and muddy as the rain began to fall in a downpour that made it hard to see.

His opponent was not a skilled warrior but what it lacked in martial ability was made up for with sheer rage accented by otherworldly speed. Those were the most dangerous foes at times, the ones that had no care or concern for their life. Most men in the ranks of his enemies would fight not to lose or fight to survive for fear that they wouldn't make it home, which ended up working against them in the end.

Jonathan had a knack for sending his mind into a place that existed outside of his personal ambitions or hopes for the future. During battle he accepted that he was already dead and the only way to return to life was to do whatever necessary to defeat his enemy. In this way he could charge a line of cavalry on foot and somehow end up atop a steed, having unhorsed an enemy. He could channel his fear into action and that made him un-beatable one on one. He would take wild risks, such as climbing a sheer rock face and sneaking into a Philistine camp with only his shield bearer and wreak absolute havoc on them creating confusion and mayhem.

Jonathan would have to use his foe's advantage of nearly unending supplies of energy against it. Instead of circling and trading jabs he began to feign that he was out of wind and slowed his movement response ever so slightly. The very next time his foe charged he dropped low and shot toward the legs. Once inside he stood up with the man on his shoulder and rolled to his side and sent him falling to his back. For the first time a look of surprise came upon its face instead of anger. Jonathan wasted no time, finding a well of energy he jumped on top of the scrambling man and attempted to plunge his dagger into the heart.

The man grabbed the dagger trying to stop the weight of Jonathan's body. He succeeded momentarily and it seemed like Jonathan would not have the strength to finish his attempt as he let out a yell that came from the furthest regions of his body, spit shooting from his mouth onto the man's face as the rain poured over them both. Jonathan leaned into the knife and pushed with all his might until the tip of the dagger pierced the skin on the man's chest. After that, the enemy lost his grip and threw a few misplaced haymakers that glanced off Jonathan's face, doing little to stop the dagger's path into his heart.

The man let out a loud screech that half-sounded like a dying man, and half like a roaring bear. Jonathan leaned into the dagger and with both hands turned the blade a quarter turn opening the wound to gush blood from the heart. The beast fought for a few more seconds, clawing Jonathan's face, but it soon gave up and after a few seconds more the heart gave out and it exhaled for a final time. The raspy breath trailing off into the ether.

Jonathan withdrew his dagger and looked around the vicinity and heard others struggling. He rushed off into the camp and began dispatching attackers one by one as they were overtaking his own kinsmen. With each kill he rallied men to his side until he had gathered thirty or so around him. There were a few creatures attacking the flanks. And he directed them to form a square, two ranks deep. In the middle he placed four men with bow and arrow and directed them to assist the sword and spearmen as the enemy closed in on them.

Moments later an onslaught of the black-cloaked beasts crashed upon their ranks and the melee resumed in full force.

Jonathan barked orders as he assisted on all sides of the square. "Hold your ranks, men! Archers aim for the vital organs. Second line, Conserve your energy! Be ready to step forward!"

For what seemed like hours, Jonathan fought as men fell to his left and right and all around him. The attackers had changed tactics and were now trying to attack one side at a time. The enemy casualty number had been high as Jonathan did his part to kill as many as he could while protecting as many of his men as he was able. Still, the enemy had whittled them down to ten or so and they now stood with their backs facing each other as the beasts circled around searching for the weakest victim.

It was then that he realized the sun was beginning to rise in the east and he heard another dissonant blast of the shofar that signaled the end of the attack and sounded a retreat. The attackers stopped at once and melted off back into the camp and disappeared as if they had accomplished what they came here to do.

An eerie quiet fell over the camp as the cloud covered sun peaked up on the horizon though it was still dark in the twilight hour.

He pulled his dagger from the last attacker he had killed and cleaned it off using the man's black cloak. He also picked up the jagged dagger with a bone handle on the tine and looked it over. The Hebrew word Tsalmaveth was etched into the blade which was crudely made. He could see pitted spots along the blade, and it was not very well balanced. This was not the work of a skilled blacksmith by any means though it was sharp.

As the minutes passed, the light began to rise and he could better see the havoc wreaked on his very own camp. He washed himself in a basin and cleaned his weapons. Putting on a fresh tunic he donned his armor again and began to prepare himself for the ugly scene that was before him. A half hour later he was walking through the camp which looked like a rubbish heap characteristic of the slums in a major city. There were survivors tending wounds and others carrying bodies of the fallen to carts that would return them to their respective tribal lands for burial in the next few days. By last count nearly one thousand perished in the attacks last night. Only one hundred of those beasts had been killed, though dozens were wounded and escaped. Most of these dead were at the hands of Jonathan and the brave men he had rallied.

The camp was in tatters. The organization typical of a camp was nonexistent. Not that it was before the attacks, but the aftermath of the attacks settled any attempt to make it so. The men all around looked defeated. No doubt many survivors would desert if they hadn't already.

He stopped a group of officers who were trying to decide the best course of action, "Call the men to ranks, I will address them in a quarter hour."

Jonathan said this as he walked away, grateful that at least the rain had subsided for now, though the sky seemed to be teeming with another deluge. He walked over to where the lined-up corpses of their enemy were laying. One killed by an arrow to the eye, another dismembered and crushed by horses, and the ones he had slain laid there amongst others with various fatal wounds. By any standards, the attack on their camp had been a total defeat. Had it not been for the sunrise it may have ended in thousands more lost as they were nearing their end of their strength and energy.

He used his foot to roll the one he'd killed onto its side and then to its back. The face was pale as a ghost and clearly demonstrated that this former man rarely saw daylight, if ever. All three had black lips and black veins running out from their mouths down their faces and necks. Had he not known that they were Israelites formerly he would not have even been able to tell. The eyes were drawn and face gaunt from starvation and the hair bedraggled and caked with grime. The pungent smell of sulfur emitted caused his nose to burn. He knelt next to the corpses and said a prayer for their souls even though they were likely cursed for eternity. These were men once, now they were demons, twisted and turned into an instrument of death and destruction.

Jonathan left them to rot in the field where they lay at the edge of the camp and walked back toward the center of camp. As he walked, he saw that the remaining soldiers had fallen into ranks and were awaiting him. The men watched him with long faces and some of them displayed an angry countenance as he mounted a horse that awaited him. The rain clouds chose this moment to open up again as a steady, soaking rain began to fall over the throng of men, as if to accentuate their dampened morale.

Rain dripping from his face, Jonathan projected his voice, "Many of you are wondering if Elohim has abandoned us. Many of you are wondering why this calamity of the last few days has been brought upon us to foment this terror that we experienced last night. I am here to tell you that this was not the work of Elohim but the work of darkness and evil. I am here to tell you that Elohim has not abandoned His people, the chosen people of Israel. We will rebuild, we will recover what we have lost ten-fold, and we will defeat this darkness, Lord willing." There was a hushed murmur rippling through the camp as many relayed what Jonathan had said.

He waited for a moment longer and then continued, "For now, it is my order that this army be disbanded from the immediate hour. Return to your homes and families and bury your dead. Tend to your harvests which will be ready in the coming weeks. When we march again months from now, we will drive this evil from Israel once and for all."

Jonathan didn't expect anyone to be uplifted in such a time, so he was not disappointed when the men heeded his order silently and solemnly. He looked toward the south and maneuvered his horse through the camp that had already begun to pack up.

He set his course to Hebron and rapidly put the camp behind him, needing to return home to his family and hopefully find his father recovering. As he came to the top of a ridge he stopped and looked back in the direction of Jebus. He silently uttered a prayer for his brother David who he was certain was alive and would prevail. That being done, he doubled his horse's pace and raced toward Hebron and the mad King Saul.

Jonathan determined as he set out that he would arrive in half a day if he paced his horse steadily, but not long into the first leg, he paused to water his horse at a secluded spring off the beaten path, realizing that his horse hadn't been watered properly due to the attacks on the camp last night.

As he led the horse to drink, he noticed footprints leading down the path toward the spring. Several sets of footprints intermixed indicated that there was some sort of skirmish here. From what he could tell there were several against one. His stomach turned into knots as he turned down the path and stopped short. His horse startled and reared up as he pulled back on the lead and calmed him. There was a tree nearby, so he tied up the horse securely and crept forward towards the scene.

What he could now see was three of the same creatures from the attacks of the last few evenings. One of them lay face down on the path, clearly dead. The second he came upon was near dead and had both legs and arms immobilized by blades and a dagger in the chest. Jonathan drew his sword and ran the tortured creature through its eye, killing it for good and all. Next to the spring, the third one lay across the body of another man. He knelt beside the pair and checked the creature first. Satisfied that it had been killed, he pulled it off the man and dragged it away from them. Next, he grabbed the man's wrist and checked for a heartbeat. He saw that the man had shallow breathing. Several cuts could be seen on the arms and legs including a bad one on the chest that would need stitches and from the looks an infection had set in on the large gash. His head was slick with sweat, and it seemed as though he had a fever.

Did this man kill all three of these? He wondered as he looked the wounds over. None of the wounds seemed to be critical so he was puzzled why he was unconscious. *It must be the infection,* Jonathan thought as he felt the forehead and confirmed the fever.

That is when Jonathan realized this man was actually a teenage boy, judging by his face, and seemed to be fourteen or so years of age. However, the boy's tall and muscular stature was a great deal larger than any teenager he'd ever seen. This was no ordinary youngster, he thought. If not for the boyish face he would've thought that this was a grown man.

In a flash, Jonathan suddenly jumped back, raising his sword to block a wild swing from the boy as the boy woke and gripped his sword, eyes wide with surprise.

"Easy there, I just happened upon you here." Jonathan said as the boy scrambled backward against a boulder and raised his sword in his direction. The boy looked terrified to say the least.

Confused, the boy looked at the dead creatures and then looked at his own body. Jonathan backed off a few paces and put his sword away on his belt and squatted low, hoping to make himself appear less of a threat.

Jonathan motioned to the bodies of the creatures and then said in an encouraging tone, "Is this your handiwork young man? Very impressive if it was, I must say."

The boy just nodded and seemed to relax a little as he lowered his blade, but kept it at hand, ready to raise it again at a moment's notice. Jonathan could tell the boy was weakened by the fever.

"Have you eaten boy? I have some rations left if you want them. The water in the spring looks good, thankfully those bodies didn't land in them or else this would be contaminated for a month." Jonathan said, as he slowed back away to his horse and accessed the pack drawing out a skin of water and the rations he'd spoken of. Doing this, he untied his horse and led it to the spring and allowed it to drink freely while holding onto the lead lightly.

He flashed a kind smile in the direction of the boy and tossed him the cloth that held the rations. At this point, the boy was squatting down with his elbows resting on his knees, using his sword to lean forward on. As the rations skidded to a stop in front of him, he opened the cloth carefully and withdrew a piece of unleavened bread. The boy placed the bread on his knee, wrapped up the cloth and tossed it back at Jonathan. He sat there waiting, looking at Jonathan, not eating the bread. For a few minutes he just stared until Jonathan realized that the boy, untrusting, would not eat until Jonathan ate the bread first.

Jonathan chuckled quietly, "Smart young lad, I wouldn't want to eat food from a stranger either. No telling what bad intentions people have out on the roads these days. Well, let's fix that right this moment."

He tied his horse to a downed limb and reached for the bread. He took a bite from the bread, chewed, and swallowed. Then said warmly, "The name is Jonathan."

The boy watched for a moment longer and then must have decided the bread was indeed edible as he broke chunks from them and attacked them voraciously, barely chewing as he devoured the whole piece of bread before Jonathan's eyes. The boy coughed a bit as he choked on a crumb. Jonathan stepped forward and offered the boy his waterskin which the boy took and drank deeply to wash the dry bread down.

After his coughing fit, he finally spoke quietly, "I am Baaldir. Thank you for your aid." He winced as the deep gash on his shoulder pulled a little.

"That's a nasty wound on your shoulder there Baaldir." Jonathan said concerned. "From the redness around it you could have an infection starting."

Baaldir looked at his shoulder and then back to Jonathan, "It's a recent wound that was mending but I must have aggravated it during the fight with these, these...." He motioned to the dead creatures nearby as the descriptive words would not come.

Baaldir's face grimaced and his skin turned gray and paled. Jonathan, realizing that the boy was about to collapse, ran forward as Baaldir fell unconscious, barely reaching him to stop his head from hitting the ground. Jonathan felt the boy's pulse and listened for breath and determined that the fever from the infection was driving this. He needed to get him to a healer as soon as possible as he was not trained in herbs and their uses.

Working quickly Jonathan brought his horse over and picked the very heavy boy up over his shoulders and eased him onto the horse, tying his arms to the saddle to keep him from slipping off. Just before leaving to lead the horse back to the main road, he dragged the three dead attackers from the spring area so they could not contaminate it for the next weary traveler. He would have liked to say a quick prayer for their souls, but hurried on his way, knowing that Baaldir, who was now in his care would need help as soon as possible. His journey to Hebron would have to wait as he thought of a healer a few hours away and hastily walked up the path to the main road and set out in the opposite direction toward Kiriath-Jearim.

CHAPTER 22

The Palace

K ing Adonizedek watched his dream as a lucid spectator. It was the
same dream he'd had for the last year, constant and unchanging; he
wished he had more answers. It was so vivid that he had a tough time
differentiating the dream from real life. The first part, he was watching his
own funeral and the funeral of Thoros. Vithas drew his bow and lit an
arrow from the brazier at his side. He loaded three arrows onto his bow
and pulled back. With tears in his eyes, he shot the arrows toward the pyres.
The dried kindling lit fire and soon was engulfed in flames. He and Thoros
would soon be ash in the wind, as was the custom. Then Adonizedek
would turn and look at the walls made of hardwood and see the towers of
the city behind him jutting up into the sky. This was the city he had told
the council about days ago. At this point in the dream he would suddenly
revert to what he assumed was the battle leading to their deaths.

In this part, he rose above the landscape in the form of a raven as he
watched his son and himself face down a retinue of impossible creatures.
All the great men of renown were there fighting as a swarm of hell descended upon them. He saw Lox standing atop a boulder in the middle of the
swarm, holding a staff with a glowing red stone embedded in it. He seemed
to urge the swarm on towards them. Clearly, he had betrayed them.

Adonizedek sidestepped an attacker and swung the butt end of his spear
to trip the assailant sending him sprawling onto the ground where he was
killed by men behind him. He jabbed his spear into another and drew
his swords. With both hands he began to pick apart the enemy as their
onslaught reached fever pitch. In a blur he sent ten creatures to meet
whatever god they worshipped. One after the other he dispatched them.

Thoros was knee deep in close combat as the enemy swarmed him.
Jarnsaxa stood back and picked apart the swarm with her bow as they tried
to overtake Thoros. Just as the swarm would cover Thoros, he would burst

forth from the fray and bodies would scatter to the four winds. He swung a hammer that shimmered in the firelight. It connected and destroyed the body of one assailant and dispatched another with every swing of the powerful hammer.

They were beginning to push the horde of creatures back just as the earth began to quake. Fire erupted from the earth and molten rock spewed from fissures and plates that opened before his eyes.

Suddenly the dream jumped forward to his son fighting a massive serpent creature that had a lion's head, venom dripping from the teeth on its powerful jaws. What manner of creature was this? Then he watched his dream-self face down an impossibly huge dire wolf, black as night. The wolf bounded up to him and opened his mouth to swallow him whole.

Normally, this is where Adonizedek would wake every time in a cold sweat, heart racing. Instead, he was ripped into a dark room with only a candle for light at the center. Was this a new part of the dream he thought? He walked towards the candle and picked it up. Using it, he scanned the large room which consisted of four walls and a door at the end of the room. He walked forward and searched for a handle. Finding none he tried to pry it open with his fingers. That's when he heard a sinister laugh from the other end of the room. His blood ran cold as he whirled around at the sound. The room, outside the candlelight was so pitch black that he couldn't see the other side.

"Who's there! Show yourself!" Adonizedek demanded, his startled panic evident in the shakiness of his voice, which was a rare occurrence indeed to hear a man such as him betray a hint of fear.

The laugh started again, only from above him this time. He held the candle up above his head just in time to see a pitch-black creature descend on him from above.

Then he was suddenly floating above his body in his chamber. A man stood over him releasing a black substance into his mouth from a wineskin.

All he heard was the low chant coming from the man as a chorus of dark cloaked men stood in the corners of the room droning a horrendous tune.

His body began to float above the bed almost as if the sound from the men lifted him as their frequency got lower, creating a slight vibration of the room and air around him. He soon realized that this was no dream and that he was indeed disembodied.

"Stop! What are you doing!" But the men didn't hear him or if they did, they didn't pay him any mind.

He willed himself down to the ground where he clawed at the cloaked man's shoulder. Then, in a horrific way, that man's head turned completely around to face him. But his face was no face; instead, it was a black void that would swallow him whole. He scampered backward, frightened by the sight and the head turned back to the business at hand.

Suddenly black smoke poured from the man's mouth and swirled in front of his hands. He encompassed the smoke in his hands and began to chant, squeezing down on the smoke like you would if making a ball of mud as he'd seen his grandchildren do often.

The man released his grip and revealed a black orb that reflected the candlelight in it. He then placed the orb into Adonizedek's mouth and with the other hand he plugged the nose by pinching the nostrils and held his other hand over the mouth.

Adonizedek watched in horror as his body's eyes opened wide with shock. Unable to breathe, he fought the black cloaked man until finally he swallowed the black orb which sent a shockwave through the room. The man released his grip as the chorus of shadowy men around the room started to taper off returning his body to its resting place on the bed and then one by one formed a line shoulder to shoulder at the foot of the bed.

He heard the black cloaked man say, "In two nights, Jebus will be ours."

Then, he was suddenly back in the black room again with the same candle sitting on a pedestal like he'd never left in the first place. This time no creature was there to haunt him, but rather he could sense that the room he found himself in was a prison of sorts, meant to hold him there forever. He once again picked up the candle and walked forward to a wall. Adonizedek couldn't describe what the wall felt like, just that he realized he was unable to walk forward. He turned around and saw the pedestal sitting just a few paces away and then put his right hand out, walking along the edges of the strange room. Eventually, he realized the room was five-sided, encased in some sort of dark energy that surrounded him above and below as well. He walked back to the pedestal and set the candle down on it once again,

Crouching low, he contemplated his situation and realized that there was little he could do as he remembered seeing the red sky as the sun began to rise. It reminded him of an old saying from the Phoenicians: Red in the morning, sailor takes warning. Another storm was coming.

<hr />

Meanwhile...

Tsalmaveth smiled as he now had Adonizedek trapped. Now he would search his mind for any information regarding the boy, Baaldir. If he was correct, Baaldir should be somewhere in the palace recuperating and once he found him, he would use him to locate Nathan. The two were bonded by blood through their ordeal in the caverns and a simple spell would reveal the thread that connected them, leading him directly to the Key.

"In two nights, Jebus will be ours." Tsalmaveth gloated out loud, not really addressing anyone other than himself and perhaps Ahmet, his vessel as he leaned over Adonizedek and placed his hand on the forehead and lightly squeezed his temples. Tsalmaveth then began chanting a spell consisting of a dead language spoken a hundred thousand years ago by a long-forgotten civilization. Moments later he was looking at Adonizedek in the black room. This room would be a prison for his mind until he died or was released, however Tsalmaveth now had unfettered access to all of Adonizedek's thoughts.

Tsalmaveth phased through the dreams and conversations the king had over the last day or so and stopped on one particular conversation from this last day with Adonizedek, David and several others. His blood boiled as he saw David standing there, virtually unharmed but for a black eye and head bandage. Not a day ago, he nearly caught David in the dungeon, and again in the stable before David bested that cursed cyclops that he had hastily inhabited, when he was evicted from Ahmet's body the first time. David was an enigma that he did not care at all to understand but would rather destroy over and over again.

After stewing over the recent events with his nemesis, David, he focused on the conversation. It seemed they were all piecing together the revelation that they were facing a new enemy, and they seemed to be on track to discover his new temple if they hadn't already. This was problematic but he would ensure that they never had the chance to capitalize on whatever intelligence they gleaned from the subsequent search. What Tsalmaveth was now focused on most, seeing through Adonizedek's eyes, was the shadow of a figure peering around the doorway of the room watching and listening to all of the goings on outside.

Adonizedek dismissed his men and the Israelites to their search and entered the room once again. There lay Thoros, wounded and unconscious, breathing slowly. His wife and mother sat nearby cradling two children and another younger boy who resembled Adonizedek.

"Father, what are we going to do about those creatures. They killed my friend. Nearly killed me and my brother. We should be marching below with a thousand men stamping them out for good." Baaldir, said excitedly.

Adonizedek chided Baaldir gently, "My son, you need to rest and recover. We will make our move once we know what we are dealing with. Until then we will all stay close and protect one another. The siege is over, finally, and now we must learn about our newest enemy. If they are truly underneath our feet, then we should seek to understand how extensive their ability to enter our defenses is. Further we must know what their goal is or if they even have one. Running off to battle is almost always the wrong choice, my dear boy."

Baaldir clearly disagreed, evident by the incredulous look on his teenage face. "The beasts that attacked me were the same ones that beat me and Nathan up a year ago. Only they weren't them any longer. It wasn't enough. I tried to use the skills you and Thoros and others taught me, and it wasn't enough." Baaldir was beginning to shudder as a tear welled up in his eyes.

Adonizedek pulled Baaldir by the shoulders into an embrace, "Oh son, a boy of fourteen should not have to experience what you have. Stay with your family and help us figure things out."

Baaldir sniffled and through tears said, "I killed a man father, and I would've killed more if not for my injuries. They escaped and I had no choice but to try and save my friend and get him out of there."

"It was hard for me the first time I had to kill a man Baaldir. I agonized over it for months afterwards. Eventually, and it pains me to admit this, it got easier and then it became a fact of life. This fact, I hoped to spare you from until you left for your initiation. Sometimes son, it is kill or be killed but what I want for you is to hold on to your humanity throughout it. If we lose our humanity, we will become like those men you had to face."

Tsalmaveth phased away from this heartfelt and simultaneously sickening father and son moment. *When I get ahold of you Baaldir I will rip your humanity from you like a weed,* Tsalmaveth thought.

Then, Tsalmaveth came to a memory of Adonizedek just after nightfall. Jarnsaxa was filling him in on the discovery below, and the sighting of Ahmet and the Shades exiting the temple. The fact that they were leaving to attack the Israelites at their camp a few miles away from Jebus seemed to be unknown.

When Jarnsaxa finished her report, she asked, "How's Baaldir doing Your Majesty? I have a gift for him," she said, producing a figurine of an archer that she'd whittled from a piece of wood.

"Very good work Jarnsaxa, that is a great gift for a boy who's been through what he has. I had him stay with Siv and his mother if you want to go and take it to him." Adonizedek turned to walk away towards his chambers.

"Your Majesty, forgive me, but I just came from there. Baaldir wasn't there, Siv said Baaldir went to find some food. I figured he'd be over on this end of the palace. No?" she said puzzled.

Adonizedek returned the puzzled look and thought for a moment before finding a guard and beckoning him over. "Search the palace and find my son Baaldir. Report back to me when you find him and preferably escort him to my wife and daughter in the lower palace."

"I will look for him as well Your Majesty." Jarnsaxa said with a bow and salute before running off in a separate direction as the guard.

This was just too exciting now, Tsalmaveth could hardly contain it. Somehow, he deduced that Baaldir had left the palace. If he had the boy figured, Baaldir would not have sat still. Tsalmaveth had seen many of the adventurous type over the millennia and if he knew one thing, it was that they did not allow grass to grow around their feet.

Tsalmaveth pondered the information. *Now where could that boy have gone to? I would think he would go back to the tunnels. My Shades should be returning from their attack in a few hours. I'll look in at them and see how it's going and have them search the tunnels for the little rat.*

Tsalmaveth released his control on Adonizedek, closed his eyes, and was soon watching the attacks on the Israelites through his many Shades. Glimpses of carnage flashed through his mind as he cycled through them one by one.

A little more loss of Shades than I hoped, being a surprise attack. But I suppose I can't be surprised with that blood brother of David there fighting. Tsalmaveth ordered his entire army of Shades to focus on subduing and kidnapping more Israelites to bring back as slaves. He would use this opportunity to replenish his forces. Tsalmaveth began to laugh as, two by two, the Shades grabbed badly wounded soldiers and dragged him from the camp towards Jebus.

Cycling through the Shade's minds once again, he soon came to a group of three Shades separated from the main attack and there he saw him. *Baaldir...There you are my little rat.* Tsalmaveth smiled excitedly, *this has been easier than I expected, for a change.*

Tsalmaveth watched anxiously as the Shades attacked Baaldir, he relayed an order to them at the speed of thought. *That boy is to be captured and not killed, do what you must but bring him to me alive!*

The first Shade surprised Baaldir and tackled him, but Baaldir, being twice the Shades size and strength, easily reversed the attack and sent the Shade flying. He arose with a sword in one hand and a dagger in the other and crouched into a fighting stance. The three surrounded him and weighed their opponent cautiously for a moment now that their objective was capture and not destruction.

One by one they attacked but Baaldir wounded and repelled each of them in turn. He threw his dagger at one and buried it in the Shade's chest at fifteen paces. The Shade fell to his knees and rolled onto its back, not dead but unable to find the strength to continue after having a dagger in the heart.

The second Shade to fall had its throat slit as the third flanked Baaldir and tackled him to the ground. The third Shade attempted to grapple him and subdue him, readying a strike to the head with a stone but Baaldir produced a smaller dagger and plunged it into the Shade's eye. Tsalmaveth watched in disbelief as a boy of fourteen managed to defeat three Shades. The last thing he saw from the third Shade as it died was Baaldir falling unconscious as he left the dagger and allowed the Shade to fall across the chest.

No! These Shades are supposed to be trained Israelite warriors. How is it possible that this boy prevailed?

Tsalmaveth looked to the Shades in the room with him. These were the very ones Baaldir had referenced in his conversation with Adonizedek. Each of them stood ready for their next order.

"Go and find Baaldir. When you find him, bring him to me. Off with you!" he shouted as the three dispersed to do his bidding. It was still dark yet and they may just be able to finish what those others failed to do. Tsalmaveth relayed a final order, *do not stop even if the sun comes up. Use the energy you need to sustain your search. I need that boy brought to me alive.*

The fact that the Shades would retreat at sunrise was due to the reality that Tsalmaveth had to recoup his energy throughout the day, drawing a small amount of power from each and every shadow and a larger amount from each and every death he caused. During the battle with the Israelites Tsalmaveth caused a thousand deaths. It had fueled his power to the point that he felt as though he could sustain himself at full power, but that would wain quickly since he was not yet bound to Ahmet. Patience was key here. It wouldn't work to haphazardly throw himself into the daytime operations until his power was fully unlocked.

With that, Tsalmaveth patted the sleeping Adonizedek on the shoulder saying, "Sleep well king, I have plans for you. See you in two days." After saying this he turned and exited with a bounce in his step, almost skipping with joy. He would be there to welcome his Shades back and set to work breaking the new captives down one by one. This had been a fruitful night.

Tsalmaveth could almost see the Key in his grasp already. As if to accent this sentiment, a low rumble of thunder in the distance rolled in shaking the nighttime landscape, foretelling even more rain to come.

The Palace Infirmary: Jebus

Two nights and most of a third day had passed in the palace after the news of the King's condition swept the palace grounds. Two nights ago, the king had been found to be in a deep sleep and nobody had been able to wake him yet, though all signs pointed to him being in good health. King Adonizedek had never been sick a day in his long life according to Frigg and Siv. Every available healer was there at this very moment trying to figure out what could have caused him to be in such a state. Ide had even sent for help from the Philistines and any kingdom nearby not under the control of Israel. So far, no response was brought to the Council of Jebus.

Orvandil and Ide were now effectively ruling the city and tending to state matters. David noticed that the two of them were like an odd pair of old hens always picking at one another or tripping the other up with contradictory edicts. That wouldn't last long before the chaos spilled over into the city itself. David could almost see it happening before his eyes.

To their credit, guards had been sent to permanently barricade the tunnel entrance that Lox had opened up; not that Bulwark and Jarnsaxa would have allowed it to be ignored after seeing what they had seen. That ordeal had lit a fire in them that caused them to work day and night. The fact that they were uncertain about the sovereign rulers of the city made these things even more important. David had also mentioned to Bulwark that there was a passage under the prison that led to a room full of scrolls and artifacts. Bulwark had secured the doorways of the room with reinforced iron gates, and David had been permitted to peruse them.

David was astounded by the information he'd gleaned. Firstly, Lox had been all over the known world, and even further, collecting information and knowledge. From what he could tell, he was trying to find references to a lost people that had a white wolf as their banner sigil. Scroll after scroll with fragments of information painted a picture of an obsession that Lox clearly had.

David had even found reference to the Ark of the Covenant and the power it held. On it, Lox had written a question: *Who is the Son of Cain?* Several of the scrolls had ink on them asking comparable questions or had notes related to it. Today he had found scrolls referencing Tsalmaveth and something called The Key. Pictograms detailed a sacrifice of blood to open a portal that brought forth a being that looked much like the one he'd seen in the temple. These last two days he'd been able to piece together a theory of what Tsalmaveth and maybe Lox had been up to.

David now sat on the floor at the foot of Thoros' bed, listening to the rain outside that had started two days ago and had scarcely stopped. After he'd heard the news that King Adonizedek was now incapacitated, coinciding with the continuous rain, he could feel the darkness of the Shadow of Death's hand on the very air they breathed, thick with dread as the rain seemed unnatural to him. Every healer and shaman in Jebus had attempted to wake him and treat him to no avail. David even began to wonder if this is the same darkness that polluted King Saul's mind, causing him to forsake God and his commands. He had found a lyre in one of the rooms adjoining and sat there plucking the strings, softly playing a melody he'd thought up.

Siv had come back with the children, and they were gathered around. The two children, Magni and Thrud sat on the ground watching David pluck the strings. Siv sat next to Thoros staring off into space, lost in contemplation.

It had been several days since he'd done anything musical. Normally, even while on the run, he would find something to make a melody with or a rhythm that soon fell into a song structure. One time he used reeds and bamboo to make a pan flute. Fortunately, as he got the itch to play music, he found the lyre collecting dust in a corner and couldn't resist the pull of strings calling him. Magni seemed to take an interest in the lyre music, and he intently watched as the melody began to take shape.

David was beginning to think up words to layer over the melody as the progression gradually became more complex. He plucked three strings at a time and added in a suspended note here and there to fill out the chords. All at once the words came to him and he began to sing:

I will bless the Lord at all times. His praise will continually be on my lips.
I praise the Lord, let the suffering listen and rejoice.
Magnify the Lord with me! Together, let us lift his name up high!
I sought the Lord, and he answered me, and He delivered me from all my fears.

Those who look to Him are radiant; their faces are never covered with shame.

This poor man called, and the Lord heard him; he rescued him out of all his troubles.

The angel of the Lord encamps around those who fear Him, and he delivers them.

Taste and see that the Lord is good; blessed is the one who takes refuge in Him.

Fear the Lord, you his holy people, for those who fear him lack nothing.

The lions may grow weak and hungry, but those who see the Lord lack no good thing.

Both children lay on their mother's lap as he continued the song. They were enraptured by the melody. Siv shifted in her seat a touch and leaned forward.

Come, children, listen to me; I will teach you the fear of the Lord.

Whoever of you loves life and desires to see many good days, keep your tongue from evil and your lips from telling lies.

Turn from evil and do good; seek peace and pursue it.

Suddenly, Siv shrieked and jumped up. "He squeezed my hand! He is waking up!" Both children stood up and rushed to their father's side.

David stopped playing as soon as Siv shrieked. At first, he thought something was wrong. Once he realized what she had said, David hurriedly placed the lyre on the ground and stood up.

David could see now that Thoros was indeed beginning to wake. He heard a faint mutter from Thoros that didn't remind him of any known words as Thoros began to slowly open his eyes. The light of the sun shining through the window would be very bright to a man that had been in darkness with eyes closed for days on end.

Thoros, who was bewildered, began to try and sit up and Siv was there to gently push him back down onto the cot. "Rest my love, you cannot be on your feet just yet."

Then, she shouted towards the door. "Guard!"

The door swung open, and two guards burst into the room with hands upon their swords, ready to unsheathe them at a moment's notice. "Yes milady. What is wrong?"

"Everything is wonderful, please, one of you go fetch a healer. The prince has woken up from his fever."

"Right away milady." They turned and exited rapidly. One stayed behind and took up his post outside the door.

"Where am I?" Thoros said, gruffly with a weak voice. Siv pulled a ladle full of water from the pitcher next to the bed and gave it to Thoros to drink. He guzzled it down and nearly choked on the water as it moved into his parched throat. He'd been days without a drink of water, his only fluid being the sponge of water that the healer used to wet his lips as he was incapacitated.

Siv pulled the ladle away and refilled it. "We are in the palace. Take it slow my love; you'll need to ease into it." As she brought the ladle back up, he propped himself up on his elbows and allowed her to slowly drain the ladle of water into his gullet.

Magni and Thrud rushed forward and wrapped their arms around Thoros' neck. "Abba, I thought you'd never wake up again!" Thrud said with tears in her eyes.

If Thoros was in pain, he didn't betray it as the kids squeezed his neck. David crouched low, last he saw Thoros conscious they were enemies, and he was David's captive. The movement in Thoros' periphery brought his gaze over to where David crouched.

Thoros abruptly sat up and ushered the children to his side. "What is the meaning of this. Why is this man here?"

Siv placed her hand upon Thoros' bare chest, bandaged and mending, and calmly explained that David and his men had found him injured outside the walls and had brought him into the city.

"He is our enemy Siv. Yet he roams our palace freely?"

David interjected, "Simply put, you saved my brother Jonathan a few nights ago in an attack. We repaid that debt by saving your life in turn."

"Then your army has occupied Jebus, where is my father?" He put his feet on the ground and began to stand but quickly realized he'd need a little time to get the blood flowing and regain his balance after being laid up.

David shook his head, "On the contrary prince. Until three nights ago I was a prisoner of your father's. My men found you and brought you here. They did not know I was captive but knew that a debt was owed because you saved my brother Jonathan's life. Your father and I have discussed an alliance though the details are yet to be worked out." He didn't go any further, preferring Siv to be the one to tell him of his father's condition.

"Where is my father?" Thoros demanded.

Siv put her hand on his bicep. "My love, your father is sleeping."

"What? How can that be? It's the middle of the day" Thoros was dumbfounded as he gestured to the late afternoon sunlight coming into the window.

David interjected with one word, a name. "Tsalmaveth"

Thoros looked puzzled so David asked a question. "Do you remember anything of the attack on you outside the walls?"

Thoros took a moment to decide if he would speak to David and finally spoke. "Not much, I remember the road, I had just lit fire to the siege camp, it had already been attacked and massacred. Then I remember fighting a bunch of feral creatures that didn't seem to tire. They stabbed me many times and I thought to myself that I would surely die as my wounds bled out."

David slowly stood and walked over to a table at the far end of the room and retrieved a cloth that had something wrapped in it. He walked to Thoros and handed him the cloth and motioned for him to unwrap it. Thoros took the item and pulled back the folds of the cloth to reveal a dagger.

Thoros looked puzzled, "What is this?"

"That is the dagger that wounded you in your chest, you are very fortunate that they missed vital organs, or we would not be here having this conversation." David offered. "Do you see the inscription?"

Thoros turned the blade over and over and looked at the crudely forged dagger with a handle made of bone. He wasn't sure how to pronounce the word, so he looked back at David waiting for him to clarify.

David continued, "The dagger has Hebrew characters etched into it. The word you see there is Tsalmaveth, The Shadow of Death or, Death's Shadow."

Thoros was still a little slow on the uptake with David's words, his energy and strength being limited after waking from a three-day sleep. He held the dagger up in the light and turned it over and over. "So, this Death's Shadow is what? A god of some sort? A secret military group?"

"Of a sort, Tsalmaveth is an adversary of my God. You may recall the plagues of Egypt when my people were enslaved by the Pharoah?"

"Aye, there were many plagues that afflicted the people in Egypt. I was little more than a boy then, about Magni's age."

David paused to remember that Thoros was quite a bit older than he looked. He looked as though he was in his thirties when he was really five hundred years old. "Do you remember the final plague?"

David waited for a few seconds then continued. "The final plague was Death itself using what we call Tsalmaveth. God allowed Death's Shadow to be released onto the earth for one night. The spirit descended on Egypt like a cloud and moved through the upper and lower residences, killing any first-born child that it encountered. You may remember that Pharoah's own son was taken by Death that night which led to his grief and subsequent release of my people from captivity. One thing you may not know is that our people were spared because we painted lamb's blood on our door frame. We celebrate with a feast of unleavened bread called Passover once every year since. Because Death passed by our house and did not enter."

Thoros was silent, contemplating. David noticed that he did not appear to be convinced just yet.

"The angel Michael captured Death's Shadow and locked it away in a deep place or so the legend tells it. It hasn't been seen again until now. Your brother Lox unleashed it and with it took hundreds of our men and turned them into the monsters that you saw a few nights ago. They are thralls, indwelt by its spirit or at least under control by Tsalmaveth."

"How am I supposed to trust what you are saying here? Not three days ago you were a mortal enemy placing me in captivity. You say your God allowed this Death's Shadow to manifest, how are we supposed to believe that this isn't from His own hand?"

David curtly replied, "Because the army of Israel was defeated two days ago by those very creatures. My men and I defied King Saul and are no longer welcome in Israel while Saul reigns. We defied him to save your life. My men are now without a country, their families may even be in jeopardy. How many more things do I need to explain before you realize that despite our being your enemies a week ago, we are on the same side now. We need to work together to defeat this evil, for the good of all in this city and in Israel."

Thoros groaned as he tried to stand, "Be that as it may, we shall see if an alliance between us will come to anything fruitful. Meanwhile, I need to see my father, help me up so we can go and see him."

Siv was not happy with that idea, "Thoros, you mustn't strain yourself. Soon you will have your strength back and then you'll be better able to help. And besides, my love. I need to tell you what has befallen your father. Since two nights ago he has been in an unending sleep. No healer can solve the mystery."

Thoros continued to attempt to stand, looking angry and worried simultaneously. "Then if this was an attack from this Tsalmaveth that our Israelite friend mentioned, then we had better assume it was only the start. Either help me or stand out my way." He limped toward the door.

Siv relented and quickly came to his side propping him up. David took this as a queue and joined her on the other side. His much smaller stature provided an elbow shelf for Thoros on his shoulder. They made their way through the door and turned to the left and made their way towards the main palace where Adonizedek lay sleeping. The late afternoon sun blazed as they arduously made their way. David noticed the oppressive humidity due to the deluge of the last few days.

Magni and Thrud ran ahead and Siv called out to them, "Children, stay within my sight. Do not leave it, do you understand?" She said this with apparent worry at the seriousness of the current situation within the palace. Frigg was walking toward the children and walked right past them in a daze not looking at anyone.

"Mother, what is it?" Siv said, now motioning for her children to come close to her.

Thoros waved his hand in front of his mother's face, and she suddenly snapped out of her stupor. Upon seeing Thoros she wrapped her arms around his neck and began to sob.

"What has become of my family, one son is saved, and now the other is missing since last night. And my husband hasn't yet awoke." She said through her tears and sobs mixed with short breaths.

Thoros, confused said, "Mother, what do you mean by this?"

Frigg suddenly began to smack Thoros' face and screamed, "Why must my sons act this way? It's your fault, he takes after you, always running into danger!" Her smacks did not damage Thoros physically, but he was visibly taken aback as he tried to gently grab her hands while trying not to strain his barely healing wounds.

"Mother, tell me what has happened and how can I help?" Siv said, trying to console her. Frigg collapsed at their feet and beat the ground, tears flowing freely.

"Love, go on ahead, the kids and I will keep her company and see that she is taken care of," Siv said to Thoros as she knelt to comfort Frigg.

David, arduously supporting Thoros' weight on his shoulder, took in all the information. Now young Baaldir, whom he'd met briefly just before they went to explore the dungeon, was missing. Apparently, secrets could be kept in this palace.

David hated the fact that he could not anticipate the events that continued to happen outside of his own ability to control them. In fact, he felt as if he'd been a step behind ever since they were in the dungeon days before when he'd had that panic attack. Ever since then he'd dealt with bouts of anger, doubt, sadness, loathing, hatred, and contemplating violence on those that were doing this to all of them. He felt as though a shadow was hanging over all of them as they started off toward the palace residence where Adonizedek lay unconscious. He had put his trust in Elohim to deliver them and he couldn't deny that he'd seen His hand work more than once on their behalf. Jeroboam's ordeal was just one example proving this.

So why do I suddenly doubt or question His power? David thought with a frown. This bothered him greatly as he lumbered on helping a groaning Thoros who was attempting to quicken his pace, impatient to see his father after seeing his mother in such a sorry state. Several minutes later, they finally reached the residence of King Adonizedek and entered the chamber. Inside, there were several healers pouring over scrolls and deliberating with one another on strategies and treatments that they had yet to implement to cure the king of the sleeping spell. The king lay in the bed with hands at his side, shallow breaths the only evidence that he yet lived as his chest slowly rose and fell with each breath. The late afternoon sun rays illuminated his face as the sun began to set on yet another day.

Thoros limped over to the bedside and grabbed his father's hand, "I will find who did this to you father and they will pay dearly."

David could notice something on the king's face. His lips had grayed, and several thin black lines had begun to extend from the corners of his mouth, almost giving him the look of a frown. Dark rings around the eyes looked as if he'd been punched in a fist fight yet there was no swelling.

"Look at the sorry state of my father, David. This is not a natural ailment, I'm sure of it," Thoros said matter-of-factly.

David was unable to respond as he was lost in thought yet again. Thoros, under his own power walked out of the room and turned to walk toward the council chambers. Soon David came to and hurried to join him. They needed to come up with a way to combat an unnatural enemy and he feared their swords would not be enough.

CHAPTER 23

Deep Inside the Caverns: The Temple to Yaldabaoth

Two nights after Tsalmaveth indwelt him, Ahmet built a fire in the new temple below the city of Jebus, using dried wood and dung. Once he got the fire roaring, Ahmet built a stand that held a small metal pot over the fire filled part way with water. The water started to heat up as he set to work preparing the ritual. He was aware of all of this but had no idea how he knew what to do or what to say, but somehow Tsalmaveth had given it to him. Ahmet had prepared ingredients that consisted of venom from six vipers, squid ink, and dried hemlock flowers. With a mortar and pestle he ground them up and stirred them until they became a singular ink-like liquid.

The Shades, in black cloaks, began to assemble around the firepit until they surrounded him. There were hundreds of them, as Lox had done his part, turning over three hundred captive Israelites into thralls of Tsalmaveth. They had lost a third of their number attacking the fleeing Israelite army two nights past, but the number of captives dragged back, too wounded to resist numbered around two hundred. Tsalmaveth had informed him that once the binding ritual was complete, they would be able to create Shades and replenish their numbers at a fast rate.

This new temple to Yaldabaoth deep in the ground underneath Jebus was now complete after the swarm of Shades had made short work of moving everything. Lox's masons from Tyre had moved the angelic statues and reinstalled them under duress from the Shades and then once the skilled work was complete, they were killed unceremoniously.

Hesitation gripped Ahmet as he finished mixing the concoction. He wasn't sure how he had come to this point. He thought about refusing to perform the ritual but then his son and wife's faces would flash through his mind.

Ahmet, continue with the ritual, Tsalmaveth said in his mind.

Tsalmaveth sat across from him, having created an illusion in Ahmet's mind that made it look as though the Shadow of Death was sitting on a chair made of stone, observing the ritual from a throne. Tsalmaveth was leaned back nonchalantly and shot Ahmet a look as if to say, "I'm waiting."

Ahmet delayed for a moment longer and then placed the bowl on the ground and repositioned himself on his knees. He slowly pulled his tunic down from his shoulders until his chest was bare. Tsalmaveth began to hum a low-pitched melody that came from his throat.

The Shades swayed back and forth and began to hum the same melody in unison with him at first. Eventually a chorus of discordant harmonies that, by themselves sounded striking but together they were altogether terrifying, began to layer over the melody. It was a horrifying sound, which penetrated deep into Ahmet's gut as his blood ran cold. The Shades began to voice their parts in such a way that it seemed like the sounds were a living and breathing thing. The discordant voices held the last note longer than humanly possible before beginning again. It gave the sensation of hearing a man shrieking in horror.

This pattern repeated as Ahmet drew the dagger from his belt with the words 'Tsalmaveth' inscribed on it in Hebrew. With it, he cut his left hand deep and allowed the blood to flow into the bowl of ink, then plunged the blood-soaked blade into the hot embers of the fire as the blood sizzled and smoked.

Ahmet suddenly thought, *Bound with Darkness, our Fate is Death. Shadow of Destruction. Tsalmaveth.*

"Say the Words, Ahmet." Tsalmaveth said from his illusory throne.

Ahmet cleared his throat and shakily said, "Bound with Darkness, our Fate is Death. Shadow of Destruction. Tsalmaveth."

"Yessss. That's it. Repeat it over and over."

Ahmet repeated the line. "Bound with Darkness, our Fate is Death. Shadow of Destruction. Tsalmaveth."

"Good, keep repeating it and carve my name in your chest with the knife." Tsalmaveth leaned forward, pointing at the knife. Ahmet hesitated and Tsalmaveth prodded him, "Do it now, Ahmet."

Ahmet, shakily picked up the red-hot blade from the fire and repeated the lines again. This time, using the razor-sharp tip of the knife to cut his chest. The skin around the cuts sizzled and hissed and the pain was so sharp that he struggled to continue.

Painstakingly, he outlined in Hebrew characters, the word Tsalmaveth into his chest, carving from right to left. The burning skin and hair filled his nostrils with an unpleasant aroma and the pain made it nearly impossible to hold in a scream, but he persisted. When he finished, Ahmet placed the knife on a cloth next to him and picked up tools, which consisted of a small wooden stick and a separate piece of wood with a sharpened obsidian shard affixed to the end. With these tools he began the process of using the ink to tattoo over the incisions he had made.

This is going to hurt, he thought, as he dipped the obsidian into the ink and raised it to his chest.

Good, he thought, but he realized that it wasn't his thought. It was Tsalmaveth responding almost joyfully to see his servant in pain.

Ahmet heard the chorus of Shades crescendo and decrescendo several times, mimicking an inhale and exhale. He placed the obsidian to the first character and began to firmly tap with the stick, causing the ink to penetrate deep into the burned flesh. Blood flowed from the burned flesh, and it stung terribly. The venom in the ink immediately went to work, but not in the way venom usually would. It began to smoke, bubble and hiss, almost as if the viper was on his chest. The burning sensation was excruciating but he pressed on, dipping the shard, and tapping the venom ink into the characters. The process took several minutes that felt like hours.

Upon finishing the last character, he dropped the stick and the tattoo instrument to his side. The venom, now in his blood stream, caused writhing pain as he was thrown to his back, gripping his chest. The tattoo began to pulsate and all at once Ahmet heard a voice in his head begin the chant again.

Bound in Darkness, our Fate is Death. Shadow of Destruction. Tsalmaveth.

Then Ahmet heard the chant alternate with a chant in a different language. It sounded like some of the words were Hebrew.

Agudah, Khoshekh! Perthro, Eihwaz! Hagalaz, Isah! Tzel Mavet!

He was so disoriented as the world spun and he couldn't tell if the words were audible or not.

Upon the last syllable the pain increased ten-fold as his body was pulled in every direction, almost as if making room for someone else. His body began to levitate, and the tattoo began to glow as it rose from his chest. The ink floated above his chest and kept the word Tsalmaveth intact, glowing a deep violet. As it hovered above him, black smoke filled the cavern. It swirled round and round and sent tendrils of smoke into Ahmet's nostrils, ears, eyes, and mouth. The smoke pushed its way into his body. He let out a blood-curdling scream, but no sound escaped, it was trapped in his mind.

Just when Ahmet didn't think he could stand any more pain, the smoke began running through his veins and arteries. The veins on his body turned black and bulged out and they looked as if they were going to explode. The pain increased over and over until the entirety of the smoke had entered Ahmet's body.

He heard a voice that was not his say, "You're mine, Ahmet. Your body is now my body, your soul is now my soul to do with as I please, and you will witness the world that Yaldabaoth will create. You'll be there at the end when all is destroyed by fire."

The Shade chorus held a low-pitched note in unison as Ahmet's body returned to the ground and as he descended the tattoo ink returned to his chest. Fully healed, it was now just a tattoo.

Ahmet slowly sat up, but not too quickly. His head was spinning, and his stomach felt queasy and then he realized he was going to be sick, so he rolled to his right and vomited on the cave floor. A black tar came up from his stomach as he wretched until nothing else came out. He dry-heaved several more times until his stomach returned to normal then rolled to his back and stared at the dark ceiling of the temple, just barely lit by the now waning fire.

"You're not going to lay there all night, are you?" Tsalmaveth queried, sounding rather annoyed.

"What did you do to me?" Ahmet pleaded as he pulled himself to his knees.

"What did I, do to you? Nothing. This is all your doing." Tsalmaveth said.

At that moment Ahmet realized the sound of Tsalmaveth's voice was coming from his own lips instead of across the room as before.

He shook his head, "No, I never wanted this...I just..."

Tsalmaveth rolled Ahmet's eyes, "Relax Ahmet, the regret will go away before long and soon you will have all you ever desired."

Ahmet began to sob uncontrollably. The weight of what he'd just done was too much to bear. He cursed himself for being so selfish, so cowardly, so stupid. In his anger and grief, he'd fallen off a cliff and felt as though he would never stop falling.

"There There. It will be all right," Tsalmaveth said almost sympathetically. Then the corner of Ahmet's mouth rose into a toothy smile, "What your experiencing is phantom pain from having your soul ripped from your corpse!"

Ahmet shrieked with horror and began to hyper-ventilate as Tsalmaveth voiced a sinister cackle.

Tsalmaveth sat forward, "Seriously Ahmet. You wanted this. You wanted power, you wanted wealth, you wanted fame. I knew that of you the first time I saw you spying on Lox and me over the altar. Now you'll have them all if you just do as I say. Not to mention, revenge on those Israelites that killed your dear son."

Ahmet persisted, "No! Not like this! I didn't know...I didn't." However, deep down, he knew this was where this path led, but he'd justified it with his desire for revenge. What could he do now? He looked at his hands and arms, then his bare chest which bore a gruesome tattoo, raised up on his skin which in this lighting now looked gray. All over his body Ahmet could see that his veins had turned black, making him look like an unusual species of man altogether.

Tsalmaveth scoffed, "Ah! But you did Ahmet. YOU said the words at that altar that gave you and I, our start. I must say, your pleas were original and nearly brought a tear to my eyes. Lox tried it several times, but we have other plans for him. I'm glad I held out because I knew you were special the moment you crawled your scrawny body to the altar, bleeding out from your stomach. Now it's natural for you to go through the pain and regret phase, but do you think we could grieve while we move one foot in front of the other...Hmm?"

Ahmet started to make another argument, but Tsalmaveth cut him off.

"Ahmet do not mistake my willingness to have this conversation as a cue that you can do anything other than my will. If you do not figure out a way to swallow this and accept your very prosperous future, then I will make good on my promises. I never break my word."

Ahmet new this was a reference to the threat to make him kill his wife.

"Y-Y-yes master." he said, dropping his shoulders in surrender.

"That's better already!" Tsalmaveth stood up and walked through the fire toward Ahmet. "Stand up, grab that bowl of ink and pour it into the hot water."

Ahmet did as Tsalmaveth commanded, pouring the venom ink into the water. It sizzled and began to glow a mixture of green and purple hues. He saw his reflection in the bronze bowl through the filter of the dim firelight. Staring back at him was Tsalmaveth and his vacuous void that one would be hard pressed to describe if the word 'face' had never existed.

All at once, the Shades, having no tongues, began to take up the foreign chant. Ahmet could only guess that Tsalmaveth was speaking through them.

"Agudah, Khoshekh, Perthro, Eihwaz, Hagalaz, Isah, Tzel Mavet."

The Shades repeated it over and over again, increasing their fervor with each repetition. The flames began to rise underneath the pot and soon the liquid was boiling and roiling a murky violet mixture. The smell was palpable in the air and Ahmet couldn't decide if it smelled sweet or altogether rancid as the waves of heat moved into the cavern temple.

Vlulor, across the temple, began to stir at the smell and was soon at the end of her chains smelling the pungent odor. A worried look came across her face as she whimpered and shrank back against the temple walls.

"Don't worry about that beast, Ahmet. Focus on the task at hand." Tsalmaveth ordered.

When Ahmet looked back, he saw that his right hand had a dagger in it. Under the control of Tsalmaveth, Ahmet raised the dagger and sliced his left hand deeply, then sliced his right hand before dropping the blade. He then watched his own hands reach over the cauldron, covered in pitch-black blood. He squeezed his hands into fists which caused the blood to flow from the open wounds into the boiling cauldron. As his blood, now Tsalmaveth's black blood, entered the mixture a massive black figure exploded up from the liquid with a mighty roar.

"With this shadow, I will bring all men under my heel! Agudah, Khoshekh, Perthro! Eihwaz, Hagalaz, Isah! Tzel Mavet! Tzel Mavet! Tzel Mavet!"

The Shades replied in unison, "Agudah, Khoshekh, Perthro! Eihwaz, Hagalaz, Isah! Tzel Mavet! Tzel Mavet! Tzel Mavet!"

The chorus of Shades repeated after Tsalmaveth three more times as the black figure above the mixture descended into the purple liquid and disappeared.

Tsalmaveth shouted the chant once more. "Agudah, Khoshekh, Perthro! Eihwaz, Hagalaz, Isah! Tzel Mavet! Tzel Mavet! Tzel Mavet!

Upon finishing the last words of the chant, the flames erupted, sending coals flying into the air and the force of the explosion sent Ahmet and the Shades closest to it flying back several cubits. Ahmet landed in a heap on the floor, lying prone on his stomach. It took a few moments for his senses to return as he slowly stood up.

Tsalmaveth picked up Ahmet's arm and pointed at the Shades. "Fill those wineskins over there with the potion."

Looking around the room at the hundreds of Shades standing like statues, Ahmet noticed their faces for the first time and could only describe it as though they had ingested poison. Ahmet could see their lips, dried and cracked, had turned a dark grey and the same black fingering of veins ran outward from the sides of the mouth, reaching out towards the bottom of the neck.

As the Shades set to work ladling the hot mixture into the skins Tsalmaveth joyously spoke to Ahmet. "Let's say we give your new powers a try...Hmm?" Tsalmaveth said excitedly.

"New powers?" Ahmet asked, unsure he heard him correctly.

Tsalmaveth replied, "Indeed! Choose one of my Shades, any one of them, and have them move forward and stand in front of you. But here's the fun part, only think it."

Ahmet scanned the front row of Shades. He closed his eyes and imagined himself pointing toward the Shade and telling it to move to a position in front of him. When he opened his eyes, the Shade was standing precisely where he told him to stand. Ahmet looked surprised and it was Tsalmaveth who smiled a sheepish grin.

"Ready for the next?"

"The next?"

"You've only just begun using the power I've given you. Strangle that Shade standing in front of you. But don't touch him. Raise one hand and imagine how you'll do it. Then, do it!"

Ahmet closed his eyes, and he heard Tsalmaveth say, "You don't have to close your eyes but if it helps you focus, go for it."

Ahmet tried keeping his eyes open as he raised his right hand. He extended his hand toward the Shade who was standing there betraying no emotion. He focused on the creature's throat and slowly curled his fingers as if he was gripping a ball. The Shade began to choke as he doubled over clawing at the air. His eyes bulged out of his head and his pale face turned purple. He was trying to draw breath but was unable. Ahmet squeezed harder; the Shade was now on the ground.

"That'll do Ahmet. I need that Shade for our next assignment." Ahmet released his grip, and the Shade suddenly could breathe again. It stood up and returned to the statue-like stance in front of him.

Tsalmaveth feigned stretching his arms above his head. "You see what power I've given you? You now have all the knowledge I possess apart from proprietary secrets, and you now have control of an army of obedient killers at your disposal. Think of the impact you'll have on the course of the world."

Ahmet bowed his head and thought for a moment. He was always the brunt of jokes with his supposed friends, was beaten by his father daily for being a weakling and had nearly lost his life a day ago at the hands of the only friends he truly had, Vlulor and Flagor. True, they were beasts, and stupid ones at that, but he had grown fond of them during his time tending to the dungeons at Lox's behest. He was the one that named them, fed them, cleaned their bedding area. They even allowed him to sit with them while they played with their toys. Lox didn't care for them. Ahmet did.

Lox, for the most part, didn't even notice that he was there taking care of them. Ahmet was a nobody that no one ever noticed, apart from his wife Ramah and his boy, Nathan, who was now dead. Dead at the hands of Israelites.

"That's it, you're starting to understand." Tsalmaveth urged. "You are a nobody, no more. With me, you will bring Israel and their weakling god to its knees."

Ahmet stood up straight and pulled his shoulders back while taking in a long deep breath.

He exhaled quickly and said, "I'm ready Master. What will we do next?" Above ground he could hear the rolling thunder shaking the earth as another storm began to gather.

Memphis, Egypt

Lox awoke in a dank cell deep in the bowels of the temple. It had been two days since anyone had come down to give him food or water. He had yelled for Astarte repeatedly to no avail. She would not come to him even after nearly a thousand years. He thought about how impossible it was that she still lived, no doubt because of the amulet's power, and grew angry when he thought about the possible reasons for her disappearance. It all pointed back towards deception. As he tried to make sense of things, memories came back to him.

I saw her burned to ash. How? How is this possible? Lox thought.

Lox suddenly realized a growing hatred for her. How could she do that to him after sharing the time alone and professing her love for him all those years before, only to take what belonged to him and his heart with it. The way Lox saw it, Astarte had conned him, using her wiles to lull him into a stupor of love that removed his ability to see the danger she was to him. He'd stupidly given her the amulet to wear after she had asked to borrow it for a ruse and promised to return it to him upon their being wed.

Clearly that was a lie. She never loved him. She had used him to take the power of the amulet for herself. The fact that she was using it in the service of the very same god he'd actively been working for, stung even more. He felt betrayed by all of it, unable to divorce the two from each other.

During the last few days, he had gone through several phases of grief. First, he'd denied that she really was there in that garden or that she'd stolen his power for her own selfish reasons. Eventually he reasoned himself out of that thought and moved onto severe anger, pounding his fist on the stone wall, to no avail. Now he felt guilt and shame that he'd been so naïve and such an easy mark.

Lox reasoned that he hated himself more than he hated her. Every time he thought about his hatred for her, he would end up circling back around to the times they'd shared and he'd end up weeping in anguish because he loved her still. That is where he found himself at this very moment. Hopeless and doomed and unequivocally in love with Astarte which seemed liked its very own type of doom. *You're pathetic, Lox. You deserve to be made a fool.*

Lox thought back to the very first time he'd met her after he'd traveled the world for many years following the fall of Babel, which was where he'd first met a younger Adonizedek in the court of Nimrod. After Babel, the people scattered to the far reaches of the earth. With his amulet he was able to speak and understand any language as well as perform magical wonders and transformative spells using the power it exuded:

***

Astarte was a girl of twenty-nine who lived and was supported by her father for selling his wine and olive oil as well as fresh grapes and olives at the local market in Ai. Lox came upon her in the market and was captured by her striking beauty and fiery countenance. She would argue and haggle with the best of them and come out on top. She always got the better deal. The fact that men were putty in her hands only helped her sell out of her father's harvest daily. Lox had become smitten almost immediately, to the point that he would wait hours for her to come to the market, just to watch her, as she drove the cart pulled by a donkey into her stall each day.

One day, he was working up the courage to speak to her when he noticed her having a tough time speaking with a foreigner. The foreigner sounded like he was from the Far East based on his dialect. She hopelessly tried to communicate to no avail. Lox, not thinking this was a way to introduce himself to her, walked up and began to translate for the man. The man was shocked and overjoyed that someone finally understood his words.

This was a common occurrence in the wake of the fall of Babel in many of the area cities and states. As the years wore on, these cities turned into nations and centered around their own ethnic culture and language. Few people had the ability to read and understand the many dialects that now blanketed the earth. Millions of people confused and unable to communicate had created an opportunity for Lox.

After she'd happily done business with the foreigner, she introduced herself to Lox and thanked him profusely. She couldn't say how many times a sale had been lost due to the language barrier. For weeks after, he would meet her there and help with the stall and translate for her. Business was booming. They instantly had a connection and would talk long past when the stalls had closed for the afternoon. There was no shortage of things to talk about with her, from food to politics, literature to astrology. She was able to converse at a deep level on any subject. Astarte lit his mind on fire as he walked her to her father's home every afternoon. This went on for many weeks, walking to her home, leaving her at the gate only to meet her at the market the next day. Life seemed to slow down for him for the first time in a very long time.

One day, as they walked arm in arm towards her family compound, Lox looked at Astarte with her skin glistening in the late afternoon sun. They were playfully teasing one another about the failed sale that had caused much laughter throughout the day. Suddenly, without any thought, Lox pulled her close and pushed her body firmly against a stack of crates, completely enraptured by her beauty. Bringing his body close to hers he leaned down and pressed his lips on hers and kissed her for the first time. When Lox pulled away, he felt as if sparks of flames were trailing from their lips. Astarte blushed as he pulled away, pink coloring showing through her olive skin.

Lox thought at the time that he may have overstepped by misreading the signals he'd picked up on over the last month.

"Apologies Astarte, I was too forward just..." but Astarte stopped him midsentence, placing her fingers gently over his lips then grabbing his face and pulling him to hers, kissing him deeply. This time their faces hovered near each other's. Lox remembered the smell of her breath, cool and sweet as cane sugar and as intoxicating as the finest of wines.

"Astarte, I love you." Lox said lowly, his heart racing as if he couldn't believe he'd said those words just then.

Astarte then buried her head in his chest and was silent though her chest was heaving as if she was crying. Lox pulled her away to reveal tear-filled eyes.

Worried he'd made an error with his confession he attempted to apologize again, "Astarte, I should have been more careful with my words."

Astarte once again stopped him, "I love you also, Lox." She kissed him again, her tears wetting his cheeks.

"Then what are these tears for?" Lox asked softly.

"It's complicated, my father..."

Lox at the time assumed that she was worried about her virtue, so he clarified his intention, "I love you Astarte and I want us to be married."

Astarte looked pained as if she wanted to be joyful but was unable to, "You don't understand. There is a reason I am nearing thirty and yet unmarried."

Lox looked at her and replied, "I don't care, what reason could there be that would stop me from having you as my wife? There is nothing I wouldn't do, no one I wouldn't speak to. Take me to your father. I will ask him for your hand today."

Astarte turned away, tears welling up again as she walked away a few paces and stopped with her back to his. "Lox, my love, I have a confession to make, and you'll see what a predicament I am in afterwards." She turned back to him with a look of dread on her face. Lox remembered that look and how he felt so much anxiety for her as she began to explain.

In their conversations he remembered that she explained about her father being a reclusive type who never left the house. Which was a big part of the reason she'd not been married off yet. No man could gain an audience with her father to put forth a request as a suitor. All the eligible and wealthy men had tried, and they had all but given up. The older she grew, the less and less worthy suitors would show up at the gates, only to be turned away by the house staff.

The issue at hand was not that her father would not entertain suitors but that her father had actually died ten years prior. She'd been carrying on the operation of the vineyard and olive grove ever since and the servants of the house, knowing that another man would seize this property and they'd likely not have the good life they currently had, willingly played into the ruse. Her father had always been a solitary man after her mother died giving birth to her, so it was no surprise that no one questioned it when the servants at the house told them he would not see them. Her father had no friends to speak of, and no close family members, so not a soul had called upon his wellbeing. It had been all too easy to fall into the role she found herself in.

Within the city of Ai and surrounding territories a woman could not own property unless they were married to the owner of said property. In the case of a death such as her father's, any man that could find some way to establish kinship would be given the property and she would lose it all and be put out or be forced to marry him to avoid being cast out onto the street.

"This is why I cannot be married, in order to make a marriage proposal official, both the father of the bride and suitor must publicly declare it with our magistrate. It's an impossible situation." Astarte said, defeatedly. As they talked, they had both found a crate to sit upon as Lox listened intently.

Lox nodded his head, understanding the predicament, "That is quite a tricky situation indeed. But not impossible. I may have a way to solve this."

That is when he revealed that his skill in language was derived from an ancient amulet that he had received when under an old crone's tutelage. As she told of her plight, an idea had struck him. They found a secluded area away from onlookers and he showed her some of the other things he could do from illusions to shapeshifting into any manner of creature. Though he did not reveal that the amulet only enhanced the powers he already possessed and made them possible without a blood sacrifice.

Basically, his natural ability boiled down to what you kill, you can become. Lox remembered that was how he'd been able to transform into a common *house fly to escape doom at Jericho so many years ago, having lost the amulet. The downside to this was that it only lasted for a few hours after which Lox would revert back to the previous state, only he would be racked with pain and nausea for days afterwards. He only used that ability under extreme or dire circumstances.*

However, with the magical amulet, all he had to do was set his mind to it and it would happen. His idea was that she could use his amulet to transform herself into her father. In this way he could register with the magistrate that he would have a new son-in-law who would assume the management and co-ownership with his daughter. This was the only way for a woman to own property. If her mother had been alive, she would've retained ownership even after taking another husband.

She was uneasy about it but reluctantly agreed to the plan. They had decided to have one of the servants that resembled her play the part of the daughter, and she would play her father in a wedding ceremony and the customary feast to follow. It was all too perfect as he thought back to the way she took to using the amulet so effortlessly, convincing the whole town that she was indeed her father, the wealthy reclusive vintner. The town was abuzz that someone had finally conquered the most beautiful and hard-to-get woman in Ai.

They were overjoyed and offered their congratulations to them every day thence, as they sold wine, grapes, olives, and other produce. A month later, on the day of the wedding and feast, Lox walked up to the door and knocked once.

No answer came. He knocked twice, and thrice. Still no answer.

Lox thought this was odd since there was always a servant to answer the door, so he ran around to the back of the house and burst through the back gate to the compound. When he went inside, he hoped to find servants and Astarte preparing for the wedding and feast, instead he found an empty yard. Once inside the house he found it completely empty, without a soul inside. Nothing except a papyrus notice nailed to the front door, which he hadn't seen when he'd knocked moments before.

It read: This house has been confiscated by the Magistrate. Convicted of black witchcraft and fraud, the witch Astarte has been taken to be executed at once. An auction shall be held tomorrow to liquidate the property and its contents. The giant, Lox, is wanted for questioning.

Lox sank to the floor. His first thought was that this must be an elaborate ruse. But then he realized that his amulet had probably been the cause of her being accused of witchcraft. He screamed in anguish as he read the notice again. Maybe someone had come to collect a debt from her father and realized he was gone and so their scheme had become known.

It wasn't until he went to use his amulet to change into a bird and take to the air to find her, that he remembered that his amulet, which had been with him for more than two thousand years, was left in the hands of Astarte.

At that moment, Lox screamed with rage and shook his fists at the sky, cursing every god he could think of. He was stuck in this human form, a much larger than normal man, on the smaller side of what was considered giant during that time. His true form would've been able to smell her scent from miles away and he would've been able to track her to the ends of the earth. Now he was left with nothing but above average strength and an unquenchable desire to hurt someone.

Filled with anger, Lox stirred up the hot coals in the hearth and set fire to anything that would be considered fuel for a fire. The roof ablaze and timbers engulfed, he walked through the front gate to the road out front. People were running up from the town to see what the black smoke was from. He just walked past them and headed toward the town. As he walked into the market, which was just about to close for the evening, he saw the empty stall where he had spent three months of his life with Astarte, whom he believed was the answer to the question of purpose he was plagued with until meeting her.

At the center of the market stood a pyre of ash, still smoldering. This must have been where she was killed while he was away daydreaming about a life that Lox would never have now. He should have been here to protect her.

All at once, rage filled his body. Lox pushed it down and pushed it down again and again until it had nowhere to go but outwards as he exploded in the middle of the market, turning stalls on end, destroying people's wares. He picked up a club and began smashing whatever stood in his way. People ran up to him to stop him and he responded by crushing them with the club. He was lost in a bloodlust that wouldn't subside until he had killed anyone and everyone that presented themselves in the market. Men, and women lay around the market dead or dying. The whole thing happened so fast that his mind couldn't keep up with his body. It was like another person was controlling the movements.

Eventually, when Lox had run out of things to smash and murder, he collapsed onto his knees, covered in blood, none of it his. There he shuddered as the jolts of energy pulsed through his veins and began to settle in his stomach. He suddenly felt sick and wretched as the jolts subsided and left him feeling weak. His senses returned after a minute or two and that was when he heard shouts and horns blowing. They were coming for him with weapons. He'd heard many a call to arms to know that he needed to leave and leave quickly. He picked up his club and ducked into an alleyway just as the militia came running into the square, leaving behind shrieks of horror and cries from women realizing their husbands had been murdered in cold blood by some monster.

Lox, having activated his blood magic transformed into a fat man that he had just bludgeoned, and then he walked down an alleyway until he came to the street that ran parallel to the market.

Lox didn't stop to listen to whether or not they were on to him; he knew he must leave Ai and make himself scarce. Someone would no doubt have witnessed him and there would be no escape if he showed his face in any nearby town. He headed for the hills and found a cave where he shivered and sulked for a few days. He remembered transforming back into his giant *form and the sickness he felt for days afterwards. Coupled with the grief at the loss of his one true love he contemplated finding a high cliff and throwing himself from it.*

Lox had given himself over to love a woman and he loved her so completely that he would've renounced his vow to avenge his mother if it meant staying with Astarte for all time. They could've shared the amulet and lived a very long life together. These emotions churned in his gut for days and he let them fester, not even leaving the cave to seek food or water.

When he was delirious from lack of water and weak from lack of food, Lox fell into a dream-like trance where he found himself standing on a snowy bluff looking down upon a nomadic village. The tents flew a flag above them that whipped in the winter wind and upon that was a symbol of a white wolf, jaws open and teeth sharp. He whimpered as he thought about his mother being murdered and burned three nights before. He was a young pup then, unable to defend himself, so he ran when they attacked and hid away.

Next to him stood an old crone, the one that had given him the amulet. "Lox, one day you'll have the power to avenge your mother. Do not shrink from your vow. I did not give you that amulet so that you could live a happy life. When I found you as a young wolf cub, I took you in and raised you and worked spells on you to unlock your power. I loved you as my own son. Your promise of revenge was made to me as well as to your dead mother. And here you sit, letting yourself waste away. Get up! This is not over!"

Lox remembered jolting awake from his stupor and crawling to a stream and drinking his fill of the cool water. He found berries and nuts and ate them, replenishing his strength.

Afterwards he had wandered around Canaan and desert towns of the south near Egypt for years on end, stealing food and shaking down travelers for their coin. All the while, he searched for the old crone from his dreams. After a few hundred years the memory of Astarte faded, and he only thought of her on very rare occasions. He had even forgotten her face for a time.

One day, He came upon Adonizedek, who was traveling north with a party of warriors to take Jebus from a defunct king who had been weakened by corruption and revolt of his people. Adonizedek offered him a horse and told him that he should meet him in Jebus if he wanted to make something of himself, no doubt realizing the sorry state of his friend from years back. Lox accepted the horse but simply said he would think about his offer. A few years went by, and he decided to retire from the bandit life and take Adonizedek up on his offer. He'd heard of his success and wondered if there was more for him in this life and whether it could be found in Jebus with King Adonizedek. That was seven hundred years ago, which seemed like yesterday to him.

***

Now here he sat, captive in a damp cell, with his amulet and a woman he loved once upon a time only a few hundred cubits away. Time seemed to have slowed to the point that he could not bear it any longer. The solitary quiet was deafening to his mind as he could hear the drip of water far down the corridor outside his cell.

The steady *drip...drip...drip...drip...drip...drip,* continued until he couldn't stand it anymore. Just as he thought he was about to go mad; he heard a *clack...clack...clack...clack,* mixed in with the, *drip...drip...drip,* almost like a syncopated drumbeat.

Clack...Clack...Drip...Clack...Drip...Clack...Drip...Drip...Clack

The approaching footsteps made their way down the corridor toward him. Eventually, a torch light could be seen as two guards walked to his cell and stood on either side of the barred door. Standing before him was Astarte, she was dressed in a black cloak that covered her body from head to toe.

Astarte pulled the hood from her head and to the guards she said, "Leave me. Say anything to anyone about me being here and I'll turn you into a pile of mucus."

The men obeyed without question and left her a torch in the holder on the side of the door, they hurried away no doubt because of the threat. There was a stool in the corner which she picked up and sat down, keeping her distance from the cell bars. Neither spoke as the sounds of the guards shutting the door to the ward echoed through the dungeon.

Below the Upper City, Near the Spring

Tsalmaveth and Ahmet stood on the edge of the underground spring that flowed from the Kidron Valley. The entire city of Jebus was fed by an underground spring called the Gihon Spring just inside the city limits. Every single resident of the upper and lower city of Jebus came there several times a week for water, filling buckets to take back to their house for washing and cooking, since the pool at Siloam had dried up during the drought. The last few days of heavy rains had begun to fill the underground river that flowed to the other pools and springs in the lower city.

The whole city was on the verge of ecstasy as they reveled in the return of the plentiful water that once supplied their prosperous city, no doubt it had returned thanks to the gods whom they worshiped. Before the sun rose today, Tsalmaveth began his preparations and by the time the city awoke to fill their water buckets his plan would already be working.

With a thought from Tsalmaveth, six Shades lurched forward carrying the wineskins containing the black liquid he'd made during the binding ritual; the same liquid was used to enslave Adonizedek in a deep slumber, though he'd used the liquid left over from the binding ritual with Goliath two decades ago on Adonizedek. During the ritual with Ahmet he'd instructed him to brew an entire cauldron of the liquid rather than a little bowl of it as he had with Goliath. With this he would bring the city and its people to its knees before him.

The Shades pulled the cork that capped each and began to pour the liquid into the spring water. It had thickened considerably in the skin, so it poured slowly, almost like a black colored blood substance. In all they had six of the seven skins. The seventh was around Ahmet's waist.

"All of it." He ordered without an audible voice. "I require the whole of Jebus under my rule before sunset today."

They emptied the wineskins to the very last drop and then stood awaiting orders. Tsalmaveth flicked his wrist toward the Shades, gesturing for them to leave his presence, and pointed back into the cavern. "Await sunset and then join me on Mount Moriah."

Once they vacated, he walked over the pool which had turned black in the firelight, and he could see it was starting to flow toward the Pool of Siloam similar to fingers spreading out to grab a large object. By the time it reached the pool it would be dissolved and dispersed so completely that it would be hard to notice it to anyone that did not know of it. All he needed now was enough of them to drink the water and give him control of the population.

Drinking the potion would cause the subject to surrender to him. They would carry on life as normal if he wished but would be solely connected to the Shadow of Death in body and mind as long as they drank the water regularly. They would have no choice but to do their bidding day or night. As they drank the water each day the effect would be renewed. He planned to make more of the potion once he'd solidified his conquest. He held back one wineskin of the pure potion in case he found a need for it. The people of Jebus would perpetually be enthralled as long as they drank the water daily.

With any luck, the three Shades he'd sent out to track that troublesome whelp, Baaldir, would return with him, and he'd be well on his way to finding the Key. Even heaven could not stop him then. Tsalmaveth was elated at the hopeful possibilities as he climbed up through a cistern and sunk into a shadow near an alley way. In just a few hours, he would move forward and take the city of Jebus.

<hr />

The Palace Council Chambers

The Council Chambers bustled as the court of officials and aristocrats gathered at the far end near King Adonizedek's throne. Only one thing was on their minds as they spoke of the king's condition. Servants had found him two mornings ago just after sunrise, asleep and unresponsive. Healers and shamans had come and tried to revive him, but he was in such a deep sleep that no medicine or shamanic ritual could touch it. He was still alive, with normal breathing and a steady heartbeat. Orvandil and Ide motioned for all to quiet. Once they'd settled, Orvandil spoke to the assembly. There were nearly one hundred in attendance.

Orvandil cleared his throat and straightened his posture. "You all have undoubtedly heard of the condition of our king, Adonizedek. I am told he is in stable condition but the slumber he is in is untouchable. We still do not know what caused this, but we called this assembly to put these matters before you because we are now left without a ruler. His son, who is the heir to the throne, is currently on a hospital bed with an uncertain condition as he is fighting for his life after injuries sustained a few nights ago outside our city walls."

Ide interjected, "The matter before us is the administration of the court and city whilst our king is under this sleeping spell. Should he recover, then all will be well, but we need to have a successor in place in case, perish the thought, he should not recover."

Someone spoke up, "Baaldir is the next in line if Thoros' does not recover. The next would be Vithas"

Ide responded, "Quite right, but he is yet a child. He cannot rule until he has been initiated as a man according to our customs. And Vithas would be ten years behind him. We would need someone to act as Regent until such a time that he comes of age. That is our law as it stands."

Orvandil interjected before anyone else could, "We must form a quorum of votes to select the Regent from amongst us. I would like to put my name forward as a candidate. I have been at the king's side for many years. I know the inner workings of the court and I know the king's mind on many matters. His Majesty would want me to fill this role."

Ide interjected in turn saying, "Just because you know the strings of the king's purse does not make you qualified as a temporary ruler and guardian of the true heir to the throne. This responsibility should go to me, clearly. I have long been involved in the rearing of young Baaldir. I have tutored him and saw to his training and education. There is no one in this room that can claim so."

The two of them glared at each other as murmurs arose throughout the room. It seemed that their tolerance of one another was solely connected to their shared ambition. Those who knew them knew this, and the running joke in the court was that if either one of them said something, the other would surely repeat it as though they had only just come up with the words.

Each of them started a chorus of huffs and puffs that seemed as though it was a competition to secure the title of most insulted. Soon, Orvandil exploded.

Exasperated, he replied incredulously. "You? The man who wears paint and women's fashion in secret. I'll not have it. Not ever! No man such as you should influence a young king. If you can even call yourself a man, being the eunuch that you are!"

Ide was taken aback. "That is a scurrilous accusation coming from you, the man that has never taken a wife nor sired a child. I hear you prefer stranger company. Well, I'll not have it. If you are to be the guardian of young Baaldir, I'd swallow my own foot first."

The two men turned varying shades of red and purple. Orvandil was the first to completely lose his composure as he picked up a chair and threw it at Ide. Ide just barely dodged the chair, and it slammed into a pillar and shattered into splintered boards. Then, the two men rushed each other and began to kick, punch and slap each other in a painfully unskilled way. Any warrior onlooking would surely laugh at their ineffectual blows on one another. Orvandil and Ide fell to the ground and struggled, their hands pressing into the other's face. In a most ugly fashion they grappled, neither one having any skill to overtake the other.

Suddenly, the doors at the end of the room slammed open and in limped Thoros using David and a palace guard for support. Orvandil and Ide regained their feet and did their best to recover their dignity from their disheveled appearance.

"My Prince! You're awake. Gods be praised!" Ide was the first to speak as Thoros limped forward, taking longer than usual due to his wounds.

Orvandil, spoke right on cue, not wanting to be upstaged, "Our prince is awake! Gods be praised!"

Thoros shot the two of them a tired and annoyed look. "I will not ask why two elderly men were fighting in front of my father's throne. But you will tell me now how you'll wake my father, or I will remove your heads where you stand!"

Orvandil stuttered but quickly recovered, "My Prince. We were meeting to make decisions on who would rule in your absence since our king, and you were incapacitated. We meant no disrespect. Have we not had every available healer and shaman allocated to the purpose of doing just that, curing our king's condition?"

"NO! You are all useless. Why should I keep any of you around? My father is laid up, after being attacked and my brother Baaldir, whom you all were just scheming to control is now missing." Thoros shouted and then instantly regretted the exertion. He steadied himself as he became lightheaded. Jarnsaxa rushed forward and pulled a chair up to Thoros and begged him to have a seat, which he did reluctantly. Those in the room gasped at the statement that Baaldir was now missing as murmurs began throughout the room.

After a few moments Thoros regained his composure. He calmly spoke, "In light of this attack on my family and apparent kidnapping of my brother I expect every man and woman in this room to mount a search throughout the palace and fortress this instant. Those responsible must be found and brought to me. Go now! Get out of my sight!"

His rage reached a maximum crescendo the more he spoke, as his booming voice rattled the furniture and echoed off of the vaulted ceiling and granite walls.

The members of the court, stunned at Thoros' sudden entry, gathered themselves and began to exit haphazardly, bumping into one another.

Afraid that if they were unable to move fast enough Thoros would single them out in another outburst.

Thoros then said, "Jarnsaxa, Bulwark, and you two idiots, Orvandil and Ide. Stay here and speak to me."

Jarnsaxa and Bulwark took seats next to Thoros. They regarded David with a nod and turned to watch Orvandil and Ide slink into seats just out of reach of Thoros.

"David, would you and your captains like to have a seat?" Thoros said wearily, motioning to an empty chair next to Bulwark. David walked over and took a seat and scooted his chair up to a taller than usual table. Joab, Jeroboam, and Uriah walked up and followed suit.

Thoros looked at each one as the sun was rapidly setting, "We have a problem. I was nearly killed by Tsalmaveth which is Hebrew for Death's Shadow, according to David here. What is most troubling is that there is now a veritable army of what we are calling Shades, made from tortured captives. These beasts are men no longer and have instead been taken over by Tsalmaveth. To make matters worse, my brother Lox had a hand in this, at least in part, we still do not know to what extent. If I knew Lox, this is likely the result of unintended consequences to a scheme gone awry. There is no telling what he intended when he unleashed this evil, and he is not here to ask. I'm told that he disappeared the day after I was captured. That was four days past. Now my father is incapacitated, and my brother Baaldir is missing as of last evening. We are quickly losing control, and we don't even know who or what this enemy is or how to defeat it."

Jarnsaxa spoke, "Where could Baaldir have gone in his condition? Perhaps he went to explore the city again, in any case, his personal weapons and other items he possesses are missing. This fact leads me to think he wasn't kidnapped by this Tsalmaveth, but rather, he took it upon himself to go and search for something. He's been out of sorts after this whole ordeal."

Bulwark interjected, "I believe Baaldir is back in the caverns. After his friend was killed, he likely wants to find the culprit and take him down. I say we take a few hundred warriors and go through the barricades I made and take them out once and for all. We all saw those creatures and we know where they are gathering."

Just then a voice from the entrance echoed through the chamber, "You may want to post some guards at all the fortress entrances first. Anyone can just walk in at any time of day."

Thoros looked up and seeing a man in a black cloak standing at the entrance he stood and drilled the man with a stare that could freeze water.

David looked to his right and jumped back from the table sending his chair toppling over. He recognized the bound man that was being transported to the prison when those beasts attacked.

The man walked forward, almost floating the way his black cloak billowed as he walked. "I'm interested to know how it is you intend to 'take me out'?" he said mockingly.

"Tsalmaveth, I presume." Thoros queried.

"In the flesh young prince." The man smiled and shivered almost gleefully, and then said, "It has been many years since I could say that!"

David slammed his fist onto the table, ready to confront Tsalmaveth. Joab motioned for David to calm himself, which David did, knowing that this was not his own residence.

Tsalmaveth, seeing this looked at David up and down and smiled, "David, it's very good to finally meet you again. You've grown since last we met. Still on with the righteous anger?" he said mockingly as he turned toward Thoros at the head of the table.

"What have you done to my father?" Thoros demanded, interjecting snidely.

"For me to know, and for you to find out, boy." he said with a snarky and sheepish grin. As several palace guards came up behind him and formed ranks behind him, each one with black sludge running from their eyes like tears.

Thoros pounded on the table, sending Orvandil and Ide scurrying for cover under the tabletop. "Do not play games with me! What have you done to my father?" The ranks of guards simultaneously lowered their spears toward the group at the table. David noticed the men had gray eyes and the black veins running down their neck similar to the Shades he'd seen below. Thoros was visibly shocked to see his own guards following the man before him. "What sorcery is this?"

Tsalmaveth walked to the other end of the table, ignoring the question, pulling out a chair and sitting comfortably slouched to one side. He just looked at everyone and their stupor as he helped himself to a glass of water. He took a sip and smacked his lips together several times, "I must say, Jebus has the best water on this side of the valley. Don't you think?"

Then, he drilled Thoros with the same stare that Thoros had leveled minutes before. "Your father is mine to do with what I wish. This city is now under my control. If you do not concede to my rule, I will kill everyone in this room, one by one."

Orvandil found a spine suddenly and shouted, "You cannot stand against our mighty Thoros and the army of Jebus. Who are you to threaten us?"

Tsalmaveth chuckled as he raised his right arm. He pointed towards Orvandil as his grin turned into a horrifying smile. "Who am I?" he said and then raised his right arm, "I am someone who can do this..."

Tsalmaveth reached out into the space between he and Orvandil and grasped something, invisible to anyone, from the air. Instantly, Orvandil's face contorted as he began to gasp for air, except no air would enter. He grabbed his throat and tried to pull the imaginary fingers from his throat. His face turned three different shades of red and then three different shades of purple as his eyes became so wide that they looked as though they would pop out of their sockets. Tsalmaveth twisted his hand and clenched it into a fist. Everyone watched in disbelief as they heard a snapping sound come from Orvandil's neck. He fell to the floor, dead. Ide, seeing Tsalmaveth kill his counterpart, shrank further under the table saying, "No...Master...Please...".

"Apologies young prince, I had hoped I wouldn't have to demonstrate just how serious I am. But I think I've now made my point. Do not give me cause for further demonstrations."

Tsalmaveth stood up and placed his hands down on the table. "Now, I want you all to listen to me. Tomorrow at dusk I will return to the gates of the fortress. You had better be ready to submit." He shot a look toward David, "You however, I will make you beg me for death."

David scoffed, "How about you try me right here and now Shadow..." as his hand went to his sword at his side.

Tsalmaveth cracked a wry smile and scoffed, "In time boy. I'm in no rush."

Thoros stood and placed his fists on the table and stared at him while everyone else sat silent, except Ide who was shaking with fear behind his chair. All the while he was pleading for mercy from Tsalmaveth.

Then, Tsalmaveth turned and walked toward the exit, stopping to look over his shoulder, and raised his left arm as if to signal that they should listen for something, holding three fingers up before counting down, "Three, two, one."

On cue, a blood curdling scream from a woman sliced through the room, coming from the direction of the courtyard. Thoros acknowledged that Tsalmaveth continued walking, laughing a boisterously sinister laugh that layered over the continued screams of horror. In a few seconds he disappeared through the door which stood ajar, the guards following behind him in a column. David noticed that they were Jebus' own palace guards, doing his bidding.

Thoros was already starting to follow. "Bulwark, Jarnsaxa. Run ahead and see what that scream was about. David, could you lend your shoulder once again?"

The two of them ran like the wind toward the courtyard as David and Thoros limped down the length of the room. Just as they reached the door Jarnsaxa came back in, white as a ghost. She just shook her head, warning that Thoros and David did not want to see what the scream was due to. This made Thoros even more anxious to reach the courtyard as he left David's shoulder and made his own way as rapidly as his torn body would allow. David ran behind, unable to imagine what could cause the look of fear in someone as powerful as Jarnsaxa.

Thoros pushed through the pain and pressed on, descended a set of stairs, and rounded a tree that blocked the view of the center of the garden. The lighting was very dim as the sun completely set in the west. Ahead of him he could see the ash tree at the center of the garden, towering over the courtyard. But the tree looked odd. For some reason, the tree had taken the shape of a weeping willow.

Bulwark walked up to him and took his arm and threw it over his shoulder, "Brother, I'm so sorry. I'm sorry brother." He said, as if that was the only thing to say.

"What is it?" Thoros urgently asked, doubling his pace. A few moments later they were standing in front of the tree and Thoros fell to his knees in shock.

David walked up behind him and gasped as he looked up at the branches of the tree. From the highest branch hung a figure from a rope with a noose. Anyone could tell in the dark, by the size of the frame, that it was King Adonizedek, King of Jebus hanging lifeless from the great ash tree.

The reason the tree looked like a weeping willow became apparent as David also fell to his knees. Hanging with Adonizedek on their own individual branches were the members of Joab's search party; twelve in all. Cries of anguish followed from his three captains seconds later as they too realized what had become of their comrades.

They all looked on in shock, realizing that Adonizedek, Lord of Righteousness and King of Jebus and offspring of the great Nimrod was now dead, hung like a common criminal.

CHAPTER 24

The Temple to Yaldabaoth: Memphis, Egypt

L ox stared at Astarte through the bars of his prison cell. He said nothing as she leaned forward on the stool. Her amber hair betrayed a
strand of gray randomly which was the only attribute that gave her away
as aged, not that it detracted from her beauty in any way. A thousand years
and her skin still looked like the fine pottery from the Far East. Smooth
and unblemished, pale by most accounts based on the regional ethnic
groups that inhabited Egypt, but still the almond tint he remembered.
Her eyelashes were longer than he remembered and rouge on her cheeks
brought out a slight pink melanin in her skin. Her emerald, green eyes
glinting in the torchlight. Any man looking upon her would assume she
was a middle-aged woman of forty or so.

An uncomfortable silence stretched on for what seemed like several
minutes to Lox. Really, it was mere seconds before Astarte was the first to
break the silence.

"I was beginning to think you'd never find me." She spoke.

Those words in a sentence formed the way they were, puzzled Lox.

He curtly responded, "Supposedly, you were arrested and burned for
witchcraft. I saw the pyre in the marketplace. Yet here you are..."

"I wasn't given a choice Lox. There were things at work that you would
not understand if I told you."

"Do you expect me to believe that?" Lox said incredulously. "You left
me and what's more, you stole the amulet from me. Was that your plan all
along?"

Astarte shook her head violently, "No Lox, you are mistaken. I wanted
to marry you; I did. And I would have had I not been taken."

She proceeded to recount those few days before she'd disappeared. According to her, one of her servants, the one that was supposed to pose

as her during the wedding ceremony, was a devotee to none other than Yaldabaoth, a fledgling god that had recently gained followers in the region. The morning before Lox came to the compound several men showed up and ransacked her home. Astarte came in from the fields to find them in her courtyard. She tried to run but one of them tackled her and ripped the amulet from her neck. They detained her and tied her up while they loaded her furniture onto a cart to be sold. The magistrate was also devoted to Yaldabaoth and concocted the scheme to burn her at the stake. However, they had burned an obscure leper in her place instead and took her away against her will.

It all sounded so improbable to Lox. What would they want with a young woman? She recounted the betrayal of her servant who was in fact a priestess of the local shrine to Yaldabaoth. These men were her bodyguards. She'd never seen them before and had no idea that she was not just a devotee but was running the whole operation for her god in that small town. The young woman appeared before her holding the amulet in her right hand. She held parchment and a piece of sharpened charcoal in her hand as she wrote the letter that Lox had found on the front door.

One of the men then forced a liquid into her mouth and as she swallowed it partially sedated her. The next few days were a blur, but she awoke days later, on a ship pulling into a port in Egypt. The woman that had betrayed her had done her part and handed her off to handlers that would take her to her fate. She was taken to this very temple and forced to play her part with the amulet ever since. They treated her like royalty, but the truth was she was never allowed to leave the temple without an entourage that prevented her from seeing or speaking to anyone outside of the temple.

Astarte told him that she often wondered if Lox was still living, but as the years wore on she soon gave up any hope. She had no idea that he was tens of thousands of years old. The amulet rejuvenated her every time she was made to wear it, which had slowed her aging process to almost none. In seven hundred years she looked as if she had only aged ten. Here she was, one thousand going on forty years old. And here Lox sat, ageless and helpless to say anything that resembled a coherent response.

"Lox, I want to know how you are still alive. I had hoped you would try to find me but after the years wore on, I feared you had long been turned to dust. But here you sit."

Lox still said nothing. He drilled her with his eyes and tried to determine if anything she said approached the truth.

"Say something Lox. The better part of one thousand years, and a love like ours and you have nothing to say?"

She choked back tears as one fell down her cheek. Seeing this tore into Lox. He had never stopped loving her even when he tried to hate her for leaving him alone. Somehow, for reasons unknown she was alive and sitting in front of him now, very much alive. He wondered for a moment if he was hallucinating, and she wasn't there after all. Maybe the fall on his head had damaged him. But seeing that tear roll down her cheek instantly softened his resolve to shut her out.

"I am at a loss for words, Astarte." Saying that name before her for the first time in several mortal lifetimes ripped through his body and ravaged him. He could hardly bear it.

Finally, he mustered up words, "To answer your question, I do not have an age. I cannot die by any natural causes save beheading. I've put that to the test more times than I can remember. I wanted to die after you died, or were taken, or whatever it is you say happened. But my curse is to live forever." Astarte took in that information and waited for him to elaborate.

"Astarte, I don't know what else to say. Yesterday I was trying to find my amulet, or what I suspected was my amulet. Today I find that the love of my extraordinarily long life has been here all along. I tried to fill my heart with emptiness and forget about you Astarte, I even succeeded for a time. And here you sit, very much alive and I'm sorry, I just don't have words to express what I'm feeling at this moment. You seem to be doing well for someone that is held against their will." He was beginning to raise his voice as the emotions came through as words.

Astarte motioned for him to quiet down and paused for a moment, "There are many things that you won't understand. I will try to explain them to you, but time is short. I can't be found down here talking to you. They will punish me if I'm found outside of my quarters. I had to threaten and bribe my way into this prison to see you."

She then stood, "I must be getting back to my quarters before they find me."

Lox stood and approached the cell door and placed his hands upon the bars. Astarte stepped forward, placed her hands upon his and stared into his eyes. The touch of her hand made his mouth go dry and his tongue stuck to the roof of his mouth.

"I will return Lox. And I'll see to it that you get food and water. I don't know how but through some miracle we are here together."

Lox pulled away and retreated to the far end of his cell and squatted down and placed his elbows on his knees as she turned and walked away taking the torch with her. Her footsteps barely made a noise, and he only knew she was gone by the sound of the door opening and being locked again.

His mind raced. Astarte was alive. She was being held captive all these years if he dared to believe her. Which he decided in that moment that he did. The only question he had now when thinking about what Astarte had told him was, to what end? The coincidences tore at his mind as he heard the monotonous drip of water return to the silent prison. He wanted to believe Astarte, but he also wanted to be angry and now he had to consider that this whole thing had been a setup from the start. That possibility angered him the most. He loathed being the plaything of gods and other beings. Somehow, he would take back control of his own destiny with or without a god's favor.

The Palace Garden, Jebus

Thoros pounded the ground in front of him with his fists as tears and spit flew from his face while he screamed in rage. His face had turned multiple shades of red as he began to heave and struggled to take in a breath. Soon after the uproar and shouting began, Siv and Frigg came running with Magni and Thrud in tow and Vithas straggling behind timidly. Seeing Adonizedek hanging from the tree, Siv began to scream and wail while the young children cried in terror at seeing their grandfather hanging from the tree that they had spent hours playing under with him. Frigg held onto Vithas and had a blank look on her face as she walked forward and looked up at her husband hanging from the great tree, her face drawn and pale as a ghost. Over the last week she'd endured more than a mother should and as of now she was completely drained of emotions. She just turned and walked over to a bench and sat there and looked as if she was somewhere else. Ide walked over to her and offered her a drink of water from a pitcher, a pained look on his face. She reluctantly accepted it and drank deeply before returning to her catatonic state, eyes narrowed at the tree where her husband hung like a common criminal.

Thoros was able to quiet himself and rose to his knees and sat back on his heels, looking up at his father and mentor hanging from the tree that he had planted before this place became the palace where he'd raised Thoros. He looked over at David who stood there speechless, unable to take his eyes from those hanging there. He just shook his head and muttered unintelligible words to himself, his fist tightly clenched on the belt where his sword hung.

David began to pace around the base of the tree looking at the ropes that were anchored to a low hanging branch and tied around the massive trunk. He traced one back to one of his men and slowly untied the rope and used the limb to lower the man to the ground. Soon Joab, and Jeroboam joined and lowered the other twelve men to the ground before heading to the rope that held King Adonizedek. Bulwark and Jarnsaxa met David there and placed their hands on the rope, gesturing that they would be the ones to handle the lowering of their king from the tree, which they did gently. Soon all who had been hung were lowered. The men set to work moving the men to a central location where they fetched linens to cover the bodies fully. They brought some to Jarnsaxa who spread them over King Adonizedek, having to use three pieces to cover his large body.

Thoros felt his torso and his fingers came away bloody through his tunic. The extra exertion had no doubt torn his sutures in the delicately healing wound on his stomach and chest. Siv, pulling the children with her, ran to

Thoros and helped him up to his feet and ushered him slowly to the bench near where Frigg sat, shallowly rocking back and forth.

"Bring me some water." Thoros said with a parched voice. Siv motioned to Ide to bring the pitcher of water he held which he immediately did, filling a cup and handing it to Thoros. As he held the cup to his lips, just about to take a drink, he felt a swift hand come into his periphery and smack the cup from his hands.

"What is the meaning of this?" Thoros yelled, ready to fight. Inexplicably he turned as saw Bulwark's massive hands enveloping David who was wildly kicking and screaming, "Don't drink the water!"

The Palace Garden...

David felt like he was watching this whole scene unfold in slow motion as moments later, Ide moved to provide Thoros with a cup of water from the clay pitcher he held, after taking a drink from a cup himself.

David felt himself acting upon pure instinct as he lunged forward smacking the cup from Thoros' hand, sending it skipping across the ground. Something about the way Tsalmaveth talked about the water and how those soldiers seem to be enthralled by him came together in that instant as he yelled, "Don't drink the water!"

Bulwark was upon David instantly and restrained him, pulling him away from Thoros, But David wrestled free and ran over, grabbed the pitcher away from Ide, pouring it on its side and sending water spreading over the clover that blanketed the ground. "The water is poisoned!" David yelled.

"What is the meaning of this?" Thoros yelled, ready to fight.

To David it seemed like time had slowed to a halt from the moment they entered the garden and found the dead hanging from the tree. He felt like he was observing all the movements of those in the vicinity simultaneously. Bulwark grabbed him, this time throwing his arms around David and picking him up from the ground. David kicked and thrashed to free himself but to no avail. Bulwark would not fail a second time to restrain him.

Joab and the other two ran up just then and squared off with Bulwark who was twice his size.

"Release him, this instant!" Joab roared, showing he would not back down.

Bulwark was incredulous, "I will not, he's gone mad!"

It was then, even in the darkness, that someone realized the ground where the bucket had dumped over had turned black, killing everything it touched on the surface, "Look at the ground! The water is poisoned!" someone said. Thoros leaned forward and put his son on the ground, reached down and touched the ground with his fingertips. As he came away from the ground with them his skin began to sizzle. He quickly wiped his hands over his tunic and looked at David.

"Put the man down Bulwark, we owe him our lives yet again it seems."

David dropped to the ground and recovered his balance. At this point, Siv and the children were huddled behind Thoros.

"They've poisoned the wells. I just put it together after seeing the way those guards were under the control of Tsalmaveth. This is how he was so sure the city was his." David slouched and hung his head as he thought about the men laying across the yard not thirty feet away.

Thoros was visibly affected by this revelation. "Did anyone drink the water?" The few who were present looked toward his mother who sat only feet away.

Siv placed her hand on Frigg's lap, "Mother, are you okay?"

Frigg lightly smiled, "I'm feeling okay, just a little tired is all," was all she could muster for a response. Siv felt her forehead and stepped back for a moment, "She is burning with fever. Someone, bring us a healer!" She shouted at others to run and do her bidding which they did at once. David watched as Siv looked her mother-in-law over as Frigg sat there calmly allowing her to do as she wished.

David looked at the elderly Ide standing off to the side, "You there, where did you get the water? I saw you drinking it just now as well." He peppered the man with several questions in quick succession and waited for any kind of response, remembering the moment when Tsalmaveth placed the pitcher of water on the table next to Ide and made a comment about the water.

Ide looked at him, taken aback by the barrage. "What? The water? I. No, I found it in the throne room from the table is all."

"Who else have you given it to? Tell me now!" David demanded.

Ide looked at his feet for a longer time than any normal person would when asked a question. Ide's shoulders tensed and he began to chuckle lightly while looking back at David; but his eyes were not human any longer. They were the blackest black David had ever seen, hollow and infinite as if they were a bottomless pit.

"Of course, I drank the water, It's the best water this side of the valley after all." He said with a derisive smile. David noticed that, by the second, black veins and what could be described as bruised skin traveled from his eyes and mouth and traveled down his neck, disappearing into the clothing.

Just like the guards who were with Tsalmaveth in the council chamber, David thought, as his eyes narrowed on Ide.

Siv interjected, "Ide, what nonsense are you speaking?"

"No. This is not Ide." David said before grabbing Ide's shoulders and shaking him violently and shouting, "What do you want Shadow?"

Tsalmaveth used Ide's belly to laugh haughtily. "All that, and you've found me out before I had the chance to really have some fun. Had your keen senses not noticed it I would've had you all before the night's end, but you always were a special case weren't you, David? That is why bringing you low and making you bow before me will be so sweet in the end."

"You have no real power here Shadow, only cheap tricks." David retorted.

"What about my mother, Shadow." Thoros retorted. "What has your poison water done to her?" He was now weakly standing up approaching a much smaller Ide.

Tsalmaveth looked up at Thoros, "Oh, you'll see. For now, let's just say her well-being depends on your actions over the next day."

Thoros reached Ide and picked him up by his shoulders and raised him, but not without wincing in pain due to the wounds on his body, "I do not take kindly to threats, even in my weakened state. What is the antidote? Tell me!" Thoros raged.

Tsalmaveth lifted Ide's arm clumsily and pointed to the wall that surrounded the fortress below before turning and taking a few steps in that direction.

"Follow me, and you'll see that you have no choice but to do as I say."

Siv stepped forward and placed a hand on Thoros' back, "Remember this is Ide, not this Tsalmaveth. You should set him down before you injure yourself and must start the healing over."

Thoros apparently saw the sense in this as he set the man down and took a few steps back. David watched as Ide turned and took a step toward the fortress. He curiously noticed that Ide's steps were far larger than normal and looked as if the control on his limbs were from outside the confines of the physical body. Ide's arms would flail from one side to the other as if he was trying to balance the movement. In any case, the movement was unnatural.

David thought back to the meeting where he first saw Ide and the moments when they'd been in the garden. He seemed to move about fine, betraying no sign that he was under control and David reasoned that this was yet another way that Tsalmaveth could control someone after they drank the water. Perhaps Ide, after drinking the water and being placed under control, was commanded to give the water to everyone, which he then carried out naturally as if it were of his own volition, likely not even knowing what he was doing.

Once David realized the water was poisoned and confirmed that Ide drank it, Tsalmaveth had switched to a direct kind of control as if he were a puppeteer, pulling strings up and down. If that was the case, then there was no way to know for certain how many inside the palace were under control as of now. David shuddered as he looked around at those surrounding him, looking for similar black veins of those he knew to be infected.

"Let's follow the lunatic," David said as he confidently followed Ide through the fortress and down the winding terraces, the place looked deserted and not at all like a well-armed fortress. At the edge of the fortress, they reached the final gate house that would look to the south over the city. Thoros and the others followed behind slowly. Thoros looked as if he'd prefer to keep up with David but was limited to limping behind with the help of Jarnsaxa and Bulwark. He stopped briefly and looked back at Siv who was carrying their children not far behind.

"Siv, you must not come with us. Stay in here and find a place to hide if it comes to it." Thoros said pleadingly.

"You know I am as capable a fighter as anyone else here." Siv protested.

"Then use your skill to protect our children and Vithas. Please Siv, I cannot go out there worried that you will be in the line of fire." Siv bowed gently and retreated with the children.

As David reached the top of the rampart where Ide had led them, he stopped and gasped and took a step back instinctively. Before him, over the expanse of Jebus was a sea of torches that blanketed the entirety of the city streets of upper Jebus, as if everyone in town had turned out tonight to gather in front of the fortress. Two hundred feet in front of the gate was a raging bonfire with flames licking the heights of the fortress walls. Standing in front of it, was Tsalmaveth and several hundred black cloaked figures, as well as several ranks of Jebusite soldiers, holding a torch in one hand and spear in the other. Thoros and the others reached the top moments later and audibly gasped as David had.

"What sorcery is this?" Jarnsaxa exclaimed, running up the parapet and craning her neck to look at the city before her. Bulwark growled as he turned and ran down the stairs and disappeared into the fortress yelling over his shoulder, "We need to shut the gates, I know a siege when I see one!"

Jarnsaxa looked up and down the wall and spoke quietly to Thoros who shook his head. Thoros looked out over the city and said, "This is great, just great!" he said before shouting to the throng outside headed by Tsalmaveth and his shadowy entourage, "Say your piece, Shadow!"

Tsalmaveth stood there stoically with arms crossed in front of him, saying nothing.

David noticed immediately upon seeing the palace guards and other soldiers with Tsalmaveth that there were only about a dozen archers on the walls above at their post. The whole of Jebus' army was now in the control of Tsalmaveth, and they were left virtually defenseless. Jarnsaxa immediately went to gather the archers that were left and positioned them as Joab, who had mended from the arrow to his leg nicely, looked them over for signs that they'd been infected similar to Frigg and Ide. Both of them now had black veins visible around their collar bone and down their arms. David was glad to have Joab here as he marveled at the man's instinctual ability to take charge and use his intuition to see blind spots in the defense, one of them being not knowing who was and wasn't infected. In mere minutes, the gates were closed, and Bulwark managed to rustle up seven spear-wielding guards who had yet to be infected, which he set to work gathering weapons to bring to the walls where they would need them should the enemy outside attack.

Soon, Jarnsaxa, Joab, and Bulwark returned along with a wounded, but mending, Uriah who was helped by Jeroboam.

David, seeing this said, "You shouldn't be here Uriah. You are seriously wounded."

To which Uriah replied curtly, wincing through the pain of hobbling up the stairs, "With all due respect my lord, if we are to be overrun, I'll not die on a hospital cot. Give me a bow and some arrows and prop me up. It's only a broken leg."

Jeroboam interjected, "I will watch over him my lord. Just tell us where we'd be best used."

David looked at the pair proudly and turned to Thoros and said, "This is your fortress, what would you have us do?"

Through all this Tsalmaveth stood there silently with a sinister grin exuding a patient, if not amused aura.

Thoros thought for a moment, "Apart from the few archers and the few guards we've managed to gather it seems we are scant on weapons." Just then, some of the guards ran up to the platform and dropped piles of tools, a few daggers, Bulwarks massive hammer, and a mess of other knives and damaged swords.

"Bulwark, is this all we have for weapons?" Thoros said, drawing out the last word to convey his doubt.

Bulwark nodded defeatedly, "My prince, nearly every weapon we have is out there in the city among those with that shadow man. These are what was left in my blacksmith stall. They no doubt overlooked these."

"Not hard to see why." Joab said as he picked up a set of daggers and a club, tucking the daggers into his waist band.

"We'll make the best of it." David said as he picked up a pair of swords with pronounced chunks missing from the blade that looked as if someone had tried to chop granite with them. "These will do, no cracks despite the damage and they look to be sharp." He swung them about, loosening up his shoulders and trying to get a feel for the weight and balance of the blades.

Bulwark reached into his pockets and pulled out a set of iron knuckles that fit around his gigantic hands as he clasped them tightly a few times and beat his fists together. "I'll be using my fists." He said as he picked up his hammer from the pile and offered it to Thoros. "I think this one will suit you prince."

The hammer looked like a normal maul in Thoros' hand which meant it was nearly the size of David's head. David watched as Thoros accepted the hammer and gripped it tightly, letting the handle rest on his other hand. "Thank you, brother. I'll be sure to return it to you."

Bulwark feigned indifference, "It was a gift to me from dwarves in the mountains far to the north. It is a perfect blacksmith's tool and now we will see what kind of a martial weapon it can be. I can think of no better man to wield it."

"If your quite ready now I had a whole monologue prepared." Tsalmaveth suddenly said clearing his throat. His voice was amplified somehow making it as if he were standing upon the rampart with them.

David and the others turned to face their foe as Tsalmaveth began to speak, "But, seeing as you've squandered much of the night, I will condense it down so that we can get down to business." He raised his arms from his side and turned to his right and left as if presenting and said, "before you, the city of Jebus and everyone in it is under my control. Whether willing or unwilling they are mine to do with as I wish."

As if to prove his point he pointed at Ide, closed his eyes, and opened them. With the snap of his fingers Ide's neck broke with an ugly snap as he fell over the parapet to the ground below. He was dead long before his body landed with a thud.

"Now that you understand what I am able to do you'll remember that I have your lovely mother under my control."

"If you harm a hair on her head, I swear to all the gods that I will make you suffer in ways you cannot imagine!" Thoros raged.

"Oh. I shall not harm her, yet. First, I must be sure you are willing to do as I say. That includes the little professional killer next to you." Tsalmaveth 'said, nodding towards David.

As he said this his body began to transform, growing a whole head taller, his face changing from the gaunt, pale-faced man into a pitch-black figure. Tsalmaveth's face looked like there was a waterfall of smokey shadows flowing from it to the ground, blanketing the area with a low-lying black fog. From Tsalmaveth's back grew a pair of black wings that looked feathered, but somehow seemed that if you ran your hand through it, then it would disperse.

David was rendered speechless as Tsalmaveth held up his hand and continued, his voice a whole octave deeper than moments before, "Tonight I have a test for you, after which, I will have an offer for you that you will not be able to refuse. Now the time for talk has passed, let us commence with your test!"

With that Tsalmaveth raised his hands and shouted, "Attack!"

As he dropped his hands the Shades and palace guards under his control surged forward. Some of them were carrying ladders and others carrying jars strung through a rope sling and a torch in their hands.

"Fire!" Jarnsaxa said, firing a volley of three arrows toward the Shades who were advancing just behind the ladder carrying soldiers. A rain of arrows dropped several of the soldiers as others behind picked up the ladders and continued forward. Fortunately, the gated area was narrow by design requiring the attackers to bunch up. The walls were much too high on the edifice of the fortress to use ladders effectively. Jarnsaxa continued to rain arrows down in varying quantities, most of them finding their marks on vital parts of her targets. Her aim was deadly accurate and to David it was thrilling to see someone fight who was born to do such things. To his right was Uriah, doing a similar job, though only firing one at a time, as Jeroboam took to hurling stones with his sling with a look of determination on his face.

David turned his attention to the coming onslaught as the soldiers carrying the jars lit the tops with their torches and twirled them about rapidly before releasing the jars. The jars arced into the air and crashed against the wooden gate, the liquid inside exploding and sending burning liquid everywhere. A droplet landed near his hand as he jumped back just in time to avoid it touching him. It had been a good long while since he'd been on this end of a siege, and he now felt pity on those he'd defeated over the decades. This was a new kind of feeling for him, being on the receiving end of siege ploys such as the flammable liquid. Soon the gate was ablaze, and the ladders were just starting to rise and slam against the parapet above.

"Get those ladders off of the wall!" Thoros shouted as he used his strength to push it back upright just as a Shade made it to the halfway mark on its climb. The doomed creature betrayed no emotion as it fell backward to the ground below, lost in the black fog that was just beginning to make its way up the inclined path. As soon as that ladder was down, another rose in its place. This time three Shades climbed together and made it nearly impossible for Thoros to lift effectively with his many injuries.

Joab, thinking quickly, grabbed a pole that held a banner and used it to hook onto the ladder and push it up with the newfound leverage. Thoros helped as the momentum gathered and they were able to push the ladder upright and finally backward, but not before a Shade made it to the top and vaulted from the ladder, just barely reaching the parapet and struggling to pull itself up. David was there with his dual swords as he swung them at the Shade and managed to cut the hand off causing him to fall to the ground. Three more ladders hit the parapet and before they had a chance to push back, three Shades ascended followed by a trail of soldiers. Daggers in hand, the Shades began to attack viciously and recklessly, with no care for their own lives. Thoros met one of them with his newly acquired hammer and to say that it was effective was an understatement. The Shade before him crumpled to the ground where it once stood, with its chest completely caved in.

"Bring me more! This hammer is hungry!" Thoros cried as he kicked another soldier in the back, knocking him down. He smashed the soldier's head and roared with excitement. It seemed as if this hammer had been wasted being beaten on an anvil for so many years.

Bulwark picked up a Shade by its neck and used his iron knuckles to crush the face as he threw it from the wall like it weighed nothing. For such a large man his dexterity was impressive. David watched Bulwark spin around and block a dagger blow from a Shade, then use his heel to kick the Shade in its chest, sending it flying. It slid to a stop and began to advance toward Bulwark again but not before Thoros crushed it with the hammer from behind with a mighty roar.

"There you go Brother, feed the hammer!" Bulwark said with a boisterous laugh. David slightly smiled listening to the banter as he cut down enemy after enemy, but they kept coming. At this point they were two deep on the wall, and more were swarming up over several ladders. There was no way they could hope to vanquish this many foes with such small numbers of their own even with so many legendary warriors facing them back-to-back.

"There are too many! We need to fall back!" David shouted.

"Fall back to the next rampart!" Thoros roared, echoing David's observation, before crushing another Shade where it stood.

Immediately, the archers with Jarnsaxa ran behind Thoros, Bulwark, and David who stood in between them and the enemy. Joab protected the flank while Jeroboam picked Uriah up over his shoulder and ran down the stairs. Uriah continued to fire arrows even as Jeroboam carried him clumsily. One by one they peeled off as the other inched closer to the stairs. Once Jarnsaxa and the archers reached the other gate they began to concentrate their fire on those closest to Thoros and the other melee fighters. A dozen enemies fell at once giving them just enough time to jump down the stairs and run through the gates of the other rampart. They attempted to close the gate but there were enemies right on their tails, so the spear men formed a line and locked their shields to meet them. Jarnsaxa and Uriah continued to fire away from above, but it was hopeless as hundreds more burst through the totally burned gates of the other rampart. A tough situation had turned into a hopeless one very quickly.

"We need a way to stop them so we can regroup, or escape. We are outnumbered ten to one here." Bulwark shouted.

"That or find a place to fight where their numbers don't count as much." Joab countered.

Thoros barked at the spearmen, "Form a shield wall! Close off the rampart! Lock shields and brace yourselves!" The warriors fell into place seamlessly and shouted their determination with their prince at their back encouraging them.

"We'll hold them here. Bulwark, take Joab and find a way to quickly barricade the next rampart." David said.

Bulwark looked at Thoros who nodded for him to do as David ordered. They at once went to carry out the order as the wave of enemies crashed into them. David used his swords to slash over the top and then slash at the legs to maim them while Thoros pulled them through the shields one by one and killed them with the hammer.

"Jarnsaxa, Uriah, Jeroboam! Come down here and take down any who make it through. Be ready to retreat!" David shouted.

Jarnsaxa wasted no time as her archers ran down with an arm full of arrows from the rampart. Uriah and Jeroboam were close behind. It was a good thing as two of their soldiers in the shield wall fell allowing several to squeeze through. The throng of enemies pushed relentlessly as David picked up a shield and filled the gap, using his sword to make any that crashed into him pay with their lives. Jarnsaxa ordered her archers to kill any that made it through as she began to pick off ones near to Thoros, one by one. Soon, they were locked in a close battle at the bottleneck of the gate. The outside yard between the first and second gate was now full to the brim with soldiers. David, looking through the gate to the former rampart, saw Tsalmaveth and several of his Shades standing at the top like statues, surveying the battle from above, not taking part in the carnage. The moon passed behind him casting an eerie glow over the nighttime battlefield.

"We must hold them! My wife and children are behind us in the palace!" Thoros shouted as he crushed another at his feet that had scurried through.

"There are too many! We need to start thinking about a way to escape!" Jarnsaxa said, striking another who'd managed to slip by and was only steps from her. "We are running low on arrows!" she warned. "Conserve your arrows, be prepared for close combat!"

David looked back at the gate behind them, it seemed as if Bulwark and Joab were able to find enough things to barricade the opening. "Archers, retreat back to Bulwark!" David shouted. "Keep going to the main gate!"

"Thoros! On the count of three we need to retreat!" David said looking at the few men left fighting next to him.

The one in the middle shouted, "We will protect the prince!" as the others seemed resolved to do the same, understanding that their fate was sealed, and they would not be retreating with their prince.

"ONE!"

"TWO!"

"THREE!" David said as he slashed the one in front of him and broke off, sprinting toward Bulwark and the others. Thoros was not far behind and soon his long legs carried him past, but he stopped and turned just long enough to watch his guards fall to the ground and be swallowed up. He ducked through the opening and Bulwark pushed a wagon full of straw over while Joab lit it with a torch. Soon the whole gate opening was ablaze as they retreated further into the fortress as quickly as they could.

"Hurry! Everyone through! Close those gates!" Thoros shouted as he stopped once again to see that the advance of their enemy had at least been temporarily delayed. David ran up to the top of the rampart as Thoros entered and the strong gates closed behind him. This was the last gate to the fortress, and they were now sealed inside.

Reaching the top, he was able to look downward at the advancing forces and could see Tsalmaveth and the fog surrounding him moving onto the next rampart. Even from hundreds of feet away, David could make out the vicious look of the true form of Tsalmaveth, complete with black smoke falling to the ground continually and adding to the low-laying fog on the ground. He began to think back to the stories he'd heard growing up about the Israelites and the plagues of Egypt. The Shadow of Death had moved through the land like a fog searching for firstborn creatures. Not only men but cattle and other animals considered firstborn were slain as the fog reached them. Only the homes of the Israelites were spared because they had obeyed instructions to cover their lentils with lamb's blood. The spirit was unable to pass through any opening that was surrounded by this.

Suddenly, an idea arose in David's mind as he shouted excitedly, startling Joab who had made his way up to the rampart.

"I may know a way to stop their advance for good!" he shouted to Thoros as he ran down the steps to the gate below. The horde had passed the burning gate below and was now making their way to the main gate rapidly.

"What is your idea then?" Thoros said, sounding hopeful.

"Lamb's blood. We need lamb's blood." David said hurriedly, "I don't suppose you'd have any in the fortress?" he asked.

Thoros was visibly confused, "Lamb's blood? What for? What could that possibly do?"

"Trust me! Time is of the essence! Tell me man, where are the livestock kept?" David said again, this time more panicked.

Thoros was at a loss for words. Jarnsaxa interjected, "There is a pen in the palace where livestock, sheep, and goats are kept. I'm not sure if any are lambs though. Does it have to be a lamb?"

"It must be a spotless lamb. No blemishes. Take me there now! We don't have time to waste!" David said as he ran off in the direction of the palace. Jarnsaxa shouted orders to her archers and ran after David as Thoros and the others went atop the rampart.

David ran as fast as he could and Jarnsaxa soon caught up, "This way David" She shouted, darting through a doorway, and taking some stairs that led into the palace. David hoped against hope that this idea he'd been given would work.

As they reached the quarters near the kitchens and food garden, they saw a pen across the yard and ran up to it to look over the rails. Finding nothing but a few goats, he went the next few until he finally came to the very last one. Inside it was a single lamb, sleeping on a bed of straw.

Jarnsaxa came near and he turned to her, "We'll need a bucket and some brushes or rags." She nodded and ran into a little house near the yard as he sat on the rail, kicked his legs up and over and spun his body down into the pen. The lamb woke and started to bleat, scared that someone had entered its pen.

David, using a soft voice crouched while slowly creeping forward, "That's okay, I'm just going to come to you and pick you up."

The lamb stirred and stood up, backing up to the wall looking concerned but did not try to escape as David reached for it smoothly talking the whole way. As he picked it up the lamb began to bleat and squirm a little. He grabbed it tightly, restraining the feet and carried it to the little gate, unlatched it and exited. He walked toward the palace once again and Jarnsaxa met him there holding a bucket and broom.

"Sorry, this is the best I could do." As she offered up the bucket. David worked quickly, setting the lamb down and holding it tightly between his knees, he reached for his belt and grabbed a sharp dagger. "I'm sorry to do this little one but you will help save our lives and for that we are grateful."

The lamb bleated wildly as he slid the dagger across its throat, cutting deep and the bleating ceased instantly. The gentle creature fell limp and David picked it up, allowing the blood to flow into the bucket. It filled up a quarter of the bucket before the blood ceased flowing. It wasn't a lot, but it would have to do with their purposes. He waited for a few moments more to gather every drop he could. Normally, if time allowed, they would hang the sheep to let it drain completely before butchering it. But this was an unconventional use and time constraint, so he settled for the amount he collected, laid the sheep on the grass, closed its eyes and grabbed the bucket.

"Let's go!" David said as they ran back towards the fortress. Hopefully, he hadn't taken too long.

<hr />

Meanwhile, On the Rampart

Tsalmaveth watched impatiently as the soldiers and his Shades advanced. Like a swarm, they began to overwhelm the first gate, which led to a series of gates on the long climb to the main gate of the Citadel Fortress. Once they passed this, they would have access to the palace. After that was occupied, there would be nowhere for David and the former ruling family of Jebus to run.

He'd mulled it over, during the day, whether he should provoke them by killing Adonizedek, but his reasoning for that was two-fold. First, it would break them and make them act out of emotion. Tsalmaveth relished a beaten and broken foe that he could spring his own kind of trap on, so he'd decided on toying with them.

The other reason was that, through Lox's research, it seemed that The Key he sought was hidden by a Guardian. This Guardian must be of royal blood. At first, he thought maybe Thoros was this Guardian, but soon settled on Adonizedek, due to his kingly nature that lent itself to stewardship. Killing Adonizedek would hopefully clear up any obstacle that would stop him from obtaining The Key. If Nathan was truly lost, then another would take his place, eventually. His Shades would comb the lands looking for the Key through their vantage in the Shadow Realm which paralleled this natural realm.

His other stronger inkling was that Baaldir was The Guardian because of the foul taste of his blood. But as of yet, the three Shades he sent out had only reported tracing him to the water hole. It appeared that Baaldir had some help judging by the footprints and horse hoofprints. The only thing the determined was that Baaldir and whoever he was with rode Northeast. If Baaldir was indeed the Guardian, then he would kill him as well. Killing Adonizedek would be a waste of a good puppet King, but he decided it didn't matter in the long run.

Things just needed to happen in a certain way and before he knew it David and his companions would be defeated. Not only would they be defeated but he would force them to do his bidding. And Thoros would do nicely as his new puppet.

His failure with Goliath, at the hands of David, had led him to this city when Lox brought him to the dark temple in the dungeon and it had turned out to be a serendipitous failure. Not only had it resulted in him having an army at his disposal, provided he could solidify control, but he'd briefly glimpsed the energy source needed for the next part of his plan. However, through some rotten luck, he'd lost it nearly the moment he'd gained a body with which to move his plan forward.

Coincidentally, that same power ran through Ahmet's body, but only as a vessel capable of holding his power, while his son Nathan, who was now lost, was The Key that would act as a conduit opening up the veil to the other dimension where The Betrayer, Yaldabaoth was imprisoned and had become the ruler of the Shadow Realm during his time there. The energy from The Key was merely a potential energy that needed a suitable circumstance to unleash it, in this case, a blood sacrifice under a full moon, if the research was accurate.

His Shades hadn't returned from pursuing Baaldir, so he assumed the trail had gone cold. It didn't matter because he knew The Key was out there and alive. All he needed was the right circumstances to locate it. Something told Tsalmaveth that one of them here would provide him with the necessary circumstance and lead him right to The Key.

The point of this exercise was to give David and company a false sense of being able to resist. Once they looked like they believed they had a chance to fight this army off he would give the order to ramp up the attack and overwhelm them. He wouldn't kill them though; he had plans for all of them. Moments later he saw them retreat to the greatly fortified main gates of the fortress and shut them while his forces lumbered through the previous gate which was now ablaze due to an inventive barricade. He had to hand it to these humans. They were nothing if not resourceful, even if they were unable to understand when they were already beaten. Their tenacity was admirable.

Tsalmaveth smiled as his forces finally cleared the barricade, opening the way for them to advance together. He raised both of his arms and focused his aura on the Shades who were peppered in the advancing army. They stopped altogether as Tsalmaveth transmitted his wishes to them. As he lowered his arms the Shades advanced once again and began to make their way to the front. It was time to crush them like maggots.

CHAPTER 25

Memphis, Egypt

L ox leaned forward on the stool in the corner of his cell after hearing the rusty door at the end of the corridor clink open. It was likely the guards with a bowl of gruel attempting to be soup and a piece of stale moldy bread to soak up the broth. He had to guess that many days had passed since Astarte had visited him. Soon he saw a torch coming rapidly down the corridor. The contrast of light to dark made it hard to tell who was approaching, but his question was answered as a frantic Astarte ran up to his cell, trying to unlock his cell door.

Lox jumped up and approached the door, "Astarte, what's happening?"

"We must go, I've bought us only a few moments until they realize I've gone. We don't want to be here when they send them after us."

Lox understood as soon as she said it. She was talking about the very same ones he'd made over the years and sent them out to spy for him. At the time he didn't know what they were but after many weeks of filling the dungeon cells with Israelite converts, he understood all too well that these creatures did not do his bidding but the bidding of Yaldabaoth at the behest of Tsalmaveth. He hadn't put that together until now when he'd received the scroll with the message about the amulet that they were likely leading him here for whatever reason.

Thousands of years on this earth and I'm as gullible as a toddler, He silently cursed his naivety.

Lox watched as a panicked Astarte fumbled with the keys, failing to find the correct one after six or seven attempts.

"I wondered if you'd come back to see me. It's been days Astarte."

She stopped briefly and looked up at him, worry showing in her eyes, "I had to prepare. It's no easy task when every minute is watched so closely by the temple acolytes. I get one hour to myself per day apart from my sleep."

She went back to work on the keys and finally found one and turned it as the lock made a familiar click and the door swung open. He stepped onto her side of the bars for the first time. She looked up at him and threw her arms around his torso and stood on her toes to reach his lips with her own. For the first time in multiple centuries, they kissed for what seemed like an eternity as all the imaginations Lox had in his mind regarding her motives evaporated.

She pulled herself away and picked up the torch, "Follow me, Lox. We must hurry."

Lox was stupefied by the kiss and was slow to respond as she made her way down the corridor.

"Lox! Follow me! Quickly!" she yelled back at him, snapping him from his stupor. He responded by putting one foot in front of the other and caught up with her almost immediately.

She ran to the door at the end of the corridor and pulled it open, revealing a set of stairs that led upward to a well-lit landing. They ascended the stairs two at a time and made it to the top where she veered to her right and burst through another door. This door led to another corridor that was open to the outside air. It was broad daylight, and his eyes flashed green and orange as the sun blinded his eyes that had been in total darkness for more than a week. Astarte pulled off her outer cloak and threw it up over Lox's head and grabbed his hand, pulling him down the corridor as he struggled to see his own feet.

He gradually regained his sight and took in the surrounding buildings. It looked like they were in temple grounds somewhere, but he wasn't familiar with the layout. Soon they came to a wooden gate that was occupied by two guards within.

Astarte pulled him into an alcove and ducked behind a pillar, "Through that gate is the city proper. I have a wagon prepared with an ox for us and I've paid a trusted man to wait outside the gate."

"What's your plan for getting past those guards?" Lox asked.

Astarte peeked around the pillar at the guards and whispered, "There will be a guard change soon. We have a half-minute window to slip past them before the next set of guards comes around the corner. If we are not out of here by then we will be caught with nowhere to run."

So far, his escape and her help with it hadn't raised an alarm and he hoped that her plan would work. His hopes were dashed that very instant when he heard a horn blow from within the temple, almost as if the very thought of hope had caused the worst to manifest. Shouts could be heard from the direction of the temple where Astarte resided. Apparently, they'd realized she had absconded, there was no telling if that would lead them to his empty cell.

"We've been too slow!" Astarte said frantically, "They leave me to myself for one half-hour and that time has passed."

She peeked around the corner again as two more bleats from the horn echoed around the compound and rapidly jumped back. "I think they've seen me." She said, face flushed with panic as she pushed him into the alcove and attempted to make them disappear in the shadows.

It was no use of course because there was ample light in their hiding place. They stood like statues, hoping the guards would assume they had seen a rat and walk past, or return to their post, but they soon heard footsteps and typical armor clank as they approached.

"Take my hand" she whispered. Lox grabbed her hand from behind.

The guards walked up suspicious of their peripheral sighting. They both looked right at Lox and Astarte, as if looking through them and seeing only an empty alcove. The two men turned and walked further down the way to other alcoves and searched, he could hear them conversing as they went. Astarte squeezed his hand and lunged forward pulling him with him.

"What? How?" Lox said quietly, stunned and confused.

"Let's go." She whispered as she hurriedly ran towards the gate, all the while holding onto his hand. Lox followed, puzzled by what he'd just witnessed. They reached the gate seconds later and she reached out and unlatched the bar that ran into the frame. The door swung inward toward her, and she pulled him through, hurrying out into a bustling marketplace.

Lox heard shouts from behind, no doubt because the guards saw the gate open, but they were lost in the crowd of people the moment they exited holding their swords. She ducked behind a vacant stall and pulled him down with her, motioning for him to stay silent and hidden with her other hand.

There they waited for a few moments as the guards searched the immediate area around the market. There were so many people here it was a losing endeavor to try and pick a specific person from the throng of people. The guards would not be able to leave their post for long, which could work to their advantage.

Astarte held onto Lox's hand tighter as the guards looked behind the stall and looked right at them. Not seeing them, they turned and left, shouting at the other guards as they walked back to the temple.

"She's not here! Let's search the temple again!" one guard shouted, his voice trailing off as they all hurried back to the temple through the side door.

Astarte let go of his hand and weakly said, "Find the old man, with a mark on his neck," before collapsing in his arms unconscious.

"Astarte!" he said worriedly, keeping his shout a little above a whisper. He lightly shook her and listened to her breathing. Lox detected light breaths and sighed in relief as he realized whatever power she'd just used must have drained her energy. He delicately laid her down and stood up to survey the market. There were hundreds of people bustling around conducting their business with one another. One man haggled with a woman over some spices as another shouted at passersby to lure them to his stall to purchase the fabrics he'd brought.

"The finest silk from the far east, luxurious linens made on the looms of Numidian royalty! Come and see their quality!" he shouted to anyone and everyone as they passed.

Another woman haggled with a woman at her stall, selling oil, "This is the finest oil in Egypt! I'll not take less then fifteen."

The other woman scoffed, "The oil in the market at Thebes sells for less. I'll pay no more than five!"

"Five! No way! Not for this type of quality." the stall owner said, "I'd lose money at that price. Just this once I'll sell this oil for twelve. Think about it for a while if you like but I cannot guarantee it'll be available once you've realized my fair offer."

"Twelve? I'll pass." the customer said as she turned to walk away.

The woman made it three or four steps before the stall owner shouted, "Wait! Ten! Final offer."

The woman stopped and turned, "Seven." A slight smirk on her face betraying a hint of knowing that she had the upper hand.

The stall owner agreed with a smile, betraying the fact that she too expected this exchange to end this way. "Seven it is." she said, taking the coin from the woman and handing her a bottle of oil with a polite bow of thanks.

Lox scanned the market several times not seeing anyone that matched the description. He was concerned that walking through the market, with his imposing size, carrying a woman would attract the wrong kind of attention. He was at a loss as to what to do.

Suddenly, his eye caught a man at the far end of the market walking with a staff, leading a wagon pulled by two beasts. The man was hunched over severely and had a beard down to his waist and wild hair that stuck out in all directions around a mostly bald scalp. Down his neck he had a birth mark that likely went up onto his face but was hidden by the facial hair. The man continued to lumber through the market, careful not to get in the way of those conducting business until his wagon reached the middle of the yard and stopped. He looked to his left and right and back again searching for something. Lox stood tall, and waited until the man looked his way again before he gestured and mouthed the name "Astarte" in a hushed whisper to the man.

The man nodded and hobbled to the back lowering a gate and pulling back the flap of the canvas that covered his wagon. He turned and motioned with his head for him to come. Lox wasted no time picking up Astarte and hurried to the man, placing Astarte in and climbing into the wagon which was surprisingly big enough for him to lay down in a curled position. The man pulled the canvas over them and shut the back hatch, securing it with a tassel. Lox could then hear him walking to the front and coaxing the oxen forward as the cart began to roll.

The man, after exiting the market climbed aboard and then cracked a whip on the rump of the oxen as they lurched forward with a little complaint from one of them. Through a slit in the canvas, he watched as they rapidly exited the market and began to make their way through the streets of Memphis.

Astarte began to stir, and she weakly said his name as she came to. He was glad to see her awake finally and after a few moments she seemed to be revived.

"How long was I out?" Astarte said quietly.

"About an hour, was that due to that trick you pulled making us invisible? How ever did you manage that?" Lox said curiously.

From beneath her cloak she pulled on a gold chain until an amulet came into view. It was apparent that the power she'd used had been from the amulet.

"Every time I use the amulet, it exacts a toll once the effect is through." she said tiredly.

Lox stared at the amulet which he'd not seen in so very long. It used to call for him whenever he was apart from it. But now, he heard nothing. He looked at Astarte with her green eyes sparkling as she looked at him. He thought about how she'd had this amulet and been using it in the temple all along and then thought about how many times she must've experienced the drawback to using its power over the years. He reached for the amulet, wondering what it would be like to touch it again after all this time. As his fingers reached for it, he felt an overwhelming energy push his hand back. Astarte tried to warn him and, seeing this, touched his hand to check that it hadn't been hurt.

Astarte then said hopelessly, "The amulet is ritually bound to me somehow. I cannot take it off if I tried. And believe me, I've tried. Every time I remove the amulet, it reappears around my neck as if I never removed it. The only way I can remove it is if the High Priest in the temple removes it with a ritual. They did this to me so that I could never be apart from them. And using the amulet to escape is pointless if I can't sustain its power without losing my own ability to stand."

Lox was stunned. Any doubt that she had willfully taken his amulet was destroyed as he realized her predicament. Having a magical amulet that gave a person god-like power was too much for most mortal humans to manage long-term. What strength Astarte must possess to hold onto this relic for so long and be made to use it day in and day out, little better than a slave.

"I'm sorry that I gave it to you back then, it seems it brought much hardship to you. Can you forgive me?" Lox pleaded, suddenly realizing he had been the cause of this.

"There is no need, Lox. It was not you who kidnapped me and bound me to this. However, it seems that through either coincidence or fate we were always destined to meet once again."

Lox was silent for a moment as he pondered this. For what reason? He thought, not believing in coincidence. He hated feeling like his strings were being pulled by an unseen force leading him to and fro, wherever it may lead. For all his own effort it seemed that he too was a slave to fate.

For an hour or so the wagon lumbered along hitting every rock and pothole along the way. Gradually he got used to the rhythm and began to doze off a bit. He hadn't really slept soundly in several days and did not realize how tired he actually was until he was able to sleep in the jostling and jarring wagon. Astarte had long fallen asleep in mid-sentence, wore out from the amulet's power.

After a period, he awoke to the old man halting his oxen and pulling the cart to stop as he heard voices outside along the road. Lox opened the slit in the canvas ever so slightly. The light was beginning to wane in the late afternoon as he was able to see a few lightly armed men speaking to the old man in the front of the wagon while a few other stood nearby.

Astarte had woken when the wagon stopped, "Can you see anything?" she whispered.

Lox shook his head, showing her that his view was limited but he listened in as closely as he could. Moments later he heard one of the men speak in a gruff tone as he approached the wagon to speak to the old man who greeted him with a quivering voice of an advanced aged man.

"What have you in the wagon old man?" the guard asked inquisitively.

The old man stuttered then found his rhythm, "W-W-Which it is my own belongings. Nothing of worth to anyone but a poor old man such as myself."

The guard nodded and cocked his head sideways before asking, "I see, you won't mind if I have a look myself before allowing you passage to the harbor then?"

The old man protested, "I most certainly do mind kind sir. What would the possessions of a nearly dead old man be of any interest to the likes of you?"

Lox held his breath waiting for the guard to push back and help himself to the wagon but surprisingly the guard refrained, instead asking for a writ of passage. The old man grumbled at the imposition but did not argue as he reached under the canvas into a satchel and removed a scroll tied with a string. Lox noticed the man's gnarled hands as he grasped the scroll, with fingers riddled with arthritis, so much so that each finger was swollen and twisted upon one another making his hand look like a hoof or a claw rather than a hand. It was a wonder that the man could grasp anything at all, yet he did with extraordinarily little trouble. The man produced the writ to the guard.

"Says here you'll be headed to the sea harbor a little farther to the north, be off with you then if you want to make it before the high tide ebbs." The guard rolled the writ up and handed it back to the man. Lox and Astarte both looked at each other wide-eyed, relieved to have passed undiscovered. As the man coaxed his oxen forward, the guard took his sword and flatly rapped it on the canvas as it passed by. The sudden disturbance of the canvas caused a small amount of dust to fill the space where they hid.

Lox felt the dust enter his nostrils almost at once after the last ripple in the taut canvas happened. He became wide-eyed once again as he realized the urge rising in his head and transferring to his lungs. He silently cursed at the ill timing of this as he tried to hold in the pressure that was building, and he breathed in hoping to let it pass. Astarte leaned forward and pressed her hand over his face hoping to muffle the sneeze. Lox inhaled deeply again in one last attempt to stave off the inevitable.

Suddenly his body involuntarily constricted as the overwhelming pressure finally burst forward, "Ahh-Cheeet!" he sneezed, loud enough for the next town over to hear. The sneeze carried forward with a well-placed swear word mixed in as the guards heard it one by one.

"Stop this instant!" the guard shouted, running up to the wagon. "I'll ask again, who, or what is in your wagon, traveler?" He didn't wait for an answer as he sliced the tether holding the canvas and began to rapidly throw it up over, exposing the contents underneath.

Just as the man was starting to open the canvas, Lox was already preparing to fight. He would kill them all if he had to. But just as he was about to lurch forward, he felt Astarte wrap her arms around his chest and whispered, "Don't move or make a sound."

For a second time today, a guard looked him dead in the eyes and turned away to address the old man who was far too calm for someone who had been nearly found out.

"That was some sneeze old man. I hope you are well?" the guard said politely as he pulled the canvas back and did his best to secure it.

The old man waved him off, "Which it is just the time of year. Pollen and what not wreaking havoc on my nose. Now, I'll be on my way if it's all the same to you? Time is shorter now on account of you twice delaying me."

The guard sheepishly bowed, "Apologies old man. Be on your way and travel well."

Without another word the old man whipped his oxen harshly and the wagon sped off down the road. As they put some distance between them the old man shouted back, "That be the last guard check before we make port. You can come out now."

Lox looked at Astarte who looked flushed after using the amulet again for the second time today. He pulled back the canvas and sat up to take in the surroundings. The sun was beginning to set as they drew closer to the port which was nestled into the reeds of the Nile Delta. He spied traders carrying their wares on their backs and workers toiling away along the banks of the river, pounding reeds into papyrus and drying them out on racks. Astarte was able to sit up as she regained her composure, thankfully the drawback was only minor given the brief time she'd drawn the amulets power this time.

An hour later, the old man pointed ahead, "There she be. The boat what will take you away from here."

Lox turned his head to look and noticed the boat was quite large, but would no doubt need to stay close to land given the smaller draft of this ship. It could travel the seas close to land but would not do well in the open ocean, especially if the water got choppy with rolling waves. This type of boat would land on a beach so if the seas got rough the crew would row it to land safely and wait for more favorable conditions.

Lox did not enjoy the ocean to say the least. In the many times he'd sailed he always felt as if it were a test of survival even though he was likely never in great danger. Further, during the nights he would stare into the blackness, and he got the feeling the ocean would stare back at him, calling him to it. It unnerved him greatly, so he only sailed when necessary.

The wagon pulled up to the pier and came to a stop. Lox hopped out and helped Astarte jump down. The old man climbed down and immediately went to the ship captain who was checking over a manifest of goods and supplies that were being secured on the ship. Several men loaded crates and sacks of grain, and casks of wine, placing them in the shallow hold below. The old man handed the captain a sack of coins and motioned for them to come forward.

"The good captain here has graciously accepted your passage on his vessel. He'll take you as far as Philistia." The old man said, reaching out for Astarte and patting her on the arm. "This old man will say goodbye now, Astarte. Good luck on your journey lass."

Astarte leaned forward and kissed him on the cheek. "Thank you, Simeon. I'll never forget your kindness these many years."

"All aboard if you're coming. The tide waits for no man, nor woman." The captain said as he stashed the coin and walked up the gangway to the ship deck. He stopped to help Astarte over the step and beckoned her and Lox to the quarters at the rear of the ship. They stood and watched the old man who had already climbed into the wagon and sat watching the boat shove off and separate from the pier. A final wave to the old man and they made their way down the Nile to the great seaway. In four days, they would be in Ashdod. From there they would lie low and decide what course of action to take.

CHAPTER 26

The Citadel Fortress, Jebus

Tsalmaveth moved through the throng of men as they overran the final gate. There, Thoros and David had put up a valiant effort to stave off the assault but, in the end, there were simply too many men against so few. The Shades were currently racing forward in pursuit of them, as they retreated into the palace, and would soon overtake them. Tsalmaveth had made sure to instruct them all not to kill them. He had uses for them alive and would prefer to exact his own brand of punishment on them.

As Tsalmaveth entered the gates of the fortress and started to walk to the palace gradually, he noticed a gathering of Shades and enthralled soldiers at the main entrance to the palace compound. For some reason, the advance had halted.

"Why have you stopped?" Tsalmaveth barked, elbowing his way through the throng of near-comatose soldiers. When he reached the front, he saw several of his Shades throwing themselves at a door only to be repelled repeatedly.

"Step aside." He ordered as they halted and parted instantly as if controlled by an unseen hand. As he walked forward to the open entrance, he saw a man standing on the other side of the doorway holding a sword with a calm and relaxed demeanor. He stood there inches away from the door opening with an amused smirk showing from the side of his mouth.

Unbelievable, Tsalmaveth thought as he reached for the door opening with his long skinny fingers. A spark jumped from the air and struck his arm, throwing it back from the opening. He didn't need to try again to know what he was dealing with. This he'd seen before centuries ago.

"Do you really think you can stop me, David?" Tsalmaveth said, seething. There was no way for him or his minions to pass due to the use of lamb's blood on the doorways.

David laughed as he replied, "I WILL stop you, that is a promise, Shadow." Just then, from behind Tsalmaveth a horn blew three times as the sun could be seen coming up over the hills below Jebus.

Curses! Tsalmaveth thought, as he now realized his window for capturing the city tonight was closing. One by one the Shades turned and ran away from the palace headed to their underground abode. The enthralled soldiers stood there, unmoving, and unaffected by the horn blow that signaled the sunrise. If he did nothing they would stand there indefinitely. However, they must drink the water daily to continue their enthrallment. Tsalmaveth made a quick decision to send half of the throng to drink water and then return, bringing water for the rest of the army to drink as they stood sentry outside the palace, trapping David and his cohorts inside.

Tsalmaveth growled with teeth clenched, "Hear this, you impudent fool. One day. You have one day to decide what you will do. I may not be able to enter but," Tsalmaveth raised his hands to display the throng of soldiers, "you cannot leave either. If you don't decide then everyone you are protecting here will die one way or the other. Do you hear me?"

David stoically looked Tsalmaveth up and down, betraying a wry smile from the corner of his mouth. This was the same smile he remembered seeing on David's face when he beheaded Goliath. "Go back to your hole Shadow. The day belongs to us." He spat at the ground near Tsalmaveth's feet.

"And the night belongs to me you little twerp. I'll wipe that smirk from you face sooner than you think when my Shades return." Tsalmaveth threatened, but he could tell that David was unaffected.

"I will never submit or give in to the likes of you, Shadow." David said mockingly.

Tsalmaveth was inwardly enraged, but he kept his demeanor calm outwardly, staring coldly into David's fiery eyes. Since he was bound to Ahmet through a binding ritual, he would not have to go dormant after the days end as before, however the use of his power was limited to just being able to control and telepathically communicate with those under his control. This was a temporary condition until he was able to fulfill his mission to bring Yaldabaoth to this plane and sever the invisible tendril that tied him to his corporeal half, Azrael, the angel of death. This was the promise made to him by Yaldabaoth eons ago when he entered a pact with the god deep in the bowels of Sheol. He would blot out the sun and bring night to the earth for eternity. Then he would have unlimited power on the earth.

For countless millennia Tsalmaveth was bent to the will of Azrael whose own existence was to see to the transition of souls to the underworld to await judgement by Elohim. Yaldabaoth had offered him a way to sever his tie to Azrael if he went rogue and carried out his plan, which was to bring him to rule the earth in a physical manner. Yaldabaoth had many names over the millennia, claiming to be the true creator of the universe, only to be locked away by his friend and counterpart, Elohim hundreds of thousands of years ago. The grudge between the two was older than mankind itself and Tsalmaveth had come so close to achieving full autonomy before he was crushed by Michael at the end of the war and bound to the stone box.

Yaldabaoth claimed to have in part created the earth. His domain was the underworld and the earth itself. Elohim was said to have created the heavens and the foundation with which the universe would hang upon as it constantly expanded. The two deities were meant to be a balance, neither good nor evil. This was the status quo until Yaldabaoth and Elohim disagreed on the creation of human beings. Lucifer, one of Elohim's closest creations, secretly agreed with Yaldabaoth and made a move against Elohim. This sparked a multiple millennia-long war between the two, culminating in the fall and exile of Lucifer and the subsequent imprisonment of Yaldabaoth in Sheol, guarded by Azrael or Malakh ha-Maveth as some called him. Sheol was also known as the Shadow Realm and it not only paralleled the earth realm but it was layered under and over many other dimensions and realms.

Tsalmaveth resigned himself to retreat for the day, he would spend his time monitoring his connection to his thralls in hopes of discovering information on the location of The Key. He would leave the daily tasks to Ahmet.

"You may escape me today with your tricks, but no matter, I have time. You do not on the other hand." He sneered as he backed away and melded into the throng of Jebusites, careful to leave his control active on them by ordering them telepathically to surround the palace and not allow any to exit. This he imparted to Ahmet as he felt his own control of the body wain.

"Yes master, I will not let one pass on my watch." Ahmet said as they descended the mount into the city proper and back into the cavern depths where his temple awaited him. Today he would forcefully make more Shades and tonight he would swarm David and his ilk like locusts on a harvest. Behind him marched a throng of soldiers, black veins and eyes all. These Shades would be the most formidable he'd ever created.

Kiriath-Jearim, The House of Abinadab

Outside, there were people and carts wheeling by on the way to the tiny marketplace at the refuge outpost of Kiriath-Jearim. The small village of about four hundred souls worked away peacefully in the mid-afternoon sun. Jonathan sat near the bed where Baaldir lay sleeping. It had been more than a day since he arrived with him splayed across the top of a horse. The infection seemed to finally improve as the fever had broken overnight, thanks to the medicine given to the boy by the healer here. He'd written and sent word to Hebron of his whereabouts and intended to see to the boy's welfare.

Truthfully, he wanted to speak to the boy and understand what he was doing out there. His clothing was intricately woven, and his build and facial features did not lend to the theory that he was of Israel. The boy looked to be around fourteen years of age though his size was more of a grown man's stature, a large grown man. Jonathan's instinct told him that the boy was from Jebus and judging by the fabric of his tunic the boy was likely part of the wealthy class of citizens. What he couldn't figure out was why the boy was outside the city near the retreating Israelite military a few leagues from the safety of the walls.

After waiting another half hour, Jonathan decided to go outside for some fresh air. The temperature was cooler than normal for this time of year and the rain that had covered the region had breathed in new life to the landscape as the sun retreated from its noontime zenith. There was a garden not far from the house and he figured it wouldn't hurt to stretch his legs a bit more, so he walked that way taking in the sights.

There were a handful of homes about that made up the small hamlet built around the tabernacle which housed the Ark and the Covenant. In the center was a modest marketplace that provided the residents with food and textiles as well as a central water well. On every street corner were a pair of guards standing sentry and at the ready should a need arise. At the other end of the small village was a barracks that housed a garrison of troops posted there by Abner years before when the Ark was brought there for safe keeping. After the Philistine's debacle in which they captured it only to return it months later after mysterious deaths and illnesses, the decision had been made to hide it away in this unassuming village.

Kiriath-Jearim was only a stone's throw from Jebus but was virtually ignored by all surrounding inhabitants not of Israel due to the presence of the Ark and its infamous power that struck fear into the hearts of enemies of Israel. Only a fool would send an army of bandits into the hamlet being assured that one wrong step would awaken the wrath of Elohim. For this reason, the hamlet was very peaceful and was the antithesis of the state of the rest of Israel under his father's rule these last few years. Jonathan sighed to himself as he thought about his father and king: the man anointed by God and chosen by his people to be their first king after a dark period in their history. Saul was a fierce warrior, and a giant of a man compared to others in Israel but his disobedience to God had placed him on the edge of ruin time and again.

Jonathan wondered if his father would ever come to his senses and repent for his disobedience but knew that for some reason this was a vain notion. His father's mind was so riddled with depression and anger that his heart had become like a stone in a furnace; untouchable and fragile, ready to explode at the softest of prodding or a sudden change in temperature that would make a rock with moisture explode into a hundred pieces.

Jonathan said a silent prayer to Elohim for his father as he reached the garden.

As Jonathan entered, he saw a woman sitting there with her son, a boy of thirteen by the looks of it. The boy looked to be bandaged up and had bruises visible on his arms and face. The woman pulled her shawl up over her head and beckoned her son to sit near her as she watched him carefully. He walked to the right and surveyed a grove of olive trees. One of the limbs appeared to be bare and upon close inspection he realized it was a dead branch stemming from the trunk, probably due to the once in a century drought that had struck the region. Jonathan pulled up his knife and carefully sawed at the limb. The decaying wood was cut easily until he was able to remove it from the rest of the tree that was still very much alive. The pair on the bench eyed him curiously.

"It's best to remove dead branches. It allows the tree to direct energy to the other parts and helps reduce the risk of disease. Plus, olive wood is particularly good for carving." Jonathan said happily, proud of his acquisition, as he sat down under the tree and began to whittle the limb down, slicing and chiseling the rotted parts from the limb until it was shaped into a block the size of his foot. He eyed the boy and his mother and smiled at them when he felt their gaze. The woman looked away and whispered to her son not to stare at the man.

"It's quite alright ma'am." Jonathan said kindly as he turned the block of wood in his hands.

He looked at the boy and asked, "What should I make with this olive wood block?"

After a moment, the woman nodded her consent to the boy to speak to Jonathan. The boy stuttered lightly, clearly nervous, but overcame it quickly as he said, "Y-y-you might be able to make a boat from it, sir."

"Ah, a boat? I see it now! You have a good eye, young man. A boat it shall be!" Jonathan said warmly as he held the block up to his face and looked at the contours closely. He set to work with a flint knife shaving with the grain until a rough shape of a boat appeared. Long and sleek with a medium draft, the kind of boat you may see on an inland lake or river. He turned it around and around checking for symmetry and made slight adjustments. Once he was pleased with the shape, he began to hollow out the boat with his knife, using his thumb to help plunge the knife into the wood, carving out chunks of wood along the diverse wood grain. Jonathan enjoyed carving with olive wood because it was a solid wood that was easy to work, and the grain of the wood allowed for smooth carving that required minimal sanding if done properly. Back home he had several fine tools for such a task, but he rarely used them being out in the field most of his life. He'd learned to use a small knife he carried to deftly carve his creations.

Jonathan hollowed the boat out with the same care as the outer part, checking different angles for symmetry. Soon he'd turned a dead chunk of olive wood into a simple boat. Given time he could also fashion crew members and a mast with a sail from the remaining pieces of the limb. Pleased with his work he stood up and dusted off his tunic, letting the shavings fall to the ground. He picked up the chunks of dead wood and chucked them into a dense thicket of bushes and used his foot to rub the smaller pieces of wood into the soil. He was never one to leave a mess in his wake.

He held the boat up and made believe it was on the water moving up and down with the waves. He cracked a smile at the boy who stared wide eyed at the creation, awed by the transformation of a block of wood into a toy boat.

"What's your name young lad?" Jonathan asked, stooping down in front of the boy at eye level.

"N-Nathan, sir." The boy replied.

Jonathan smiled and offered the boy the newly carved boat, "Well, young Nathan. Would you like to see if this boat will float? Let's see what kind of shipwright I make!"

<hr />

Meanwhile, Near Sunset...

The sun was descending at a pace that could be seen with the naked eye, with just a faint ring of light escaping from around the edges of the cloud covered sky. It caused the buildings to take on a gray and black shade that steadily darkened, even though it seemed like mid-afternoon to him. The absence of any color, including his own skin, was unsettling.

Baaldir ducked into an alcove as the Shades ran by searching high and low. He was out of sight just in time to evade them, waiting for a moment longer listening to see if they doubled back towards him. He trained his ear on the other buildings in the city and, hearing nothing, decided to return the way he came and then cut over into another street. The whole city was deserted, without any signs of life to be seen. As he recognized the street as one that would take him to the palace he boldly ran, silently searching for the Shades hoping to see them in time to avoid detection. They'd chased him for nearly the whole day, snarling and lashing at him as they pursued him up and down the streets of Jebus. He'd narrowly evaded them several times only to be found again and the chase resumed.

Baaldir couldn't make sense of the world he found himself and for some reason he understood that this should be a dream. But it was not like past dreams where he might have a tough time running, feeling like wading through mud, or speaking feeling like his tongue had molasses on it as it hampered his ability to form words, especially in moments of surprise or distress. Here, in this dream he was fully aware and able to control his movements as though he was awake. He knew this wasn't real because he could remember meeting the man at the waterhole and the fight with those

Shades just beforehand. He remembered passing out and found himself in Jebus again. Only this was not the Jebus he knew. It was a dream, and he was the dreamer except everything felt real, apart from this place being void of any color whatsoever.

His muscles ached from strain. His heart pumped like a racehorse and sweat poured down his reddened face as he ran. These were never present in a normal dream. Above all, the city was exactly as he knew it to be from his many days exploring it with Nathan. Baaldir knew this city like the back of his hand and hoped that this advantage would work in his favor to help him escape those frightful creatures he'd somehow come to know as Shades. He was unsure if they could harm in this dream or if he'd wake up just before as he had in previous nightmares and he didn't want to find out.

Baaldir thought back on his fight at the watering hole where he'd killed three assailants after trailing the main group of Shades through the night. Hundreds of them ran south and he soon realized they meant to attack the Israelite army. He watched the night attack from a distance, torn between one enemy fighting the other enemy. One enemy had likely killed his best friend and the other threatened to overrun his city and harm his family. However, he had seen several Israelites be taken into the palace and cared for and even allowed to roam the palace at will. The warrior David was one of them and for all he could tell, they were now allies to his father. The politics of Canaan and Israel astounded him and made him acutely aware that he had a lot to learn.

But here, in this dream, he was uninjured though completely unarmed. As he ran down the street, he wondered why this world had no people, yet Shades existed to attack him. It made him think that there was more to this dream world. For one, he was lucid. He knew he lay unconscious somewhere that the Israelite had taken him, having woken briefly before slipping into the dream world yet again. And he had discovered that his body, though able to experience fatigue, was able to perform at a much higher level than his body while awake. He tested this out as he leapt across an entire intersection and landed on the other side. The leap was better than thirty feet and was many yards further than his real jumping skill. With this realization his energy was renewed as he began to run faster and faster toward the fortress and his family's palace. In no time at all he reached the entrance of the fortress. What he saw made him skid to a sudden stop. Hundreds of bodies lay at the gates, and he could see the next set of gates was much the same. Crumpled in a ball face down on the dirt was Ide, his father's creepy advisor. Flashes of Ide's dealings with Lox came to him in that moment.

What happened here? Baaldir thought as he cautiously stepped forward.

The best he could determine was a battle of some sort at the fortress gates. Mingled within the corpses were a handful of Shades like those that were chasing him in the dream. However, the dead around him looked to be mostly Jebusite soldiers and civilians. Dumbfounded, Baaldir stepped over bodies and made his way carefully through the gates. One gate at a time, he surveyed the carnage, relieved not to see his brother or anyone else he knew well. Passing through the final gate that opened into a yard in front of the palace, he stopped with a cold shudder down his spine.

Before him were thousands of men, woman, and even children standing shoulder to shoulder. They stood there catatonic and emotionless facing the entrance to the palace. Baaldir's height advantage allowed him to see for a good distance to his left and right and he could see that the throng was packed tightly as far as the eye could see. It was highly likely that the people surrounded the palace.

What magic is at work here? Baaldir thought as he quickly backed up, not sure what to make of the scene.

The people all seemed to have the same countenance. From the side he could see that their eyes and skin around them had turned gray and the skin around their mouths had veins of black originating at the corner and descending onto their necks. It looked like some kind of mass disease.

Baaldir turned suddenly, sensing a presence behind him. Standing before him was a man he recognized, kind of anyways. Ahmet, Nathan's father, stood ten paces away with a retinue of Shades on his flanks. He wore a dark cloak that covered his head and body completely. Ahmet's eyes flitted around as he looked Baaldir up and down with a puzzled look on his face.

"Nathan is dead." Ahmet said flatly, making clear that he recognized Baaldir. This statement shook Baaldir. He'd held out hope that this was not true but hearing Ahmet say it just drove reality home. A tear welled up in one of his eyes as he scowled at Ahmet.

"And here you are, standing shoulder to shoulder with the scum that did it," Baaldir said accusatorily. He was outwardly disgusted at the sight.

Ahmet shot him a puzzled look. "What nonsense are you speaking now boy? It was the Israelites your father allied with not two days later."

Baaldir shook his head, "You are deceived Ahmet." he said, pointing to the Shades at his sides. "These were the murderers; I saw it with my own eyes Ahmet."

Nonplussed, Ahmet began to pace in front of the Shades. After a moment he came to a stop. "We will just have to see who is telling the truth now won't we? Capture the boy!" he said, throwing his hands toward Baaldir as the Shades surged toward him.

Baaldir had only a moment's notice to react as he turned and dove into the crowd of civilians elbowing and pushing his way through. The people moved aside easily as they were clearly not cogent enough to react to being pushed and soon several of them fell over causing a series of others to fall like dominoes. Behind him he could hear Ahmet screaming for someone to stop him, but he kept pushing. The further he went into the crowd the more the crowd closed in behind him and eventually all of them, receiving orders to detain him, started clawing at him. One grabbed his wrist, and he shook it loose. Another attempted to throw their arms around him and he ducked to the ground and shot under the legs of another in front of him.

Eventually he stood and started to wildly swing his arms and kick at those around him while trying to make it to the palace entrance.

After fighting the crowd for what seemed like forever, he finally saw the arched entrance to the right and made a beeline for it, knocking over a man and woman while throwing his elbow into the jaw of another who tried to grab him. The thought crossed his mind that these were innocent bystanders, unable to control their own actions. Somehow their will had been taken or suppressed by whatever this dark force was, and it made him pull his blows slightly so as not to mortally injure anyone. In a matter of seconds, he was to the arched opening and happened to look over his left shoulder and saw a wave of Shades closing in on him. They were not so careful with the lives of those enthralled by them as they trampled, bludgeoned, and sliced their way after him. For a moment he thought he should turn around and face them with the hope of saving lives, but he realized that there was no proof that this was at all real. However, he was not going to let them capture him in order to find out, so he ran through the arched opening and into his home of fourteen years.

Once inside, he ran forward but looked over his shoulder just in time to see a group of Shades slam into an unseen force that knocked them back, violently suffering broken bones and smashed faces.

Someone else has some magic to counter them, Baaldir thought as he watched Ahmet come to the opening and stop just outside.

"You are just as much responsible for Nathan's death boy; filling his head with adventure and taking him places that you both had no place being." Ahmet said venomously as he smacked the invisible wall with his palms and pushed with all his might, to no avail. Baaldir listened to the accusation and recognized it as one that he had told himself these last few days. The guilt, grief, and anger he directed at the Shades he also had directed at himself which was why he felt he needed to follow those Shades the other night; to do what, he was unsure at the time but was acting on his own intuition.

"You cannot come in here Ahmet," Baaldir taunted. "I'm going now, for what its worth, I'm sorry about your son. He was like a brother to me and I miss him."

"Spare me your apologies, boy. One day soon you and I will have a reckoning." Ahmet smacked the invisible wall once more for good measure.

Satisfied that Ahmet and the Shades could not come through the barrier he turned and headed deeper into the palace. Maybe he could find his brother and his mother and father. They might have a plan to escape to safety. It didn't take long to cross the palace as he came to the garden where the tall ash tree was. The noonday sun showed brightly in a cloudless sky, allowing him to see clearly to the other side of the garden which was not nearly as beautiful in these shades of gray he saw in this dream. There he saw his brother and his sister, Siv, there and those Israelites, one of whom was David the mighty warrior. He ran towards them shouting.

"Brother! Sister! Where is mother and father?" he shouted at them as he closed the distance. Neither of them turned to acknowledge him. As he reached, he went to throw his arms around Thoros but went right through as if his body was not corporeal after all. He wondered at this especially since the throng outside was more than capable of touching him. He tried again, shouting at them, and attempting to get their attention. He waved his hands in front of their faces and even resorted to throwing a punch at Thoros' gut.

Thoros, with a grim expression, spoke to Siv and David as others looked on. Baaldir, realizing the futility of trying to get their attention, decided to stand by as an unseen eavesdropper.

"There is no telling how long the lamb's blood will hold them off, we need to think about an escape plan." Siv said, always the voice of reason.

"But we can't travel with mother in her state. And my father... I'm not leaving him or my mother behind!" Thoros responded.

"We may have no choice but to leave him here Thoros. I only have enough lambs blood to wet the lentils one more time all the way around." David said somberly. "It will only buy us another day at most."

Jarnsaxa spoke up next, her voice shaky, "We have few weapons, even less men to defend with, and our water is poisoned. The only water we have is what was in our lambskins at the start before the poisoning happened."

"What about, 'I'm not leaving my father behind', don't any of you understand?" Thoros raged, his face turning red with anger.

Baaldir listened to their back and forth and then found himself focused on a hunched over figure lumbering about among the bushes on the periphery. His curiosity peeked, Baaldir slowly crept over to the side of the garden and standing there was Skald, the crippled seer that his father kept around. Skald stood there calmly as Baaldir happened upon him.

"You best be going back boy, lest you be swallowed by the darkness." Skald said, knowing more than he let on.

"What about my family. I need to help them." Baaldir said frantically.

"There is nothing you can do here. Go back to your body Baaldir. Walking in the shadows is not for boys. Sooner or later, you'll lose yourself. This is for men such as me to do, NOT boys." Skald said, warning evident in his tone.

"I need to see my father. What is Thoros talking about? Why would they have to leave them behind?" Baaldir asked, not willing to listen.

Skald sighed, clicked with his tongue, and lifted his staff and pointed toward the ash tree, "Follow me, foolish boy." He walked rapidly for a crippled man leading the way across the garden to the great tree.

Skald stopped once he rounded the back side of the tree and placed his staff on the ground, leaning into it to steady himself. Baaldir, close behind rounded the tree and stopped suddenly. On the ground lay a body, an exceptionally large body, covered with a shroud.

"Your father Baaldir, or what was his body." Skald offered even though Baaldir was more than able to understand what he was looking at.

"He is...dead? But...how?" Baaldir said, at a loss for words, tears welling up in his eyes.

"The how does not matter. His body is here, and your father is not. Now. Off with you, foolish boy!" he said as he used his staff to tap Baaldir on the forehead.

Baaldir awoke suddenly in a soft bed covered in bandages and blankets.

"It's about time you woke up boy." A man said, leaning forward on a chair.

He was an exceptionally large man with a chiseled jaw and muscular features on his black colored skin. Long blonde hair, almost white hung well past his shoulders. Baaldir sat up on his elbows with a puzzled look, not sure what to make of the man sitting before him.

The man betrayed a wry smile through his stern countenance which was softened a bit due to his bright blue eyes, "My name is Azrael, and you and I have much to discuss. And you've kept me waiting."

CHAPTER 27

The Palace, Jebus

David shouted, "Okay! That's the last of entry points," as he jumped down from a second-story balcony overlooking the courtyard where thousands of enthralled citizens and soldiers of Jebus stood emotionless. The lamb's blood was now gone but for a few brushes full, enough to do the main entrances one more time, maybe. The sun was on its descent to the horizon and darkness would give way to Tsalmaveth and his Shades yet again. Through several heated conversations amongst those inside the palace grounds, they still had not come up with a solid plan to escape being surrounded. Thoros didn't want to leave his father's body behind even though taking it would mean they were severely hampered in their escape.

"We have one day starting now. If we are to escape it will need to be during that window." David said, walking up to Thoros, Siv, Jarnsaxa, and his companions: Joab, Jeroboam, and Uriah.

"Great, now all we need is an escape plan." Uriah said defeatedly.

Just as he said that Bulwark came over, walking briskly from the other side of the palace. "I have the answer. But you're not going to like it brother." he said addressing Thoros.

"I already told you. He goes with us, or I stay." Thoros said, motioning in the direction of Adonizedek's body. "I'll not leave my father's body to be desecrated by those animals out there."

"Siv, talk some sense into the man. He's not thinking straight." Jarnsaxa said curtly.

Siv sighed heavily, "My dear, let's at least listen to what Bulwark has to say."

Thoros looked at Bulwark, giving a slight nod as the only confirmation that he was willing to listen.

Bulwark wasted no time, "Behind the throne room is a secret staircase that descends to a corridor which leads to the stables. It was built for such an instance where the royal family and court may need to escape in the unlikely event of a failed defense."

"I'd say that the unlikely is upon us already." Joab said, looking at David then back to Bulwark.

"How many of us are there?" Siv asked the group.

Jarnsaxa replied, "Forty. Counting all present, the nobles that were not infected, and servants. Also, a handful of guards."

"I'm waiting for the part where you tell me how my father's body will be carried with us." Thoros said impatiently.

"Brother, there is not a way to carry him. The stairs are steep and narrow." Bulwark said apologetically. "If there was a way you know I'd be the first one to carry him."

Thoros' face began to turn red as if he was about to explode in anger and just as he drew in a breath, he heard a voice from near the body of Adonizedek.

"Foolish boy!" said the voice as all turned to see Skald turning around walking toward them carrying his gnarled staff. He shook his head in frustration. "Must I tell you the same thing I told Baaldir? Your father's body is there." he said, pointing a mangled finger. "HE is not. That body is not your father, foolish boy!"

Thoros rapidly shot out questions hearing the name of his brother. "Baaldir? Where is Baaldir? Is he here, has he been found? What do you mean by this old man? If my father is not here, then where is he? Is this another one of your riddles? Because I swear, I'm in no mood..."

Skald interrupted, as he was wont to do. Only he was allowed to interrupt the king or any official. This was his way when relaying his messages from the gods.

"You waste time worrying about a body that has no meaning any longer. Your father's spirit is no longer bound to it. Therefore, funerals or burials or a pyre will not bring him any peace. It will only waste time."

Thoros was taken aback but he finally seemed to allow the notion to sink in as he exhaled and allowed his shoulders to relax for the first time since he awoke more than a day ago. But then he remembered Baaldir.

"You mentioned my brother. What of Baaldir?" Thoros asked.

"Baaldir is on his own journey. He will be for quite some time. You have your own journey to worry on." Skald offered.

Thoros was annoyed at the vagueness of Skald. That was one of the reasons he disliked and dismissed the old man's rambling predictions. They could apply to any infinite number of people or places.

"I am the heir to my father's kingdom Skald. I won't be going anywhere but to the battlefield to defend what my father built." Thoros responded matter-of-factly. Then added, "I'll not be leaving on a journey anytime soon old man."

Skald burst into a mocking laughter before replying, "Hear this, King Thoros. To stay here would be rule to over a pile of your family's corpses. Your destiny lies far from here. Fight if you must but know that in the end it will not stop you from that journey I spoke of. This much I know Thoros, if you stay here and guard your father's corpse your own corpse will be added to it. You must live to establish your own kingdom to rule over a new people. Your choice *King Thoros*." The last words carried a hint of mockery.

Siv stepped forward and placed her hand on Thoros' chest and whispered to him, "My love, we need to think of Magni and Thrud. Your father would want them to be safe. Not to mention young Vithas. You will be like his father now."

Hearing the appeal of his love for his two children, Thoros softened and turned to look at his children who were sitting with their grandmother and their nurse who helped look after them daily. But they were not there.

"Where are my children? Where is Vithas?" Thoros thought frantically. "Where are the children!" he shouted, noticing that his mother and the nursemaid were no longer sitting on the bench that was but ten feet away. Moments ago, they were there and now they were all four missing.

Siv started to search around the nearby area thinking they may have been playing hide and seek with the nurse. Frigg had been catatonic for the last day and had not moved a muscle as she sat there staring off into space. Even she was nowhere to be found.

"Magni! Thrud!" She shouted as Thoros began to fear the worst. The sun had just begun to set. Thoros joined in the calls, "Magni! Thrud! Vithas! Mother!"

Soon every single one of those in the garden began searching high and low.

"They're gone Thoros! Please tell me we will find them!" Siv cried, tears now running down her cheeks. "Thrud! Magni!" she screamed, panic evident in every syllable. "Vithas!"

Jarnsaxa ran to Siv and hugged her, "Siv, my dear. We will find them. They probably went further into the palace."

Thoros, now fearing the worst, began to bark orders. "You! Check the throne room and living quarters. You! Check the upper levels, take two or three people with you!"

Just then someone shouted, "We found the nurse!" Thoros ran toward the shouting. As he ran up, he saw a young lady crumpled up on the ground. Blood was leaking from her head. She was conscious but very shaken up.

"I tried to stop her, but she hit me with a rock and took them." The nanny who was named Lydia said.

"Took them where?" Thoros shouted. The girl began to cry and shook her head.

Almost as if to answer his question Thoros heard a loud amplified voice shout from outside the palace.

"THOROS! Do bring your wife and friends to the front entrance!" came a man's voice that sounded like none other than Tsalmaveth. Thoros' face flushed and the strength left him the moment he heard him say his name.

David was already running, followed by Joab and Jeroboam who lent his shoulder to a hobbling Uriah, their swords drawn. Thoros gathered himself and began to follow; Siv and the others came close behind. As Thoros came to the entrance, he saw that David was already there with a blade drawn. Standing at the entrance just outside the palace was Tsalmaveth and on his right and left were two very scared children being held at the shoulders by two Shades. In front of him was Vithas. Tsalmaveth stood there smugly with his hands upon the boy's shoulders.

Behind him were thousands of people holding torches. So many torches lit up the area as shadows danced on the walls of the palace. Thoros' heart sank as he realized his son and daughter were those children.

How could this happen? Thoros thought as he went to step forward.

"If you harm a hair on their heads there won't be a shadow where you can hide!" Thoros yelled.

Tsalmaveth wore a sardonic smile as he patted the tops of the kid's heads gently. Vithas was not one for words or outward emotions, so the boy stood there stoically. Though he was no doubt terrified.

"Papa! I'm scared!" cried Magni as Thrud cried inconsolably.

"Be a brave boy Magni. I'm going to make sure you are safe." He said and then looked at Tsalmaveth. "They are just children, Shadow. Surely you are not so depraved as to hurt an innocent child?"

"This is your fault Thoros. Well, yours and David's fault actually. Now I'm going to tell you how you can save your children's lives. Listen carefully because if you deviate in the slightest, I will kill your offspring. Better yet, she will do it." Tsalmaveth motioned for the crowd behind him to disperse and out walked his mother, Frigg. Her eyes were vacant, and anyone could tell she was under full control of the Shadow of Death.

Joab shouted in confusion. "How is that possible? She hasn't drunk that water in a whole day. His hold over her should have worn off by now, I was sure of it!"

As if to answer his question, a slight young woman with a burn scar on her neck pushed past him and crossed the barrier.

Siv reached for her but was too late. "No! Lydia! What are you doing?"

Lydia did not respond as she walked straight over to Tsalmaveth and turned around by his side. She said, "I made my choice years ago, Siv. I serve Yaldabaoth now and always."

Tsalmaveth clapped his hands joyously. "Ha! Splendid! The wonders never cease! Even I was not aware that He had devotees in the palace! Now, what was I saying about your children?"

A Shade stepped forward and handed Frigg a jagged dagger and melded back into the crowd.

Thoros stepped forward and scowled at Tsalmaveth and through gritted teeth he said, "You wouldn't dare..."

"Oh, this is no threat Thoros." Tsalmaveth said as he snapped his fingers. Upon doing this Frigg moved forward, emotionless, toward the two children who squealed in horror. "It's an assurance."

"Okay! Stop!" Thoros shouted. Tsalmaveth raised an eyebrow and snapped his fingers when Frigg was only a hair's breadth from Magni's throat. Frigg froze in place, unmoving. Tsalmaveth allowed a wry smile to escape from the corner of his mouth.

Through squinted eyes, Tsalmaveth stared at Thoros, taking a step forward so that he was just out of arm's length from him. For a moment Thoros had thoughts of lunging forward and grabbing Tsalmaveth by the neck and twisting mercilessly, but then he heard Thrud whimper and all thoughts of solving this with violence escaped his mind.

Thoros told himself, *I need to stay calm and think. Think Thoros. Your children's lives depend on it.*

But Thoros was at a loss as his heart ached and began to beat faster, panic starting to set in. For the first time in his life, he realized that his strength and speed would not save his children. His brute force, and his mighty voice would not save his young brother from this evil. He could hear his father's voice ringing in his ears telling him to control his temper and he finally understood what he'd meant. To save his children he needed to stay calm and level-headed. He needed to use his mind and not his sword arm.

"Now, Thoros. I may be a lot of things, but I am not one to break promises. I will always do exactly as I say. Let's see if we can find a way out for your precious son and daughter."

Through gritted teeth once again Thoros said, "What do you have in mind?"

Tsalmaveth's eyes brightened at the question, "That's more like it. What do I have in mind?" he said, raising his hand to rest on his chin while resting the elbow in his other hand as if to say he was thinking about it. Seconds later, the dark eyes returned to gaze at Thoros.

"Thoros, Jeroboam, Jarnsaxa, Bulwark, and..." he let his fingers alternate as they tapped his cheek rhythmically. "David." The last name he called with jovial laughter playing on the somber tone of the other names.

"Come before me, front and center now. Make haste, I am not patient," Tsalmaveth ordered.

Thoros looked at those whose names were called. David stood there with clenched fists, clearly locked in the same dilemma as himself. He heard David whisper something to Joab about finding his men in the hills and rallying them to fight before he exited through the barrier, following behind Thoros.

David stepped forward; his eyes locked on Tsalmaveth in a hateful glare. Tsalmaveth took notice and said, "I don't like the way this dog is looking at me. Maybe I ought to just go ahead and kill the kids?" He raised his fingers ready to snap. Thoros elbowed David and said under his breath, "My children David, don't do anything rash." Meanwhile Siv shrieked in horror seeing her children in the grasp of Tsalmaveth. She hit her knees pleading and asking for mercy.

"You should heed his caution, David. I know how much of a cold-blooded killer you are but even you should realize that to defeat me you'll have to soak your blade in the blood of these thousands of innocents first. Are you willing to have their blood on your hands David, son of Jesse and slayer of giants? Will you have the blood of these children on your hands as well? Will you add a line to the famous song the people sing about the tens of thousands you've slaughtered?"

David relented and allowed his shoulders to drop as he averted his gaze ever so slightly, signaling that he would not be acting at this time. Thoros sighed, relieved for at least a moment.

"That's better, dog." Tsalmaveth said condescendingly. "Now, for the reason I have called you five. Here is what you will do to save these children and those behind you in the palace. I know about your escape tunnel and rest assured the exit to that near the stables is being located as we speak. Do not allow for the illusion that you have any choice other than what I am about to give you. This will be your one and only chance to save lives. Understood?"

Tsalmaveth began to pace in front of them as if he were a General inspecting his men, his chin held high, and hands clasped behind his back. Bulwark stood next to Thoros. Then David, Jarnsaxa and Jeroboam stood on his left. Each one wore a worried look.

Tsalmaveth stopped in front of Thoros and David. "On your knees, all of you." He stepped to the side to reveal Frigg with a blade at the throats of both of the young children. A thousand Shades had filtered through the crowd and now lined the area in front of the throng, nearly filling in the space making it feel very constricting. Thoros' eyebrows widened and then furrowed as he realized these Shades were formerly Jebusite infantry. To a man, they were armored and heavily armed with swords and shields with the odd man bearing a spear or poleaxe.

There were not this many last night, and now he has made more with my own soldiers, Thoros thought as he looked them over. He noticed that their faces were contorted and drawn in as though they had been starving for months, the skin was gray colored as the black veins traveled down their necks. Blood ran from their mouths and dried a rusty brown.

Defeatedly Thoros hung his head, *they've cut their tongues out. What sorcery could make a man do this to themselves? I don't have a choice; this enemy cannot be beaten by natural means.*

Thoros had no hesitation as his thoughts ran rampant ranging from defiance to complete surrender, seeing his mother about to kill his children. He hit his knees and dropped his arms to his side and pleaded with Tsalmaveth.

"Please spare them, I'll do whatever you tell me to do," Thoros offered with a tear running down his cheek, hopeful that his plea would be accepted. He didn't care that he was bending the knee, something he swore he'd never do. The others soon followed though David stood there like a statue; the look of hateful disdain returned.

Tsalmaveth looked at David for a moment and sighed. He snapped his fingers, and three Shades lurched forward and grabbed Jeroboam and dragged him over to their ranks. Another Shade brought a stool out and produced a rope.

Meanwhile, David and the others who were still behind the safety of the barrier shouted in unison, "NO! NO! NO!"

"I told you dog; watch the way you look at me. Now Jeroboam here will have to take the punishment for you." Tsalmaveth taunted.

"No! Take me. I'll bear the punishment for him!" David pleaded. "Don't kill him!" The Shades continued, pulling Jeroboam's right arm down to the stool and tying it to the top while holding his head in the dirt, knees on his back.

"It's too late for that David. You will learn this lesson and then we will try this over again." Tsalmaveth snapped his fingers and a Shade with a sword raised came forward and in one fluid motion chopped Jeroboam's hand off from his arm. Blood spurted from the limb as Jeroboam's cries of anguish faded into unconsciousness. Working quickly, a Shade produced a leather cord and began to tie off the limb, stopping the bleeding. Another Shade came forward with a red-hot iron and quickly cauterized the stump. Once the tourniquet was secured two Shades dragged the unconscious body of Jeroboam across the yard and dropped him in front of the doorway before returning to the ranks.

David was raging, his face red with anger as he said, "You MONSTER! You didn't need to do that!"

David hit his knees suddenly, anguish and regret written on his face. Thoros now knew this enemy had outmatched him. How had Tsalmaveth anticipated David's actions to the point that he had a red-hot iron ready for the moment it was needed? Thoros thought this as he regretfully remembered Skald's erstwhile warning just a few short minutes ago.

Tsalmaveth knelt down face to face with David. "Men like you only understand one language, it is that of the sword. Now that you and I speak the same language we can have a productive conversation, no? Or should I choose another body part to remove?" David heaved as Thoros noticed he was trying to hold it together.

"NO! I'm sorry, it won't happen again. Just don't harm anyone else." David said frantically, averting his eyes from Tsalmaveth.

"It could have been worse David, fortunately for Jeroboam I like him. He has provided me with amusement these last few days. Defy me again though, and I will take more than a dominant hand. I'll think up new ways to torture you and those who follow you." He said this while shooting a glance toward those standing in the entrance safely behind the barrier.

"I have to give you credit David; the lamb's blood trick was inspired. It had me going for a moment or two. Reminded me of those days back in Egypt." Tsalmaveth snapped his fingers, and two more Shades came forward with skins of water and two chalices. They concealed the cup and the skins as they poured water into both cups and handed them to Tsalmaveth while two more produced a small table and set it down in front of everyone.

Tsalmaveth raised his voice to address those standing before him, "Let us play a game. In my hand I hold two cups of water. One is pure water, fit for drinking. The other is my water which I need not explain further," motioning to the throng behind him with torches flickering as if to accentuate his point.

"What I am proposing is a game of chances to decide your fate. The game is simple: choose one cup and drink from it. If you choose pure water, you are free to go. I will clear a path for you to exit the city and you will be allowed to leave safely and unmolested. Choose the other and you will remain here as my servant, forever. This goes for all of you, apart from Thoros and David."

Thoros was starting to get his hopes up, but they were dashed as soon as they arose. He looked back over his shoulder at Siv who gave him a worried look.

Tsalmaveth continued, "Thoros and David, you both will not be playing this game. You will watch your comrades and loved ones, even your children choose their cup and when all have won or lost then you will drink the cup that I give you. The children will remain until the end as assurance of your cooperation. Your friend, Jeroboam, is free to go either under his own power or over someone's shoulder, once you've done as I've asked. As you can see, I am being more than fair to all of you. I could simply wait for your barrier to fail and then kill you all. But what is the fun in that?"

Tsalmaveth snapped his fingers once again and the crowd instantly began to part, creating a path that opened to the gates of the fortress lined with a thousand torches. The heavily armed Jebusite Shades marched single file on both sides of the crowd and lined the path to the gate, making a wall on both sides our of the shields they carried.

"Once you drink you are to place the cup down and walk forward. If you reach the gate and are not under my control, then you know you've chosen wisely and are free to go. If you don't choose wisely...well, you likely won't know it anyhow. Now. Who would like to go first?" Tsalmaveth clapped his hand joyously as he stepped back and allowed his Shades to set up a table with the cups upon them.

Thoros had mixed emotions because his wife and children would have a chance to escape but it seemed to him that David and himself would not be given the same chance. He chose to at least be hopeful that his loved ones would survive even if he didn't.

Thoros decided to speak up on the other's behalf, "Someone gather up every person in the palace and tell them to come to the entrance." He heard several footsteps behind him run off to carry out the order. Soon everyone was gathered at the entrance, they weren't far off to begin with, knowing that their only protection was there. They mostly stayed behind the barrier for fear that Tsalmaveth would renege on the agreed rules of the game and kill them outright.

"The servants and nobles will go first in no particular order," Thoros ordered as he looked at the entrance over his shoulder. Tsalmaveth seemed amused with his ability to give orders even while on his knees and still be sure they would be followed.

David looked at Joab who was standing nearby, fingers hovering near his sword. Uriah stood with him, propped up by crutches, nursing a broken leg.

"I have a better idea, King Thoros. David's men will go first, followed by your nobles, your close associates will be the last," Tsalmaveth said with a surprisingly polite tone, making sure to emphasize the title of King.

Joab spoke up, "We will go last and see to our lord's safety."

Tsalmaveth's face darkened as he chuckled, "Oh Joab. You will go when I say you go. Understood? Why don't we start with the crippled boy there? Uriah, is it? You'll need a head start. I'm tempted to just give you the pure water so that I don't have to risk having your pathetic hobbling corpse amongst my thralls should you choose poorly."

Uriah hobbled forward on his crutches trying to keep his broken leg from hitting the ground or anyone else and once he reached the table, he looked at each of the cups separately, weighing each in his hand, and even pouring a little in his cupped hand.

Tsalmaveth, growing impatient snapped, "Choose a cup and drink. Don't overthink this, boy."

Uriah set one glass down and picked up the other glass and raised it to his lips, "Here goes nothing." He said as he took a drink of the water and set the cup down.

Tsalmaveth pointed to the path and flicked his wrist, "Get moving hop-along."

Uriah hurriedly hobbled down the path toward the gate. Tsalmaveth stood by looking directly at David with an annoyed look on his face, tapping his foot all the while.

As Uriah made it to the gate, he stopped and turned around. "I will wait here for my comrades. If you don't like it, you can kill me now."

Tsalmaveth chuckled, amused at the obstinance, uncaring that Uriah chose to stay close by. Tsalmaveth turned to Joab and motioned for him to take his turn.

"Joab. I'll up the stakes on yours seeing as you have family ties to our man David here. Once you drink you will take that sorry little man, Jeroboam, and carry him with you. No need for him to drink. If you make it out then you both are free but if you don't then I will have my Shades tear him apart, limb from limb and you will be my slave for eternity. Do we have a deal?" Tsalmaveth beamed with a smile that told Thoros that he enjoyed having power over everyone.

Joab, making no comment, walked forward as the Shades picked up the cups, concealed them briefly, and placed them back in front of him.

Following Uriah's lead, he quickly chose a cup and drank deeply. He then walked over to Jeroboam and pulled him up over his shoulder and carried him. "Remember what I told you Joab." David said as Joab passed by and limped down the path with Jeroboam slung over his shoulder like a sack of grain. Joab nodded and said, "I'll see you again cousin, either in this life or the next."

Luckily, Joab made it to the gate and joined Uriah, turning back and hesitating as he looked at David kneeling.

"Go! Joab. Do not worry about me! That is an order. Get those men to safety!" David shouted.

Joab nodded and saluted David before tapping Uriah on the shoulder and turning to leave them behind. Thoros hoped whatever David ordered would succeed. He felt like it may be their only hope after all this was over.

After Joab and Uriah, the others in the palace filed in one by one. Skald was the first though he chose a cup with his eyes closed and drank until it was empty. "Good water." He said, as he used his walking stick to navigate the path to the gate, safe and clear. Thoros marveled at the man's trust in fate so much so that he felt choosing a cup and its contents was predetermined. He knew of warriors that fought in this way, knowing that their death or survival was predetermined regardless of what they did. In a way it was a freeing notion that allowed a man to give oneself over to battle and let it sweep them away, creating acts of heroism and bravery. For the first time he felt, as he watched Skald awkwardly saunter down the path to freedom, that there was something to it.

Perhaps a little too late, Thoros thought defeatedly.

A dozen or so passed freely, choosing the correct water, and escaping to freedom. Just when Thoros was starting to think this was all a ruse and the water was pure after all, he saw a woman walking down the path. At the halfway point, she stopped and stood there for a moment swaying back and forth. Finally, she turned and walked straight into the crowd of people and disappeared among them.

From there, it seemed like every two or three who drank turned and did the same. Clearly, Tsalmaveth had not been bluffing about there being a one in two chance of choosing the pure water. Eventually all that was left was Siv, Jarnsaxa, Bulwark, and David kneeling next to himself. His children stood there with drawn faces, likely tired from all the happenings.

"Siv, you will go next. I'll allow you to say goodbye to your husband. Also, given how smoothly this game has gone I'm feeling generous. I'll not have your children drink the water. Instead, if you succeed in freeing yourself through the game, I will send them to you safely. However, I will only release Vithas once your husband completes my demand. But not until then." Tsalmaveth gave a haughty expression as though he was proud of his display of mercy.

Siv walked forward and got down on her knees in front of Thoros, wrapping her arms around his torso with her head buried in his chest. Thoros felt as if he would fall to pieces in her arms as tears from her cheeks wet his tunic. She looked at him with her watery green eyes. The torches nearby glistened as he looked deeply into them. "Take our children to safety Siv. I know not what will become of me here but knowing that they are safe will give me the courage to face anything."

Siv nodded and buried her head into his chest again and squeezed him. She then kissed him deeply and lingered there for a moment longer as he felt the invisible tie pulling him closer to her. Then, as if her mind was now made up, she stood up and walked away toward the table. She picked up a cup, looked at him one last time and drank deeply. As she set the cup down, she turned and walked around the table, stopping in front of Magni and Thrud, "Your mother loves each of you more than anything else in the world. I'll be waiting for you at the gate. When he lets you free don't hesitate and run toward the gate." She tried to reach out and hug them, but a Shade swatted her hand away and pulled them away from her.

Thoros watched as she began to walk down the path. Siv walked purposefully, and when she reached the gate she turned and shouted, "I've made it to the gate Shadow, will you honor your word?" Thoros exhaled as she turned and spoke, relieved that she was not infected by this evil.

Tsalmaveth grinned from ear to ear. "You really have all the luck Thoros," he said as he looked at the children, "Release the boy and girl to their mother. I'll not renege on this promise." The Shades immediately released the children, and they crept forward, unsure if they were really free. They decided to run to their father and threw their arms around his neck.

"Papa, why can't you come with us?" Magni asked through tears.

Thoros gritted his teeth and looked at the two children as he held them tightly, "Your father loves you very much, but I cannot go with you this time. Run to your mother and you make sure to do as she tells you. Do you understand?" The two nodded, tears in their eyes and ran down the path to Siv who scooped them up with tears of her own soaking her cheeks.

Thoros hated that he'd been unable to protect his children from the horrors and that their innocence had been stolen so young. He was a young teenager at least before he witnessed the sorts of things these two had witnessed. A tear welled up in his eye as he choked it back down, willing himself not to cry. Tears would serve no purpose now.

"Jarnsaxa, Bulwark. Let's get on with it." Tsalmaveth said impatiently, tapping his foot as if to say his good mood had just been a ruse.

The two arose and walked toward the table. "I'll go first." Jarnsaxa said.

"You will not. I will and I'll wait for you at the gate, friend." Bulwark said, already reaching for a cup and taking a drink, emptying the cup. He slammed it down on the table causing both cups to spill over. The water ran onto the ground from the other cup and began to sizzle on the ground, instantly killing whatever plant life had grown up between the cobbles. Bulwark walked away shooting Jarnsaxa a look that said, "I'll see you soon." The Shades with the skins rushed forward and filled the two cups again, mixed them up and set them back down in front of Jarnsaxa.

Thoros looked down the dark path and saw the shadow of Bulwark passing through the gate and breathed a sigh of relief that at least he would be there for his children and Siv after this. Jarnsaxa breathed a sigh of relief that brought Thoros' attention back to her.

"Bottoms up." she said as she drained a cup and walked toward the path throwing the cup at a Shade who narrowly caught it before it shattered on the ground. Tsalmaveth laughed at this and clapped his hands together.

Thoros watched Jarnsaxa walk toward the gate, stop ten paces from it, and turn. She pointed at Tsalmaveth, "When I am free from your grasp, I will kill you and all your Shades."

Just like the others, those words and expressions darkened and completely erased from her face as she turned slowly and walked into the crowd, towering over the rest. Jarnsaxa was lost. Thoros heard wails of anguish coming from Bulwark as he heard a commotion at the gate, but no sooner had it started than the path of enthralled citizens closed up, leaving Tsalmaveth standing in front of a kneeling David and Thoros. Bulwark, no doubt realizing that he would not be able to do anything, had retreated into the city to find Siv and the others.

With the snap of fingers, Shades rushed forward and grabbed David and forcefully held him from being able to move his limbs and placed a dagger to his throat.

"The dog will bite if I don't muzzle it." Tsalmaveth said to Thoros.

"What of me, why have you not muzzled me? Some would say I bite harder." Thoros said.

Tsalmaveth chuckled, "Because I have your little brother, Vithas. You'll do what I say without hesitation. This one on the other hand," he motioned to David, "he is unpredictable. I don't trust unpredictable."

Tsalmaveth produced a cup and reached toward Thoros, "You will drink this now and I will release your brother."

Thoros took the cup, "So, I really don't get a chance to choose?" he said defeatedly.

"No. You will serve me as my slave. An immensely powerful slave, King Thoros. As will the dog next to you. The two of you will bring about the kingdom of Yaldabaoth for me."

Thoros shook with nervousness as he held the cup, trying to figure out something, anything that he could do to kill their captors and escape with his brother. Maybe he could grab Vithas and run back through the barrier. But his hope was dashed, all notions that he could do anything disappearing as Frigg, his mother, held the daggers close to her youngest son's skin. The blade touched just enough to break the skin causing a single drop of blood to appear on Vithas' neck. The young boy's whimpers of fear were enough for him to realize it was futile. He'd been defeated and had only one chance to save his brother.

"Drink the cup Thoros." Tsalmaveth said.

"Don't do it Thoros. He can't be trusted. He will not release your brother," David said through gritted teeth, a Shade wrapped around his neck in a chokehold.

"Oh, but I will most certainly kill your brother if you don't drink. That is assured Thoros. I held up my end of the bargain and allowed well over half of your people to leave the palace, did I not? Did I not give your children over to your dear wife and allow her to leave?"

"He's a liar Thoros." David said as the chokehold tightened, turning his face red while a Shade walked forward holding a cup and forced David to drink the liquid. David fought it the whole way but soon he lay on the ground convulsing and coughing. A minute later he lay there, catatonic.

Thoros' hand shook holding the cup, as water splashed onto the ground and sizzled, dashing any hope that this was a ruse, and the water was instead drinkable.

"This is not just poisoned water Thoros, it is straight from the source. Not only will you be my slave, but you will also be my general during the day. You will lead my armies and conquer in my name. You will be feared the world over. Those that drank from the wells will eventually return to their pathetic existence none the wiser of their involvement. But you all will never escape. I will see to it."

Thoros closed his eyes and thought of his mother Frigg, and his dear friend Jarnsaxa. Somehow it comforted him to know that he would be amongst them even if he wouldn't know it. He could only hope that Tsalmaveth would not harm his loved ones after he was gone. Resigned to his fate, Thoros thought once more of Skald and his surrender to fate an hour ago. With this thought in his mind, he raised the cup and drained it dry. The effects were immediate as the burning sensation entered his chest and stomach as if he'd drank a potent alcohol. He began to cough and choke as the substance felt like it passed through his stomach and into his blood stream. Soon the burning sensation reached his head, and he began to see flashes of red behind his eyes as the burning intensified.

"Release my brother Shadow. You promised!" Thoros shouted with a shrill tone, gasping for air. He could hear Tsalmaveth laughing insidiously though his eyes had blackened at this point. "Please, please, please. Vithas, run!"

"Vithas, you'll be staying with me young lad. I have use of you still." Tsalmaveth walked over and placed a bony hand on the boy's shoulder. "Do as I tell you and you'll see your family again boy." He then motioned for a Shade to take the boy away. Vithas betrayed no emotion save bewilderment, crediting the stoic teaching of his late father, and walked away with the escort toward the palace.

Tsalmaveth stood next to Thoros who now sat up, blank-faced and vacant, as all senses began to bleed together and fade into nothing.

Thoros woke suddenly in a cold and dark room with only a candle on a pedestal in the middle. Unaware that he was no longer in control of his body but was trapped here, he attempted to find a way out. After hours upon hours, he gave up with a loud scream that bounced and echoed around the black room.

———◄—◇—►———

Meanwhile...

"All hail King Thoros of Jebus!" Tsalmaveth cried loudly as the chorus of voices behind him shouted in unison. "ALL HAIL KING THOROS OF JEBUS!"

The laughter from Tsalmaveth was insidious as the chants rang out in unison as if one voice amplified by tens of thousands was speaking.

Tsalmaveth snapped his fingers and Jarnsaxa walked from the crowd and stood in front of him awaiting orders as the nursemaid who had watched the children for years was on a stool cleaning the blood from the lentil, breaking the force that kept them out.

"Thank you, Lydia. Your loyalty will not be forgotten. Come to my chambers later tonight." Tsalmaveth said as she bowed low and replied completely lucid, "I live to serve, master."

Tsalmaveth turned to Thoros and said, "King Thoros!" Thoros stood up at the mention of his name. "Congratulations on your recent marriage to Jarnsaxa and your ascension after the death of your father. The entire world rejoices and hopes your reign will be a prosperous one and that you will soon have an heir."

Thoros bowed regally and stood up straight, looking about the palace. When he saw Jarnsaxa he ran to her and joyfully kissed her. "My wife, and my queen!" He shouted as he beamed.

Tsalmaveth inwardly smiled at how easy it had been to control everyone. The fact that he could destroy Thoros' life while him being totally oblivious saddened him a little so he decided that he would find a way to rub it in his face when he paid him a visit in the Shadow Realm from time to time.

He walked up to King Thoros and put his hand on his shoulder, having to reach rather high to do so, "In the coming days, the populace will return to normal and be none the wiser. You and I will come up with a story to explain the death of Adonizedek. You will rule them and use the Jebusite army to carry out my will."

"I will do as you command, Master." Thoros said obediently.

"Very well, King Thoros. I bid you good night." Tsalmaveth said as he walked away and entered the palace. He stopped for a moment remembering something, "Come with me dog!" Tsalmaveth shouted while snapping his fingers. David followed behind enthusiastically, veins of black traveling down his legs and arms.

Tsalmaveth stopped as a fun idea struck him, "Dog. When you are in my presence you are not to stand and walk on two legs. Instead you will walk on your hands as well like the good dog you are."

As he entered the palace, Tsalmaveth took in the sights, reveling in the success of the last night. Tsalmaveth was one step closer to his goal, now that he had David and Thoros under his control, Vithas as his captive, and control of the whole city and its military. He would double his efforts to locate Baaldir once again as he was now sure, after Ahmet's exchange with the little Shadow-walker just before their little water cup game came about, that Baaldir was indeed The Guardian. Where there was a Guardian there was bound to be The Key. It was a pity that Ahmet and the others were unable to capture him as he waltzed around Jebus in his spirit form. That would have given them a direct line to his location and thus the location of the elusive Key. In the coming days and weeks, he would find ways to use Vithas and even King Thoros to lure Baaldir and the Key to him.

As he made his way to the throne room he stopped to take in the view of the garden in the midnight moonlight. The large tree stood there looming over all of Jebus. With just a thought several Shades appeared before him as if through a shadow.

"Hang the former king from the highest branch and the others from the lower branches. Hang Ide up there also, on the lowest branch." Tsalmaveth ordered.

A few minutes later, King Adonizedek, late king of Jebus and offspring of the great Nimrod hung from the tree once again, the other occupied branches now taking on the form of a weeping willow in the full moonlight.

Such a beautiful sight, Tsalmaveth thought as he turned and walked into the palace proper and began to plan his next steps.

CHAPTER 28

The Great Sea, Near Philistia

T he ocean surged, lifting the boat before launching it up and over the swell. The upward motion left the vessel suspended for ever-so-slight a moment before the sea dropped out from under the hull, forcing the boat to plunge nose first into the swale that was created by the opposing waves.

For a slight moment, Lox felt weightless as he grasped the rail of the boat with all his might, just as the wave crashed up over the rails, drenching those aboard with salty water and nearly knocking them all from their feet.

During the last several hours the seas had progressively gotten worse, and the boat had taken on water, flooding them out of their quarters below deck. To make matters worse, four of the crew had been swept overboard and the sail had been ripped off by a sudden gale force wind that snapped the riggings like a twig. The captain had required him to help even though his skill at sailing was virtually non-existent.

"Man the oars, all of you!" the captain shouted over the roaring ocean and deafening winds. "We need to stay clear of the reef or we'll be torn to bits!" he shouted to his first mate who barked orders at the sailors.

Lox assumed a place on the starboard side of the vessel and grabbed an oar that was lashed in place with hemp rope. Five others joined him, and they prepared to row. Lox looked over his shoulder and saw Astarte huddled in the opening to the lower deck. She had wrapped her arms in a rope and tied it to a timber so that she wouldn't be washed away the next time a wave crashed over them.

"ROW, men! Your life depends on it. Hard to starboard! ROW!" the first mate shouted.

Lox rowed as hard as he could and couldn't tell if the boat was turning or if their efforts were futile. Soon he was able to match the rhythm of his comrades as their oars raised and moved back to engage the waves. He did his best to copy the man in front of him so as not to impede their progress.

Soon he was rowing with all his might as wave after wave crashed upon them.

"We're going to run aground! Prepare yourselves!" the captain shouted.

Lox's blood ran cold at the words. He had no time to brace as he heard the boat scrape along a reef, making an eerie sound that was akin to thunder rolling and a pig squealing simultaneously. Suddenly the boat lurched forward, and the nose shot up towards the sky. Everyone was thrown forward as a wave surged over the deck and threatened to wash them all away. Lox held on for dear life as the wave passed, pulling at him violently. As soon as it passed, he jumped to his feet and clambered his way over to Astarte who had fallen unconscious due to hitting her head while being thrashed about.

"Astarte!" he shouted. Checking her vitals, he was relieved that she was still breathing. The blow to her head looked serious but not fatal. They needed to survive this somehow though he accepted that the duration of the storm would determine whether their boat held together. They were probably close to land, being that they had been pushed into a reef. So if the boat could just hold for the duration, they could likely find a way to shore or find help.

"Hold fast men! Prepare for a surge!" the first mate yelled as another wave surged over, rocking the boat atop the reef, each movement causing the hull to break apart slowly. Another wave crashed in as if to respond to the other wave's attempt and rocked the boat nearly ninety degrees on its side. Lox held onto whatever he could while holding Astarte securely in his arms.

"She'll never hold! Prepare to abandon ship!" the captain cried. Lox couldn't believe their awful luck. Another wave surged and righted the ship except in righting itself the hull completely fractured, sending splinters of timbers flying through the air like arrows. One struck Lox in the arm and he winced. Fortunately, it was a glancing blow and only caused minor injury. He began to hurriedly untie Astarte's arm and was able to free her just as another massive wave surged. This time the two halves of the boat separated and were hanging by a thread on the reef. There was no saving this vessel, and it was highly likely that all aboard would perish.

Lox thought to himself, *if only I could use the amulet! Astarte is unconscious and cannot use it to save us. Think Lox. There has to be a way. Think!*

Working quickly, Lox tied a rope around his and Astarte's waist hoping that at least it would keep them from separating. But, as if to mock his attempt to find a solution, another wave that was bigger and more violent than any previous one loomed over the vessel like a giant behemoth ready to devour them whole.

Lox knew at this moment that he would die and all he could think of doing was to laugh as the monster swallowed them in the torrent.

Well that just figures, what with my luck! Lox mused before he was knocked out cold by a stray timber and pulled into the water with Astarte tied onto him. They sank into the raging sea and were lost.

Kiriath-Jearim, The House of Abinadab

"You've kept me waiting." A voice said as Baaldir sat up abruptly to see the man across the room speaking. Moments ago, he'd had a dream, but to call it a dream was a gross understatement. Skald had tapped him on the forehead in the dream, and he could still feel the knob of the gnarled staff touching him ever so slightly.

"I kept you waiting...who are you?" Baaldir asked, while looking the large man up and down. The man wore a plain brown robe and an unassuming tunic that he'd seen monks and priests wear occasionally. It had a hood that sat around his shoulders, and it appeared that it was wrapped around his shoulder in such a way that once undone it would open up like a cloak or a cape of some sort. The man's square jaw tightened as he leaned forward placing his forearm on his knee and looked at Baaldir's confused look for a moment.

"As I said, my name is Azrael. I apologize if I came off brashly. I'm told my skills with speaking to others could use some work."

"Well, Azrael. What is it you wanted to discuss?" Baaldir said. He had lots of other things to work out, chief among them his dream and his feeling that not only was his father dead but that his brother and whole family was in jeopardy at the hands of those Shades.

"Yes Baaldir, your father is dead, and your brother is soon to be defeated by Tsalmaveth and his Shades. I am here to pass along instructions that only you can carry out, Shadow Walker. There is not much time so please don't ask questions even though you no doubt will have them."

Baaldir was reeling at the confirmation, for a second time, that his father was dead. It threatened to overwhelm him here and now as he thought, *how could this be?*

Could he have prevented it had he not left the city to follow the Shades? Was his desire to avenge Nathan the cause for his father's untimely passing?

Azrael, seemingly sensing the grief, shifted in his seat and lowered his voice, "I know this will be hard to take in given the news of your father. I am deeply sorry for your loss, Baaldir." Baaldir nodded, choking back tears.

Azrael shifted again and cleared his throat, "What I am going to tell you is for your ears only. You are to speak of this to no one. When I say no one, I mean not even your most trusted friend or family member can know of this."

Azrael paused for a moment to see that Baaldir was engaged and listening, but not long enough for Baaldir to interrupt with a question.

"Baaldir, you are able to walk in the Shadow realm where only a handful of mortals have ever gone before. As you see from your dreams, the world is similar to this one and indeed runs parallel and it is every bit as real as this one. In your case it is accessed when you sleep and it can also be accessed, with training, through meditation. Your father's seer, Skald is such a man, though his path deviates from yours greatly Baaldir. He is neutral in this realm whereas you are an adversary to Tsalmaveth. Your presence there is a threat."

Baaldir couldn't help it as he blurted out a barrage of questions, "An adversary? Shadow realm? What? Why me? I'm just a boy! How is it that I'm able to go to this Shadow Realm?"

"As I said Baaldir, there is much to say about this, and it will become clearer if you allow me to say it uninterrupted." Azrael stretched his fingers and cracked his knuckles before continuing, "Simply put, you are an adversary. Not that you intended to become one, but fate has decided it because you are a Guardian of The Key. Don't worry about this particular detail for the moment. As I said, once I've explained it, all will become clear to you."

Azrael stood up slowly and walked to the window and looked through the shade that covered it. Satisfied that there were no eavesdroppers he returned to his seat and continued once again. Visions of meeting Ahmet, Nathan's father in that space haunted him. Was this man now his adversary? Judging by the response to him and attempt at capturing him it certainly seemed so.

"You are a special case Baaldir. The injuries you sustained allowed trace amounts of your blood to mix with the blood from another. As a result you are now linked to this world you dream of now. Though, as you've already realized, these dreams are every bit as real as this world. Think of it as an alternate plane of existence. Where you sit right now is also an identical bed that looks and feels like the one you are sitting on, apart from the absence of color. There is no true light there to reflect in order to create the rainbow of colors you see with your normal eyes; instead, it is shades of gray."

Blood from another? Baaldir thought as he was already astounded at the overload of information this man was giving him. It helped him to understand, if only partly, the reason for his dreams. It had become a bit of a burden to him in his waking hours since he didn't seem to sleep. He was always awake both here in this realm and in what he now knew as the Shadow Realm. Now Baaldir was sitting on the edge of the bed with his feet on the ground listening to Azrael explain.

"Now, this Shadow Realm is extremely dangerous, and you mustn't spend too much time there, lest you lose yourself. You must stay grounded here in this reality. To do this you must learn to travel there through meditation."

"But I dream of this Shadow Realm each time I sleep without fail. I can't control it."

"You must learn Baaldir. Going there in your sleep and unaware is dangerous. If you die there, you will die here. Remember that. Anyhow, I will leave a pouch with you. In it are many common herbs. Brew tea with a pinch of herbs before you sleep, and it will keep you from dreaming. This is important because while you are there you are not sleeping, really. This will have consequences here in this world as well." He produced a leather pouch and tossed it to Baaldir. "You may have noticed that these last several days have felt rather restless even as you slept many hours a day," Azrael added.

"But why do I need to travel there? Why can't I just take this herb and never go there again?" Baaldir asked, unable to refrain from asking.

Azrael, growing used to the interruption took it in stride this time, "At least you ask good questions young Baaldir. I suppose I should answer your 'why you' question. The simple answer is that, by your actions you were chosen to bear this task and walk in the Shadow Realm to protect your loved ones and the entire world at large. You are to become the Guardian of the Key."

Azrael must've been able to sense another question coming so he pre-empted a response, "Do not ask me what this is. I am not permitted to impart more than this to you. This is your journey and as you discover the answers it will become clearer to you. For me to explain it all to you would rob you of the experience necessary to fulfill your purpose in this task."

Azrael continued, not waiting for Baaldir to interrupt, "Tsalmaveth has found a vessel and is now able to operate more widely as a result. Before he was confined to a stone vessel created by myself and others like me. His plan is to bring the Shadow Realm into this one. To do that he needs The Key. Once he has The Key, he will tear a hole in the veil between the two worlds. Once that happens a creature more powerful than him, or anyone you know, will be unleashed to bring a hell onto earth and its inhabitants. If they kill you, the Guardian, it will make obtaining The Key much simpler. This is why you must listen to me. This is also what your father unknowingly gave his life for. He had the potential to be the Guardian, but Tsalmaveth got to him first. By the way, your father was also stricken with similar dreams as you."

Now Baaldir had so many more questions hearing him talk about his father, whom he hadn't even had time to grieve properly. He figured it would be best to try and find out more about his father's killer, "So, these Shades that Tsalmaveth commands; I've fought them in this world, and I've escaped them in the Shadow Realm. What is to stop them from seeking me out here and killing me as well?"

"This place is holy ground they will not dare to come within a mile of it. Call it a refuge of sorts. As long as you stay here, they cannot harm you. You are to stay here and learn to meditate. Being able to access the Shadow Realm at will is crucial to you being able to carry out this heavy task. You cannot do it if you are not able to understand the evil that is rising in the land."

Baaldir let this roll around in his mind as a thousand questions came to him. He decided that he'd leave it be, though he did have a curious question, "Who are you, Azrael?" This question would nag him if he did not ask.

"In addition to my name Azrael, I am also called: Malakh ha-Maveth. If you know your Hebrew it would mean 'Angel of Death'. However, I am a messenger of death, not death itself."

Baaldir was visibly startled as his face flushed at the mention of this. Thoughts of Tsalmaveth and David's explanation of it meaning 'Shadow of Death' made his blood run cold.

"Angel of Death?" Baaldir repeated as Azrael looked at him stoically, no doubt allowing the emotions to do their work on him.

"Yes, Baaldir. I am an angel of Elohim, created to be a messenger of death and see to the transition of souls from this realm to another realm. Every single death that ever was or ever will be. I am at them all."

"But Tsalmaveth is the Shadow of Death. You are the Angel of Death. Am I seeing a relation here or am I crazy?"

Azrael scoffed, "That is another story for another time, young Baaldir.

"If you are an angel of Elohim, why don't you use your power to defeat this evil? Surely, with his power you could achieve this. Why put this task on a fourteen-year-old boy's shoulders?"

"As I said, I am a messenger of death. I started our conversation informing you of the death of your father, King Adonizedek. That is my job, mostly behind the veil unseen, but on occasion I appear in human form to men to inform them of a death and even their own impending death. It may be unfathomable, but I am there at each and every death since time immemorial. I suppose it would help to answer your question as to why I don't just call down the power of Elohim. The simplest answer is that as angels, we cannot interfere with humans. I've used your shadow walking as a reason to intervene and give you information. Call it a bending of the rules if you will. But even I have limits, I cannot share certain things with you, and I cannot physically intervene on your behalf unless ordered to do so."

Baaldir now only had one question for Azrael, "Were you there with Nathan?"

Azrael cracked a smile, "I did not help anyone named Nathan cross over."

Baaldir was visibly shocked as his mouth hung open. *Could it be?* He thought as his heart began to race.

"Before I leave, I will show you some techniques to access the Shadow Realm through meditation." Azrael motioned for him to sit on the floor with him. "Do as I do, and I will walk you through it."

Baaldir watched how he sat on the floor with his legs crossed, back perfectly straight, shoulders relaxed and hands upon his knees. With that completed, Azrael began to explain the process. Baaldir closed his eyes and visualized the room he was in while deliberately placing any other thought he had in his mind inside a box which he'd visualized in front of him. He did this as many times as he needed to until his mind only thought about the room he was in. Then he visualized the room without color and heard Azrael say, "Open your eyes."

Upon opening his eyes, he was shocked to see that he was in the Shadow Realm. Azrael sat across from him and nodded his approval.

"Follow that process each time and soon it will be as natural and easy for you to come here as breathing. Let's go outside and look at the surroundings." With that, Azrael stood up and walked through the wall without using the door. Baaldir tried to do the same thing but ran into the clay brick wall with a thud.

From outside he heard Azrael, "You still have to use doors, Baaldir."

Of course I do. Couldn't be that simple, he thought to himself as he opened the door and walked out, feeling a little foolish.

"Okay, out here in the Shadow Realm the surroundings are identical to your reality with the exception of the color. Your body is still where you are meditating so you should be certain to be in a safe place when you cross over. All you need to do to return to your body is shut your eyes and visualize your body in the room. Also, if your body is disturbed while meditating it will forcefully remove you from the Shadow Realm, although this will cause you great fatigue. Try to avoid that."

With that in mind, Baaldir and Azrael walked through the town of Kiriath-Jearim. People walked by them without noticing them and spoke as if they were not there. Baaldir could see how this would be useful for espionage and eavesdropping.

"These people cannot see us. Did they also see us open and close the door?" Baaldir asked curiously.

Azrael shook his head, "Think of that door as a separate door that coexists with the door in your own reality. If you open a door in this one you don't see it open in the other. The reverse is not true, however. If someone opens the door in your reality you will see it open in this one."

Baaldir was catching on, "So is that how the Shades were able to chase me in the Shadow Realm?"

"Precisely, very well deduced. You may have noticed their abhorrence to sunlight at some point? They can operate in the Shadow Realm only during daylight hours and both simultaneously during nighttime under the control of Tsalmaveth."

"Does Tsalmaveth have the ability to control them during the day as well?"

"Now that he has a vessel, he is able to control them by proxy using the vessel during the day and directly during the night, but he is almost always aware. What one Shade sees; he sees as well. It's a terrifying notion that he can order his Shades or any thralls around with just a thought. As fast as he can think he can control them. This is why you must use caution, Baaldir."

Azrael walked with him as they made their way through the little hamlet. Just before they came to the center of town he spoke, "Baaldir, this is a lot for any man to handle, let alone a child. Be careful who you trust and don't be reckless. Use your head and listen to your gut."

Baaldir was thinking about his brother and sister, Siv and had a thought that he hadn't seen his brother Vithas when he was in Jebus earlier. He turned to face Azrael to ask but he was gone as if he had never been there.

Baaldir took a moment to think of his family and wondered how or when he would see them. He wondered what this key was supposed to be and realized that Azrael had given him no information on locating it or even recognizing it. Apparently, he was supposed to find it, protect it, and find a way to defeat Tsalmaveth.

Baaldir decided to think about what he knew and determine how it connected:

Let's see. I know what the key is for, though I don't know what it is. I don't know how the key is used, but I know why the key is needed. Tsalmaveth needs the key to destroy the veil between reality and the Shadow Realm and bring hell on earth. My father was killed by Tsalmaveth. Thoros and my family are surrounded and likely to be overrun. There are some good Israelites, Jonathan is one. David is another, maybe. This town is a safe place within walking distance of Jebus, Tsalmaveth and his ilk won't come here. Maybe I can bring my family here and build a resistance.

Baaldir was lost in his thoughts as he walked around the town in the shadows. Suddenly he tripped over a bench and fell face first into a small pond. Soaked, he stood up and trudged back up to the land and realized that everything around him within twenty feet or so was full of color. At the outside of that radius it was the same gray, which he had gotten used to in the Shadow Realm. Even his skin was the usual tan pigment.

Dripping with water and covered in muck, he whirled around to look at the sight, marveling at the delineation of the color, with sun shining on him and the absence of light in the shadows. In the middle of that radius, he saw a woman sitting on a bench with a boy, their back was to him. Then he saw the man called Jonathan laughing and chatting with them. He handed the boy a boat carved from olive wood and motioned for them to go to the pond and try it out to see if it would float.

The moment the boy and his mother turned, Baaldir's head started to spin at the sight of them. He took two steps backward as he fainted and fell into the pond once again with a great splash.

When he awoke again, he was lying on the floor of his room again, completely soaked and covered in mud.

The first thing he thought as he pulled himself up was: Nathan is alive and he's here in this village.

* * *

Outside Jebus

The tapered walls of Jebus loomed large in the moonlit sky as Siv made her way with Magni and Thrud. Bulwark walked behind them and ushered them down the main road south. The night sky was clear for the first time in a few days, but a steady breeze came from the east and Siv could feel the temperature dropping a little, evidenced by the cold chill that ran up her spine. Soon they were nearing the remains of the Israelite camp. There were empty crates and torn tents strewn about and it looked as if someone had summoned a tornado the way items were scattered left and right, showing just how hastily the Israelites had broken camp three nights ago.

"Siv, we should see if we can find some shelter here and wait until morning to decide where to go." Bulwark said as he walked over to a collapsed tent post and stood it back up.

Siv shook her head disagreeably, "I need to get my children as far from that evil man as possible. What if he changes his mind and comes to force us back into the city?"

Bulwark let the post fall back to the ground and surveyed the surrounding area that he could see well in the moonlight, able to make out shapes and basic outlines of objects, "Well at least we ought to scavenge for a blanket or two; maybe a weapon or other supplies. Something to give us a chance out here."

Siv relented, "You're right Bulwark. Let's stay together while we search because I don't want to be separated." The whole ordeal in the palace with Thoros had shook her to the core. The doubt and worry crept in with every step that they took away from her husband and the city that they had called home for many years. She counted her blessings as she pulled Magni's ear, drawing him close to her as she squeezed, then doing the same to Thrud.

I would do anything to see you two safe, she thought.

"Children, go with me and Uncle Bulwark and stay within sight of us at all times. Do not wander, do you understand me?" Siv asked and the two children silently nodded that they had understood.

Siv and Bulwark slowly walked into the wreckage of the former Israelite camp picking up any item that might be useful. She found a blanket and put it around the children's shoulders and told them to share it. Next, she found a rope and bucket filled with water. It was then that she realized how thirsty she was. The experience of the last day forced her to be weary of it, and instead of drinking the water, she kicked the bucket over, dumping the contents of it onto the ground. Siv picked up the bucket by the rope handle and decided to use it to carry any other smaller items that she may find.

Bulwark found a small pull-cart that seemed to be in good condition and said, "This will make a fine cart for supplies." He then pulled it behind him to the next pile of rubbish and pulled another blanket from it. Next, he found a waterskin.

Bulwark poured some water onto the ground and realized it was wine. "I'll hang onto this one." he said shamelessly as he poured a few swallows into his mouth, the wine dripping down his beard.

In the same pile he found a loaf of stale flatbread and some dried fish that looked edible. Bulwark passed it to Siv, and she sat with the children and broke a piece of bread off for each of them. They gnawed at it without complaint and soon they had devoured the bread as if it were the best they'd ever tasted. Siv was now realizing that it had been over a day since they last ate or drank anything.

"We need to find clean water." Siv said urgently before giving the last of the flat bread to the children. She wrapped the fish back in the cloth and stuck it inside her bucket. Bulwark nodded and came back with another bucket with a little water inside it.

"Don't dump this water out like the last one, my queen. It's clean; rainwater most likely," he said with a smile. She poured the water into a cup she'd found nearby and gave it to Magni and told him to pass it to Thrud after he'd had a drink. Once he'd done that, she retrieved the cup and took a drink herself. She offered it to Bulwark who declined, instead tapping the wineskin on his belt three times and gave a wink of the eye.

"Bulwark, Siv. It's good to see you made it." Someone said quietly in a forced whisper.

Both of them spun around and assumed a defensive stance as she pulled the children behind her, in the process knocking the bucket over accidentally. A moment later, a man walked forward, and they breathed a sigh of relief. It was the Israelite, Joab.

"Looks like you all had the same idea. Sorry about the water bucket. We've managed to find supplies if you want to join us?" Joab offered.

"Has anyone else made it out?" Siv asked, hopeful that they weren't alone in making their escape from Tsalmaveth.

Joab shook his head defeatedly, only a handful of the nobles but most of them decided to take up residence in the lower city, something about mounting a defense.

Fools, Siv thought. There was no safety in that city now. They'd be devoured sooner rather than later and be in worse condition than they were in now.

"We'll join you. Children?" she said, ushering the children in front of her as they followed Joab back to where they'd made a temporary camp. Uriah sat on a stone with his broken leg in a splint and Jeroboam laid back against a pile of straw with his right hand missing, finally conscious and clearly in pain. Jeroboam managed to politely nod towards her, as they entered the makeshift camp. They had a small fire going which was mostly glowing embers.

"Are you sure a fire is wise being so close to Jebus?" Bulwark asked worriedly.

"We are sheltered by the hills, and we've only been burning clean dry wood, so the smoke has been minimal." Uriah offered, poking at the embers to get them to ignite a pile of sticks he'd tossed onto the fire.

Siv was satisfied with the explanation, "May we?" she said, pointing to a log.

"Please, our camp is your camp." Joab said, motioning for all of them to sit.

Silence filled the space in between the crackles of the wood burning, with the occasional pop that sent sparks flying a few feet into the air. Magni and Thrud soon fell asleep on their mother's lap near the warmth of the fire while Bulwark sipped on wine from a cup, he'd gathered up a bunch of wood and was feeding the flames little by little, keeping the fire going.

Joab broke the silence eventually, "Tomorrow we plan to find David's Gibborim. They are to the west in the hills, maybe a half day away according to David. What will you do?"

"We haven't decided what we will do just yet. I had thought Philistia might be a refuge for us, but I can't be certain who is our enemy or ally these days." Siv said.

"It is the same for us, we are no longer able to travel freely within the lands that King Saul controls. Perhaps these two could as they weren't involved in defying the King, but I doubt either one could get themselves home alive at this point." Joab said, gesturing to Uriah and Jeroboam who had both fallen asleep.

Siv thought on this for a few minutes as she stroked Magni's blonde hair. The fact was they needed to find a place that was safe for her children.

"These Gibborim, are they warriors?" Bulwark asked, weighing into the conversation.

Joab leaned forward and cocked his head, "Aye. You could say that. Not only are they warriors, but they are handpicked by David himself for their renown in battle. My brother is there with them along with a thousand other warriors loyal to David alone. At least that is my hope."

"Your friends will need a healer. Do these Gibborim have a healer among their ranks?" Siv asked while glancing at the bloody bandages on Jeroboam's arm where his hand used to be.

"That I do not know. All I know is that David's last order to me before..." Joab paused and choked back his emotions before continuing, "before we left him in Jebus was to go and find The Gibborim."

Siv could relate. She had left Thoros and his mother at the mercy of a madman. She worried for her husband, wishing that she'd had the power to fight back and defend him. Thoros was her rock, and she didn't know what she would do without him, but she had to figure it out for the two children on her lap. If the gods were favorable, she would see Thoros again one day.

Siv motioned to the two sleeping near Joab. "Jeroboam there does not look well. Do you know of a healer nearby?"

Joab shook his head as he looked over at Jeroboam, "I don't know..." Joab sulked before a streak of brightness entered his eyes, "Kiriath-Jearim has a healer, the House of Abinadab is there."

"Perhaps we should go there first, then look for these Gibborim. Is it close?"

Joab responded, "Only a few leagues away from Jebus. On our way to the hills where the Gibborim should be located. We'd have to move quite slowly to keep these two from being harmed any further."

"It's settled then, let's rest and leave before daybreak. Who will keep watch?" Siv asked.

"I'll take watch Siv. I don't sleep anyway." Bulwark offered. It was true, Siv could not recall ever seeing Bulwark shut his eyes to sleep. For some reason he didn't need much sleep if he slept at all.

Siv nodded, "Very well, wake us before sunrise. We'll set out for Kiriath-Jearim first thing in the morning."

Everyone, apart from Bulwark, fell asleep within moments of the decision being made. In the morning they would all set out to find help and hopefully an army to rescue David and Thoros from the grasp of evil.

CHAPTER 29

The Palace, Jebus

One week later...

For the last week, the armies of Jebus had reformed and order had been restored to the city proper, much to the amazement of Ahmet who stood upon a balcony overlooking the city below. It was astounding how quickly Tsalmaveth's influence had permeated every facet of life in the city at large, making it impossible for any single soul to move about without him knowing it. The populace had all returned home and awoken in their beds with no recollection of the events of the night before. While still infected, Tsalmaveth was not actively controlling them unless he needed to; in which case, he could do instantly since they still unknowingly drank from the tainted water supply.

At Tsalmaveth's order, he had made more of the concoction with the binding ritual down in the temple and now had an ample supply of the black tar substance that when diluted, was colorless and tasteless in the city water supply. Each day the Shades would pour the magical liquid into the spring and it would flow to the pools in the lower city, insuring that not a single soul could live in Jebus without being enthralled. Their gray veins and darkened eyelids the only evidence to outwardly show any proof. Of course, with everyone the same it wasn't even a question on anyone's mind. It was as if it had always been that way.

Next to him was a catatonic David, who sat there on all fours as a dog would, facing forward, emotionless. Under normal circumstances, Ahmet would be terrified to be in the presence of the legendary warrior, but several nights back, Tsalmaveth had done something he thought impossible a few days ago. In just a week, the Shadow of Death had turned Thoros into a puppet and David, the renowned Israelite warrior, into little more than a guard dog.

"Come with me David. We have much to plan before we leave the city." Ahmet said, leading him away by a cable tow around his neck. Once they reached the Council Chamber, they walked to the head of the table where Thoros stood next to the chair that would normally seat the King of Jebus during a meeting.

As Ahmet reached the head seat, Thoros pulled the chair out and helped him sit down before lightly pushing the chair into place. Thoros then went to a chair on the side and sat down next to David, who knelt next to Ahmet blank faced. It was interesting to him the level of control Tsalmaveth had over those that drank of the essence filled potion, undiluted and full strength. For instance, he ordered Thoros to function as king and continue as he would if it were his own idea and that it had always been this way.

The most amusing however was the control over David. Instead of having him function as he normally would with exception of doing Tsalmaveth's bidding, he had him follow around on a lead like a dog or a beast of some sort. If Ahmet wished for David to fight or kill for him, he needed only to think it. The only condition was the potion must be ingested every day. As long as they did this, their every movement was ordered by Tsalmaveth's power, and obeyed without question.

This was also true for any of the Thralls outside the palace that Tsalmaveth wished to keep enthralled indefinitely. He need only command them to drink the potion periodically and their enslavement would continue. By this point, the nobles and servants of the palace that were enslaved were back to working in the palace and keeping it functioning as it normally would, none the wiser to their enslavement. This detail also gave Tsalmaveth a way to know the goings on of the city at all times from several viewpoints. The common people of the city would drink the tainted water daily not realizing they were one command away from returning under Tsalmaveth's control. However, it took a great deal of concentration and energy to maintain this control on such a large scale, so Tsalmaveth had reserved this option in the event that he needed to mobilize the city against a threat. For now they would carry on as normal, unaware of the goings on of the court and royal family, which was not unusual.

To further bolster his protection, Tsalmaveth had turned nearly three thousand Jebusite soldiers into what he was now calling *Vigamadr*. Ahmet wasn't sure what such a word meant but he surmised that is was to mean "slayer or killer." The Vigamadr patrolled the city and walls throughout the night. He even had archers and calvary units under his banner. The warriors were all turned into Vigamadr in the same way as the Shades were, only without the torture and starvation, and were now a kind of undead elite military guard.

Ahmet cleared his throat and signaled to those present that they were going to begin the meeting. "As you know, our Master has ordered that King Thoros train up and field an army of elite forces, in order to protect our lands from the Israelite scum that has surrounded us. He has also been overseeing the restoration of normalcy in our great city." He turned to King Thoros, "Please inform us of your progress this last week."

Thoros stood and spoke, "Gladly. I am happy to report that our water and food supply has stabilized, which has helped the city begin its transition back to its peacetime operation. Trade with Philistia and the Phoenicians along the coast are resuming as we speak. Our military suffered only minor losses in the battle to fend off the Israelite hordes, so I am also happy to report that our military capability is fully restored at this moment. To that end, I believe the wisest course of action would be to deploy a force to protect our trade routes so that we can allow goods and grain to begin to flow in our granary and markets once again without fear of harassment from the Israelites." Thoros sat back down and nodded to Ahmet that he had finished.

"Splendid!" Ahmet said, beaming with joy. "Our Master will be thrilled at this news when he visits tonight. Until then we must begin to mobilize. I've received a message from King Achish in Gath that he requires help to beat back the Egyptians from their borders. Our Master is inclined to answer this request. I want a force of one thousand warriors ready to ride by tomorrow morning at first light."

"Certainly. It would be my honor to lead this force and fulfill the Master's wishes." Thoros said proudly, chest puffed out. Ahmet marveled that even as Tsalmaveth had complete control over Thoros he had withdrawn the effects of the poison so as not to show the typical black veins seen on the Shades and David himself. In this way, a curious person would be none the wiser as it would seem that Thoros was acting of his own volition.

"There will be no need for that, good King. You are needed here to insure the stability of the kingdom. Our servant, David, will lead them as you are well aware of his abilities. The Master and I will be going with him to assess his every move." Ahmet said cordially. "We have business with King Achish that requires our presence in Gath."

Thoros looked disappointed but took it in stride and nodded, his acceptance of the decision. Ahmet, just a few weeks prior would've messed his undergarments in the presence of these men. Now, with the power and confidence Tsalmaveth had granted him he felt as though he could command Thoros to fall on his sword and he would do it without question. Ahmet could feel the power running through his veins and the confidence sharpening his mind and reactions. At the beginning, when he'd first given his life over to Tsalmaveth he'd felt the pang of guilt and despair that accompanied the loss of his soul to the darkness.

But now, he felt as if he was on the verge of a type of ascension that would set him free. He was beginning to love his power and the abilities it afforded him. He'd lost his son. He'd lost his wife to only the gods knew where. But now he had the power to make those responsible pay for it with their lives. And the payment would be costly if he had anything to do with it.

Ahmet rose from his chair, "Make the preparations, we ride at dawn." he said as he walked away snapping his fingers, signaling David to follow.

David followed dutifully behind his Master as they walked out to the garden to admire the great ash tree. One week had passed since it was transformed once again after the defeat of Jebus. The branches were full-up, and he thought it was a pity that more bodies could not be accommodated on the tree. He stared at the lifeless face of Adonizedek who casually swung there with the wind. It was then that he noticed that two ravens sat on the branch above him. They squawked what sounded like a curse as they took to the sky and flew out over the city and disappeared.

Ahmet turned to David and, in a gloating tone said, "What do you think of your countrymen hanging here?"

David looked up at the tree, shook his head and said, "Nothing. They died a traitor's death. All who resist Tsalmaveth deserve the same fate."

Ahmet chuckled, "Quite right dog. Quite right. Go and arm yourself and your horse. Tomorrow we will ride for battle."

"Yes master. I will go now and prepare." David stood up, and turned to walk towards the armory in the fortress.

Ahmet remembered something as David was leaving, "David. Before you go, drink this." He pulled a small bottle from his pouch, uncorked it and handed it to David who drank it without hesitation, tipping it upside down to show that it was empty. "Do you have men loyal to you David, seeing as the main army has fled?" Ahmet inquired, an idea beginning to form.

David shrugged, "If they are they will be in the hills of Ephraim awaiting my orders."

Pleased, Ahmet said, "Good dog. Now you may go prepare."

Ahmet chuckled to himself as he now had figured out what his next step toward avenging his son and stolen wife would look like.

Inside a mysterious black room

"Let me out of here!" Thoros yelled again for the thousandth time; so much so, that his voice was nearly worn out. He could feel the hoarseness creeping in as the hours and days of constant yelling had taken its toll on him. Somehow, he had found himself in a room that could only be described as never-ending darkness. It was the kind of darkness that he could feel, similar to being caught in a late winter rainstorm with the cold moisture permeating the bones. No number of blankets and fire from the hearth would warm them. The only light, if you could call it that, came from a single candle that was set upon a pedestal. He could walk up to it but as he walked a distance away no matter how far he walked, he realized it would stay within his view at all times.

Where is my family? The last I saw Tsalmaveth was taking Vithas away and everything had fallen to pieces.

Just then, Thoros was startled as he heard a low growl mixed with a guttural laugh somewhere in the darkness.

"Who is there?" he shouted, taking on a defensive posture, facing the direction he thought the sound had come from. Seconds later, he turned around completely after hearing the growling laughter behind him followed by a scampering series of footsteps. It was mixed with a clacking sound that sounded like claws tapping on the floor. Thoros was about to shout again when, for a third time, the growling laughter repeated, except it was right behind him. His heart raced as he swung his elbow around only to find nothing but air.

"Your guilt and shame are like lightning to my veins, Thoros" a voice said audibly though no one had shown themselves. It was a voice that he had not yet heard.

The mysterious voice added, "You and I are going to become well acquainted with your shame and it will fuel my conquest," the growling laughter began again from all directions. Thoros, at this point, could not tell what direction the laughter or voice was coming from, and he was totally disoriented as he craned his neck and spun about trying to locate the origin.

"What have you done to me? Where is my family and...my brothers?" Thoros said, trailing off on the last words.

"What have I done? Don't you see? It's what you didn't do that has caused this calamity?" the voice said mockingly.

"I always did what I thought was best for them." Thoros retorted, and added, "Release me from here and face me like a man. I'll tear your limbs from your scrawny little body!" The rage built up in Thoros and exploded at that moment.

"Good! Good! Let it consume you Thoros! Let the guilt at not being enough to save your father, your mother, your brothers, your city, your kingdom, your own miserable life, your friend's lives...Let it consume you, Thoros!"

At this point, the mighty Thoros hit his knees as the guilt he'd felt crushed him as if it were an elephant sitting on him. Thoughts began to flood his mind as he grabbed his head and squeezed, hoping to make the pain stop.

I wasn't enough. I should have done more. I let my anger get me captured which led to being mortally wounded. I should have never gone off in anger but instead should have stayed to protect my brother, Baaldir. Oh, Baaldir. Where is he now, is he even alive?

Soon, Thoros was lying on the floor curled up and muttering to himself while the voice chortled and shouted, "Yes! That's it! Your finally understanding, Thoros!"

Meanwhile...

Time passed unnoticed in the darkness as David sat in the room staring at a black pedestal that held a candle that burned with a flame. It did not shed any light and if he had to describe it under normal circumstances he would call it a black flame. He knew he was trapped somewhere after being forced to drink that burning liquid. The thing is he'd lost track of was how long it had been; for all he knew he'd been here for days or even months. Time seemed irrelevant here. When he'd first found himself in here, he frantically tried to find a way out but couldn't seem to even locate a wall. It seemed as though the darkness extended out to infinity. And no matter how far he walked the black flame was close by as though he'd never moved. Soon the feeling of futility caused him to squat down with his knees in his chest. David was lost in contemplation, staring at the black flame that flickered menacingly, giving no comfort of light that a normal candle would in a dark room in the middle of the night.

This must have something to do with the liquid I was forced to drink, he thought even as the memory of it was hazy, almost as if thinking of a dream an hour after waking. He couldn't even be sure that he'd drank liquid. He wasn't even sure if the life he'd lived was real.

Think David. Think. Why am I in this darkness?

A voice spoke in his mind, not his, "You love the darkness, David. Its why you spend so much time flirting with it."

David looked around and thought, *What? Who is this? What are you talking about? I don't love the darkness. Who are you?*

The voice chuckled softly, "I'm a part of you, David. I'm who you really are. I'm the part of you that loves the darkness. I've been waiting so long to have this time with you. It just so happens we'll be spending a lot of time together getting to know one another."

No offense, but I won't be staying here long enough to become well acquainted, David thought.

The voice began to laugh boisterously, "Do you really think that you'll be rid of me if you leave here? I am you, David. And right now, I'm in control of your body. And let me tell you, I'm not disappointed. I've waited for this opportunity for a long time. You've dabbled with me for years David. And now you will set me free once you help my minion locate The Key." The voice laughed again, "Correction. You will set yourself free, David. No longer will you be constrained by virtue, or the laws that you followed so rigidly."

David's heart was beating so fast listening to the voice that his next reply was out loud even as he knew the voice was internal, "No! I will not stand for this! I have always followed the laws because that is what my God requires. In return, I have been favored. I have been blessed. Elohim has used my talents to work His will on this earth. I've seen it firsthand. I'll not turn my back on that no matter who you say you are!"

The voice began to laugh and laugh as if coming from the belly as it replied, "Well we shall see, won't we? One thing I do know is that you do not have control any longer, Tsalmaveth does; and don't you worry, I will bring you news of the ways he uses your sword and talent for death."

The voice trailed off as if walking down a spacious hallway, laughing haughtily all the way.

David lowered his head into his hands and thought, *I have to find a way out. I have to find a way out.*

For the time being he was at a loss for any semblance of a plan as he lightly rocked on his heels in the darkness.

------◆◇◆------

Kiriath-Jearim, The House of Abinadab

Awaking from the Shadow Realm, Baaldir was soaking wet and covered in muck and pond scum. He didn't bother to clean himself off or dry himself as he threw open the door and raced from the house toward the garden he'd just seen, although now, the world in his view was bright with vibrant color in the late afternoon sun.

Baaldir winced as he realized that his injuries, which were not present in the Shadow Realm, were very prevalent in this reality. *Easy Baaldir, or you'll be laid up again*, he thought as he slowed his pace and walked more deliberately toward the garden at the center of the hamlet.

The hamlet was now full of color and was like an oasis with plants growing everywhere, a complete contrast the shadow version of the village. Had he not been on a mission he would've spent time admiring the tranquility of the village.

Nathan is alive. And he is here. What are the odds?

Baaldir slowed to a stop as he entered the garden. Sure enough, across from him near the same pond he just took a fall into, was Nathan and his mother Ramah laughing at the boat that now floated in the pond. The man Jonathan, who brought him here, stood by smiling and commenting on how he should've been a shipwright.

As Baaldir stared he began to walk forward, unaware that his feet were moving. He was also unaware that he did indeed break the stitches on his wounds for a second time as a splotch of blood began to slowly form on his soiled tunic. He approached Nathan who's back was turned to him.

Ramah saw him first as he said, "Nathan?" her hands went over her mouth in surprise as she gasped.

Nathan, hearing his name from behind him, turned and nearly went as white as a ghost when he saw Baaldir. His arm was in a sling, and he was bandaged on his head and other arm with yellowing bruises on his face and neck, injuries from his battle in the caverns.

Barely able to form a word at the shock of seeing him, Nathan with a tear forming in his eyes finally said, "Baaldir?"

Jonathan, stupefied at first that Baaldir and Nathan seemed to know one another, noticed the blood on Baaldir's tunic and also that he was soaking wet and soiled with pond scum.

Jonathan stepped forward, "Baaldir, your stitches..."

Baaldir was in a whole different world and didn't hear Jonathan as he walked forward and embraced Nathan, tears in his eyes.

"I'm so sorry brother. It's all my fault," Baaldir said in between sobs. "I thought you were dead. They said you died!" he added.

Nathan was crying also but was better able to speak now, "It's not your fault Baaldir, it was those creatures. I'm alive and it's a miracle. A man came to see us in Jebus. He said it wasn't my time to die, and he brought us here where we will be safe."

Baaldir was joyous as he separated and ran to Ramah and hugged her, "I have missed you and your pastries as well," he said as he kissed the top of her head.

"Baaldir..." Jonathan said once again.

Finally, Baaldir paid Jonathan heed. "What is it, sir?" the last few words weaker as he spoke. Baaldir suddenly realized that he was getting dizzy.

"Your stitches." Jonathan said rushing forward, arms outstretched.

"Yeah. I'm going to need a healer." Baaldir said as he fell over, unconscious and Jonathan caught him before he hit the ground for a second time in a week.

<hr />

The Shadow Realm

Suddenly Baaldir was awake in the Shadow Realm again only he didn't recognize any of his surroundings. He was standing at the bottom of a massive pyramid with stairs that ran up into the clouds. All around him was the densest forest he'd ever seen. He looked around and decided a higher vantage point may give him a better sense of his surroundings. Before ascending he had a passing thought about lying unconscious in Kiriath-Jearim. He thought about the joy of seeing his blood brother, Nathan again. He needed to figure out a way back and remembered that all he had to do was close his eyes and focus on his own body.

Baaldir closed his eyes and stood there clearing his mind as Azrael had shown him. When he opened his eyes, he was still standing at the base of the strange pyramid. Apparently, the state he was in was preventing him from crossing back from the Shadow Realm. He was confused by why he would've ended up in a place he'd never seen before. The way Azrael made it sound; Baaldir should be able to travel to any place that he could visualize.

Apparently, there was still a lot to learn about his 'shadow walking', as Skald had called it.

Not sure if he had any time to waste, he began his climb up the narrow and steep set of stairs. It took him more than an hour to reach the summit and when he finally reached the top, he realized it was big enough for a small city to be built upon a plateau that was far longer than it was wide. But it was nothing but sand. Visibility was limited as clouds were low to the ground moving across the summit slowly. As he walked forward the clouds felt cold and wet and he shivered, not wanting to stay in and among them for long. The clouds would break up sporadically, revealing shapes in the distance. He saw a central building in the distance and decided to approach it with caution, not that he could hide anywhere but a cloud here or there. Still, he walked softly and kept himself ready for an ambush or a surprise. When he reached the building, he noticed that it appeared to be a temple of some sort with columns at the front and side. The condition of it seemed to be long abandoned as cracks and crumbling facades were prevalent.

Ahead of Baaldir was a set of doors that were already open. No signs of life were detected as he crept forward into the ruined temple. On his right and left were statues of winged serpents and other monsters meant only for scary stories or myths told by travelers and sailors. Still, he pressed on, thankful that the partially caved-in roof allowed for what passed as light in this gray landscape. This at least gave him some ability to see the deeper he went in. Dust covered everything from the walls, statues, and floors and he was sure that no one had been there for many years.

What is this place? He thought as he came to the back of the main chamber.

Here there was a giant statue of a serpent with wings and long claws protruding from the arms and legs. The head of the serpent was a lion instead of that of a man-eating serpent or reptile. The torso of the serpent looked humanoid and from the looks of it wore some kind of armor. It looked so lifelike that he couldn't tell if the eyes were watching him or not.

Stepping up onto a dais at the end of the chamber he couldn't help but note that he might be the only one to have set foot on this place in eons. He used his hand to wipe an inch of dust from the floor at his feet. Baaldir realized it was sand, not unlike the sand outside this temple. This told him that a sandstorm had likely happened at some point, causing the sand to settle on the summit of the pyramid. Baaldir imagined that thousands of years ago this land was a desert or a barren area, perhaps from fires.

As he wiped the sand from the floor, he was surprised to see Hebrew characters that said: "Mashchith," which should be translated as: "The Destroyer." It was followed by several other indecipherable characters, likely worn away from repeated sandstorms.

There were also some incomplete characters that seemed to read "Behold the Betrayer." He sounded out the Hebrew, "Hinneh Yaretz Ha-Bogeid."

Baaldir made a guess that the whole inscription read something like: "Here lies the Betrayer, defeated by the Destroyer." The last part was hard to decipher due to the worn-out characters. His lessons in Hebrew, which his parents insisted upon, had taught him that the title 'The Destroyer' could mean one who subdues, defeats, or subjugates. That is how the Israelites saw their god, Elohim. He was a destroyer who subjugated those that stood in the way of Israel.

Logically, Baaldir made the guess that 'The Betrayer' must be someone or something related to the Shadow Realm, since he had been transported to this place in the same realm after falling unconscious in his own reality.

Thinking back to what Azrael claimed the aim of Tsalmaveth to be, he reasoned that this place would be significant in the Shadow of Death's plans. Now the question was how to find a way back to his own reality to search for The Key. That was the other part Azrael had told him.

Baaldir turned this over in his mind. *Tsalmaveth needs The Key to merge this world with my world. Whatever The Key is it probably unlocks something terrible here. But where is here?*

Baaldir was lost in his thoughts as he swept more sand from the dais hoping to find more characters or clues as to his purpose here. Lately it seemed like every action he took, or event that happened to him, had this tinge of fate attached to it, as if he couldn't escape it if he made any number of choices. Regardless of the choice Baaldir would've ended up here anyways.

But for what purpose? Surely my only purpose isn't to be The Guardian. Why am I here? And why now?

He decided to try and look at it from a different angle, but as he stepped to the right, he felt a stone sink under his foot and a click that followed.

That can't be good, he thought as he stepped from the dais and looked around frantically, hoping he hadn't just triggered something deadly.

Baaldir's heart sank as he heard a rumble underneath the floor. Dust and sand began to kick up all around from puffs of air and the ground began to change right under his feet. The floor began to open in multiple different areas and shifted to the left and right. Soon a great staircase opened up in the chasm and descended into a black abyss, which he could not see the end of.

Eventually the trembling subsided which at least made him feel like the whole place wasn't coming down around him. He could not see a single way back to the other side of the great chamber and it now looked like his only choice was to descend the stairs. As he took the step, a torch on the wall of the stairs lit. Soon the flame spread into a seam of oil that ignited down the entire staircase.

It is even longer than I thought, he said to himself as he looked at the staircase that was so long it appeared to come to a point in the distance.

Baaldir walked downward for a few dozen steps and stopped to listen. The eerie silence quite unnerved him as he took one more step. As he put his weight on the stairs, he heard another puff of air, and a telltale click. Seconds later the floor above began to close over his head.

"Not AGAIN!" he shouted, as he vaulted up the stairs, trying to make it to the surface before it closed. However, just before he made it to the final stairs, the floor completed its movement, and he nearly ran headfirst into the stone ceiling.

"Come on! Good grief!" he said, muttering more choice words under his breath. Not that he didn't swear, it's just that he didn't do it out loud for fear of the strong backhand from his mother who detested foul language. Baaldir pounded his palms on the stone to no avail and realized that he well and truly only had one path before him now.

Shouldn't have expected anything else, the way my life has been going these last few weeks, he thought as he sulked his way back to descending the stairs one at a time.

Baaldir walked and walked, wondering just how deep this staircase went. When he looked back up, he could no longer see the ceiling or the top of the staircase. As he started to descend again his ear picked up a faint vibration coming from below and a little further beyond it started to sound like a low growl.

And here I am, walking right towards it, Baaldir said, shaking his head in disbelief.

Finally, several minutes later he reached the bottom of the stairs and came to a door. He didn't have to decide on opening the door because it opened automatically and the torchlight along the stairs began to flicker as it went out, reinforcing the fact that he was not allowed to go backwards.

Baaldir stepped through the door and once through, the door closed behind him. He found himself in a large room with a black pit in the middle that seemed to be so deep he could not see the bottom. No light escaped from within it.

"It's about time you made your way here, foolish boy." a voice said from the far end of the dimly lit room. Baaldir heard a tapping of a staff echo as he saw a hunchbacked elderly man hobble forward from the shadows. He recognized the voice and soon his guess was confirmed as the old man known as Skald the Seer stood before him on the other side of the chasm.

"So. The foolish prince wants to be a Guardian? Are you ready to see if you have what it takes?" Skald said with a serious look on his face.

Baaldir, mouth hanging open, came to his senses, "If it will help me save my family and those I care for, then I would do anything."

"We'll see, Baaldir, we shall see," Skald said before he waved his staff and appeared next to him. With another wave of his staff, Skald pushed Baaldir off-balance and into the chasm. Baaldir screamed, "SKALLLLLLLLLL-LLLD!" as he disappeared from sight.

The Shadow Realm

Adonizedek sat in a stoic silence staring at the center of the room, which was pitch black, apart from the only light coming from a black onyx pedestal that held a single candle with a black flame. He stood up and walked over to it and bent over to inspect it again for the hundredth time. The candle gave off so little light that he could not see more than an arms length in front of him. Every time he tried to walk away from it to search for the edge of the room he'd feel an invisible tether keeping him within the small ring of light, if one could call it that.

I wonder if there is there any way to escape this, Adonizedek thought as he took a few steps back and sat back down. All the while his eyes were trained on the candle that did not appear to flicker. There was no telling how long he'd already been locked away in here and he worried for his family and his people. He supposed all he could do now is trust that Thoros would recover and that David would prove to be the ally they so desperately needed.

Most of all he was worried about Baaldir who had gone missing again. Quietly, he said a prayer to a God he'd only occasionally paid homage to. Elohim was this God's name and now he was certain this God was his only hope. That is if Elohim could hear him, wherever it was he was held captive.

"Elohim, I beseech you. Please defend me and my family and move your hand against my enemies," Adonizedek pled as he reached his arms around his knees and drew them to his chest.

Almost as a retort, he heard a sinister laughter come from just outside the perimeter. "Your going to need more than prayer to get yourself out of here. You're mine now, King Adonizedek. Your kingdom is mine and your son is now mine as well. Even if you escape this prison, you won't have anywhere to go. "

Adonizedek's blood ran cold and sent a shiver down his spine at the sinister voice making itself known for the first time since he watched Tsalmaveth trap him as the black substance was forced down his throat.

I have to find a way out, Adonizedek thought as he narrowed his eyes at the candle again.

He shouted at the unseen entity, "We shall see, Shadow. We shall see."

A vicious cackle was the reply as it trailed off into nothingness leaving him there in silence once again.

To Be Continued...

Thank you for reading *Awaken The Dark*.

This story will continue in *Book Two: Awake In The Dark.*

Awaken The Dark is the exciting beginning of a trilogy called *"The Shadow of Death"*

For more information and updates on the writing progress or for future release dates please Email at: theshadowofdeathtrilogy@gmail.com

Acknowledgments

First, I want to say thank you to my wonderful and beautiful wife of seventeen years, Danielle Swartzell. Your support, advice, and many hours sitting at the dining room table listening to my story and my passionate ramblings of the research, have helped change my writing for the better. Your help in keeping me focused through this as I set the goal to finish this, after my many years of dabbling in the art of writing, cannot be appreciated enough.

Secondly, I owe a debt of gratitude to Grandpa Joe Coti, one of the most interesting men I have had the good fortune to know. For the last several decades, he has been teaching at Southwestern Michigan University, after a full career as a chemist and serving in the Marines. His passion for creative writing and literature was a driving force in my initial development as a writer. When I brought him the first one hundred pages that I felt were solid he spent his entire vacation here in Georgia reading it on the porch with coffee every morning and made notes, comments, and suggestions as a professor would a student. He even shared it with his independent creative writing group in Michigan when he returned home and provided me with their thoughts and suggestions. My appreciation for this cannot be overstated. His help on these first one hundred pages changed my writing and opened up the potential for the story of Baaldir and Nathan and in many ways, the villains, Tsalmaveth and Ahmet.

Thirdly, much gratitude goes out to the podcasts I listened to at work each day and on my commutes. They discussed the symbolism and allegorical themes in The Prose and Poetic Edda. Particularly the 'Northern Myths Podcast' and the 'Viking Age Podcast' and so many others. Their discussions lit my mind on fire with possibilities and in many ways helped me to focus my writing through that inspiration. Many thanks also go out to a Dr. Jackson Crawford for his wonderful translation of the Poetic Edda in which that aforementioned podcast discussed in depth. My copy of his translation is a treasured part of my library.

When I set out to author this book almost fifteen years ago, I was only doing it as a hobby because I was interested in Norse mythology and had always been enamored with the stories in The Bible I read over and over growing up. What struck me as I formed this idea was the space in between the lines that left so much to the imagination. It was a space where giants roamed the earth, characters had flaws and internal struggles, and a space where Norse Myths could stand next to the historical and Biblical stories of the Middle East and ancient Canaan. I hope the readers of my books will appreciate this and be as excited about it as I have become.

Lastly but most importantly, I want to thank you, the readers, for your support and I look forward to sharing more with you in the future. I hope to see you walking with me through the Valley of Shadows real soon. Awaken The Dark was just the beginning. Keep an eye out for the second installment called "Awake In The Dark" With God's help, I will finish and publish as soon as possible.

Kindest Regards to All,
Jeremiah K. Swartzell